LLOYD KAUFMAN and **ADAM JAHNKE**

THUNDER'S MOUTH PRESS
NEW YORK

The Toxic Avenger: The Novel

Published by
Thunder's Mouth Press
An Imprint of Avalon Publishing Group, Inc.
245 West 17th Street, 11th floor
New York, NY 10011

AVALON
publishing group incorporated

First printing, May 2006

Play-Doh is a trademark of the Hasbro Company.

Library of Congress Cataloging-in-Publication Data is available.

ISBN-10: 1-56025-870-5
ISBN-13: 978-1-56025-870-4

9 8 7 6 5 4 3 2 1

Book design by Maria Elias

Printed in the United States of America
Distributed by Publishers Group West

This book is dedicated to my beautiful wife, Pat, who has inspired so many wonderful cellu-Lloyd head crushings, mutations, and dismemberments . . . and to the memory of my dear mommy, Ruth Lisbeth Fried Kaufman, who taught Charles, Susan, and me the true art of head crushing . . .

Contents

Acknowledgements

Lloyd Kaufman makes the following Ecch-nowledgments:

A Toxic Thank you to Tisha Jahnke for allowing Adam to work on this book . . .

Thank you to Adam for not allowing me to work on this book . . .

Thank you to Michael Herz for being the true the Toxic Avenger . . .

Thank you to Jerry Rudes for making this tomb . . . er . . . tome a Toxic reality

Thank you to John Oakes for Toxifying the publishing world.

Thank you Lily-Hayes, Lisbeth, and Charlotte for tweaking this Toxicity . . .

Thank you to Sigrun for tweaking moi . . .

Thank you to Gabe Friedman for your talent and for not killing me . . .

Thank you to the Troma Team, and the cast and crew of the original Toxic Avenger movie; otherwise we would have had to come up with ideas of our own.

Thank You Roger Kirby and Jon Foster . . . true toxic friends

No Thank You to Sony, Viacom, Time Warner, News Corp., and the other devil-worshipping international conglomerates sucking us all dry of our economic and spiritual capital.

Preface

What the Hell Is This Thing?

Many years ago, the marketing experts at the big Hollywood studios discovered something that came as a tremendous shock. Unlike the marketing experts themselves, most of the people who went to the movies knew how to read. What's more, they actually enjoyed it.

In a perfect world, this realization would send the studios into a new golden age of literate, sophisticated filmmaking. The suits in the boardrooms would suddenly wonder why they were wasting their time churning out billion-dollar crapfests aimed at mildly retarded hillbilly children. If it turned out that the audience was significantly more intelligent than they'd been given credit for, then perhaps it would now be time to raise the bar and produce entertainment that challenged, provoked, and stimulated the intellect.

In a perfect world, we'd all crap thousand-dollar bills and drive orgasm-powered automobiles.

What actually happened was that the marketing experts realized there was a completely untapped advertising space out there just waiting to be exploited. The average American child had already been turned into a walking billboard, wearing movie imagery on their T-shirts, carrying them around on their lunch boxes, lining their shelves with them on toys, games, and model kits. With the introduction of movie-tie-in cereals and candy, kids were actually staining their underpants with reminders of their favorite movies. If people were going to read anyway, why shouldn't they read regurgitated versions of the latest Hollywood bullshit? Never mind the fact that the average

Hollywood movie has less plot and character development than a standard VD pamphlet from the free clinic. All the studios had to do was hire some starving writer for pennies a day and voilà!—instant publicity. Thus was born the novelization.

This is not a novelization.

"Kaufman, you shameless, self-promoting dipshit," I hear you protest. "I've seen novelizations for everything from *Star Wars* to *Showgirls* and I think I know a movie tie-in when I see it. And this, my friend, is obviously a movie tie-in. Don't lie about it. It just makes you look even more pathetic than you already are."

For one thing, I doubt anything could make me look more pathetic than I already am, but that's beside the point. Yes, the novel you hold in your hands retells the origin and adventures of Melvin the mop boy from the original 1985 movie *The Toxic Avenger*. So in some circles, that makes this a novelization. And in true Troma style, it's showing up a good twenty-plus years after the movie it's supposedly novelizing.

But that's not how you should think of this. Instead, think of this book as the big-budget Toxie remake no studio would ever green-light in a million, billion years. Over the years, we've flirted with the idea of remaking *The Toxic Avenger* several times.[1] We've come close to making it happen, but at the last minute the deal would always be undermined by typical slimy Hollywood double-dealing and back-stabbing. Also, once we got over the initial shock of seeing so many zeros in front of the decimal point of the figures being discussed, we realized that real Troma fans, the ones who made Toxie into a household word and had stood by us through thick and thin, would hate us forever if such a film were ever made. You'd call us sellouts and whores and rightly so.

If Hollywood was to make a *Toxic Avenger* movie, the first thing they would do is get rid of me, Lloyd Kaufman, Toxie's creator. Now, that

1. We've also personally flirted with many of the executives at the studios we've been dealing with, which may be one reason the remake never got off the ground.

might not seem like such a horrible idea. Hell, I got rid of myself pretty early on in the writing of this novel. In the long tradition of such celebrity "novelists" as Marlon Brando, William Shatner, and the hot chick who wrote all the Nancy Drews, I didn't write one word of this book. I didn't even write this part here where I'm telling you I didn't write the book, for fuck's sake. That name beneath mine on the cover? That's Adam Jahnke, the guy who did most of the work on my last book, *Make Your Own Damn Movie!*, and wrote every word here. And an outstanding job he did on both, even if I/he/we do say so ourselves.

Anyway, the point is that even though I, Lloyd Kaufman, didn't actually write this book, at least I, Adam Jahnke, kept me, Lloyd, in the loop. I consulted with me throughout the writing process, often while pleasuring myself.[2] There would be no such happy moments if this were a big-budget Hollywood movie. If I were lucky, they'd keep me on as an "adviser." This would mean they'd ask my opinion on a couple of inconsequential points, ignore me when I said I thought they were assholes if they did something that stupid, and prop me up in a deck chair to give interviews on *Access Hollywood* when the movie came out. Lucky me.

Besides me, the next thing to be cut out would be Toxie's glowing green balls and his big, hairy mop. If this were a studio-financed movie, the corporate, bureaucratic, and labor elites would castrate the screenplay, removing anything that might offend the various corporate entities that line their pockets. Here, the targets of our satirical wrath will be spared nothing. You can get away with that kind of thing in a book because, as far as the elites are concerned, the only reason people buy books in the first place is to line their mahogany shelves with them and look smart at cocktail parties. Nobody actually reads the damn things.

So while the idea of a big-budget Toxie movie is mighty tempting in theory, the odds are heavily stacked against it being worth a damn. The

2. Don't even try to figure it out. I'm so goddamn confused with the pronouns at this point, I don't know if that refers to masturbation or some kinda gay sex deal or something else entirely.

only way to avoid it being as lame as a polio victim is if some eccentric zillionaire gave Troma the money to do whatever we wanted and ordered some major studio to distribute whatever bizarre, splatteriffic, stream-of-consciousness opus we turned in to them uncut and unmolested. On our own, Troma just doesn't have that kind of money or power. Hardly anybody does except for maybe Oprah and she hasn't been returning our calls since she got cut out of *Def by Temptation*.

But in a book, money is no object. This, then, is the movie *we* would make if we had unlimited money and freedom. In this book, Toxie looks more realistic than if we hired twenty years' worth of Oscar-winning makeup designers. We have the best-looking Tromettes in our history, with the biggest, most expensive breasts money can buy. Or, if you prefer, they have smaller, more natural breasts and an androgynous, boyish quality. Whatever turns you on. The action is colossal, with explosions that would land our entire crew in the burn ward if we attempted them on a real set. The sex is uncensored unless you, the reader, are such a total prude that you imagine these scenes with black bars covering up the action.

Yep, technology has made leaps and bounds in recent years, making it possible to capture just about anything you can imagine on celluloid. Leave it to Troma to introduce the latest technological breakthrough in cinema. The do-it-yourself movie. All you need is this book and the ability to read it and voilà—you've got the cheapest multimillion-dollar feature film ever made.

However, despite all these advances, the head crushing still looks like a melon with a wig on it.

1.

The Town

This is the story of a town.[1]

Tromaville, New Jersey, lies just across the Hudson River from New York City. No working-class rock stars ever came from Tromaville. Neither did any movie stars, politicians (either corrupt or honest), astronauts (either corrupt, honest, or immolated), or any celebrities of any kind. Some of the folks who live in Tromaville commute into the city every day for work, but none of them is an executive, banker, or anyone of any import or consequence whatsoever. Zack Raymer, who lives above the pet store on Reed and Fiftieth, rides the train to Wall Street every day, but he scrubs toilets at the New York Stock Exchange. Part of him hopes that someday he'll get promoted to the team that cleans the world-famous bullpen. A very small part. Most of him hopes

---

1. Well, no . . . actually it's the story of a poor, pathetic dork who gets dumped into a vat of toxic goo and transforms into a hideously deformed creature of super-human size and strength. But we can't just come out and say that. Not if we want to have a hope in hell of being reviewed by the *New York Times*, anyway. So for the sake of all the effete snobs out there, let's just say it's the story of a town.

that he gets home in time to stroke one out to *Real Sex 17* on the HBO he steals.

Tromaville was named after the Troma Indians, whose land this once was. The Troma had been dying out for years prior to the arrival of the white men, due in no small part to their ritual of manhood. When a boy became a man, he was sent off to live off the wild for seven days and nights, eating only what he could find, forage, catch, and kill. When the boy returned, the elder would grasp the boy's head tightly between his hands and squeeze with all his might until either the boy entered manhood or the head crushed like an overripe melon. In retrospect, it was a poor choice for a ritual but it did begin a long history of Troma head-crushings.

The original European settlers were a peaceful (in other words, cowardly) people and had no desire to fight the Indians[2] for their land. Instead, they vowed to live in peace with the Troma and work together to forge a new, perfect society.

It worked well for about five years. The settlers and the Troma exchanged ideas almost as frequently as they exchanged fluids. The Troma men taught the white men[3] how to hunt and fish with handmade tools and weapons. The whites taught the Troma how to say "Fuck that" and use guns. The Troma braves schooled the whites in the ancient tribal tradition of casino gambling, while the whites taught the Troma how to drink alcohol and sit around for most of the day doing

---

2. In the real world, of course, I would never use the offensive term "Indian" to refer to our Native brethren and cistern. But since this is a work of fiction, the term is perfectly acceptable, keeping in the tradition of such novels as *The Last of the Mohicans* by James Fenimore Cooper and *Kill All Them Wily Indians* by Louis L'Amour.

3. Another note on word usage for the sensitive. When the word "white" is used to describe skin color, it is considered offensive and politically incorrect. The proper modern term for such people is European Americans. We only use the term "white men" in this context as both a reflection of the period in which this chapter is set and to avoid having to keep trying to spell the word European over and over again.

nothing. Meanwhile, the Troma squaws demonstrated how they were able to get along without the men while they were off providing for the tribe. The white women paid careful attention to these lessons and soon realized they had little to no use for their men.

As with any idyllic society, this one couldn't last for long. After a few years, the Indians fell victim to a surprisingly wide array of new and exotic venereal diseases brought over from Europe. The settlers mourned, buried their new friends, and in tribute, named the town after the tribe who'd taught them so much. Granted, the tribute would have meant more if they'd been paying attention to a single fucking word the Indians said. Without the Troma to teach them, the Europeans fell back to their old ways almost immediately. Their inept hunting methods (which consisted mainly of wandering into the forest and shooting at anything that moved, be it a bird, a deer, a branch, or a fellow Tromavillian) resulted in most of the big game abandoning the area. Eventually they began to go into the city for food but for a few decades, they lived on squirrels, fish that had been half-destroyed by buckshot, and the occasional foray into light cannibalism.[4]

Today, the descendants of those genital-wart-infested, ass-munching pioneers have overcome most if not all of the obstacles their forefathers and mothers had endured. Things weren't great, but the town limped along, and the citizens rarely had to eat each other anymore.[5] The town enjoyed a brief economic high point during World War II. The country was encouraged to collect materials that could be used to make much-needed equipment for the boys overseas. These materials then had to

4. "Light" cannibalism, or Kosher cannibalism, as it was also defined by the early Tromavillians, involved eating only those parts of the body that the settlers would put in their mouths anyway, if the unfortunate victim (or main course) had been alive—i.e., no brains, eyes, or feet, except for a few hard-core foot fetishists.

5. By which I mean they rarely had to literally eat each other. Sapphic love, however, was one lesson from the Troma that had taken hold in Tromaville and would never really be forgotten.

go somewhere, and a lucky few towns were appointed to take care of these conversions. One got metal, another got paper. Tromaville was stuck with rubber. And while the economy flourished, the town was covered by the stench of burning rubber throughout the 1940s and into the '50s.

In their defense, the town's leaders, headed by Mayor Eli James Fuller, made some attempt to capitalize on this unforeseen boon. They cluttered the town with brightly colored, flag-waving billboards riding the crest of boosterism, sporting slogans such as "Bouncing Back from the Axis!" and the unsuccessful anagram "TROMAVILLE—Turning Rubber into Munitions And Vehicles In Light (of the effort to) Liberate Europe." Unfortunately, these pro-Tromaville slogans were overshadowed by those created by naysayers. Things such as "Visit for a Day, Stink for a Lifetime" and the blunt but effective "Tromaville—It Smells Like Burning, Toxic Shit!"

The result of this half-assed war of the words was a mass exodus of the population out of Tromaville. No one particularly liked being associated with a town that was a punch line to a nationwide "Who farted?" joke. Tromaville's coffers were full of foul-smelling rubber money that could have and should have been used on improvements to the schools, roads, and the rubber plant that caused all this in the first place. But when longtime residents abandoned the town, Mayor Fuller shrugged his shoulders and decided these ungrateful motherfuckers didn't deserve the money anyway. Thus corruption slouched its lazy, apathetic way into Tromaville's local government.

Fuller died in 1958 and was succeeded by a series of handpicked status-quo maintainers, each one more dishonest and unethical than the last. Sure, Tromaville continued to have apparently democratic elections, but the candidates in those elections were individually selected by a very powerful few, representatives from Tromaville's three elites: corporate, bureaucratic, and labor. The elites continued to live the high life and ignore the problems of the town, never realizing that the war had been over for sometime and their one big industry had long ago teetered over the brink of bankruptcy. To the surprise of nobody except the city council, in the mid-1960s all that rubber cash turned into a series of rubber checks. Tromaville needed another industry, preferably one led by billionaires as corrupt and immoral as they were themselves.

A committee swung into action, leading a nationwide search to attract a new major player to reenrich everybody who deserved to be rich. They did not lack for corrupt and sleazy candidates. However, the two favorites of the committee proved unfeasible. The tobacco industry was pretty well locked up in parts of the country where . . . you know, tobacco could be grown. A brief flirtation with the entertainment industry ended in disaster after Tromaville alderman Bob Sandowski was caught with his sweet Jersey lips wrapped around the package of Hollywood up-and-comer (so to speak) Anthony Perkins. The whole affair was hushed up to everyone's satisfaction, the only exception being *Tromaville Times* editor Sam Huggins, who was forced to kill a front-page story with the headline "Sandowski Masters Bates."

Having struck out twice, the manic-depressives on the city council began to despair. They hadn't counted on the agricultural technicalities of the tobacco industry or the hypocritical morals of the entertainment industry. Maybe, they thought, they were out of their league. Well, not them personally, of course. They considered themselves to be renaissance men who could accomplish pretty much anything if they bothered to put their minds to it. But the sad sacks and dipshits who lived in Tromaville had proven themselves to be really good at just one thing: melting shit down into slag. They needed an industry that could put that skill to use. Soon after the Hollywood debacle, they found one: nuclear power.

It didn't take much imagination, money, or skill to convert the old rubber factory into a fully functioning nuclear reactor. Well . . . a poorly shielded, cheapjack reactor, one that required several thousand more dollars in hush money to the appropriate government officials, but a nuclear reactor nonetheless. The idea was that Tromaville would supply a big chunk of energy to the citizens of New York, not to mention taking care of most of Jersey. It was a fine idea and it worked for a couple of years. Until three little words scared off the New York contingent: Three-Mile Island.

Three-Mile Island terrified most of America. All it did in Tromaville was piss people off. Just because one lousy reactor had some troubles (a reactor well known to be operated by drunks, junkies, and goat fetishists, the Tromavillians would often add), why should the entire industry be punished? But the damage had been done. New York City broke their contract with Tromaville, and millions of dollars evaporated in a puff of green radioactive smoke overnight.

Undeterred, new mayor Howard Schiffman and plant C. CEO Bradley Drysdale scrambled to come up with a new source of income. Surprisingly, Drysdale was not an idiot and had actually picked up a few things about how nuclear power works in the few years since he'd taken over the operations of the plant. In conversations with other plant managers from around the country, a common concern had cropped up again and again—namely, what to do with the toxic by-product of all this fabulous energy. Now, Drysdale hadn't exactly realized this was a problem until now. The converted factory had come with a lot of underground storage space, and there was plenty more where that came from in Tromaville. All you had to do was vat the goop up and lock it away. No big deal. If they started seeing humongous super-rats roaming around the plant and biting the heads off of babies, then they'd figure out another option, but until that day came, everything was swell. Drysdale couldn't really understand why the other CEOs were nervously wringing their hands and sucking the blood that was flowing freely around their badly chewed fingernails.

Drysdale and Schiffman took this new information and in about forty-five minutes had formulated a plan.[6] Tromaville would accept the

6. It could have happened sooner than that, but Schiffman's cook had made ribs that night, and both these boys loved their ribs.

toxic waste from every other plant in the U.S.A. . . . for a steeply nom-
inal fee, of course. And unlike other radioactive dumping grounds,
there'd be nothing clandestine or secretive about it. Schiffman immediately ordered a new sign on the outskirts of town: "Welcome to
Tromaville, The Toxic Waste Capital of the World!" For the third time
in the town's history, the money poured in, and also for the third time,
none of it went anywhere except into the pockets of the labor, bureaucratic, and corporate elites.

Of course, you can't turn a whole town into America's toxic shithole
without a few repercussions, and yes, there were incidents. There were
some mutations at the local high school in the mid-'80s,[7] but as far as
Schiffman and Drysdale were concerned, no humongous super-rats =
no problem.

So as Tromaville limped into the twenty-first century, things pretty
much stood in exactly the same place they had fifty years earlier. The
fat cats were getting fatter, while the regular folks got screwed on a regular basis. Like most American towns, the status quo had been in place
for so long that most people had forgotten how to hope for anything
better. Like most American towns, crime ran rampant and unchecked[8]
because the police had better things to do . . . like hauling barrels of
toxic waste to and fro and accepting kickbacks from the people who
were committing the real crimes against humanity. Like most American
towns, Tromaville needed a hero.

Unlike most American towns, they actually got one.

His name was Melvin.

---

7. Not to mention two less well-known but equally popular sequels to the mutation incidents a few years later. A third follow-up to the mutation incident has been
planned for a number of years but, as of this writing, those responsible have been
unable to get their shit together well enough to actually produce the damn thing.
8. Truth be told, crime didn't exactly "run" in Tromaville. The criminal element was
only slightly less apathetic than the law-abiding citizens, meaning that they at least
had enough energy and creativity to beat the shit out of somebody once in a while.

2.

The Nerd[1]

There are few jobs in the world less glamorous than being a janitor. Some, but not many.[2] But as with any job, there's a definite pecking order, and in the field of custodial services, your status depends almost entirely on what kind of establishment you clean. Janitors at huge corporations in fancy glass towers rank near the top, since they

1. Editor's note: Webster's defines "nerd" as "a socially maladroit individual whose poor grooming, inarticulate speech, and lack of social and/or physical graces is directly proportionate to their ability to earn wealth and power." To call someone a nerd is widely considered to be as offensive as calling a Hispanic person a spic, a lesbian a dyke, or a priest a pee-pee-fondling church monkey. It is against Troma policy to use terms that might cause offense to certain segments of the population. For years, the Troma Team has employed "Gyno Americans" to describe U.S. citizens of the feminine gender, thus avoiding use of the male suffix, as in "woman" or "female." If this were a film, we would, of course, describe Melvin as a "socially impaired individual" instead of a nerd. But since this is a book and likely to be banned, burned, or censored anyway, we'll use whatever offensive phrases we like. Perhaps the most offensive phrase you're likely to see is the description of Lloyd Kaufman as "author."
2. A few jobs that are less glamorous than janitor are fish sexer, janitor's aide, and any position with Troma Entertainment, including president.

don't tend to handle anything more disgusting than discarded evidence of insider training. The bottom rung of janitors consists of those poor bastards who are forced to clean up bodily excretions. These misfortunate fuckers work in hospitals, rest homes, XXX-rated theaters, and health clubs, the sum total of all human detritus.

Melvin Ferd had been the janitor (or, as he was unaffectionately referred to by the clientele, "mop boy") at the Tromaville Health Club for almost five years. It had begun as a part-time job. Just a way to make some money so he could support his loving mother, a possessive, smothering cunt of a bitch. As a side benefit, it was also Melvin's way to get as close as possible to those who were more popular than he was. Granted, just about everybody in Tromaville was more popular than he was, so he really could have taken a job just about anywhere and achieved the same goal.

But the sad fact was that Melvin, unlike a lot of nerds, geeks, misfits, and dweebs, simply wasn't all that smart. Often an annoying laugh, bad hairstyle, and/or ill-fitting and unwashed clothes will mask an intellect the size of New Hampshire. Not in Melvin's case. With Melvin, what you saw was what you got. Not that that should be a problem. In a perfect world, personality and disposition should carry you pretty far. And if that were the case, Melvin would be the All-Seeing Overlord of the Universe at this point. They don't make them much sweeter or more inherently decent than Melvin Ferd. Let's face it: it takes a remarkably goddamn even-tempered person to collect other people's sweat-stained jocks and wipe down their shower leavings eight hours a day without complaint.

But this is an imperfect world, and even by flawed standards of comparison, Tromaville was a pretty fucked-up corner of it. Back in high school, Melvin had attempted to demonstrate just what a good-hearted person he really was. One lunch period, as Melvin was chowing down on his banana-and-liverwurst sandwich, he spied something across the cafeteria that struck a chord. A number of seniors were playing keep-away with a new transfer student's lunch tray. For the first time in his life, Melvin's blood boiled with anger. Or perhaps it was jealousy, since ordinarily the seniors would be tormenting him instead. But Melvin had been around for a while, and it was at least momentarily amusing to see how a kid with only a tenuous grasp of the English language would respond to a bullying.

Either way, Melvin felt he couldn't simply sit idly by and let the new kid suffer. Unseen by anyone, Melvin stood up and marched over to the melee. As the tray passed from hand to hand, Melvin sneaked in between and lunged for it. Milk, creamed corn, and tuna casserole splashed everywhere as Melvin rescued the lunch and returned it to its rightful owner. Sab Sada, the Asian transfer student, accepted his ruined lunch with no small degree of amazement. Melvin turned and faced the bullies head on. "Hey," he squeaked. "Leave him alone. He didn't do anything to you guys."

The seniors looked at each other, then back to Melvin, struck dumb(er) by the fact that Melvin had willingly put himself in the line of fire. Fortunately for Melvin, before they could retaliate (as they surely would have), all eyes returned to Sab, who had become hysterical.

Sab sat at the long table, weeping into his lunch tray. "What you do?" he cried.

Melvin didn't know what to say. "I . . . hey, it's okay. Sorry your stuff spilled. You can have some of my lunch."

Sab slammed his palms down on the table and stood, eyes blazing with red fury at Melvin. "You . . . big nerd! You dishonor my family! Sab Sada descendant of long line of samurai. Sada clan not be rescued by nerds!"

The seniors began to laugh, now a bit sorry that they'd picked on Sab Sada. Looked like he was one of them after all. Melvin glanced behind him, his bravado deflating quicker than a blow-up doll in a cheap motel. "Look, I'm sorry . . . I didn't . . . I mean . . . I was just trying to help. How was I supposed to know you were a samurai?"

Sab's head rolled back on his neck as he let loose with a primal scream of embarrassed anguish. "Sab Sada looks weaker than puny Yankee dog nerd?!"

"Well, no . . . not weaker," Melvin backpedaled. "Maybe as weak as."

Sab reached down and grabbed a butter knife from his tray, holding it out to Melvin. Melvin's eyes grew wide with fear as he flinched back a step. Sab breathed long and deep, peas and white sauce dripping from the end of the knife. "You dishonor Sab Sada. You dishonor Sab Sada's samurai ancestry."

The seniors pressed against Melvin and shoved him forward. One of the more creative bullies started a chant that quickly engulfed the entire cafeteria. "Fight fight fight fight Fight FIGHT FIGHT!!!"

"No, Sab Sada, I'm sorry. No dishonor intended. Honest."

"Stupid, stupid nerd. Remember Sab Sada. Remember!" With that, Sab Sada flicked the knife around and plunged it into his own stomach.

Those standing closest gasped. Melvin shouted "No!" and reached to pull the knife out. Sab and Melvin's eyes locked as they fought for control of the stainless steel weapon. Instead of pulling it out, the struggle wedged it in deeper, turning a small puncture wound into a gaping abdominal cavity. Blood began to spray from Sab Sada's stomach, hitting Melvin in the eyes and face. The appearance of blood in the cafeteria got everyone's attention, and that's when the screaming started. The screaming . . . and the vomiting. After all, everyone in the room had just filled their bellies with school cafeteria tuna casserole. That alone is enough to precariously put your stomach on the verge of revolt. But following that up with a ritual disembowelment for dessert was too much.

When it was all over, Sab Sada lay dead on the puke-slick floor. Melvin sat next to him, covered in blood and in a state of complete shock. Teachers, paramedics, cops, and reporters came in waves, and each new arrival started off a systematic chain reaction of regurgitation as the newcomers were overwhelmed by the sights and scents of the cafeteria.

So ended Melvin Ferd's career as a hero, not to mention his academic career. While Sab Sada's death was eventually ruled a suicide, the board of education felt it was perhaps a preventable one. For everyone's benefit, they expelled Melvin six weeks later. Even if they hadn't, Melvin probably wouldn't have come back to school. It isn't easy to concentrate in class when half the student body calls you names such as "Gutbuster" and "Dr. Ke-dork-ian."

Although most of Tromaville had long since forgotten Melvin's inadvertent role in the hara-kiri death of poor Sab Sada, his life had not exactly improved by leaps and bounds. Even as a janitor he was subpar, and in any rational corner of the galaxy, Melvin would have been fired a long time ago. Or, considering the disdain in which he was held by both his employer and the clientele, he would have quit in a glorious rainbow of "fuck yous" and "eats shits" hurled at every man, woman, and child who was unlucky enough to be in the building when Melvin reached his breaking point.

There had been plenty of opportunities for either scenario to play out over the years. As an employee, Melvin was loyal to a fault, but his actual work was . . . well, somewhat flawed. Not that Melvin didn't have what it took to be a good janitor. It's just that Melvin was a dreamer, and like all dreamers, he tended to lose focus on the task at hand.[3]

It wasn't uncommon for Jerry Wilkins, who owned the place, to see

---

3. Not that we would know anything about losing focus.* The authors of this book are pragmatic, steely-eyed individuals who hone in on a goal and accomplish it no matter what the cost. This single-minded determination can be seen in the narrative clarity of such films as *Sgt. Kabukiman NYPD* and *Terror Firmer* or in the total lack of tangential footnotes and asides in books such as the one you're reading right now. Present footnote excepted, of course. What were we talking about, anyway? Oh, right, Melvin's career at the health club, right. Okay, so Melvin was not the best janitor in the world. . . . Wait a minute, is this still the footnote? Goddammit! *Focus* is also not a term frequently used in descriptions of the breathtaking cinematography in most Troma films.

Melvin cleaning a window as Jerry was heading out for lunch. Jerry would then cruise down to the other side of town, enjoy a leisurely blow job from Pepper, his favorite pre-op transsexual hooker, drive back to the club, and find Melvin still standing at the window, wiping the same square foot of glass. On more than one occasion, Melvin had been distracted while restocking and put Deep-Heat Penetrating Muscle Relaxant cream in the soap dispensers. And Melvin's mop had been accidentally rinsed in the jacuzzi so often that most everyone knew to stay out of it past one in the afternoon.

But Jerry had other reasons for keeping Melvin around. He knew that the vast majority of his image-obsessed customers were never, ever going to see any results. Especially if they kept on buying the repackaged candy bars and milk shakes he sold as "energy boosters" and "smoothies" at the club's snack bar (which had itself been repackaged as "The Power Station"). What they needed was somebody they looked good in comparison to. Melvin was the perfect specimen of antihealth. He was scrawny enough to be mistaken for a junkie, except that one glance would tell you there was no way this guy was cool enough to score some heroin. His face was a struggle for domination between his enormous set of buckteeth and his bulbous nose. The icing on this misshapen cake was a flurry of unkempt, Brillo-pad hair. The only remarkable thing about his appearance was a strikingly beautiful, crystal-clear complexion that had never been touched by the zits and pimples that usually visit losers like Melvin in adolescence. If his skin had been wrapped around a more attractive framework, it would have been the envy of every man and woman in New Jersey. As it stood, Melvin resembled nothing so much as a rag doll made out of wet paper towels by a retarded child in a hurry. Compared to him, even Jerry's flab could be called muscle with a straight face, so Jerry kept him around for just such a purpose.

On the other hand, Melvin himself had had ample opportunity to throw this dead-end job back in Jerry's acne-scarred face. Melvin schlumped around the club, stealing glances at people more attractive than he out of the corner of his eye, and lighting up like an emergency flare at a traffic accident whenever somebody deigned to speak to him. This combination of shyness and desperation made Melvin an irresistible target for anybody who wanted to look tough without really trying. I know it's hard to imagine that a health club would attract that sort of shallow, self-centered egomaniac, but it's true. And the Tromaville Health Club had them in spades.[4]

Melvin's primary nemesis was an evolutionary throwback called Bozo. A lot of people thought Bozo was a nickname. A lot of people were wrong, which may help explain why Bozo was such an asshole. You see, Bozo's mom was a clown fetishist. A lot of kids grow up with an irrational fear of clowns, but Bozo's fear made a sick kind of sense. Bozo and his mom took in the circus on a regular basis, and every time, Bozo's mother would disappear just as the clowns ended their act. One time, five-year-old Li'l Bozo got curious and went exploring. The gruesome details of what the kid found are perhaps best left to your imagination. Suffice it to say, try to remember when you were a kid and you walked in on your parents having sex. Now imagine that same situation, only you're in a fairground reeking of elephant shit and stale cigars. Calliope music is blaring from every speaker. You've become separated from your mom and you're wandering around on your own. Suddenly you see a tiny, garishly colored clown car rocking back and forth, its windows coated with steam. The door swings open and three half-naked clowns tumble out, laughing and slapping each other on the back. You approach the car, peer inside, and there before you is your mother. Naked, red and white makeup smeared all her face and body, at the center of a clown Bukkake party.[5]

---

4. Not that it was just the black people and the shovels that were self-centered and egomaniacal. Tromaville Health Club had them in hearts, diamonds, and clubs, too.
5. Whoops, I guess we didn't leave a whole lot to your imagination there, did we? Sorry about that. You'll have plenty of opportunity to use it later on, though. We swear.

At any rate, Bozo's rather special childhood trauma didn't justify his present behavior. Besides, if Bozo had really wanted to freak out some psychiatrist, he could have whipped out a couple of dozen other "traumas" from his formative years, most of them self-inflicted. All Bozo or anybody else knew was that there were certain things that sent him over the edge. Any form of weakness or stupidity (except, of course, for his own) stressed him. And when Bozo was stressed, you paid for it.

Everyone in town had paid something for Bozo's stress, from his Pagliacci-sucking mother on down. Even the aptly named Slug,[6] the closest thing Bozo had to a real friend (due mainly to the fact that Slug would do absolutely anything Bozo told him to do), had suffered a kicked testicle or two thanks to Bozo. But Melvin had paid more than most for Bozo's stress. For though they could never admit it, Melvin and Bozo were in love.

Well, maybe they weren't in love, exactly. What happened was this. Melvin and Bozo had first made each other's acquaintance in the health club's men's room. The far stall of the men's john was (and still is) known as Plato's Retreat.[7] The reason for this was a glory hole drilled in the dividing wall between the two stalls, usually covered by the seat cover dispenser. It was understood by the club's clientele that if you were in the "receiving" stall, you were ready, willing, and able to satisfy whatever Plato happened to be in the stall next to you. Bozo considered Plato's Retreat to be his office in the club. Not that he was gay, at least as far as he was concerned. But Bozo figured if you couldn't see whoever or whatever happened to be servicing you, it didn't really

6. Slug got his name from both his apathetic nature and his usual reaction to any argument, misunderstanding, or anything he didn't understand. During Slug's tenure at Tromaville High, the school had been peppered with teachers sporting black eyes, broken ribs, and cracked teeth. These days, of course, teachers are simply shot.

7. By contrast, the far stall in the ladies' room was known as Play-Doh's Retreat.

count. At this point we should all take a moment and thank all the gods that have ever been or ever will be that Tromaville was not a farming community.

At any rate, one afternoon Bozo wandered into the men's room to see a pair of stained, untied sneakers in the receiving stall. Never one to look a gift horse in the mouth,[8] Bozo slid into Plato's Retreat, slid down his shorts, and assumed the position.

Unbeknownst to Bozo, the catcher in the next stall was none other than Melvin Ferd, hard at work restocking the ass-wipe and wiping the diarrhea off the porcelain. Of course, not being a member of the in-crowd, Melvin had never heard of Plato's Retreat or the unwritten law of the receiving stall. And not being a stickler for detail, he didn't really notice when the wall next to him suddenly developed an erect (though not as large as you've probably heard) pillar of flesh.

If Melvin were a faster worker, things would have been different. He could have finished his job and left the stall. Bozo would have been pissed that the catcher hadn't lived up to his end of the bargain and burst out of the Retreat ready to dole out an ass-whupping, but once he'd seen that it was Melvin, he likely would have breathed a sigh of relief, glad that he'd dodged at least one bullet in his lifetime. As it was, the introduction of Bozo's dick into the glory hole happened right around the same time as Melvin began to restock the seat covers. Melvin unlocked the dispenser and opened it wide, pinning Bozo's love rocket between the wall (painful) and the cold, sharp metal edge of the dispenser (agonizing).

It was the most intense orgasm Bozo would ever have.

For about thirty seconds, the men's room echoed with girlish screams. Bozo hollered first, in a depraved mixture of pleasure and pain. Melvin's screams came in stages. First, a yelp of surprised alarm

---

8. Literally. Keep reminding yourself, it isn't a farming community, it isn't a farming community. . . .

reacting to the noise Bozo was making. Next, a freaked-out shriek once he saw the ejaculating penis he'd trapped.

Melvin tried closing the dispenser, but a wedge of trapped foreskin prevented it from shutting. There was no other option but to grab the ejaculating penis and pry it loose before slamming the dispenser shut. Bozo bucked and writhed against the wall, trying to free himself from the grasp of both Melvin and the metal door. The harder Bozo struggled, the tighter Melvin held on. Bozo began to wonder if he would ever stop cumming.

With the dispenser shut, Melvin let go and collapsed against the wall, scared, sticky, and confused. Simultaneously, Bozo fell backward and lay on the floor, coddling his raw and bloody privates. After they'd recovered for a moment, they looked up. Their eyes met through the gap between wall and floor.

Melvin's eyes widened in fear to the point where half his skull was nothing but eyeball. Bozo's eyes did the opposite, narrowing down into hateful, stressed slits.

Bozo chased Melvin along the floor, both of them scuttling under the stall walls through puddles of mop water and piss. Bozo grabbed Melvin's ankle and dragged him back, hauling him up to his feet in stall three.

"Mop boy" was all Bozo could muster. The stress had grabbed hold of the tiny part of his brain that at least tried to string words into sentences.

"B-b-b-b-b-b-bozo," Melvin cleverly stammered in reply. "I-I-I-I . . ."

Before Melvin could stutter another syllable, Bozo grabbed him by the crotch and upended him, dunking his head in the toilet while squeezing Melvin's nuts as hard as he could and flushing with his foot. It was a historic moment. Melvin's first swirlie.

Ordinarily, Melvin would not have escaped this encounter with his life. But a part of Bozo realized that if he slaughtered the mop boy in the john, he'd probably have to come up with a reason. The real reason could never be revealed, of course. And coming up with a lie would require wits. Or at least half of one.

So Melvin walked away from this meeting with a noseful of toilet water, a set of aching testicles, and a sworn nemesis. Bozo would make it his duty from that day forward to make Melvin's life a living hell. And in that, he was quite successful. Ever since the glory hole incident, a typical Melvin/Bozo encounter went something like this.

Bozo is at a workout machine, concentrating on his pecs/delts/abs/fill in your own annoying muscle group abbreviation. Slug is in his usual position, spotting him.[9] Melvin enters the room, mopping the floor. As usual, he has decided to perform this task at a time when the workout room is at its most crowded.[10]

The sight of Melvin sets Bozo's eyelid to twitching. Stress begins to build.

Melvin mops away, sneaking peeks over at a couple of girls at a nearby workout station. One is doing curls, the other is her trainer, and Melvin smiles at the sprouting raisins (Melvin's euphemism for hardening nipples) pressing against their leotards. He's mesmerized at the sight of the trainer's hand gliding along the other girl's arm, feeling the muscles tighten and work. Whenever one of them makes eye contact, Melvin just grins shyly and stupidly and looks away as swiftly as his eyes can dart.

The smile infuriates Bozo, who feels that Melvin has absolutely nothing in this life or the next to smile about. He certainly doesn't deserve to get anything even remotely like the same kind of pleasure he

9. And because of the unspoken homoerotic bond between them, Slug is probably also spotting his shorts.
10. In Melvin's defense, by choosing this inopportune time to mop up, he was only following the guidelines set up in the *Official Rulebook of Custodial Services*. This invaluable manual also includes such laws as restaurant janitors must mop the dining room with the most foul-smelling mop available, and do not place the "Caution—Wet Floor" signs in the lobby until after the floor has dried and everyone has slipped, fallen, and hurt themselves at least twice.

gets from staring at women in workout clothes. The twitch becomes unbearable.

Melvin continues his work, his back to Bozo, fantasizing about an alternate universe in which he actually knows how to operate one of these machines and impresses everyone with his feats of physical stamina.

Bozo cannot stand Melvin's proximity and decides to warn him off before he gets so close that Bozo has no choice but to introduce Melvin's teeth to the back of his throat. This is Bozo's idea of a good deed.

"Hey, Mop Boy!"

Startled that somebody's actually said something to him, Melvin whirls all around, scanning the room for the imminent threat. As he does so, he swings the wet mop, dripping chemicals, dirt, and mopped-up sweat in a tight circle around him and, inevitably, slapping Bozo square in the face.

Furious, Bozo grabs the mop, leaps up, and wraps his fingers around Melvin's throat. The usual "oh, shit, I fucked up again" look takes residence on Melvin's face.

"Bozo, I'm sorry! I didn't see you there!"

"Didn't see me there?! I'm ALWAYS there! This is MY machine, Mop Boy!"

Slug leans in, grinning and practically drooling at the promise of impending violence. "That's right, Mop Boy. Nobody touches this machine but me and Bozo."

"Shut the fuck up, Slug," Bozo mutters, not grateful for the support. "Look, Mop Boy, you know this machine is here, right? So if you know the machine's here, you know I'm here! Right?!!"

"Yeah, Bozo, I guess!"

"You guess?!! NO, you fucking dimwit asshole, you don't guess! You KNOW! Look!"

Bozo shoves Melvin down and lies him on the bench. This is the closest Melvin ever gets to a piece of actual exercise equipment. And while he couldn't be 100 percent positive under the circumstances, Melvin was pretty sure he could feel a familiar protrusion coming to life beneath Bozo's shorts while he was straddling him.

"What the fuck are you lying on?"

"A machine."

"A machine?"

"Your machine, your machine!"

"That's right, shithead. MY machine. And do you have any idea what it's like to taste your fucking mop when I'm on my machine?"

"Bad?"

"Fuckin'-A-right, it's bad! Here! Try it!"

Bozo grabs the mop and wrings it out over Melvin's squirming face.

"Whaddaya think? You like that?"

"No, Bozo!"

"Yes, you do. 'Cause you're the fuckin' Mop Boy, ain't you? You love everything about this thing, don't you?"

"Yes, Bozo! It tastes good!"

Bozo mashes the mop into Melvin's face and lets him go.

"Maybe to you, you fuckin' retard. But normal people think it tastes like shit. You watch where you're swingin' that thing, or next time I won't go so easy on you."

Melvin nods and runs out, chased by the laughter of the women he'd been gawking at moments before. Slug grins and pats Bozo on the shoulder.

"That's showin' him. You okay, Bozo?"

"No, I'm not fuckin' okay! He's stressin' me, Slug. That weaselly little mop boy is always stressin' me."

"You've gotta relax, man."

"Yeah, you're right. Jacuzzi! Let's go!"

With that, Bozo and Slug would adjourn to the Jacuzzi with most of the girls.

This sort of thing happened two or three times a week.

Now, most people wouldn't put up with this kind of abuse on a regular basis. They'd find a job where they weren't required to drink mop scum all the time. But quitting would require a spine or something like it. In strict medical terms, yes, Melvin did have a backbone. It was badly curved and barely strong enough to support Melvin's ninety-five-pound frame, but it did exist. Melvin knew it was there and had read enough classic literature to know that it wouldn't take much to strengthen it and give him the confidence he so sorely needed. His readings proved that all it required was a good, healthy dose of gamma radiation or cosmic rays or the bite of a radioactive insect of some kind. But most of the radiation in Tromaville seemed to be pretty well contained and channeled through the power plant these days. And while there were probably plenty of irradiated bugs crawling around loose, Melvin was too scared of being bitten to let any of them anywhere near him.

So Melvin had resigned himself to his lot in life. Besides, a wise man once said that with great power comes great responsibility.[11] Well, fuck that! Who needs that kind of pressure? Anyway, a superhero usually requires some kind of supervillain to fight, and all Melvin had was Bozo. Melvin thought Bozo was basically a dickhead, but he didn't think he was a villain, much less a supervillain.

As usual, Melvin thought wrong.

---

11. I can't quite remember who it was. It was either Rabbi Stanley Leiber in his groundbreaking work *The Amazing Moses,* or my electrician, Butch Van Dyke, when she was rewiring my kitchen so I could install an under-the-sink garbage disposal.

3.

The Gang

Jesus, these chapter titles are about as boring as watching stink rise up off a dead cat. How the fuck did Charles Dickens get to be known as such a genius with this kind of crap? Time to ditch the high road, I think, and start spicing things up around here.

3.

Wherein Little Melvin Stumbles onto a Scene of Hot Group Sex and Discovers the Joys of Sweet Sapphic Love

Much better.

As far as anyone in Tromaville could tell, June 14 was just like any other Flag Day. The two people in town who knew it was Flag Day rose at the crack of dawn, went outside to hang up their moth-eaten American flags, then sat down on their porch with a shotgun in their lap, ready to fire on anybody who might disparage the Stars 'n' Stripes.[1] Everybody else in town went about business as usual, blissfully unaware that the nation's least observed holiday was ticking away yet again.

Bozo woke at the crack of three in the afternoon with a hard-on that wouldn't quit, no matter how furiously he jerked the damn thing. By four he'd come to the conclusion that he was going to have to get laid

1. Like everyplace else in America, Tromaville had enjoyed a brief flag-waving fad immediately following the events of 9/11. Flags were flown night and day for about six weeks. At that point, Tromavillians figured those dirty terrorist bastards had probably got the message. Besides, everybody in town had become used to the new skyline by that point and had pretty much forgotten why they were bothering with these goddamn flags in the first place.

that day, no matter how much it cost him. Not that the thought of going out to get a hooker (or "sex professional," as they preferred to be called) crossed his mind. No, Bozo knew that the most likely place to score was the health club, and the only way to ensure privacy was to slip a twenty to Jerry. They had a long-standing arrangement whereby anytime Bozo needed to indulge in a little after-hours penile exercise in the locker room, a crisp new twenty-dollar bill would rent the place for the night. By 7:00 P.M. the transaction had gone down, and Bozo and Slug were busy in the weight room. They'd pick a station adjacent to some other poor schmuck who was legitimately trying to work out and glare at him, furiously pumping iron until veins stood out in their foreheads. Inevitably the schmuck would become freaked out by this unwanted attention and cut his workout short. One by one, the club emptied out.

A word about the pecking order at the Tromaville Health Club. Anywhere people gather on a regular basis, whether it's a school or an office or a church or a men's room in a city park, you can count on one or two people rising above the others and establishing dominance. This phenomenon has been tracked by sociologists, documentary filmmakers, and other nerds looking to establish dominance in their own, considerably more geeky fields. What this theory fails to account for is a place like a health club, where every single person is so cocky and self-absorbed that they all believe they are the alpha male, female, or shemale.

To the surprise of nobody in particular, the Tromaville Health Club was no exception. Ask anybody hanging around the pool, and every last one of them will tell you that he's King Shit of Turd Island. It doesn't matter if they're grossly obese or if they leave the club, put on thick eyeglasses and pocket protectors, and report to their mind-numbing dead-end jobs as chartered accountants for the staple factory. For the hour or two a week they're hanging out at the health club, they're the coolest cats in town.

Bozo and Slug believed they had more claim to dominance than anybody else in the club. For one thing, they were there more than anybody else. The health club was the one place in town where they could remove their shirts and run around in obscenely short shorts without looking conspicuous or freezing their balls off during the long, cold Jersey winters. They weren't the strongest guys in the club, but they were the most psychotic, able to frighten most people away from their favorite machines with a glare and an occasional infantile tantrum. But the biggest thing these creeps had going for them were Julie and Wanda.

Julie and Wanda were without question the most highly desirable unitard models in the club. There was never a blond, perfectly teased hair out of place on either of these women. This was not much of a stylistic feat, since they seldom bothered to do any actual exercise. They loved the Jacuzzi and the sauna. On rare occasions they'd perch themselves atop an Exercycle and halfheartedly go through a rotation or two. But there was no real need for them to exert themselves. They had the most perfectly sculpted bodies money could buy. Their breasts were of the highest-quality silicone, their lips were puffed full of fat borne of their asses. If Bozo and Slug had just wanted to get laid, they could get pretty much the same sensation by fucking a couple of mannequins.

But Julie and Wanda had other attributes that made them perfect matches for Bozo and Slug. It goes without saying that they weren't very bright. How many geniuses do you know who are hooked up with guys named Bozo and Slug?[2] But what really made Julie and Wanda irresistible to Bozo and Slug was a complete and total lack of morality.

Julie and Wanda had met back in high school. They bonded at a slumber party, when they both thought the opening scene in *Carrie* was the funniest shit they'd ever seen.[3] The Monday after the party, they couldn't wait to try it for themselves. They set their sights on a fat girl named Twink, usually called Twinkie for obvious reasons. In the shower

---

2. Pierre and Marie Curie once had a foursome with a pair of grave robbers named Bozo and Slug, but that was just a one-time thing, so it doesn't really count.

after gym class, Julie and Wanda wasted no time bombarding Twink with tampons and sanitary napkins, screaming "Plug it up!" at the top of their lungs. In fact, Twink was about two years younger than they and hadn't even started menstruating yet, so she had absolutely no idea what the hell they were yelling about. The other girls stood by, not participating but not exactly doing anything to come to Twink's rescue either. Once Julie and Wanda exhausted their personal supply of feminine hygiene products, they decided to try to pry open the dispenser on the wall. Unfortunately, their enthusiasm got the better of them and they ended up hauling the whole damn machine off the wall and throwing that at Twink's plump little head, which split open like a ceramic doll. Twink lived, which was lucky for Julie and Wanda, who only got expelled instead of tossed in jail. Not that they cared. Neither one of them had much use for education anyway, and now they had plenty of free time to explore the erotic boundaries of each other's sadism.

In Bozo and Slug, the girls had found a pair of kindred spirits. Naturally, the guys had noticed the girls first. They'd have cheerfully given each other's left nut for a shot at pouring the pork to these two outstanding specimens of modern cosmetological science. And no doubt Julie and

---

3. For those unfamiliar with the film, we are pleased to present the following excerpt from Sir Desmond Thomason's *Perspicacious Encyclopedia of the Cinema,* 3rd ed. "Brian De Palma's *Carrie* opens with a scene of both female subjugation and feminist empowerment as young Carrie White (brilliantly portrayed by Sissy Spacek from the classic *Ginger in the Morning*) begins to menstruate in the steam-filled locker room of a public high school. Always a target for her classmates, the other students torment the poor child, pelting her with a wide array of feminine hygiene products. Of course, De Palma is working on several levels here. The steam represents the fog of adolescent confusion all teenagers stumble through. The tampons and sanitary napkins, an attempt to dam the flow of hormonal angst. Placing the scene in a high school locker room is both narratively expeditious as well as a cinematographic coup, giving De Palma the opportunity to film water-slicked young lovelies in the same manner as a Degas or Manet would paint them. The scene is, in many respects, amongst the funniest shit I have ever seen."

Wanda would have been turned on by their act of self-mutilation. Fortunately for the boys' genitals, it didn't have to come to that.

A window of opportunity presented itself when the guys spotted the gals poring over a newspaper article that visibly stiffened their nipples. Slug nonchalantly walked by and discovered they were reading about a spree of hit-and-run deaths that had recently plagued Tromaville. A spree that just so happened to be the responsibility of Bozo and Slug. Risking everything on the slightest chance that they might get laid, Bozo and Slug sauntered over and confessed everything. They were inordinately proud of the little game and the point system they'd developed. And when you realize that between the two of them they maybe had the intellectual capacity of a bottle of hand lotion, the point system was a breathtaking display of mathematical acuity.

Bozo and Slug laid the whole thing out for Julie and Wanda. Homeless people were worthless because nobody was going to miss them anyway. Old people were a measly ten points. Slow, ready to die anyway, not much challenge to be had in running them down with a speeding vehicle. Able-bodied ethnic minorities were thirty points apiece. Gays (or people who looked like they might be gay) were forty. Kids were fifty, double points if they were on a skateboard or bike. Women who were either pregnant or pushing a baby carriage were the jackpot, a whopping hundred points. They hadn't scored any of them yet, but it was important to keep it in mind as the holy grail of the game.

That night, the streets of Tromaville were safe to walk after dark. The four of them were too busy fucking each other to fuck anybody else.

After they hooked up with the two most physically desirable and dangerous women in Tromaville, Bozo and Slug's stock went through the roof. They didn't exactly run the place. There was too much dishonest, corrupt, and downright evil bullshit going on in and around the Tromaville Health Club for that to happen. But the fact that these slimy, self-obsessed lowlifes had paired up with a pair of Amazons went a long way.

Sure, there were rumors that the four of them got up to some pretty fucked-up shit whenever they weren't hanging around the gym. But nobody really cared about that. As long as they looked good while they were soaking in the hot tub, they could do whatever they wanted.

Anyway . . . what the fuck was I talking about?[4] Oh, right, right . . . Flag Day. Okay, so it's Flag Day and Bozo wants to dip his wick into some fur pie.

If there's one thing Bozo had a gift for, it was clearing a room. So after a lot of intimidating glares and a fistful of threats, everyone in the club suddenly remembered all the great Flag Day parties they'd been invited to that night. Cleared of customers, the health club closed early that night, leaving the place empty except for Bozo, Slug, Julie, and Wanda.

Oh, and one other. Little Melvin Ferd had spent most of the day out of sight and, therefore, out of Bozo's tiny mind.[5] So while Bozo and Slug were escorting their dates into the highly romantic men's locker room, Melvin was busy leaving huge streaks on the big plate glass wall by the racquetball court.

Bozo and Slug had spared no expense at transforming the locker room into a swinging love pad. They'd brought in a cooler full of the finest domestic beer on sale at the corner liquor store. Their tape player played nothing but the sweetest makeout music ever recorded by Motorhead. And the smell of sweaty jock straps was quickly overpowered by the intoxicating aroma of the grass Slug had bought from the fourteen-year-old dealer at the junior high.

---

4. Editor's note: The device of the unreliable narrator has been employed in some of the best novels of all time, from Vladimir Nabokov's *Lolita* to Chuck Palahniuk's *Fight Club*. After working with Lloyd Kaufman, we believe that this device is in fact a mask for severe attention deficit disorder and a high level of manic bipolar behavior. Thanks to the ready availability of prescription drugs, literature will soon be cured of this malady and all books will be much more reader-friendly. The new literature will be clear, bland, and concise, and in all likelihood will be written primarily by postmenopausal ladies and Hollywood movie stars.
5. Much like Bozo himself, who had spent most of his life out of his tiny mind.

The blunt was passed, the beers were drained, and the clothes began to come off. A pair of lips soon found Julie's left breast, and Bozo had extremely mixed feelings about the fact that the lips belonged to Wanda. Yeah, it turned him on, but he already had a dick so hard he could pound nails with it. Clumsily, he lunged for the free tit.

"Not so fast." Julie shoved his head away and knocked him on his ass. Slug laughed, spraying beer through his nose.

"What the fuck?" Bozo asked nobody in particular. "Whose party is this, anyway?"

Wanda turned, allowing the boys a good, hard look at her tongue circling Julie's nipple. "You'll get your turn. For now, why don't you play among yourselves?"

Julie lay back on the bench, giving Wanda the access she needed to strip the pants off her. With one last smile for the guys, Wanda slithered down Julie's long, lithe body, her fingers extending up her chest while her face disappeared between her legs. Slug's eyes grew wide and the rest of him grew in another direction. Never one for discretion, Slug made himself comfortable in the corner. Very comfortable. Within seconds he'd yanked his pants down and had begun to stroke himself with satisfaction.

Bozo couldn't quite believe what he was seeing. Who'd have thought that an orgy would be so difficult to get going? His eyes drifted from Slug's pud to the sixty-nine unfolding without him. On the one hand, his sexual frustration was so extreme that he was about ready to rape every single one of these motherfuckers, go home, and jerk off to some good, old-fashioned Internet porn. But Bozo did have a pragmatic side. Even under ideal circumstances, Bozo was good for about forty-five seconds of genuine penetration at best before he was spent. He figured if the girls got each other off, he could move in, do what he came to do, and they'd have the night free for some real fun. And if Slug was so stupid that he'd rather grease his palm than wait to get inside Wanda, fuck him. He could look after himself. So Bozo stood back, lit himself a cigarette, and enjoyed the show. And there was plenty of show to go around. Between the girl-on-girl table action center stage and Slug's one-man circle jerk in the corner, Bozo's eyes were dancing around the room like the most popular girl at the prom. He could wait to get his nut off. Briefly, anyway.

Meanwhile, Melvin had swabbed his way to the hallway connecting the two locker rooms. The women's locker room was almost always a pigsty due to the fact that Melvin couldn't quite bring himself to spend much time in there, no matter how late it was or how empty the club may have been. He emptied the trash without daring to look inside and certainly wouldn't dare to set foot in the showers where God only knew how many wet, naked women had caressed their soapy bodies. Even mopping the floor took an extreme effort of will. Somehow the tiles looked different if you knew what had been walking on them earlier.

After speed-cleaning the women's locker, he shoved open the door to the men's. Melvin had been in the men's locker room thousands of times. But nothing in his wildest fantasies had prepared him for what he saw this time.[6]

Julie and Wanda, stark naked, were completely intertwined on the bench in front of him. Wanda was on top, apparently being struck by a brilliant idea because she was throwing her head back and screaming, "Yes! Yes! YEESSSSSSSS!!!"

Melvin had never seen so much naked female flesh in his life. He had absolutely no idea what to look at. Of course, his first instinct was to look away. Too bad, because this landed his line of sight directly onto Slug's erect penis, only slightly camouflaged by the fist wrapped around it.

Melvin whipped his head back to the girls immediately. His eyes took in as much as they could before his natural shyness made it impossible to look anymore. He gallantly averted his eyes again . . . right back to the masturbator. He swung his head in the opposite direction and found Bozo, also staring intently at the masturbator. Bozo glanced up,

6. Actually, Melvin's wildest fantasies were relatively tame. His most extreme fantasies were all in the style of Japanese animation and looked nothing like real life.

and his eyes met Melvin's. At first he apparently did not recognize him, because he simply smirked and nodded, as if to say, "Hell of a thing, the human schlong, ain't it?" Then the penny dropped. Bozo's eyes narrowed and reddened, along with the rest of his complexion.

"MOP BOY!?!?!!" Bozo's voice echoed through the empty locker room, breaking the spell everyone had been under. Julie and Wanda fell off each other, but had kind of suspected Melvin was there anyway, so made no move to cover themselves up. They were enjoying his obvious discomfort. Slug, on the other hand, had no idea he was being watched, and painfully bent his dick into an unnatural shape in his haste to get it tucked away and out of sight.

Melvin's mop fell out of his hands, clattering on the tile.

"What the fuck are you staring at, Mop Boy?" Bozo demanded as he grabbed Melvin by the throat and shoved him against the wall.

"Bozo, I . . . I . . . I . . . didn't know you were . . ."

"Didn't know I was what?"

"Didn't know you were . . . busy. . . ."

"Well, we are. Very busy."

Julie and Wanda, still naked, walked over and flanked Bozo. If Melvin hadn't already been intimidated by the hand around his throat, the fact that four tits were now just inches away would have been enough to scare him silly.

"Y-y-y-y-y-y-yeah . . . I see that now. . . ."

"You didn't see nothin', did you, Mop Boy?" Julie asked.

"No, Julie, of course not. I'm sorry."

"You see, Bozo? He didn't see nothin'. Let him go."

"What? Let this fuckin' twerp go?"

"Yeah. He's not worth it."

"Okay, Mop Boy. Julie here just bought you a reprieve. But don't you EVER fucking come in here again. Got that?"

"But Bozo, I gotta come in here to clean—"

Melvin's words choked off as Bozo's fingers tightened around his larynx.

"NEVER! Got it?"

Melvin nodded, his face turning purple.

Satisfied that an accord had been reached, Bozo threw Melvin's limp noodle of a body out the door and into the hall. His bucket and mop flew out right behind him, soaking Melvin in dirty water.

Melvin wiped the water from his eyes and saw Bozo and the two naked chicks framed in the door.

"You still here, Mop Boy?"

Melvin struggled to get to his feet, slipping and splashing in the spilled water.

Wanda leaned out of the door, her hand hidden behind Bozo's back. "Now get the fuck out of here . . ."

Her hand materialized into view, a knife suddenly thrust into Melvin's face.

". . . or I'll kill ya!"

Melvin needed no more prodding.[7] He found his footing and bolted, slamming into corners and doorjambs as he went.

By now, Slug had recovered enough from his genital injury to join the others. "Is he gone?" Bozo and the others were shocked to discover that Slug had a lovely falsetto when his balls went north.

"Fuckin' mop boy," Bozo seethed. "He's stressin' me, Julie. I'm stressed."

Julie shrugged her ample frame into a diaphanous top and lit a cigarette. "Well, there's only one thing to do when you're stressed. Right, Wanda?"

"Absolutely." Wanda's hand snaked its way into Slug's pants pocket and fished out his keys. She jingled them in the air. The sound immediately made everybody's eyes light up. Pavlov would have been proud.

Bozo snatched the keys and grinned. "Yeah. Let's go driving!"

---

7. Actually, he'd needed no prodding in the first place. His feet were willing to start hauling his scrawny ass out of there the second he'd made eye contact with Bozo.

4.

Featuring the Full Head-Crushing Scene![1]

The fish lay in front of Jorge and spread its legs. Jorge's brow furrowed in confusion. He scratched his head and said, "Hey, fish don't have legs," but didn't want to look a gift horse in the mouth and fucked it anyway.

(Wait just a goddamn second . . . how'd that get in there? Sorry, folks. That paragraph is an excerpt from my unpublished book of magic realism, "One Hundred Years of Turpitude." This is what happens when you write all your books, screenplays, and suicide notes on cocktail napkins and toilet paper. We now return to The Toxic Avenger, *already in progress.)*

Melvin did not stop running until he made it into his bedroom. Not that he was a particularly good or fast runner. I mean, if anybody had actually been chasing him, they'd have caught him pretty quickly. But in his own mind, he was Dustin Hoffman in *Marathon Man*. Of course, his arms and legs were spiraling crazily out of control, and he knocked over five pedestrians, fell over several newspaper vending

---

1. Man, Dickens was an asshole. If *Barnaby Rudge* had chapter titles like this, kids would have no trouble staying awake through English class, I can promise you that.

machines and a mailbox, and stepped in a variety of animal feces. But other than that, it was just like *Marathon Man*.

For most people, their bedroom is their refuge from the rest of the world. It's a reflection of their true inner selves, their interests and desires. It's the one place where they can relax and be themselves. Melvin's bedroom was where he could relax and be an extension of his mother. He'd tried decorating it once, covering the walls with posters of places he'd like to go and movies and comic books he loved. Mrs. Ferd removed all of that while he was at work and decorated the room the way she wanted it. Macramé wall hangings, plastic ferns (because there was no way she was going to entrust the life of a real plant to her misfit son), and a cloth calendar from 1978. As long as Melvin lived under her roof, he was going to obey her rules. And part of that meant not cheapening her house with pictures of monsters and hoochie mamas with impossibly large you-know-whats. Since then, Melvin kept all of his most treasured possessions in an unmarked cardboard box in the closet, safely hidden behind a stack of board games.

Melvin collapsed atop his old lady bed, stared hard at the ceiling, and gasped for air. He hadn't run that much since . . . well, since ever, really. Exercise wasn't just a foreign concept to Melvin. Up till now, it had seemed a physical impossibility. For all Melvin knew, his heart was never going to slow down. He'd be gasping for air for the rest of his life, unable to speak or swallow. Fine by him. He'd just spend the rest of his life in this room, hyperventilating and waiting to starve to death. The only saving grace in this entire day was that his mother hadn't been home when he came racing through. . . .

KNOCK KNOCK KNOCK.

"Melvin? What are you doing in there?"

Melvin rolled over on his side, and his eyes rolled back in his head. Dammit. Why is it that the older people get, the sneakier they get? Maybe under those black masks, ninjas were really just armies of elderly people.

"Melvin! You came tearing through my house. You ran right into the china hutch and nearly broke the Princess Di commemorative. What is going on?"

Mrs. Ferd preferred to have these preliminary discussions through closed doors. This gave her son the illusion of privacy . . . an illusion that was inevitably shattered twenty seconds later, when the door swung wide open. Like now.

Mrs. Ferd (first name: Eunice) was the strongest, most capable decrepit old hag in Tromaville. She looked to be about seventy-five if she was a day, but nobody really knew how old she was. She may have been about forty and the shock and awe of having Melvin for a son aged her prematurely. Or she could have been twice that, which would mean she'd given birth in her late fifties or early sixties, a possibility far too horrible to contemplate.

Melvin had been raised solely by his mother, Mr. Ferd having disappeared shortly after Melvin's birth in hopes of setting up a couple of far more expensive but artistically inferior sequels that gave the filmmakers an excuse to go to Japan.[2] To support her family, Eunice Ferd had taken a staggering number of jobs, from riveter to exterminator, from waitress to daytime talk show host. Of course, her family consisted of herself and Melvin, so she was making a lot more money than they needed, and Melvin was left alone through most of his childhood, the TV and a dead squirrel his only companions. With all the money she'd saved from a lifetime of hard labor, Mrs. Ferd retired from the rat race and devoted the rest of her life to smothering her son with unwanted attention and henpecking.

Mrs. Ferd stood in the doorway, her wrinkled fingers curled around the glass doorknob.

"What on earth is the matter with you, young man?"

2. See *The Toxic Avenger Part II* and *The Toxic Avenger Part III: The Last Temptation of Toxie.*

Melvin's head lolled back on his pillow as he continued to gasp. He willed his throat to swallow his tongue but it wouldn't obey his wishes.

"Are you all right? The way you came racing in, I thought you must have had to go number two. I didn't hear any flush, though. Don't tell me you left one floating in there, Melvin."

"I'm fine, Mom," Melvin squeaked, surprised and a little disappointed to hear his own voice again.

"Don't you lie to me. If I go in that bathroom, am I going to have to bring a can of Lysol and a plunger?"

"No, Ma, jeez. I was just in a hurry to get home, that's all."

"Well, you should be. It's not safe to be walking the streets at night, you know. I was just reading in the paper about another one of those awful hit-and-run murders. It was only a nigger, but still—"

"Mother!"

"Oh, Melvin, you know I'm just a fadin' ole southern belle.[3] It's perfectly acceptable for ladies like me to use terms like that. But don't you ever let me catch you talking that way or you'll be eating soap soup for a week."

"Yes, Mother."

"Now give your mother a kiss good night."

Mrs. Ferd shuffled into the room and leaned over the bed for a kiss. Melvin shut his eyes tight to avoid catching a glimpse of his mother's drained, pendulous breasts as her flannel robe swung open. He endured a kiss (which was kind of like pressing his lips against a face-sized hunk of beef jerky) and kept his eyes closed until he heard the door click shut . . . just in case.

---

3. This was a blatant lie. Eunice Ferd had never been farther south than a day trip to Washington, D.C., when she was in finishing school. But she felt the name Eunice sounded pretty southern, and this combined with her advanced age gave her the right to be as despicably and casually racist as humanly possible. Not that she had any deeply felt convictions of any kind. It just gave her something to do while she was waiting to die.

Alone at last, Melvin turned to face the wall. There had to be a way out of this situation. His job would now be an even less endurable nightmare than it had already been. Bozo had merely disliked him before. Now he actively hated him. Melvin didn't know the extent of Bozo's psychosis. Frankly, he didn't want to know. When you're dealing with degrees of crazy, a couple plus or minus in either direction were worth less than a fart in a tornado.

As for his mother, Melvin loved her, but gawd-damn-it! Give a guy a little breathing room, huh? Melvin thought he was pretty lucky she didn't make him save his bowel movements in Tupperware containers so she could be sure he was feeling okay. No, it'd been quite a while since she'd made him do that.

It wasn't that Melvin didn't have the imagination to figure a way toward a better life. If anything, he had too much imagination. The spirit was willing but the flesh was weak. In his heart, he shook the radioactive dust of Tromaville off his shoulders on a daily basis, made a new life for himself far, far away, and returned a figure of respect and adoration, ready to run for mayor and clean up the town he really did love. But he was incapable of acting on these impulses. When you've spent your entire life being kicked in the balls and sampling toilet water on a regular basis, it's difficult if not downright impossible to kick back. Win one battle and you've got about a dozen more waiting right behind you. And Melvin's fantasy life didn't help matters much. All his plans of escape seemed to involve spaceships, monster trucks, or teleportation devices. When your most practical plan of action involves rolling out of town behind the wheel of a vehicle designed by "Big Daddy" Roth, you know you're in trouble.

So Melvin lay there, wishing he could sleep but knowing deep down that for the next eight hours, he'd just be watching the big red digital numbers tick away on his alarm clock, waiting to go back to work and start the whole goddamn cycle over again.

Interlude: An Excerpt from She Flies Undone by Larry Wall (A Selection of Oprah's Book Club!)[4]

I was twelve years old the year our new baby took sick.

We were living in New Jersey then, far enough outside of the city to make Mom and Dad feel good about raising us kids. Close enough so they didn't have to feel like responsible grown-ups all the time. Mom had me when she was nineteen, way too young for anyone to have to be burdened with the responsibility of a young son. For Mom, it was a death sentence she was not prepared to accept.

I had my first taste of beer when I was six. Mom had been asked out by her then current boyfriend, Scott or Stu or Mack or something like that. Ordinarily when she went out on dates, I'd get dropped off with one of the neighbors downstairs (we were still in the city at that point). But this time she couldn't get ahold of them. They weren't answering their phone. They weren't responding to Mom's desperate knocking at their door. I was closer to the ground and could see shadows dancing around in the light peeking out from beneath the door. Someone was home. They'd simply had enough. Fine by me. So had I.

We stood outside no. 401 for what felt like a year, Mom and I. Her knuckles grew red from slamming her fist on the door. "Mother-fuckers!" she yelled. "I know you're in there! Come on!" She sighed, tired, beaten at last. She looked down at me and saw a rock, a huge stone tied to her ankle waiting to drag her down just as soon as she took that last step off the bridge into the Hudson. "Fine!" she yelled at the neighbors, though she was still glaring at me. "Be that way. But don't come asking me for any favors!" No one ever did anyway.

Mom pulled me by the arm back upstairs and parked me on the couch. She switched on the TV, lit a Newport Light, and sat down to sulk. I breathed easier now. For one night, I thought, things would be

4. Oprah Jurkowitz, that is. Not to be confused with any other book clubs owned or operated by anyone else named Oprah.

normal. I had ABC's TGIF lineup on the TV. I had my mom. It would
be like it should.

Fifteen minutes later, Scott or Stu or Mack showed up, flashing
his copier salesman smile and whisking my mom into his arms.
She grabbed him by the coat and dragged him into the kitchen. I
knew what she'd say. No show, no date, no way. The kid. It's always
the kid.

Scott or Stu or Mack came back out, sat down on the couch next to
me, and switched off the set. "Hey, Skippy." He had a way of exhaling
a cloud of cigarette smoke into my face even when he didn't have a
smoke in his hand. "You like music?"

This was the first time any of mom's boyfriends had ever asked me
a question. I responded the way TV had taught me. I shrugged.

"Sure, everybody likes good music. How'd you like to come with
your mom and me to see a righteously ass-kicking band tonight?"

I looked up. Behind Scott or Stu or Mack, my mom was adjusting
her makeup and hair in the reflection of the microwave. She was going,
whether I went or not. I smiled at Scott or Stu or Mack, nodded.

"Good boy!" Mom's boyfriends tended to speak to me like I was a
dog. One time I put a collar and leash on and pretended to be a dog
for an entire night. Mom didn't like that much.

I'd been thinking about that night a lot lately. The concert, the
party, the after-hours club, the taste of beer. Mostly about the way
Mom looked with Scott or Stu or Mack. I think that was the first night
I saw her happy. Maybe the only night.

When we moved to New Jersey, Mom had married a flight atten-
dant. Trent. Trent wanted kids more than anything in the world and
treated me like I was his own. He'd changed Mom, convinced her to
settle down, move to New Jersey, and try—at least try—to raise a
family.

He talked a lot about a family. That struck me as weird. Seemed to
me we were a family. Trent told Mom he wanted more, kids of his own.

I asked him if he and Mom had a new baby if Trent wouldn't be my friend anymore. "Of course not, Skippy." He put his hands on my shoulders just like he'd seen fathers do in the movies for years. "I don't want you to worry about. Sure, your mom and I are gonna keep trying to bring you a baby brother or sister. But between you, me, and the mailbox, I don't think it's gonna happen."

"Why not, Trent?"

He pointed up. "See that?"

A plane was flying low through the clouds that always seemed to form around the reactor at the energy plant, heading into JFK or LaGuardia, I supposed.

"I work on one of those. And every time we come home, we fly right through those clouds. My doctor says that may help explain it."

"Explain what?"

"Well, Skippy . . . your ole buddy Trent's shooting blanks, I guess is what I'm trying to say."

"I don't get it."

"It's okay, Skippy. Growing up here, I bet someday you'll be shooting blanks, too."

Trent was wrong, though. Mom did get pregnant. Not long after that, Trent took off in one of his planes and never came back. But his influence lingered. Mom wanted to be a mom now. The baby was born and she was perfect. Darker than either me or Mom but that didn't matter. She was a perfect little baby girl.

When she got sick, that horrible summer when I was twelve, I'd have bet all my baseball cards that Mom was going to fall apart. It was the first major health problem either of us kids had had. But Mom surprised everybody. She pulled together and nursed that kid as best she could. When Mom had to rest, I pitched in and looked after her myself. For the first time, we were a team.

But still . . . was Mom happy? Was I?

Please look for _She Flies Undone_ in hardcover at bookstores everywhere. We now return to _The Toxic Avenger_, chapter 4.

Meanwhile, a strangely familiar green sedan[5] burned rubber down the darkened streets of Tromaville. Inside, Slug and Wanda sprawled across the backseat, making every effort to drain the last of the beer. Bozo was behind the wheel, slamming his fist on the dash in time to the pulsing vein in his forehead, while Julie sat beside him, scanning the sidewalks for points.

". . . fuckin' goddamn mop boy piece of shit cock-knockin' son of a bastard whore asshole . . ." This litany had begun to pour out of Bozo's mouth as soon as Melvin had run out of the locker room and continued pretty much unabated up through this very moment.

"Jesus, Bozo," Slug counseled. "Give it a rest, wouldja?"

"Don't you fuckin' tell me to give it a rest. Fuckin' mop boy with his stupid fuckin' mop and his stupid fuckin' grin. What's he got to be grinnin' about? Is he actually fuckin' eatin' shit with that goddamn shit-eatin' grin?"

"After tonight," Wanda purred, "I don't think he's gonna be grinning for a long, long time. We scared him good."

"Fat hairy load of monkey spunk that does." Bozo gripped the wheel tightly and slammed his head against the seat in an effort to dislodge the migraine that had taken hold. "We scare the fuckin' shit outta him twice a day and back he comes, grinnin' that twat-ticklin' grin like nothin' happened."

Julie smiled and turned around to face the whole group. "How'd you like to teach him a real lesson?"

---

5. An excerpt from _The Oxford Dictionary of Literary Terms_, 5th ed. "Foreshadowing—a literary device suggesting a later event beforehand." I.e., the appearance of a green sedan in any Troma film suggests that said vehicle will eventually flip over and explode.

"Abso-fuckin'-lutely. You got somethin' in mind?"

"Mm-hmmm . . . it's not enough if it's just us. We've got to humiliate him in front of everybody. Make it so he'll never, ever want to set foot in our club as long as he lives."

Bozo nodded and smiled. "I like it, Julie. I like it a lot."

"I haven't even told you the idea yet."

"I don't give a good squirt of runny dog shit what the idea is. As long as it does what you said, it's perfect."

"It will, baby. And you won't be stressed no more, I promise."

Bozo's smile melted off his face as he looked out the window. "Only one thing's stressing me right now. Where the fuck is everybody?"

Slug yawned and glanced out the window. "May as well call it a night, Bozo. I think we're all alone out here." Slug was only too happy to pack it in. If they didn't snag anybody tonight, he'd maintain his twenty-five-point lead over Bozo.

"Hold on a sec," Julie snapped back to her lookout position. "One o'clock."

Bozo looked down at his watch. "I've got eleven-thirty."

"No, dipshit. The one-o'clock position. Kid on a bike."

"Huh?"

Exasperated, Julie reached over and physically turned Bozo's head in the right direction. "Look! There!"

Evil laughter exploded from everyone in the car simultaneously. Bozo accelerated, pulling alongside the kid in seconds. The kid looked to be about twelve, and wherever he was going, he was in one hell of a hurry. He was breathing hard, almost as if he'd pedaled all the way over from another novel right into this one. He had reflective patches on his windbreaker and, like all good girls and boys, wore a white helmet. He threw a frightened look over his shoulder at the car.

Julie leaned out the window, the night air immediately making her thin top more of an idea for clothes than an actual garment.

"Hey, kid! What's your name?"

The kid knew he wasn't supposed to talk to strangers, but most stranger didn't have hard, pink nipples thrust toward him, either. "Skippy!"

"You're out awful late, aren't you, Skippy?"

"Our new baby's sick! I've gotta go to the twenty-four-hour drug-store for medicine."

"You hear that, Bozo? Skippy's going to get medicine."

"Better tell the brat to stock up on fuckin' Band-Aids while he's there," Bozo sneered and sped on past the bicycle. Skippy breathed a sigh of relief . . . and a sigh of disappointment because he was really enjoying the view of Julie's tits.

All sighs were canceled as soon as he saw the car brake about a hundred yards in front of him, turn around, and come racing back toward him at about eighty miles per hour.

Slug and Wanda were screaming, "Yeah, yeah, hit him! Hit him!" Julie understood that Bozo didn't need any encouragement and kept her mouth shut so she could concentrate on the ride.

The first bone to break was Skippy's left shin as it was shattered between the car's grille and the bike. Fortunately for Skippy, the bike fell away as he rolled off and onto the car's windshield. The windshield wiper caught his cheek, ripping it open and leaving a chunky streak of blood on the glass that Slug and Bozo would puzzle over later on. The join between the windshield and the car's roof was the last part of the vehicle to actually come into contact with Skippy's body, but it was a big one. It pulverized his shoulder and sent him soaring into space.

Bozo braked and spun the car around, hoping he'd be in time to see the kid hit the ground. He was, but just barely. Skippy lay still on the red and black asphalt, broken bones sticking out of his skin in half a dozen places.

Applause and cheers rang out in the car. Bozo took a satisfied swig of beer, pleased with tonight's performance. He turned around and looked at Slug, a sly smile on his face. "Double points, dude. You'll never catch up now."

Slug's laughter turned to panic as he realized that Bozo was exactly right. So it was with no small amount of glee that he saw movement up in the street ahead. He reached into the glove compartment and fished out a dog-eared spiral notebook. He flipped through the pages, trying to find the reference he knew was there.

Rule 11—If a target is carrying a briefcase or backpack, the driver gets another ten points if they can knock it open. No points if they just have bags or something that's already open.

Rule 12—The driver gets NO POINTS if the target is still moving after getting hit by the car. If the target was smart, they'd play dead and just lay still until somebody helped him. But nobody's as smart as us, so FUCK THEM!!

Rule 13—THIS GAME FUCKING ROCKS!!!!!!!!!!!!!!!!!!!!

"Uh-uh, man. Check it out. He's still moving. No points."

Bozo whirled and saw Skippy crawling back to his bike. It was a cute gesture. As fucked up as he was, that kid's bike-riding days were behind him. But you had to admire his moxie for trying to get back in the saddle.

"We'll see about that," Bozo muttered and slammed the car back into gear. He revved the engine and the car shot forward, heading straight for Skippy's head.

The last thing Skippy saw in this world was a radial tire spinning like a washing machine on acid. The front tire obliterated Skippy, bursting his head open like it was a cantaloupe filled with hamburger, cranberry sauce, and Karo syrup mixed with red and blue food coloring, topped with a wig, and a smiley face painted on it.

The car came to a stop, blood, hair, and hamburger still caught in the rims of the tires. The doors flew open and the giddy little group of psychos came tumbling out, happy as drunk chimps, which, come to think of it, they basically were.

"Ohmigod, did you see that?" Wanda shrieked to the night sky. In every group there is always a moronic inquisitor who will ask everyone if they saw what they have clearly all just seen. Wanda inevitably filled that position.

"Chalk it up, man." Bozo slapped Slug on the shoulder. Slug flipped to the back of his notebook and the two of them began to tally up the scoreboard.

Julie and Wanda each whipped out a digital camera and began to record the carnage for posterity. "Ohmigod, this is so totally amazing," Wanda kept on yammering. Julie took her pleasure more seriously and was fully intent on capturing high-quality images. "This is gonna play so good."

"Hey, Julie!" Bozo yelled. "How'd you like to see Mop Boy like that?!"

"Nah." Julie put the camera away. "He don't got no brains. There'd be no sploosh when you crushed his head."

Off in the distance, the quartet heard sirens. Maybe they were coming this way. Maybe not. Either way, they didn't intend to find out. With one last "Fuck you" at the harmless corpse, the gang reloaded the car and sped off into the night, now ready and eager to hear the details of Julie's plan.[6]

6. Oh, by the way, that baby that Skippy was going to get medicine for? She died, too. No points for collateral damage, though.

5.

Punk'd!

June 15. 1:42 P.M.

Target: Melvin Ferd, master of the janitorial arts. Melvin is in the middle of one his most complicated tasks at the health club: cleaning the rubber tread on the treadmills. This job has given Melvin trouble since day one. At first he simply couldn't figure out where to stop cleaning and spent about an hour on each treadmill. Later he discovered that he could save himself a lot of time if he turned the treadmill on and allowed the machine to do most of the work for him. A fine idea for someone slightly more coordinated than our man Melvin. At the moment he's nursing his jammed fingers for about the sixth time that day.

As Julie sees Melvin sucking on his red, swollen fingers, her resolve goes away for a split second. It'll be a fine prank, no doubt about that. But is it worth it? If he doesn't fall for it, she'll be cozying up to the biggest social misfit in the known universe for no reason. Well, all great artists must suffer for their pranks. At least she wasn't slicing her ear off like that painter dude, and that was a hell of a good prank.

Julie slides up behind Melvin and taps him lightly on the shoulder. The slight brush of human contact causes Melvin to recoil and mentally prepare for an ass-kicking. But since he's at the foot of a treadmill, he doesn't have far to recoil and finds himself tangled up on the handlebars, the moving walkway pushing him inexorably back toward Julie.

"Hey, Melvin."

"J-j-j-j-j-j-julie . . . where's Bozo?"

"Don't worry about him. I just wanted to apologize for last night. We had no right to chase you off like that. You were only doing your job, weren't you?"

Taken off guard, Melvin allowed himself to be delivered (none too gracefully) back to terra firma by the treadmill.[1] "That's right. I didn't want to see you guys . . . doing whatever you were doing. I was just doing my job, Julie."

"I know. And you're really good at it, too."

"I am?"

"Sure you are. This place would be a sty if it weren't for you, Melvin."

"Geez, Julie, thanks."

"Unlike that bozo Bozo. He's a child, Melvin. I need a man. A man with responsibilities and a steady job. Do you know anybody like that?"

Melvin gave it some thought. "Well, Jerry owns his own business."

"Jerry's an old man, Melvin. Almost forty years old. I need somebody with a future." Julie traced a lacquered finger up Melvin's palpitating chest and laid her hand on his shoulder. "And I think I know just the person."

"Y-y-y-y-y-y-you do?"

"Mmm-hmm. Why don't you meet me in the girls' locker room at three?"

---

1. As opposed to being delivered back to *Terror Firmer,* as all those who have seen Troma's 1999 masterpiece are sooner or later.

"I dunno, Julie. Won't it be full of . . . well, girls?"

"No, silly. Spinning class starts at three. We'll have the place totally to ourselves. We can talk about your future." With an extreme effort, Julie ran her fingers through Melvin's hair. A blizzard of dandruff turned his shoulders into Santa's Workshop. Julie ignored it as best she could and pressed on. "Our future."

"Jeez, Julie, I don't know about this. Bozo'll kill me if he catches me alone with you. Bozo'll kill me if he catches me, period."

In her mind's eye, Julie grabbed Melvin by the throat and screamed in his face, "What the fuck's the matter with you, you little pip-squeak? Don't you want to get laid? You're meeting me at three so we can get this over with, got it?"

In reality, Julie realized that such a reaction would make a successful pranking extremely unlikely. So instead, she just smiled and purred, "Don't worry about Bozo. This is just between you and me. Three o'clock?"

"Uh . . . well . . . um . . . okay, I'll try."

"I know you won't let me down, Melly-Belly," Julie whispered and brushed past, making sure that her artificial breasts came in contact with Melvin's bare arm.

Melvin sat down on the treadmill, willing himself to take it easy. An opportunity like this came along . . . well, an opportunity like this had never come along for Melvin. At this point he wasn't sure if he was going to go or not. All he knew for sure was that he had some serious thinking to do.

As for Julie, she took one last look at the wall clock as she sashayed out of the big room. She had just over an hour to psyche herself up for the performance of her career.

2:25 P.M.

A flatbed truck rolled into the outskirts of Tromaville, New Jersey. Inexpertly lashed to the cargo bed stood a dozen oil drums with radiation symbols spray-painted on their sides.

It had been a long, sleepless journey for the truck's drivers, a pair of rednecks-in-training who called each other Funker and Beano. They'd begun their trip at a nuclear reactor back in Oklahoma, with the drums sealed tightly and the prospect of a cross-country road trip listening to shit-kicker music on the radio dangling before them. About seven hours after they began, they pulled into a truck stop to load up on greasy food and even greasier beer. As they were swinging back into their cab, they noticed a sickly-sweet stench coming from the drums. Funker and Beano had been partners for years, so they were used to each other's stenches by now. This one was new.

A quick investigation of the drums (which was really all either of them were capable of) showed that the drums' caps were being eaten away by the bubbling ooze that they were supposed to contain.

"The fuck?" Beano asked his partner.

"I knew these things weren't meant to hold this shit," Funker gloated.

"Nice call, Dr. Science. What the fuck are we gonna do about it now?"

Funker looked up the road, scratched his nuts, looked back down the road they'd come up. "Way I see it, we've got two choices."

Beano stared at him, having absolutely no idea what those choices could be.

"Option A. We get back in the truck, drive without stopping, and dump this shit in Tromaville as soon as possible."

Beano grimaced and looked at the open road. "What's option B?"

"Option B is we go back inside and get ourselves a coupla truck stop hookers first, then drive without stopping and dump this in Tromaville as soon as possible."

Funker and Beano grinned at each other. "B!" they exclaimed simultaneously. "Definitely B!"

So by the time Funker and Beano pulled into the outskirts of Tromaville, they were strung out on uppers, had bags under their eyes the size of silver dollars, and were furiously scratching at the crotch crickets they'd picked up from Tammy and Wendy.

"Dude, what're you doing?" Beano, the conscience of the pair, muttered as they rolled into town. "There's a road around the town to the dump we're supposed to take."

"Fuck that. We gotta stop and rejuice before we dump this shit."

"Yeah, but dude, we're not supposed to drive this shit through populated areas."

"We're not supposed to drive drunk and stoned, either."

Beano nodded sagely at his partner's sound words. "What do we have left?"

Funker shook his head. "Nothin'. Don't worry, though. I know a guy in Tromaville. Jerry, he always hooks me up. Works at the gym."

The flatbed sputtered to a halt on the street outside the health club, toxic goo splashing onto the sidewalk.

"Let's hit it."

Funker made straight for the door as Beano paused, sniffing at the smoldering spots they'd created on the asphalt.

"Hold it, man. You think this crap's safe out here?"

"Better out here than up your fucking asshole, dipshit. Now you coming or not?"

"Hang on."

Beano reached back in the cab and found an empty box of doughnuts. He ripped the top off and fished a grease pencil out of the glove compartment. In big block letters he scrawled "PLEASE DO NOT TUCH" and gently set the sign next to the center drums. He stood back, admired his work, and bolted into the club.

3:02 P.M.

Julie paced back and forth, trying to figure out if any humiliation she'd ever endured would be worse than being stood up by Melvin Ferd. Wetting herself during first communion? Having her first boyfriend laugh in her face after she took off her training bra? Being asked by the plastic surgeon, "Are you sure that's all you want done?" after she went in for implants? None of that even came close. If that little wet fart didn't show after she'd all but thrown herself at him, she might just as well pack her bags and leave town immediately. She could never show her face in the club again, that was certain. For all she knew, word would spread like wildfire and she'd never be able to live this down anywhere on earth. What would be the sexiest way to kill yourself?

Luckily for her, the question remained unanswered for the moment as the clatter of a mop and bucket coming through the door announced Melvin's arrival.[2] Julie gave her hair one last fluff in the mirror hung in her locker door, switched on her thousand-watt smile, and struck her best Victoria's Secret pose. She stood alluringly for all of thirty seconds while clattering and splashing sounds continued to come from the hallway outside. After Melvin failed to appear, she decided to give him a little guidance.

"In here, Melvin!"

"Y-yeah . . . um . . . just a sec."

With a percussive slam, Melvin's mop bucket raced in and struck the doorjamb between locker room and hallway, splashing gray water on the floor and wall. A second later, Melvin himself appeared, mop held nervously in front of him in hopes of creating an impenetrable force field.

"Hey, Melvin," Julie purred. "You're late."

---

2. For those who are curious, the authors have spent a great deal of time personally researching just what would be the sexiest way to kill oneself. An overdose of pills isn't bad, providing you put the time and effort into arranging yourself on the bed just so beforehand. However, this pales in comparison to anything involving a bathtub, whether it's electrocution, drowning, or poison. While undeniably pleasurable in other regards, auto-erotic asphyxiation does not leave as alluring a corpse as you might expect and should be avoided unless you are the lead singer of a washed-up Australian rock band.

"S-s-sorry," Melvin feebly apologized, eyes cemented on his grip on the mop. "I had an emergency cleanup in the weight room."

"An emergency?" Julie smiled and stepped directly in front of Melvin, resting her fingers on the mop handle. "You take care of emergencies a lot, don't you, Melly?"

"Uh, I guess," Melvin quaked. His fingers skittered along the mop, away from Julie's. "I mean, if the equipment isn't properly maintained, somebody could get hurt or something."

"Mmm . . . I like that you're there to help people. Loyal, responsible Melvin." Julie locked her eyes onto Melvin's but to no avail. His gaze would not be moved from the mop. Her grip slid down the mop, her long, lacquered fingers wrapping around Melvin's nail-bitten, white-knuckled grip. Melvin inhaled deeply, feeling the sharp pangs of a headache from the cheap perfume with which Julie had liberally doused the room. He couldn't take the sight of his flesh touching hers, so Melvin had no choice but to look up and meet Julie's come-hither eyes.

"I need a man like you, Melvin," said Julie. "A good, hardworking, honest man. Can you make an honest woman out of me, Melvin? Can you save me from a life of meaningless sex, cheap thrills, drugs, and booze?"

"Sure," said Melvin. "But what about Bozo?"

"Jesus, Melvin, didn't you read the last scene we did together? We've been over this already. I'm sick of him. You're gonna take me away from him and his kind, aren't you?"

"Uh, okay. Where to?"

"Anywhere but here. But first I've got to be sure about you, sweetie. If you're going to be my man, you've got to do anything to make me happy. Can you?"

"Yes, Julie. Whatever you want." By now Melvin had had enough of Julie's eyes and felt confident enough to allow his gaze to wander to her tits. Julie's silicone chest missiles had a Svengali-like effect on men. When other women complained that men would never look them in the eyes, Julie didn't understand what they were talking about. It seemed to her that was like Superman complaining that being able to fly cheated him out of the complimentary bag of peanuts on airplanes.

"First I want you to prove to me what a big man you are. Seal our new relationship. I want you to make love to me, Melvin."[3]

"Oh, okay," Melvin chirped and began to slide his shorts to the floor.

"No!" Julie screamed, almost giving the whole thing away. Little Melvin hoisted his shorts back up, though not before Julie had been treated to a quick glimpse of Littler Melvin. "I mean, there's something you have to do for me first. To get me in the mood."

"Like foreplay?" Melvin had studied the pencil drawings in the library's sticky copy of *The Joy of Sex* very closely, so he knew all about foreplay.

"Kind of," Julie replied with a mischievous twinkle. She reached into her locker and brought out a hot pink leotard complete with a matching pink tutu. She held it out to Melvin who, for the first time, began to have second thoughts.

"Jeez, I don't know, Julie. People will start coming back here soon and I've got a lot of work to do. We'll get caught."

Melvin was backing up now, fishing around with his mop for the bucket in hopes of making a hasty retreat. Julie saw that she was quickly losing the fish she'd so carefully baited. Time to bring out the big guns. Literally.

Without missing a beat, Julie peeled off her top, exposing her perma-hard nipples. As expected, the fun bags froze Melvin in midstep.

3. While she had never used the phrase "make love" before, this was in fact how Julie cemented all her new relationships and deals, whether it was with a teacher threatening to fail her, a cop giving her a ticket, a priest who gave her too many Hail Marys in confession, or a plastic surgeon expecting to be paid in full.

He came back toward her as if his eyes were metal and her tits were equipped with magnets (and, indeed, they may very well have been).

"Come on, Melvin. Don't you ever feel a little bit kinky?"

"Yeah," Melvin told Julie's boobs, despite having not heard a single word she'd said.

"I love a man who's confident and secure in his masculinity. And I loooove pink. Pink gets me so hot, Melvin. Does pink get you hot?"

"Uh-huh," Melvin answered truthfully. After all, Julie's nipples were pink, and at the moment, he felt very hot indeed.

"Well, if you slip this on and meet me down by the Jacuzzi in ten minutes, you'll find out just how hot pink makes me. You'll get plenty of pink . . . all you can eat."

Julie arched her back and allowed her nipples to brush against Melvin's slack-jawed face. The effect was enough to weaken any resolve Melvin had left. His skin tingled with pleasure as he grabbed the tutu from Julie's hands and started the difficult process of extricating himself from his T-shirt.

Julie smiled wickedly and watched Melvin undress until she realized she was watching Melvin undress. "Ten minutes, baby. Down by the Jacuzzi. I'll be waiting."

"I'll be there, Julie."

"And Melvin? Bring your mop. We might be able to put it to good use, too." For illustrative purposes, she straddled the mop and eased it suggestively between her legs. Melvin giggled and nodded as Julie set the mop down and left the locker room.

3:15 P.M.

Forty-five minutes ago, Jerry Wilkins became several hundred dollars richer. And now he was working on doubling his money.

Funker and Beano were passed out on the couch in his basement office. Beano's head rested adorably on Funker's shoulder. Jerry was carefully going through their pockets, fishing out the pills and cocaine he'd just sold them.

Jerry's office was better equipped than any pharmacy in North America. As the owner of a health club, Jerry felt it was his business to cater to all aspects of physical and mental well-being. And for some people, that meant copious amounts of illegal drugs. Jerry particularly loved selling to truckers, especially stupid ones such as Funker and Beano. For one thing, truckers were in and out of town, so if they got caught with the stuff, they'd theoretically be in somebody else's jurisdiction by then. For another, stupid truckers like these two tended to come in after they'd been up driving for days on end. Inevitably Jerry would sell them the drugs and offer them a couple "on the house." The freebies were powerful sedatives, knocking out the fatigued truckers for a few hours. When they woke up, Jerry would give them each a cup of coffee and ask if they were ready to get down to business. Funker and Beano would have no memory of already buying the drugs, and Jerry would sell the same stuff to them again.

Feeling pretty happy with himself, Jerry sat down at his desk, poured himself a belt of bourbon, and switched on the TV. All things considered, this was turning out to be a pretty damn good day.

3:17 P.M.

The door to the women's locker room creaked open just enough to allow a single eyeball access to the world outside. The eyeball scanned the corridor, looking for the slightest sign of life. The spa appeared to be as deserted as an Osama Bin Laden support rally at Ground Zero.

The door burst open. There stood Melvin, clad in the ill-fitting leotard. The tutu wrapped around his hips, wide enough to touch both sides of the doorway. He held the mop like a staff and wore an expression of confidence that had never touched his face before. In the locker room he'd felt momentarily ridiculous as he assessed his look in the mirror. But the memory of Julie's breasts against his face wiped away all doubts. Despite the pink leotard and tutu, for the first time in his life, Melvin looked like a man. A man who was going to get some.

Melvin strutted through the deserted hallways, twirling his mop and only dropping it twice. In his head he walked in time to the beat of James Brown's "Sex Machine." In actuality he was walking to the accompaniment of Al Jarreau's "Good Morning, Mr. Cheerio," because Jerry insisted on piping Tromaville's "smooth jazz" radio station into the club. This is why most people in Tromaville used headphones while they were exercising. But today all Melvin heard was the sound track in his head and the sound of his blood rushing toward his gonads.

Melvin pushed open the door to the Jacuzzi room and stepped inside. The door swung shut behind him, engulfing him completely in darkness. Once again, panic gripped Melvin's hormone-crazed mind as he began to think he may have made a tactical error in agreeing to all this.

"J-julie? It's me. Melvin." He was poised right next to the door. If he didn't hear what he wanted to hear, he'd get the hell out of there and forget this whole thing ever happened.

"I'm right here, sweetie. Waiting for you."

That was what he wanted to hear, all right.

Melvin groped his way forward, using the mop to sweep the way ahead for obstructions. "Where are you, Julie? Why's it so dark in here?"

"I like the dark, Melly."

"Then how're you going to see the pink?" For a person not blinded by lust, this should have been a clue that something here wasn't kosher. But what Melvin was really wondering was how he was going to see the pink. He'd basically forgotten about the costume he was sporting.

"I'll switch the light on when you're next to me, sweetie. Don't you worry . . . I'll see some pink."

Melvin's mop plunged down and splashed into the Jacuzzi. He stopped, turned around, and sat on the edge of the tub. "I'm right here at the hot tub, Julie. Where are you?"

Julie's voice materialized in Melvin's ear, her sweet and sour breath tickling the hair on the back of his neck. "Right next to you. Can't you tell?"

Melvin felt a cold nose rub against his ear. He giggled (actually, it was more like a titter)[4] and pulled away nervously.

"You're cold."

"I was in the water waiting for you to come and warm me up."

The nose nuzzled Melvin's cheek again, this time accompanied by a tongue. She lapped Melvin's ear, sending shivers of pleasure down his spine.

"Oh, Julie," Melvin sighed and reached up to pull her closer to him. His fingers dug deep into soft, warm fur as her tongue eagerly smacked against Melvin's lips.

"Are you wearing a fur coat?"

"Something like that. Now shut up and kiss me."

"Oh, Ju-mmmph," Melvin mashed his lips against her tongue. Simultaneous with Melvin's muffled sigh, the lights snapped on. Melvin, of course, wasn't aware that most passionate kisses are performed with the eyes closed, so as soon as the lights came up, he immediately saw what was happening.

Melvin's eyes were locked onto the milky blue eyes of a purebred pygmy goat. Not to mention his lips, which were locked around the goat's tongue.

Melvin recoiled in disgust, painfully landing halfway between the hot tub and the deck. Water soaked half his tutu as Melvin and the goat bleated at each other. Melvin's bleat was one of shock and horror. The goat's was one of disappointment. She'd thought she'd made a friend.

Melvin looked at the goat, the ribbon around her neck, and the

---

4. Usually only prepubescent schoolgirls giggle or titter. To his credit, Melvin had never done either one before this very moment, but then again, he'd never had much reason to.

leash leading back to Julie's hand. Julie was doubled over with laughter. As were Slug and Wanda, standing directly behind Julie. Bozo, on the other hand, was not. He simply stood imperiously behind the goat, arms crossed and a wicked smile of satisfaction curling around his lips.

Laughter and goat bleats pealed off the tile and echoed throughout the room. Melvin, still trying to fumble his way out of the hot tub, looked around and saw virtually every member of the health club gathered around, laughing, pointing, and wiping away tears of hysterical happiness. Melvin recognized every one of them. Dominating a corner of her own was Louise, a 250-pound housewife in an ill-fitting tank top that read "Jail Bait." Her flab was rippling with reverberations from her laughter. She was probably getting more of a workout right now then she ever did on any of the exercise machines. Closer to Melvin was Doug, a spiky-haired stick figure going on nineteen who was laughing so hard he was actually pissing himself. Only those closest to Doug noticed, and even they didn't seem to care. Melvin's discomfort was the only thing worth calling attention to today.

Melvin shakily got to his feet, only to be almost knocked back into the tub by a hearty shoulder punch from Vince, a chiseled, permanently oiled lothario who seemed to think that Melvin was in on the joke. Melvin rebounded with more ease than anybody would have thought possible and attempted to make his way out.

Of course, Melvin had been humiliated before. Many, many times. But this time was different. This was humiliation on multiple levels. The pink leotard rode up his ass, giving him a wedgie reminder of what was going on. The goat's cries sounded eerily like the group's laughter. Melvin had been laughed at by people, tropical birds, even monkeys in a zoo. But this was the first time a common farm animal had conspired against him.

Bozo saw Melvin attempting to ignore the gales of laughter and escape. The hell with that! This goat had cost him twenty-five bucks for the day and he'd be good and goddamned if he only got thirty seconds of high comedy out of the rental. As Melvin tried to squirm away, Bozo positioned himself right behind him, tormenting him as he went.

"Where you going, Mop Boy? You don't just get a girl like Flopsie here all excited and then leave before she's satisfied. She's ready for some powerful deep dick action like only a superstud like you can give her."

"Lemme alone!" Melvin squealed and kept going. The crowd wasn't letting him off that easy, either. They descended on him, shoving him, and attempting to turn him back toward the goat.

"Lemme alone," Bozo repeated in a feeble approximation of Melvin's voice. "Come on, Mop Boy, you know you want some, too. Get back there and fuck that goat! Fuck that goat! Fuck that goat!"

It doesn't take much to get a chant started, especially if it uses the word "fuck," and the mob quickly picked up on the cue. "FUCK THAT GOAT! FUCK THAT GOAT! FUCK THAT GOAT! FUCK THAT GOAT!"

They say that in moments of extreme stress, even the weakest person finds reserves of strength they never knew they had. Usually when "they" say shit like that, "they" are referring to single mothers lifting Buicks over their heads in an attempt to rescue a trapped infant or presidents discovering that they can make the army go to war against random Middle East countries for no apparent reason. Melvin didn't know who "they" were exactly, but if he did, he wouldn't mind telling them that they were only half right. Melvin had never experienced a moment of more extreme stress than this one. Even so, his arms and legs still felt like they were made out of overcooked pasta. But he did realize he had one advantage over the rest of this crew. He had a weapon.

Melvin squeezed his eyes shut and swung the mop in as wide an arc as possible, poking people in the ribs and forcing them out of his way. The application of the mop had two effects. First, it disrupted the precision of the chant, turning "FUCK THAT GOAT! FUCK THAT GOAT!" into "FUCK THAT hey oof watch it goat that fuck uhh fuck goat mop ouch that that goat fuck knock it off fuck fuck goat goat that fuck yuck ew mop water fuck goat." Second and more important, it cleared a path that Melvin was able to follow back into the hall.

Bozo had never been one to let a victim go that easily and rallied the troops with a clever *cri de guerre.* "GET HIM!"

Bozo latched onto Melvin's trail and burst into the hallway after him. The mob, having nothing better to do, followed.

Melvin ran down the hall, looking in vain for a place to hide. The tutu, although it weighs less than a pound, is not built for speed, and when you weigh only ninety-five pounds soaking wet (which at least half of Melvin was by now), it's more than enough to slow you down. Melvin glanced behind him and saw Bozo, Julie, and the rest of the mob flooding down the corridor after him. There had not been time for them to gather pitchforks and torches, but rest assured, if they'd been available they would have grabbed them.

Melvin's panic and fear gripped tightly around him and he ran blindly, heading upstairs. There was a utility closet up there known only to Melvin. If he could just make it there in time, they'd never find him.

Down in his office, Jerry heard a stampede gallop across the floor directly above his head. "The fuck?" he asked the still sleeping Funker and Beano. Jerry checked his calendar. The spinning class was supposed to be going on right now. The running back and forth like a fucking idiot class didn't start till four.

"Goddamn fat-ass fucks," Jerry fumed. "Better not be wrecking my place."

As Jerry got up to leave, Funker blinked his eyes and woke up. "Jerry? What's happening?"

"No fucking idea. Sounds like a herd of rhinos running around up there. I better go check it out."

Funker's rational brain (a very, very minuscule area) flashed to his illegally parked truck. "Everything's okay, yeah?"

"I just said I have no fucking idea. Everything's probably fine. Stay here. We've still got business. I'll be right back. If it's a fire or something, I'll give you a call."

Melvin wasn't used to running, period. He certainly wasn't used to running up flights of stairs while carrying a mop and wearing a tutu while fifty people were chasing him. It was starting to seem less and less likely that he'd be able to reach the sanctuary of the utility closet unmolested.

As Melvin reached the top floor, Bozo was right behind him. The others filed in behind, creating a wall of humanity that no one could penetrate.

"End of the line, Mop Boy. Time to peel down that pretty little tutu and fuck that goat!"

Hey, the mob collectively thought. We recognize that! "FUCK THAT GOAT! FUCK THAT GOAT!"

The mob pressed in. Melvin looked behind him. The hall was a dead end, leading straight to a closed window. He had two choices. Stop running and let the mob take him back downstairs to become a goat rapist. Or . . . well, what the hell. They were only three floors up.

Melvin turned and ran as fast as he'd ever run before. He threw himself at the window with every ounce of strength and hoped to holy hell that he wouldn't simply bounce off.

Luck was with him, if you can call it luck when you have to defenestrate yourself in an attempt to avoid forced bestiality. The mob became truly slack-jawed as Melvin, mop, and tutu disappeared from view. A couple of people screamed. Others laughed. Bozo didn't know what to do. He ran to the window, hoping Julie had her digital camera to take pictures of the inevitable Polack splash of guts that would be waiting on the ground below.

Instead, Bozo saw Melvin's pink-clad ass sticking up out of a barrel of bubbling green goo. He had landed on the back of a truck parked in front of the club, and his legs were flailing madly in a feeble attempt to extricate himself from the vat.

Bozo was somewhat pleased that Melvin was still alive. The joke could keep going, assuming they could get downstairs in time.

Jerry had arrived too late to see where the stampede was heading so naturally figured they'd gone outside. But the only thing he saw there was Funker and Beano's truck with two crazy legs sticking up out of one of the barrels.

Now, Jerry wasn't a smart man or a brave man or even a particularly clean man. But he knew the kind of cargo Funker and Beano hauled into Tromaville, and although he wasn't 100 percent sure that a toxic waste shampoo was hazardous to one's health, he had a pretty good idea. Jerry leaped onto the back of the truck and started tugging at Melvin's legs. Not the safest or best way to get him out of the situation, but the only one that came to Jerry's mind.

The Bozo-led group of bozos burst out of the health club's front door in time to see Jerry give one last heave on Melvin's still-thrashing leg. Whether it was Jerry pulling from the outside or Melvin scrambling around on the inside isn't particularly important, but the result was that the barrel Melvin was trapped in capsized, spilling Melvin Ferd and fifty gallons of foul-smelling toxic waste onto the sidewalk.

Jerry fell back onto the truck, safely out of the way. The mob lurched every which way, scrambling for a dry patch of asphalt.

Melvin, wet, stinky, and in more pain than any human being should ever have to endure, shuddered and twitched alone on the sidewalk. His eyes burned and his head pounded and throbbed. He lifted his hands to his temples and sat there, head in his hands, willing the pain to stop.

Even in Tromaville, a toxic waste spill on Main Street in late afternoon doesn't go unnoticed. The first representative of law and order to realize something was going on was a beat cop, Officer Jimmy Maslin. Maslin saw the commotion from about half a block away and ran over, not afraid to use his billy club to get the looky-loos out of his way.

"All right, break it up, let me throoooooly shit!" Maslin exclaimed as he saw Melvin's crouched form. The pink of the leotard was now a dirty gray, and the tutu was beginning to smolder. On Melvin's bare arms, Maslin could see pustules forming before his eyes, the flesh seeming to breathe in places flesh just doesn't breathe.

To his credit, Maslin was a good, responsible cop and knew the first thing to do wasn't to figure out what the hell was going on here but to get this poor bastard some help. He shakily fingered the radio on his shoulder. "This is Maslin. Requesting an ambulance and a haz-mat team to the Tromaville Health Club ASAP." The radio crackled some sort of response, and Maslin leaned down to give Melvin whatever help he could.

"Take it easy, kid," Maslin said. "Help's on its way."

Melvin lifted his head. As he took his hands away, great chunks of hair pulled out of his head and chunky palmprints were left on his forehead. Bits of skin had melted off his hands and into his head. Goo dripped off him, creating a toxic curtain in front of his pleading eyes as he looked at Maslin. "H-h-h-h-h-hot . . . s-s-so hot-t-t-t."

"It's okay, you'll be okay," Maslin blatantly lied. He didn't know the first thing about hazardous materials, but he knew that this kid wouldn't ever be okay again. "An ambulance is coming."

"Ambulance?!" Bozo exclaimed. "What for? He's faking it!"

"Shut up," Maslin commanded. The ambulance's siren could be heard just down the street. Maslin breathed a sigh of relief. "You hear, kid? There it is. Let's get you ready."

Maslin reached over and gently touched Melvin's arm. Instantly, his fingers melted into Melvin's flesh, and the sickly-sweet smell of roast pork filled the air. Maslin screamed in horror, his eyes watering from the greasy black smoke that was rising from his hand.

Melvin looked over and saw what was happening. He tried to pull away but couldn't. The two were joined at the arm. Flames began to rise from the officer's hand.

Maslin knew he had about two seconds before that fire rose up and consumed both of them. He gritted his teeth and pulled back as hard and as fast as he could. The toxic fire had weakened his arm at the wrist, and the hand fell away like so much undercooked meat. Blood sprayed from Maslin's mutilated stump, dousing the shoes of at least two nearby spectators.

As Maslin fell away,[5] Melvin got to his feet. The flames still danced on his arm, spreading rapidly up his shoulder. The mob fell back screaming as Melvin whirled around, looking for something to put out the fire. The flames reached higher, engulfing Melvin's chest and face.

"JESUS!" somebody in the crowd screamed. "He's gonna hit the truck! We'll all die!"

Melvin realized there was some truth to that and figured he'd better get as far away from the truck and the rest of these not-terribly-innocent people before something happened.

"Bullshit," Bozo counterreasoned. "He's totally faking it!" Nobody paid Bozo any attention and ran into each other trying to get away from Melvin.

For his part, Melvin tucked his head down and shot through the dwindling crowd. Fire swept rapidly around him as he ran, leaving a trail of greasy smoke. Burning fragments of pink taffeta fluttered away in the late afternoon breeze as he rounded the corner and disappeared out of sight.

5. Don't shed any tears for the wounded cop, gentle reader. Remember, an ambulance is on its way.

The mob disintegrated much, much faster than it had formed. Everyone ran back to their homes, wanting to get as much distance between themselves and this incident as physically possible. Soon all that was left of the group of merry pranksters were Bozo and Julie, standing shaken by the front door.

The ambulance pulled up and paramedics ran over to Maslin,[6] still cradling his bloody stump of an arm. Jerry gingerly got down from the truck, taking his time to make sure that none of the toxic crap got on him, too.

As the disaster area became a scene of controlled chaos, Bozo smiled and elbowed Julie in the ribs. He looked down at her and gave a little nod of satisfaction, clearly pleased with the day's events. "What'd I tell you," he grinned. "Pretty funny, huh?"

6. See? What'd I tell you, you bunch of bleeding hearts?

6.

The Modern Prom[1]

EDITOR'S NOTE: Shortly after agreeing to publish this masterpiece, we received a frantic telephone call from one Dr. Zachary Douche. Dr. Douche claimed to be Lloyd Kaufman's therapist and begged us not to publish this novel. We had received the same advice from our accountants but were curious as to Dr. Douche's reasoning. He explained that Mr. Kaufman suffered from a God complex and feared that writing a novel in the third person, from the point of view of an omniscient narrator, would exacerbate this problem.

1. Actually, this chapter was originally titled "The Modern Prometheus." Y'know, like Frankenstein? But our editors felt that if we dropped the "etheus," our book would appeal to that all-important tween girl demographic. While Troma has no problem using any means necessary to promote our stuff, we draw the line at blatantly lying to the audience. So here are some tips to having a memorable prom night! (1) Spiking the punch is all well and good but a properly mixed cocktail adds a flair of sophistication to your debauchery. (2) If you aren't crowned prom queen, don't immediately take revenge on your nemesis. Stew in your own juices for a day or two. Then, when they least expect it, WHAMMO! (3) Due to safety concerns in most modern high schools, it is perfectly acceptable to wear Kevlar beneath your tux or dress. (4) Girls, make sure you put out. Especially if your date's name is Lloyd or Adam. Have fun, kids!

We thanked Dr. Douche for his advice but made it clear that we intended to proceed with the novel as planned. For one thing, we assumed that the person we were speaking to was in fact Lloyd Kaufman himself, using a high-pitched voice and a rather obviously phony name to get out of completing work on the book. Furthermore, we pointed out that Mr. Kaufman's previous books included a long list of collaborators. Therefore, we reasoned that any actual "writing" done by Mr. Kaufman would be negligible.

Whether or not we were correct in our position, we may never know. However, Mr. Kaufman did check himself into the New Horizons rehabilitation clinic two days after the phone call from Dr. Douche, citing mental and physical exhaustion. This was troubling news because as we were going to press, we discovered that chapter 6 consisted only of a title, a footnote, and ten pages of crudely drawn pornographic cartoons. We then attempted to contact Mr. Kaufman's collaborator, Adam Jahnke. During our only conversation with Mr. Jahnke, he claimed in a slurred, drunken voice to have never heard of Lloyd Kaufman. His sentences were punctuated by what audio experts have confirmed was the sound of a pistol being dry-fired near his head.

Fortunately, another of our authors had for years failed to live up to his contractual obligation. This particular author had failed to deliver a new work of fiction, making it a simple matter for our legal team to convince him to contribute a chapter to the present work. It gives us great pleasure to bring you chapter 6 of The Toxic Avenger, *as written by J. D. Salinger.*

If you really want to know about it, how it happened and what it did to me, you probably want to know about my childhood and my parents and all that David Copperfield crap. The problem is there isn't anything to tell, and I'm not interested in telling it. I never knew my dad, and my mom—well, she was my mom. I mean, she was *nice* and all but I can't say she was any different from your mom or his mom or the president of the goddamn United States's mom. I don't know them and they don't know me, right? So who are they to judge?

What I really want to tell about is all this madman stuff that happened to me one Flag Day. It started with Julie. I liked her and all that but never thought she liked me until that Flag Day when she started coming on to me all hot and serious-like, right? I guess you probably heard about all that. And I guess you probably heard about what happened next. She turned out to be just another phony, just like Bozo and Slug and everybody else I ever met at that health club. Gyms have nothing but phonies, I figure. You keep going back because you hope you're wrong, maybe someday you'll meet a person there, you know? But you never do.

So after all that stuff, the stuff you already know about, the first thing I should tell about is the burning. I was wet, wet head to toe with this goopy goop. It was in my eyes, in my nose, and it burned. When I breathed, it felt like hot, heavy snot was going down my throat into my lungs. I tried to open my eyes but they were stuck, the eyelids were stuck together. I pulled harder and felt one rip open. It hurt like the devil, too, I can tell you that. But I could see then, at least I could sort of see. Everything was green and all I could see were all those phonies from inside, looking at me, making me feel stupid again for getting all wet with this goop. I couldn't hear anything either except for ocean sounds like when you hold up a seashell to your ear. Which was weird, I thought, because Tromaville isn't very close to the ocean and I was pretty sure that there weren't any seashells being held up to my ears. Either way, I figured that sticking around here with the phonies and the police wasn't going to help me any. I wanted to get away from there. I wanted to go home. So I got to my feet and started running.

I'd walked from my house to the gym and back probably about a billion times but I'd never run the distance before. So I had to stop to catch my breath after about two blocks. Maybe it was because I was out of shape. Maybe it was because I was on fire and the smoke was making it hard to breathe. Either way, I stopped and rolled on the grass lawn of a park and let the flames die down. Nobody seemed to be following me for some reason. That was good. If they caught me rolling around on the grass, the city would probably make me pay to resod the lawn.

After I stopped burning, I took a look around as best I could. Everything still looked green to me and it hurt to live but I needed to get my bearings. Bubbles were forming on my arms. They'd grow to about two inches, then burst, splattering more green stuff everywhere. Funny thing. I'd never seen anybody's arms explode before. It was kind of nifty just to watch it for a little bit.

The park I was sitting in had this really good playground where kids could play on the swings and slides and teeter-totters and that kind of stuff. I'd played there, too, when I was a kid. In the mornings, usually, when it was too early for the other kids to come out and ruin it for me. People said you couldn't play on the teeter-totters by yourself but I figured out how to do it. It's easy, really. You just have to bounce off the ground with your legs before you land. People think things can only be used one way but if they'd just think about it, they'd figure out all sorts of good new ways to use stuff.

It was faster for me to cut through the playground to my house so I got up, wiped off more of the green stuff that was splashing out of my bubbles, and walked off that way. There was a girl playing by herself on one of the swings. I recognized her. She was about nine years old, and about a year ago or so, she fell off the slide while I was walking past. She played by herself all the time. She reminded me of my sister. Not that I have a sister. But if I did have a sister, I know she'd be it. So when she fell off the slide, I went over and made sure she was okay. She'd scratched her leg a little bit, but other than that, she was just shaken up. Since then, I'd stop and say hello whenever I saw her playing there. I don't think she liked me very much. Maybe because she remembered me from the time she hurt herself. The fact that she didn't seem to like me only made her seem even more like my sister.

Seeing her there made me forget what had just happened to me for a second, so I decided to say hello.

"Hello," I said when I got close enough. I smiled, too, real friendly-like.

She looked up and when she saw me, her legs stopped kicking. The swing slowed down and stopped so I could see how big her eyes were. Her mouth was hanging open, too, like she'd just remembered something really important and knew she was going to get in trouble because of it.

"Remember me?" What was the matter with her, anyway? I saw her a couple of times a week, and even if she wasn't always friendly, she at least knew who I was. "I'm Melvin."

She just sat there like a goddamn rock or something. That's what happened to people. They grow up and they turn into phonies overnight. I never wanted that to happen to this girl, but I guess it had. A lot sooner than I thought it would, too.

Then something really crazy happened. She was sitting there on the swing, just looking at me, and all of a sudden it looked like she was sinking. Not falling off the swing or anything. Just sinking lower into the ground. But the ground was sinking, too.

I thought maybe I was seeing things so I brought my hands up to rub my eyes. But one of them wasn't where it was supposed to be. I felt around on my face and found it. It had started sliding down my face so my right eye was right around where my cheek should be. I shoved it back up to the right spot and the girl went back up to where she was supposed to be. I guess that's when she started screaming like a madman.

I didn't like that any. Besides, like I said, everything really hurt. Maybe this green stuff everywhere was doing something bad to me. I figured I should probably get home and try to wash it off, maybe even put some bandages on my arms to keep them from exploding all the time. So I started running again. I could hear the little girl screaming still as I ran away. Later I heard she ended up in a crazyhouse. Life's sure funny that way.

I got home and went through the back door as quiet as I could. I didn't know if my mother was home or not but she probably was. She never went anywhere anymore. She'd wonder why I was home already and I didn't want to explain what had happened at work today. As I walked through the kitchen and down the hall to the bathroom, I knew I'd have to do some explaining sooner or later anyway. The green stuff on my feet was melting the tile on the kitchen floor. She'd be mad about that, you'd better believe it.

In the bathroom, I turned on the water and started to fill the tub. Then I opened the medicine cabinet, hoping to find something that would make this stop hurting once I washed it off. There were bandages and disinfectant and a whole bunch of pills my mother took for different things. One pill helped her lose weight. One pill helped her sleep. One pill helped her lumbago. One pill kept her regular. I didn't see anything that helped everything everywhere stop hurting, though. Just aspirin. I shook a whole mess of aspirin into my hand and washed them down with water straight from the tap. Mom hated when I drank straight from the tap. She said it was trashy. But since this green stuff seemed to be melting everything I touched, I figured she'd just be happy that I didn't break one of her glasses.

Then I remembered about the weird thing my eye was doing. To tell you the truth, that had actually bothered me more than I let on. I don't know very much about medicine or that kind of thing but I do know that most people's eyes usually stay where they're meant to stay. So I closed the medicine cabinet and took a look at myself in the mirror. Sure enough, my goddamn eye had started sliding down my face again. I tried pushing it back up, but it just slid right back down. That was discouraging. Sometimes when I'm worried about something, I'll bite my fingernails. It's a bad habit, I know, but it makes me feel better. But this time the whole goddamn nail slid right out of my index finger into my mouth. What the hell was going on, anyway?

I spit the fingernail into the sink and ran my fingers through my hair, trying to figure out what had happened. Whole chunks of hair came out in my hands, and let me tell you, that was something to worry about. If it weren't for the fact that they'd probably all slide out of my fingers, I would have bit my nails like a madman just then.

By now the tub was pretty much full. I didn't even think about taking off the crazy pink tutu Julie had made me put on. All I wanted was to wash this stuff off before anything else slid down or over or off. The water was hot but the green stuff was hotter. Hell, it had already started on fire once. So I climbed into the tub, crazy pink tutu and everything.

As soon as I got in and the green stuff started mixing with the water, the water started to boil. The whole bathroom filled up with steam. I don't know if you've ever accidentally spilled boiling water on your hand or something but you can probably guess that it hurts like hell. But this time the boiling water almost felt better than the burning green stuff. I sank down into the tub and let the green stuff float off me.

I guess I must have shouted or something when the boiling water hit me because I heard somebody knocking at the door. I didn't have to be Sherlock Holmes to figure out who that was.

"Melvin? Is that you?"

Who the hell else was it going to be? Is there a problem I don't know about with strange men coming in during the middle of the day and taking baths?

"Yeah, Mom."

"What's going on in there?"

"Nothing, Mom. Just taking a bath." Another big bubble was forming on my arm at that point and it exploded just when I said the word "bath," so I suppose I probably yelled or screamed more than I wanted to.

"What did you get into? You made a mess of the kitchen, you know."

"I know, Ma, I'm sorry. I'll clean it up."

"Too right, you'll clean it up!"

All of a sudden I couldn't see anything. I reached up and felt my head. What happened was that one of those big bubbles was forming on my forehead, and the pressure had forced my eyes shut. The bubbles on my arms were kind of wild, but I was pretty sure I didn't want my forehead to explode like that. So I laid down and put my whole head underwater, rubbing the bubble so it would just go back down on its own and not blow up.

"Melvin, what is going on in there? Are you all right?"

I raised my head out of the water. Unfortunately, I could feel all the rest of the hair slide off my head and land in the water. That was no good. At least the bubble on my forehead was going down a little bit. I opened my mouth to tell my mother everything was okay. But instead of hearing myself say, "Everything's fine," I heard a roar. A goddamn roar! Like a lion or some crazy animal like that, you know? Had I done that? I suppose so. At least it seemed to satisfy my mother because I heard her gasp outside the door.

"Okay, sweetheart. Mommy understands. Take your time and don't worry. Everybody goes through puberty. You'll be much happier when it's all over."

I didn't know what she was talking about but at least she was walking away now. I agreed with her about one thing, though. I probably would be much happier when this was all over. Something else had started happening now. The bubbles were forming all over the place but they weren't exploding anymore. My arms and legs and everything were blowing up and staying that way. It still hurt, and that was no joke. But at least they weren't splattering burning green goop all over the scenery anymore.

The water wasn't really helping anymore so I decided to get out of the tub. I decided not to drain the tub. My mother would really hate that. Besides, it looked like all the water was evaporating on its own anyway.

I stood up but my legs weren't really working very well anymore. The bubbles were making them wobbly and impossible to control.

They couldn't support my weight and I ended up face down on the floor, trying to get to the door. The room was really spinning out of control by now. The steam smelled like an oil slick and it felt thick on my skin. It clung to everything instead of disappearing in the air.

I tried to pull myself forward with my arms but they weren't doing what they were supposed to, either. My fingers were still bubbling and the nails were just barely hanging on to them. I didn't even have to chew them to get them out now. I reached out and felt something soft and familiar. I pulled on it and I felt it give way. The next thing I knew, I felt a long wooden stick hit me on the head.

I rolled over and looked at what I'd grabbed. It was my mop from the gym. I must have carried it all the way home for some reason. I couldn't figure why, but I was glad to have it now. It was something familiar. It was something I remembered. It was something to hold on to now that the rest of the world was swimming and sliding and getting generally weird.

I turned over on my back and held the mop to my chest. I could feel my arms and legs and everything still bubbling and moving but I didn't care anymore. Mom was right. Once it was all over, I'd be much happier. So all I had to do was ride it out. Besides, I'd probably just wake up and find out that this had all been some kind of madman dream. I have dreams like this all the time, or if I don't, maybe I'm starting to now. I really am a madman sometimes.

Special thanks to J.D. Salinger for his contributions to this book. Remember to look for J.D., Lloyd Kaufman, and Adam Jahnke on the publicity tour for The Toxic Avenger. *In addition, J.D. appears Friday nights at the Laugh Factory in Greensboro, Wisconsin, and will be starring in his own holiday special on Fox this Christmas season. Look for "A Very Caulfield Christmas," costarring Paris Hilton, Ron Jeremy, Jessica Simpson, Nick Lachey, and the cast of* The O.C.

7.

The Birth of a Notion

And now, a word from Oliver Stone.

"Thank you, Lloyd.

"In my 1991 film *JFK,* I outlined an elaborate conspiracy designed to cover up the true motives and methods behind the assassination of President John Fitzgerald Kennedy. The people behind this massive obfuscation of the truth included the global military-industrial complex; political power brokers in Washington; and, to borrow one of Mr. Kaufman's own turns of phrase, members of the cabal of labor, bureaucratic, and corporate elites.

"Even before my film was completed, keepers of this flame leaped to its defense, denouncing my theories and suggesting that it was impossible for a conspiracy of the size and scope I was presenting to possibly sustain itself. Somewhere along the lines, these right-wing apologists claimed, someone would certainly have to break the code of silence. For them, it was easier to believe that Lee Harvey Oswald, acting alone, made several shots that our best marksmen found impossible to duplicate rather than believe that people in our own government organized a coup d'état and kept it secret all these years.

"What this assumes is that everyone involved in the keeping of the conspiracy knows not only the entire truth but also the entire lie. It assumes that the point of the conspiracy is to put forward a plausible cover story to obscure the real truth. Clearly this is not necessary for the care and maintenance of a successful conspiracy. A successful conspiracy need not put forth a plausible or even an implausible cover story. All it need do is cloak the real truth in a shroud of mystery that is impossible to penetrate.

"It is certainly not mandatory for a conspiracy to be created and maintained by a global network of supremely intelligent men and women. Rather, all one needs to do is know when to be less intelligent. When pressed for answers, simply fog your memory and forget details of the event. The less people know, the easier it will be to create the shroud of mystery.

"In the absence of any real facts, many people will find it easy to believe your cover story, no matter how implausible or far-fetched it may seem. Those who choose to disbelieve the cover story can easily be branded as paranoid, as I was in the early 1990s. However, as a wise man once said, paranoia is simply having all of the facts available to you. In the case of the Kennedy assassination, we shall have to go all the way back to—"

Thanks and shut up, Oliver. We can take it from here.

Oliver Stone is, of course, as paranoid as a coked-up marmoset in a room full of monkey-humpers, but his point is well taken. Conspiracies and cover-ups are remarkably easy to create and maintain. You do not have to be a genius to develop one. Case in point: Tromaville, New Jersey. As we've seen, the town was built on a foundation of lies and deceit.[1] And it was certainly not built by a cabal of rocket scientists and

---

1. Really, it was built on a foundation of genocide and inbreeding, but it was definitely developed on lies and deceit.

philosophers. More like a coalition of the shilling. Tromaville's elites did not get to their lofty positions of power and wealth by crafting a vast network of intelligentsia with their eyes on the big picture. No; the secret to Tromaville's success was the fact that the left hand seldom knew what the right hand was doing.[2]

So in the case of the incident at the health club, it didn't take long for a completely implausible cover story to form that completely exonerated each and every person in town of any wrongdoing. Except, of course, for the victim of the incident himself. Somehow, the whole bizarre accident was all Melvin's fault, and in the unlikely event that he should ever turn up again, he would almost certainly face criminal charges.

Chuck O. Plotnick was Tromaville's chief of police,[3] and he arrived on the scene shortly after Melvin fled, to take charge of the investigation. The fact that a truckload of uncovered nuclear waste was illegally parked on a city street did not make his job any easier. But after thoroughly questioning Officer Maslin to ascertain that his arm hadn't simply melted off on its own as part of some natural process, everyone at the health club (who actually did help him quite a bit by simply acting as if they had no idea what happened), Funker, Beano, and Jerry, Plotnick was able to file the following report (with the assistance of those involved).

"At approximately 3:25 P.M., custodian Melvin Ferd was mopping the third-floor hallway as part of his regular janitorial duties."

(JERRY: Um, if he was hurt doing his regular duties, then the gym's responsible. We could be facing a helluva workman's comp settlement if you put that in there, Chuck.)

---

2. Although considering the pud-thumpers of Tromaville, the left hand could usually make a pretty good guess what the right hand was doing, and it hoped the right hand would wash itself before it made contact with the left hand again.
3. Chuck's middle name was actually Rastus, but he'd changed it to the initial "O" once he'd joined the police force, and the task of labeling all of his gear with the initials "C.O.P." tickled him to no end. Simple pleasures for simple folk.

"At approximately 3:25 P.M., custodian Melvin Ferd was performing an unauthorized cleanup of an off-limits area of the Tromaville Health Club. Specifically, the seldom-used third-floor hallway area."

(BOZO: I seen him earlier sittin' in that utility closet he's always hangin' around in. He looked out of it. More than usual, even. And I think he had a needle stickin' in his arm. That help you any, Officer?)

"It is suspected that Ferd was a heroin addict and high on the drug at the time of the incident—"

(JERRY: Whoa whoa whoa . . . don't want to make it sound like that kind of thing goes on at the club all the time, now, do we?)

"—clearly placing Ferd in violation of the drug-free workplace code set forth by his employer, Jerald 'Jerry' Wilkins. As closely as can be pieced together from the evidence on the scene, the sequence of events was as follows.

"Ferd, strung out on heroin, accidentally placed his right foot in his mop bucket. Ferd then began shaking his leg wildly in an attempt to extricate his foot. This action caused Ferd to lose his balance and fall, landing on his back with his right foot still stuck in the bucket. Trying another tactic, Ferd then used his left foot to pry the bucket off. This resulted in the left foot also slipping into the bucket, leaving him trapped on his back with both feet painfully wedged into the mop bucket.

"Using the mop handle for leverage, Ferd lifted himself into an upright position, precariously balanced inside the bucket. Keeping one hand on the mop for support, he leaned over and attempted to remove the bucket by hand. This resulted in Ferd's left hand getting stuck inside the bucket. The action of Ferd's left hand slipping into the bucket produced the reaction of his mop-bearing hand launching him toward the end of the hall.

"Ferd, three extremities now trapped, rode the wheeled mop bucket at an indeterminate speed toward the window at the end of the hallway. Hitting the wall suceeded in dislodging the bucket but also propelled him through the window to the street below. Instead of hitting the asphalt however, Ferd's fall was broken by . . ."

(JERRY: Hmmm . . . a truck full of fluffy newborn kittens?

CHUCK: Humane Society would have shit fits seven ways to Sunday.

JERRY: Truck full of down pillows?

BOZO: How 'bout a truck full of horse shit like them Back o' the Future movies? Y'know, where the faggot from *Family Ties* goes back in time in an ass-kickin' DeLorean and fucks his mom?

FUNKER: Does it have to be a truck at all? I think me and Beano would both feel a whole lot better if he just fell into a big puddle or somethin'.

CHUCK: No. No puddles, no horse shit, no kittens. Whatever it is, it's got to explain what happened to Maslin's arm.

BEANO: So what's wrong with the puddle idea? Just make it a puddle of toxic waste. You got 'em everywhere in this town.

CHUCK: And no toxic waste. We don't have toxic waste on the main streets of Tromaville. So what else would do that to a guy's arm?)

"Ferd's fall was broken by a truckload of napalm, en route from the munitions plant in Delaware to our Canadian allies in the north.[4] It is debatable as to whether being doused in a barrel of napalm saved or

---

4. Addendum to Chief Plotnick's report: "It is a well-known fact that the American military has been supporting our defenseless neighbors to the north for many decades. Recently it seems that the threat to Canada has increased substantially. North Korean dictator Kim Jong Il has sworn to destroy this bland, peace-loving land in hopes of finally getting someone somewhere to take him seriously. America has naturally leaped to our neighbor's defense, shipping hundreds of tons of surplus napalm and Agent Orange to the Canadian Air Force in preparation for a preemptive strike against the North Koreans. On behalf of the entire Tromaville Police Department, this officer wishes Canada godspeed in their mission. This information is highly classified and this report is therefore to be stamped Top Secret. Thanks to S/Sgt. Marcellus J. Funker and Lance Corporal Oswald Beanowski for clarifying this issue.

merely prolonged Ferd's life. There is little doubt, however, that he emerged from the gray barrel . . ."

(JULIE: You should make it a blue barrel. It would go so much better with the truck.)

". . . from the blue barrel a changed man.

"Upon extricating himself from the barrel, Ferd immediately began shouting obscenities and flailing wildly. Officer James Maslin heard Ferd's screams while on routine patrol and was first on the scene to provide assistance. Officer Maslin attempted to calm Ferd but was injured in the line of duty when Ferd grabbed Officer Maslin by the arm and plunged it into the nearby barrel. Officer Maslin has lost said arm and the reporting officer recommends that Officer Maslin be awarded the Tromaville Police Department's highest citation, the Ribbon of Excellence, in addition to six weeks . . ."

(CHUCK: Strike that.)

". . . two weeks unpaid medical leave.

"At this point, Ferd threatened innocent bystanders with similar treatment if they should attempt to approach him. Those standing closest to Ferd at the time also maintain that he demanded heroin through use of the slang phrases 'smack' or 'horse,' with one witness also stating that Ferd used the term 'the big H,' although the meaning is clear regardless of the specific word choice.

"Finally, Ferd fled the scene, running screaming up Main Street like a naked Vietcong little girl. At the time this report is filed, Ferd is missing and presumed either dead or jonesing. If Ferd is still alive, he should be approached with extreme caution. He is wanted on the following charges: vandalism (viz., the broken third-floor window), possession of an illegal substance, creating a public nuisance, theft of government property (viz., napalm), assaulting a police officer, and suspicion of public urination. However, considering the amount of napalm absorbed by Ferd's body, it is highly possible, even probable that he is deceased and his body has simply melted away, never to be found."

Plotnick switched off the mini-tape recorder he'd been dictating into and looked around the room at his fellow conspirators. "Now, THAT'S a cover-up!" he grinned.

Jerry, Funker, Beano, Bozo, Slug, Julie, and Wanda burst into applause as Plotnick triumphantly held up the recorder for them all to admire.

"Thank you, thank you. Just doing my job."

"So that's it, right?" Bozo asked. "Mop Boy's dead, he ain't comin' back, nothin' happened here. Case closed, yeah?"

"Just gotta type it up, but yeah. Case closed."

"That's what I like to hear."

"Hey," Jerry piped up. "What the fuck are you and the rest of the Dead End Kids doing here, anyway?"

"Don't stress me, Jerry," Bozo warned, pointing an erect finger at the vein that was starting to throb dangerously in his forehead.

"He's here on my say-so," Plotnick said, "and that's all you need to know. So. I guess the only thing left to do is to notify Ferd's . . . what. Anybody?"

There was a long silence while everyone contemplated this brain-teaser. Ultimately, Slug broke it.

"About what?"

Plotnick leaned over Jerry's desk and thunked Slug with the mini-recorder. "About Ferd's unfortunate accident and demise, asshole! Who's his next of kin?"

Another long silence, broken this time by a long, sustained squeak coming from the leather couch where Funker and Beano were sitting. Seconds later, Funker grabbed his nose in disgust.

"Fuck, man! Did ya shit your pants?"

"Little bit, yeah," Beano muttered, trying not to look at Julie and Wanda's tits but failing somewhat spectacularly.

"All right, seriously," Plotnick demanded. "Did Ferd have any family? Jerry, you've got to have some kind of emergency contact . . . JESUS BALLS, THAT'S RANK! Open the fucking door!"

With not a little bit of gagging and choking, Jerry opened the door. Bozo, Slug, Julie, and Wanda practically trampled each other in their rush to escape the noxious ass fumes Beano had so graciously provided. "Look in the Rolodex!" Jerry yelled over his shoulder before following them to fresher pastures.

Plotnick grabbed the Rolodex and ran into the hall, leaving Funker and Beano to stew in each other's juices. He flipped through to the letter "F" and found the seldom-used card for Ferd, Melvin.

"Looks like I'm notifying the mother," Plotnick said to nobody. His heart sank a little at this. Nobody likes notifying mothers, and Plotnick was no exception. He found notifying siblings was the easiest. If the victim's nearest living relation is a brother or sister, they usually don't give a shit about the vic one way or the other and take the news in stride. Mothers were bad. Fathers were worse because they usually wanted to either punch him, or worse yet, hug him. Wives were okay, especially if there weren't any kids around. You could usually count on some grief sex shortly after notifying a wife. Still, Plotnick thought, this Ferd kid was pretty young. Maybe the mom's hot. Plotnick stuck the card with the address in his pocket and headed for the showers. If there was even a possibility of some MILF-lovin', he'd better wash off every last trace of Beano's fart stinkum.

8.

Big

Unlike most of the inhabitants of Tromaville, Melvin had never come to on his bathroom floor before. So when his brain swam back up to the realm of the semiconscious, he had no idea where he was or how he'd come to be there. There were hazy fragments of a dream in which he was licking the insides of a goat cheese sandwich onstage with the Joffrey Ballet, but even those were fading into obscurity.

The first tangible piece of evidence that he was back in reality was his old, reliable mop. He felt the wooden handle in his grip and squeezed, finding reassurance when he came across the worn area where the paint had peeled away. Melvin slowly moved the mop off his chest and used it as a cane, propping himself up into a sitting position. His head swam with the effort. He tried to focus his vision but the room seemed off, slightly askew somehow, as if he were seeing things from two perspectives at once.

Melvin blinked his eyes and shook his head, but his eyesight continued to play tricks on him. He shut his eyes again and reached out, blindly finding the sink with his left hand. Melvin hoisted himself up, almost collapsing again from the wave of dizziness that crashed over him. Just the simple act of standing seemed to take forever. It was as if his legs were tree trunks and needed extra time to straighten out and find their upright and locked positions.

Melvin ran some water in the sink, opened the medicine cabinet, and found the five-thousand-tablet jumbo-size bottle of generic aspirin his mother bought at the warehouse store two and a half years ago. The aspirin had always been a last resort for Melvin. The childproof cap gave him trouble, and the effort of freeing the aspirin from the bottle seemed to just make his headaches worse. This time he effortlessly flicked the cap off with his thumb. But Melvin's victory over the pharmaceutical industry quickly turned to disappointment. Just his luck, the worst headache of his life was greeted by one solid aspirin and a few broken shards. Any port in a storm, though. Melvin upended the bottle into his mouth and greedily drank straight from the running tap. He licked his finger and stuck it into the empty bottle, coating it with aspirin dust. He rubbed the dust over his gums and tongue, not knowing if it would help but feeling pretty confident that it sure couldn't hurt.

Tossing the empty bottle over his shoulder, Melvin shut the medicine cabinet, gave the mirror a cursory glance, and ducked his head down into the sink, splashing water over his face. The water was cold and sharp against his skin. It cleared his head just enough for one question to come shooting through his subconcious and become the only thing that mattered in the universe.

"WHO THE HELL WAS THAT?!"

Melvin straightened up and found himself staring into the reflection of a barrel-chested giant. He brought his left hand to his chest. The giant in the mirror did the same. He looked down at his hand. It seemed larger, stronger . . . greener than it had before.

He looked back at the mirror. The dual-perspective trick hadn't corrected itself, and it seemed as though the lower perspective was affording him some blurry details just out of his line of sight. He put a hand over what he'd come to think of as his upper eye and forced the lower to focus on the mirror. Through the lower eye, he could make out the giant's face. He bent over slightly and the face came completely into view.

Now, Melvin had never been what you'd consider a vain person. He had never spent more than thirty seconds examining his appearance. Usually at the half-minute mark he'd be overcome by shyness and look away in a hurry. But this time he stared in the mirror for a solid three minutes. And at the end of those three minutes he had to come to the conclusion that somehow the giant in the mirror was him.

The dual-perspective problem he'd been having was now explained. His left eye had slid considerably south of his right, taking up residence next door to his nostrils. It could still see perfectly. In fact, both eyes seemed to have a clarity and sharpness that they'd never had before. He was just seeing on two levels at once.

His hair was gone, but that didn't bother him much. You could cook a three-minute egg in the time Melvin had spent fussing over his hair in his lifetime and still have to wait for it to get done. What disturbed him most about the face looking back at him was its complexion. The creamy white, smooth skin Melvin had taken such pride in was gone. His face was now a bas-relief map to a dead dog's asshole. It was mostly a dead-looking shade of brown flecked with green. It looked like a chewed-up, shat-out piece of leather stretched over a week-old bowl of oatmeal.

He traced his fingers over the lumps of his new face. He discovered a weak, translucent piece of skin near the bridge of his nose that burst open under his touch, streaming a river of sickly, yellowish pus down his face.

Melvin stood back from the mirror and looked at the rest of his body. He was definitely not the same old Melvin. He peeled the tattered tutu away from his waist and peered inside. Definitely not the same old Melvin. He was bigger proportionally all over. Even so, the fact that his face was now a diarrhea pizza with extra sauce meant that his already slim chances of ever getting laid had just disappeared entirely.

Melvin sat down on the green shag toilet seat and weighed his options. How was he going to break this to his mother? Would he ever be able to go out in public again? Melvin's mind raced through every possible scenario. So transfixed was he by his strange problem, he didn't even hear the doorbell ring.

Mrs. Ferd, on the other hand, did hear the doorbell ring. Not that she did anything about it. She was absorbed by the cross-dressing alcoholic teenagers with lupus on one of the afternoon talk shows she strongly disapproved of but watched anyway. Besides, it had been so long since her doorbell had been rung that she didn't recognize it at first. But when the rings turned into knocks, she dropped her cigarette butt into the tumbler of melted ice by her side, hoisted herself out of the La-Z-Boy, and made her way to the door.

Chief Plotnick stood on the porch, freshly showered, wearing his best Regret-to-Inform uniform and aviator shades. The door swung open, catching him in midbreath spritz. He shoved the Binaca into his pocket and tried not to recoil when he saw Mrs. Ferd, decked out in bunny slippers, housedress, and hair curlers. Tried, but failed.

"Eunice Ferd?"

"Look, I'll tell you the same as I told the last ones. I'm right with the Lord and I'm not interested in any more gospels of Jesus Christ. I can barely make it through the ones I already knew about."

"No, Mrs. Ferd, I'm Police Chief Plotnick. May I come in? I'm afraid I have some bad news."

Mrs. Ferd stood back and gave Plotnick the once-over. He didn't appear to be carrying any Bible tracts, boxes of fund-raising candy, or tickets to the policemen's raffle, so she decided to step aside and let him in. It had been a while since a man had voluntarily set foot in her house. The occasional paid escort didn't really count. After all, they were hardly more than boys.

Plotnick went inside, saying good-bye to the fresh air and hello to the odor of Lysol and fish sticks. He looked around the living room, wondering if he'd accidentally come to visit the Doily Hall of Fame instead of the Ferd residence.

Mrs. Ferd turned the television down (but not off) and took her usual chair in the recliner. Plotnick waited as long as he could to be invited to sit down, but when no such invitation was forthcoming, he gingerly sat on the edge of the plastic-encased davenport. Mrs. Ferd narrowed her eyes in disapproval but stopped short of actually telling him to get his ass off her furniture.

"What's the problem, Officer?"

"Well, Mrs. Ferd, I'm afraid there's been an accident at the health club where your son works."

At this point in the speech, the parent would usually fill in the blanks and spare Plotnick the trouble of having to spell out the messy details of their child's death. Mrs. Ferd was not so helpful. She fished another Virginia Slim out of the pack on her TV tray, lit it with an aged brass lighter that looked to weigh upward of five pounds, and just stared back at Plotnick. The expression said, "What does this have to do with me?" Plotnick was relieved it didn't say, "I heff no son!"

Plotnick chewed on his tongue and weighed his options. Ordinarily he'd start at the beginning and go step by step until the parent broke down sobbing and he could leave. In this case he guessed that Mrs. Ferd wasn't going to shed so much as a hiccup of grief unless he cut to the chase. He didn't think he'd be able to stand twenty minutes of her chain smoking and staring at his groin while he took her through his convoluted story.

"I'm afraid Melvin took a fall out a third-story window." Plotnick waited for a reaction. Mrs. Ferd scrunched her brow in confusion, but

Plotnick couldn't tell if that was because of his story or if she'd just realized there was a cigarette butt floating in the melted ice she was sipping.

"He landed in some highly . . ."

Don't say toxic, don't say toxic . . .

". . . combustible material. There was a fire. One of my officers lost his arm trying to help your boy. But I'm afraid it was too late. He was engulfed in flames and ran off down the street. We're searching for him but we have to assume, considering the extent of his injuries, that your son is most likely dead."

Mrs. Ferd took a drag off her smoke and stared at Plotnick as if she had never seen a genuine retard before and was amazed by it. Plotnick was uncomfortable enough to dig into his breast pocket and find the card with the address on it, just to make sure that he hadn't accidentally come to the wrong house. He'd done that before. Once he'd mistakenly told a couple that their daughter had been killed in a drunk-driving accident on her prom night. The couple was devastated because they didn't have a daughter. They had a son whom they suspected was gay and they completely believed the possibility that he'd gone to his prom in a burgundy chiffon dress.

Mrs. Ferd jabbed her cigarette out into a fish-shaped ashtray and leaned back in her recliner. "What in the hell are you talking about? My boy's not dead."

Plotnick had seen this kind of thing before, but usually denial took on a more hysterical form than Mrs. Ferd was demonstrating. "I'm sorry, Mrs. Ferd but it's very unlikely that anyone could survive this level of injury."

"He's not injured. He's locked himself in the bathroom. As usual."

"What?"

"He got back here about an hour ago and he's been holed up in there ever since. Spends a lot of time in there doing God knows what." Mrs. Ferd leaned in close and stage-whispered, "Masssssturbating!" Plotnick felt a little sick and wasn't sure if it was the scent of sour mash and cigarettes that wafted over him or just the sight of this awful woman using the word "masturbating." He'd never felt that self-pleasure was a sin before, but hearing her say it, he felt that it was an abomination in the eyes of God, Satan, and everybody in between.

"Is he in there now?"

"Where else? Little pre-vert. Come on, I'll prove it to you."

Mrs. Ferd winked and gestured for Plotnick to follow her. Plotnick hesitated just a moment before following her down the hall. Was there a chance that he was wrong about this? Maybe Ferd wasn't the one who fell out that window. After all, he hadn't been there, and he'd just had to rely on the testimony of dimwits and numbnuts. If so, this was going to produce a whole kettle of shit stew that wasn't likely to go down easy with the Big Man.

Melvin was still sitting on the toilet, his misshapen head resting in his oversized hands, when he heard his mother's insistent knock on the door.

"Melvin! Get out here this minute!"

Dammit! Not yet. Not now. He still hadn't figured out what he was going to do, but he was fairly certain that the only immediate solution was to sneak out of the house and not come back until his body had shrunk back down to normal.

He glanced around the room, looking for another way out. The only window was above the bathtub and less than a foot and a half wide. His old body might have been able to squeeze through. If he was naked and greased up. And willing to part with some skin off his shoulders. Maybe. But there was no way this six-and-a-half-foot tall, two-hundred-pound hulk . . .

(NOTE FROM LEGAL DEP'T.: Due to copyright issues, we strongly advise against using the word "hulk.")

. . . two-hundred-pound thing . . .

(LEGAL DEP'T.: Same problem, Lloyd. "Thing" is also a registered trademark of Marvel. Try again.)

. . . colossus?

(LEGAL DEP'T.: X-Men character. Can't use it.)

God fucking dammit! How are you supposed to write anything if half the English language is a registered trademark of other companies? Christ on a crooked cross, if these fucking lawyers had been around a hundred years ago you wouldn't be able to order a slice of huckleberry pie without paying 15 percent to the estate of Mark Twain! Melvin's fucking body was too goddamn big to fit through the fucking window, okay?! Or does Marvel have the copyright on fucking Window Man, too?!!

(LEGAL DEP'T.: Not yet. Please continue with the story, Lloyd. We're enjoying it very much.)

Yeah, I bet.

Mrs. Ferd knocked again, more insistently this time. "Melvin, pull your pants up and get out here right now! There's someone here to see you."

That didn't sound good. Nobody ever came to see Melvin. He had to get out of there. Now. All he needed was a few minutes.

"Just one minute, Ma," said a deep, reverberating voice completely unlike Melvin's. He slapped a hand over his mouth. Who the hell had said that?

The same question had entered Mrs. Ferd's mind. "Who's that? Is there someone in there with you?"

Crapola. Whatever had mutated[1] his body had obviously changed his voice as well. "Uh, no!" He tried to pitch his voice higher, but it was still about three octaves lower than it had ever been before. "Just me. Sick." It was strange watching himself speak. It felt almost like that voice belonged to someone else and had been dubbed in during post-production.

Out in the hall, Mrs. Ferd turned to Plotnick with the first signs of concern beginning to appear on her face. "That's not my son."

---

1. LEGAL DEP'T.: Watch the "mutant" references, Lloyd. We're watching.

Plotnick had kind of guessed that one. Shit, this was not turning out the way it was supposed to at all. Not only was Mrs. Ferd about as far from being a MILF as anyone he'd ever met, now a routine notification was turning into a home invasion case. And judging by that guy's voice, he was a big one. Plotnick did what any heroic cop would do in this situation. He drew his gun, backed away from the door as fast as possible, and called for backup.

In the bathroom, Melvin had opened the window and was standing in the tub, trying to decide if what he was about to do was truly impossible or just highly improbable. He grabbed his mop and chucked it outside. Well, at least that fit. Now he just had to figure out how *he* was going to get through.

A new voice shouted at Melvin from behind the door. "Listen, whoever you are. This is Police Chief Charles O. Plotnick. Within minutes, this house will be surrounded by Tromaville Police units. You have nowhere to go, buddy. Give yourself up and this can all end quietly."

Well, what do you know, Melvin thought. Mom was sleeping with the chief of police and he hadn't even known. He was impressed that she'd managed to be so discreet but knew that whatever he was going to do, he had to do it soon.

Melvin put both his hands on the windowsill and tried to hoist himself up. But instead of his body going up, the wall went down. Without even trying, he had torn a hole in the wall. The window fell and shattered, making Melvin wince. Mom would be pissed about that, no question.

Melvin could hear his mother and the cop out in the hall, trying to figure out what that noise was. His mother was screaming at the cop, asking if he even knew how to use that gun of his and how much damage he was going to let happen to her house before he did something. The cop was shouting back at her, telling her to shut up and remain calm until the backup arrived.

Melvin dropped the pieces of sheetrock and wood he held in his grip and ducked through the hole in the wall. He grabbed his mop and took one last look back into the bathroom where he'd spent some of the happiest moments of his life. Melvin didn't think he'd be changing back to normal anytime soon. He didn't know what would happen to him, but deep down he suspected he'd never use that toilet again.

"Sorry about the wall!" he shouted, still getting used to his new bass voice. He could hear sirens close by and getting closer by the second. He ran toward the back gate, leaped over it without even thinking, then paused and took one more look back at the house where he'd grown up.

Melvin raised his hand and gave a little wave, although no one was there to see it. " 'Bye, Mom."

He turned and ran like hell down the alley, just as the police began to fire tear gas randomly into his house.

9.

Gangs of New Dork

Whether you live in Mega City One or in Bumfuck, Wyoming,[1] alleyways are not considered pleasant, safe areas of town. You don't often hear people say, "This alley will be the perfect location for my Christian bookstore," or "Daddy, I want to get married in the alley." When they're discussed at all, it's usually in the context of, "I think I'll go purchase some crack in the alley" or "Hey, there's another dead body in the alley."

You can generally assume that an alley is particularly noxious if it has a name. Streets, avenues, plazas, piazzas, and promenades get names. Alleys are supposed to exist only to connect things that have names. So if an alleyway has been dubbed Crime Alley or Death Alley or Junk Alley, odds are pretty good that you should avoid it. Even if it's called Sunshine Alley or Kitten Alley, you should probably think twice before skipping naked down it on a moonless night.[2]

---

1. Actually quite a pleasant little burg, despite their long-standing tradition of ass-raping drifters.

Certainly that was the case with Tromaville's Shinbone Alley. You wouldn't find Shinbone Alley on any map. If you were looking for it, you wouldn't be able to afford a map anyway, and even if you could, you'd be so strung out on drugs you couldn't make heads or tails of it. If you weren't looking for it, you didn't want to find it and may Jesus Christ and his twelve drunken buddies help you if you did. After you stumbled across it once, it was pretty easy to remember where it was. It connected Seventh and Eighth Streets, was littered with shattered crack vials and needles, and boasted an impressive population of dealers, junkies, rapists, and pedophiles. And if you couldn't remember all of that, you just had to know it was the alley right behind the elementary school.

Nobody in Tromaville remembered how Shinbone Alley got its name, which was not too surprising. Most people in Tromaville couldn't remember what their last meal was until they drunkenly spewed it into their neighbor's front lawn. Plus, most people in Tromaville didn't have an omniscient narrator following them around to tell them that Shinbone Alley was named back in 1897 when it was the territory of a street gang called the Mud Fuckies.[3] The Mud Fuckies were led by Bob the Bitcher, a psychotic ex-boxer with a handlebar mustache who pissed and moaned about every little thing that went wrong and did basically nothing to change any of it. Bob the Bitcher ran his operation out of a second-story room above the town's tonsorial parlor overlooking what would soon come to be known as Shinbone Alley. Bob's trademark, other than his incessant whining, was his method of dealing with trouble in the ranks. The troublemaker would be invited up to Bob's room and asked to take a seat. Bob would listen to the facts of the case, then snap the bastard's leg off at the knee and

2. If it's called Kirstie Alley, it's probably really wide and vacant and opens onto a Scientology Center. Avoid at all costs.
3. So called because of their unusual and somewhat disturbing pastime of shaping mounds of wet clay in the then-unpaved streets of Tromaville into crude approximations of vaginas and . . . well . . . mud-fucking.

toss the limb out the window. It wasn't long before this practice attracted a regular population of stray dogs that would camp out in the alley below and wait for the inevitable rain of severed legs. Hence the name Shinbone Alley.[4]

The only noticeable improvements in the vicinity of Shinbone Alley in the past century or so were that the streets were now paved and there were fewer dogs. They'd all been destroyed and eaten by the booming rat population. Crime was still fairly organized, but the brains behind the operations had all moved to more upscale neighborhoods. The alley itself was now little more than a convenient place for dealers to sell drugs during the day and for homeless people to die at night. The drug trade tapered off after the sun went down for two reasons. First of all, the real money was made during school hours, so it wasn't really cost-effective to run a twenty-four-hour store out of Shinbone Alley. But more importantly, during the graveyard shift Shinbone Alley was under the protection of Officer Jake Clancy.

Clancy was an honest cop who believed in outdated notions such as truth, justice, and the law, making him quite literally part of a dying breed. Not that Clancy was the only honest cop in Tromaville. It's just that most of the other honest members of the force weren't smart enough, strong enough, or well-groomed enough to be of any use to the corrupt higher-ups. They were usually partnered with older, dishonest cops and assigned to out-of-the-way, strategically useless beats like the old folks' home and Spinal Cord Row. But Clancy was smart, fit, and genuinely wanted to help. He requested the Shinbone Alley beat specifically because he had kids himself and wanted to protect them. Granted, if he'd really wanted to protect them he would have asked to patrol the area while school was in session. But if he'd done that, then he would

---

4. Oddly enough, Spinal Cord Row on the other side of town did not have a similarly colorful history. It just happened to be home to a large number of chiropractic offices.

have had to spend his evenings with that hatchet-faced buzz saw he called his wife. And for all his good intentions, Clancy was still only human.

Still, Clancy's presence on Shinbone Alley had been . . . inconvenient. Ever since he'd taken the beat, the crack whores had become intimidated and moved to other, more well-lit parts of town where they just couldn't compete with the high-class girls. Profit margins were much bigger on crack whores than on hookers or "escorts," so the prostitution concession was definitely feeling the pinch. Also, Shinbone Alley's usefulness as a body dump had drastically declined. What had once been the unsolved murder capital of New Jersey was now just another back alley where bums could freeze to death in the winter. Tromaville had plenty of those already. What it needed was a good, centralized spot to get rid of dead stoolies, finks, and anybody who'd outlived their usefulness.

So it had been decided that Clancy, one way or another, had to go. An olive branch would be extended to see if Clancy was as uncorruptible as everyone assumed. After all, he could be a useful resource if he was playing for the right team. And if he turned down the offer, nobody would be too upset if Jake Clancy was the first new unsolved murder victim to be discovered in Shinbone Alley in some time.

Dispatched to carry out this task were three ambassadors of goodwill well known in the Shinbone Alley district. Cigarface was a compact figure of a man who apparently gained sustenance from eating the ass ends of cheap cigars, since that was all anybody ever saw him put in his mouth. He was cueball bald but sported an improbably ugly thatch of facial hair. No one would have been surprised if they'd learned that Cigarface shaved his head and stuck the hair on his cheeks and chin with epoxy, although there was no proof of that other than his patchy tufts of beard.

His able-bodied assistants were a brother-sister team known as Knuckles and Knipples. The sister, Knipples, was the more masculine of the two. Knipples was a short, stocky, obscenely hairy man with an androgynous high-pitched voice and truly terrible taste in clothes. Whereas most transvestites enjoyed dressing in sexy, revealing outfits, Knipples preferred to dress like an overweight Mexican housewife. No one thought these getups made Knipples look particularly attractive, but he did save a lot of money on clothes.

Knuckles, on the other hand, wore expensive silk pastel suits, layers of eye shadow and rouge, and sported an elaborately feathered hairstyle. He was the picture of men's fashion circa 1985. Someone who was rushing to keep an appointment with this trio would not immediately know which one was in charge just by looking at them. All three looked equally nuts in their own special way. But if you saw them loitering in Shinbone Alley on the evening of June 14, you would pay most attention to Cigarface. If for no other reason, you'd likely be attacted to the thick wad of money he was obsessively running his fingers over.

"Man, I can't believe how much cash The Big Man wanted us to lay on Clancy," Cigarface purred into the wad. "No way is he gonna turn this down."

Knipples checked his face in a compact and licked some stray lipstick off his mustache. "I don't know. An honest cop's an honest cop, no matter how much money you offer him."

"You got that right, sis," Knuckles nodded sagely.

"Tough shit for him, then." Cigarface pocketed the money and exhaled a bluish-gray cloud of cigar smoke and halitosis. "Plan B works just as good."

The three freaks pricked up their ears as footsteps and an off-key, whistled version of "Too-Ra-Loo-Ra-Loo-Ra" echoed down the alley toward them. Cigarface motioned for his backup to take up their positions, which happened to be pretty much exactly where they were already standing.

Clancy rounded the corner and found himself facing Cigarface.

"Well, well. If it ain't Cigarface and a couple of the lowest cronies he could muster. You're out past your curfew, boys."

Cigarface bit off another centimeter of cigar and sucked the tobacco juice down his throat. "Evening, Officer. We've been sent to talk business with ya."

"And what business might I have with the likes of you all?"

"A very lucrative business if you play your cards right. Ain't that right, boys?"

Knipples ran his stubby fingers through the coarse hair of his wig. "Too right, Cigarface."

Knuckles didn't answer. He just grinned, nodded, and flexed his sockless toes inside his comfortable loafers.

Cigarface came within a few inches of Clancy and held the money out beneath his nose, fanning them so the intoxicating smell of cash wafted his way. Clancy looked at the money as if Cigarface were holding a runny stool sample out for him to admire.

"What's this?"

Cigarface stuffed the wad into Clancy's breast pocket, patted it down, and smiled. "All yours, Officer. Compliments of The Big Man. Your cooperation is . . . and will be . . . very much appreciated."

Clancy hiccuped a half laugh and fished the runny stool sample out of his pocket, then tossed it into a puddle that may have been rainwater but probably wasn't. "Big Man, huh? Well, you tell The Big Man, whoever he is, that not all cops are for sale. And as long as Tromaville still has a couple of honest cops on the beat, the town don't belong to him."

Cigarface sighed and glanced back over his shoulder, giving Knuckles and Knipples a "can you believe this sorry bastard?" look. Neither of them could, so they grabbed Clancy by the arms and pinned him against the brick wall.

"Clancy," Cigarface said with a little sadness, "we were told that this money was either gonna be for you or for us. If you took it, no problem.

But if we took it, we've gotta earn it. And now our money's sitting in a river of piss. That ain't right."

"It ain't right, Clancy," Knipples whispered into the cop's ear.

"Y'see, we were told to take care of you one way or the other," Cigarface went on. "You decided against one way, so we're gonna have to do the other. It'd be nice if we didn't get paid in piss money, but, too bad for you, we enjoy our work. So we're gonna have to find some way other than money to make this worth our while."

"Easy now, boys," Clancy said, sounding surprisingly calm for someone whose arms were pinned by a hirsute transvestite and a monosyllabic Don Johnson wannabe. "Don't make things any harder on you than they already are."

"On us?" Cigarface barked a genuine laugh. "Fuck, boys, he *is* a good cop. Always thinking of others."

Knuckles knocked Clancy's hat off and stroked his hair like he'd just discovered a new pet. "Good cop."

"That's right, Knuckles. Good cop. He'd never make detective, though. F'r instance, haven't you ever wondered why they call me Cigarface?"

Cigarface took the stogie out from between his lips and gently blew the ashes away from its tip, causing the cherry to burn an angry red. Before it could subside, Cigarface pressed it hard into Clancy's forehead. The cop screamed and squirmed but was held fast by Knuckles and Knipples.

Cigarface took the stub away, revealing a blistered, perfectly round scar. Melted flesh still clung to the cigar as he stuck it back into its home in the corner of his mouth. He stepped back, admired his work, and grinned. "And that is why they call me Cigarface. Now. Let's find out how these boys got their names. Who first? Knuckles or Knipples?"

Clancy blinked tears away and looked from one to the other. Knipples licked his lips and ran his hands up his body in an obscene parody of sexuality. Knuckles just stared dumbly at him. "Knuckles," Clancy said in a voice barely above a whisper.

Cigarface smiled and nodded. "Nobody ever chooses Knipples. Sorry, sweetheart. Okay, Knuckles. Show him what you've got."

Knuckles knodded, stood back, and flexed his right hand. A frightening explosion of pops ricocheted through his fingers, making even Cigarface wince a little. A fist formed before Clancy's eyes and in a blinding instant of pain shot forward, liquefying his nose and giving several teeth a free tour of his digestive tract.[5]

Clancy's vision blurred as he struggled for air and desperately tried to get rid of the taste of blood, snot, and spit that was filling his consciousness. The only thing that would bring him fully back to reality was a shock even greater than being hit square in the face with a sledgehammer made of flesh. Unfortunately for Clancy, he got one when he heard Knipples' reedy voice ask, "My turn now, Cigarface?"

"Absolutely, sweetheart. Do your worst."

Clancy felt himself thrown across the alley. He landed in a garbage pile full of licked-clean tins of tuna fish and moldy bread and felt the rats scurrying for safety beneath him. Clancy rolled onto his back, shook his head to clear his vision, and instantly wished he hadn't. Knipples was coming toward him, rubbing his chest and crotch through the fabric of the tight sweater and flowered skirt that, thank Christ, he was still wearing. As Knipples stepped into the light, Clancy thought he could see dark, damp spots appearing on his chest.

Knipples towered over him now and began to unbutton the sweater. Clancy tried to get away but had nowhere to go. With Knipples directly over him, Clancy couldn't help but notice the tent that was rapidly being pitched in the ugly little dress. Both of Knipples' hands were busy

---

5. The teeth, which had always wondered what was down there, were duly impressed for a while. But as the tour dragged on and on, into ever fouler and smellier depths, they began to realize it would probably be a one-way trip. If you've ever taken the studio tour at Universal City, you can probably relate.

with his sweater now. It hung open halfway and he was teasing his pebbled nipples through the thatch of coarse black chest hair. Clancy was repulsed but hypnotized by the circular motion of Knipples' fingers on his chest.

As he stared, jets of rancid, yellowish milk began to shoot from Knipples' man-teats. Knipples squeezed his boobs hard enough to leave marks visible even through his fur. The milk erupted with surprising power, hitting Clancy in the face. Much of it hit in the eyes, but as it ran down his face, it crept into his shocked and gaping mouth.

The taste of the man-milk was worse than anything Clancy had ever imagined or experienced (and he'd once licked a dead skunk's puckerspot on a dare when he was twelve, so he knew a little something about this sort of thing). It was like regular milk six weeks past its expiration date, mixed with earwax and gonorrhea. It made him gag. It made him heave. It made him spew. Clancy projectile-vomited beef enchilada, coffee, a maple log, blood, snot, and teeth[6] all over himself.

"Jesus fuckin' mama in a motor home, boys," Cigarface laughed in admiration. "Looks like we got us a geyser. Knuckles, grab his gun before it gets all caked in puke."

Knuckles gingerly stepped through the still-growing puddles of milk and vomit, not wanting to stain his white pants, and relieved Clancy of his Magnum. Clancy barely registered the loss, as he was still hacking up bile and finding its flavor infinitely preferable to Knipples' man-milk.

"Give it here," Cigarface ordered.

Knuckles brought him the gun. While Cigarface inspected it, Knuckles put a restraining hand on Knipples' shoulder. His man-boobs had run dry, and Knipples had now turned his attention to his other erection, rubbing it furiously through the skirt.

---

6. The teeth, needless to say, were extremely happy to be out of there, as they were about to embark on the digestive equivalent of "Backdraft: The Ride."

"Stop being such a fuckin' slut, sis," Knuckles cautioned.

"But Knuckles . . . it's throbbin'! It wants to blow, too!"

"We'll have plenty of time for that when the job's done."

Cigarface cocked the gun. "Hey! You two fuckin' perverts wanna stop making kissy-face for a minute and haul that cop's sorry ass over here?"

The siblings nodded and grabbed Clancy under each arm, dragging him roughly back to Cigarface (and, in Knuckles' case, dislocating the cop's shoulder in the process). Cigarface leaned down, shoved the gun into Clancy's mouth, and explored it with the barrel, feeling which teeth were gone, which were loose, and which might still make it through the night.

"You have gotta be," Cigarface sighed, "the stupidest motherfucking cop I have ever seen. All you had to do was take the money. Why didn't you just take the fuckin' money?"

Clancy began to sob. "I'm sorry . . . I'll take it! I'll take the money!"

"It's too late for that, dipshit. We're deep into Plan B territory now."

"Please, boys . . . don't do it. I won't tell anyone . . . I won't press charges. Just . . . just let me go. I've got a family!"

"You shoulda thought of them before you went and pissed off a bunch of scumsuckers like us. They're not gonna be too happy about you going and getting yourself killed like this. Shit, you've just ruined everything for everybody tonight, ain't you? Left your kids without a dad and left your bitch without a paycheck. All because you thought you had you some balls. What do you think, boys? Should we take care of that for him?"

Knipples giggled and nodded excitedly. "Yeah, Cigarface. Do it! Blow his balls off!"

Cigarface traced the muzzle of the gun down Clancy's chest, leaving a clean trail in the puke shirt he'd made himself, and pressed it firmly against the damp spot on the front of his pants.

"God, no . . . .please don't," Clancy begged, knowing that it would do no good.

"Say bye-bye to the family jewels, Clancy," Cigarface smirked. "They had a good run."

Cigarface wasn't into guns like a lot of his friends were. He much preferred close-up, slow-acting weapons such as knives, lit cigars, and acid-dipped condoms. But how often did you get a chance to see a bullet rip through a pair of testicles? In this case, he'd make an exception. He thought back to his high school Hunter Safety class. Squeeze the trigger. Don't pull it.

Just as he was in midsqueeze, he felt something big land on his right shoulder. It dug into the flesh and the skin immediately began to bubble and ooze beneath it. Ordinarily he would have screamed "OOOOOO WWWWWWWW!" or something equally clever, but before he had the chance, something equally big came up and latched onto his groin, digging into the soft tissue between ass and balls. The big thing lifted him away from Clancy and tossed him into the depths of the alley. The last thing Cigarface heard before he landed and lost consciousness was a deep, angry "RRRRRRROOOOOOOOWWWWWWRR!!!!"

Knuckles and Knipples stared at the space where Cigarface used to be and found themselves staring at two tree trunks joined together at the top by a tattered, filthy pink tutu. Their eyes kept on going up. Those weren't tree trunks. They were legs. And the legs supported a thick, muscular torso. And resting atop the torso was a greenish, hideously mutated head that at that moment was roaring horribly.

They registered the fact that they were confronted with a seven-foot-tall monster of some sort, but before the fight-or-flight instinct had a chance to kick in, the monster's beefy arms swept down and grabbed them by the necks. The thugs were yanked away from Clancy and whirled around and around. The creature spun them faster and faster, so that the only thing that could stop their momentum would be running into a solid object. Like each other.

The monster cracked their skulls together, not hard enough to split them open but with enough force to make both Knuckles and Knipples stagger to their knees.

The monster dug his fingers into their scalps and hauled them to their feet by the hair. Knipples' wig came off in the monster's grip. Knipples fell back to the ground and skittered away, scrambling to get his second wind. The monster tightened his grip on Knuckles' heavily laquered Flock of Seagulls 'do and pulled, ripping it clean off his head as easily as if it had been another wig. Knuckles screamed, clutched his pink scalp, and staggered away from the monster.

The creature threw away its fistfuls of hair and turned back to Knipples. Knipples adopted a martial arts pose, learned from years of masturbating to Bruce Lee movies. He took a running start and leaped, attempting to land a flying kick on the creature's head. But there was no way for Knipples to jump that high, and his foot came just high enough for the monster to easily grab it out of the air and toss him aside. Knipples landed face first in Clancy's puke.

Knuckles was not reacting well to his sudden attack of male-unpatterned baldness. Even so, he was still smart enough to realize that he'd need a weapon of some sort to attack this thing with. He dug through the garbage and found a length of copper pipe about a foot and a half long. It felt comfortable in his hands and made a satisfying smack when he whapped it against his palm.

Knuckles grabbed the pipe and turned to the monster. With a furious yell he swung the pipe at the creature's head. It ricocheted off with seemingly no effect other than to annoy it. Knuckles looked the monster in its eyes. The eye that was in its proper place narrowed with anger, while the eye that had slid down the thing's face opened a little wider. All of a sudden, Knuckles didn't feel quite so heroic for trying to save his sister's life. Looking into the thing's eyes, he realized that he'd made a huge tactical error. Instead of attacking, he should have simply said "Fuck her" and ran. It wouldn't have been that hard. He'd been literally fucking her for years, so metaphorically fucking her would have been a piece of cake.

He never got the chance. The monster snatched the pipe out of Knuckles' hands and twirled it like a baton. The creature handled the pipe like an expert. Twirl, parry, and thrust. It plunged the copper pipe deep into Knuckles' chest, piercing his heart.

Knuckles' eyes widened as he saw the first of his blood begin to spurt out of the hollow end of the pipe. The blood splashed onto the monster's chest and it took a step back, surprised. Apparently not wanting to get dirty, it plugged the end of the pipe with the palm of its hand. Knuckles could feel enormous pressure in his chest as the blood backed up in the pipe.

The creature steered Knuckles' back up against the brick wall with the pipe. Once he was properly supported, it bent the pipe into a U shape, pried Knuckles' mouth open with his free hand, and stuffed the pipe down his throat. Knuckles felt his mouth and lungs fill with his own gushing blood.

Knipples looked over from the puke lake he lay in just in time to see his brother sag to the ground, the copper pipeline sticking out of his mouth and chest. Watching Knuckles die filled Knipples with a bloodlust that surprised even him. Without a second thought, Knipples leaped to his feet, ran, and jumped on the monster's back, intending to scratch the thing's eyes out.

The creature whirled around but couldn't shake Knipples from its back. Knipples' hairy legs were wrapped tight around its torso. His fingers were clawing over its face, not doing much damage but flailing wildly enough that he might get lucky. The monster reached back and with unerring accuracy sunk two of its massive fingers into Knipples' eye sockets.

Knipples immediately released the creature and fell to the ground, screaming. The monster glanced at the two pierced eyeballs attached to its hand, trailing optic nerves, blood, and viscous humors. For the first time, the thing made a sound other than a guttural roar. Clancy was surprised to hear it make a noise that sounded almost like "Ew!" as it shook the eyeballs off its hand.[7]

Knipples lay squirming on the ground, grasping the vacant holes where his eyes used to be. The monster slowly walked over, reached down, grabbed Knipples by the crotch, and yanked as hard as he could. The screech that came out of Knipples' mouth would haunt Clancy for the rest of his life. Dogs heard the high-pitched scream from blocks away and began to howl.

Knipples' scream was loud enough to revive Cigarface from his stupor. He staggered to his feet and looked over to the source of the commotion. Knipples lay on the ground, blood streaming out of two black sockets in his face and out of his groin. The floral skirt was stained dark with blood. For a second, Cigarface thought that the stress of the attack had been enough to finally induce a menstrual cycle in Knipples.

Then he saw the monster, kneeling next to Knipples and playing with a couple of bright red, oversized marbles. Cigarface was nobody's idea of a deep thinker, but even he was able to put two and two together and realize that the monster was playing with Knipples' disembodied balls. As Knipples squirmed beneath the monster's grip, it pried open his eye sockets and dropped a testicle into each one.

At this point Cigarface decided this wasn't going well at all. He stood painfully, cupping his own still-throbbing gonads, and shook a fist at the

---

7. The Adventures of Knipples' Left Eyeball Episode I: The orb flew off the monster's fingertip and rolled safely into the dark recesses of the alley. Its partner was not so lucky. It landed in the center of the action. As the left eye watched, the creature's foot came down on the poor right eye, smooshing it into so much jelly. The left eye gave a tiny howl of agony and swore it would have its revenge on this hideously mutated creature of superhuman size and strength. It didn't know how or when, but someday, when the monster least expected it, the eye would be avenged! *To be continued* . . .

creature. "This ain't over, freak!" he screeched in his new falsetto. "I'll getcha! I'll getcha!" With that empty threat hanging in the air, Cigarface limped out of the alley, in hopes of living and fighting another day.

For its part, the monster seemed satisfied with the ball swap it had performed on Knipples. Knipples still writhed and moaned on the wet ground but was no longer making any attempts at going anywhere. The creature stood and retrieved a pair of filthy, discarded mops out of the trash heap. Armed with the mop, the monster pressed his foot against Knipples' throat. As his mouth was forced open, the monster ground one of the mops into Knipples' mouth, silencing him forever.

With Knipples taken care of, the monster repeated the procedure on Knuckles, hooking the mop beneath the pipe and grinding it into his face before allowing it to clatter to the ground. With Cigarface having bravely run off with his nuts tucked deep inside his body cavity, the monster turned on Clancy.

Clancy was petrified as the monster approached him, too scared and too injured to move. But instead of attacking, the thing simply picked up Clancy's hat, dusted it off, and placed it gently on Clancy's head.

"Don't be afraid," it said in a low, mellow voice. "I'm not going to hurt you. Are you okay?"

Clancy nodded, not entirely convinced that any of this was real. Maybe he'd been knocked out by Knuckles' first blow and all of this had just been some weird hallucination.

"Good," the creature said. With its anger gone, the monster looked almost benign. One of its eyes still roamed about uselessly halfway down its face, and when it attempted a smile, its lips formed a weird, crooked gash that revealed a row of battered teeth. Even so, it now looked . . . friendly.

"I don't know what came over me just now," it continued, a trace of disbelief in its voice. "I've never done anything like that before. I just saw them attacking you and . . . I couldn't help myself. Anyway, you'd better get that nose looked at. Let me help."

The creature held out its giant hand and easily lifted Clancy to his feet. The cop swayed unsteadily as the monster let him go for a moment, digging around in a nearby garbage pile. When he returned, he held out Clancy's gun. It sat harmlessly in his giant palm, looking for all the world like a child's toy.

"You'll need this," the monster smiled.

Clancy nodded and took the gun from him. "Th-thanks," he said. Now he was sure this was just an extended hallucination. Why would this thing give him back his gun? How did he know Clancy wouldn't just turn around and shoot him? It had to be a dream.

The creature picked up a mop and nodded. "No problem."

Clancy holstered his gun and walked back to the street. He shook his head and turned back, sure that all traces of this weird encounter would have disappeared into his mind. All he'd see was Shinbone Alley, dark, dirty, disgusting, and empty, as usual.

Nope. There were the bodies of Knuckles and Knipples, mop handles growing out of their faces like miniature palm trees. And right between them was the monster, leaning on his mop and watching Clancy go. It smiled again and waved.

"'Bye now!"

Clancy ran out of Shinbone Alley faster than he'd ever run before.

10.

Tromaville Confidential

Tromaville P.D.:

A persistent parade of perps, panhandlers, pinheads, paid pigeons, peg-legged peepers, perfidious paramilitants, perfumed perjurers, and parsimonious pickpockets playing poke-the-platypus pretty plainly.

Drunks, deviants, devil-worshippers, and double-dealing dildo diddlers doing dirty deeds dirt cheap.

Scum-sucking sickos serving subpeonas silently so Susie Sixpack sleeps soundly.

And then there're the criminals.

Tromaville P.D.:

HQ hidden harmlessly on the ground floor of the dilapidated city hall.

Three floors up, the office of the mayor. The better to see you with, my dear. The long arm of the law reaches far. The grasping arms of the mayor reach farther.

Downstairs, holding cells. Dank. Dark. Drunk tanks in less enlightened times.

The ground floor:

The center ring. The bullpen. Ground Zero. Desks for the rank and file. Heavy wooden chairs for the vics and the families. Watery mud in a sludge pot passing itself off as coffee, a quarter a mug for both visitors and staff.

Junkies, whores, and junkie whores line the wall. Putting in an appearance for the sake of the paperwork. Joe Q. Voter has the misfortune to stop by the cop shop and sees trouble caught in the web of the law. Obviously the boys in blue are doing their job. I'm voting yes on Prop 101. More dollars for law enforcement. My tax money is being well spent.

Uniformed cops mill about, grateful they can't afford the two bits they'd have to toss in for a cup of javalike arsenic. They drop off their perps. They sign their reports. They wander back to the locker room, loitering at the entrance to sneak a peek into how the other gender lives before they dust their boxers with jock-itch powder.

Low-level detectives take statements, make calls, eat ice-cold, day-old Chinese food out of take-out buckets. Working bunco, narcotics, auto theft. None of the glamour boys sits down here. Robbery homicide. Sex crimes. Special forces. Regicide investigation. CSI: Tromaville. All these hotshots have their own bullpens, their own rings in this Barnum & Bailey big top. Shit runs downhill, so everyone's always looking to move one floor up, sure that things have gotta be better up there. And at first, they are. But sooner or later, you realize all that shit came from someplace and just because you're getting to it sooner doesn't make it any fresher.

But what do you do? Run downstairs to the asshole who's got your old job and wants your new one and tell him not to bother? The grass isn't any greener, the shit doesn't smell any sweeter, and the coffee still tastes like a reheated BM? Fuck that. Let the punk-ass figure it the hard way. Like you. Like all of your brothers in arms.

So it is, was, and always would be. Disappointment heaped on disappointment. The boys upstairs didn't talk with the boys downstairs. The boys downstairs didn't talk with the boys on the street. The boys on the street didn't talk with the feebs and lowlifes they brought in off the street. A place for everything and everything in its place.

Except today.

Except right now.

Right now, there's only one thing to talk about at the HQ. And right now, everybody's downstairs talking about, with, or to it.

Clancy.

Clancy and his run-in with the gang.

Clancy and the bribe his dumb ass turned down.

Clancy and his savior.

His savior, the monster.

Jake Clancy:

Honest. Decent. Hardworking. Compassionate.

Generally disliked and thoroughly unpromotable.

Clancy made a name for himself a few years back, volunteering for an assignment nobody wanted. Notifying a ten-year-old kid that his mother had been found dead. Naked. Cut in half. Cops were operating under the assumption that Mom had been a two-bit whore and her last john's other names were Wayne and Gacy.

Clancy believed the kid was man enough to hear the grisly details, and he spared none. Gave the kid a ride to his dad's house. Told the whole story again. Ruffled the kid's hair and gave him a Lik-M-Aid Fun Dip to soothe the pain.

Only problem was the dead woman didn't have any kids.

The kid's real mom was at the grocery store buying string beans and applesauce.

Clancy made a name for himself on the force.

That name was Lady-killer.

Now it looked like that name was going to get changed. No consensus had formed yet about what it should be changed to. Batshit-crazy was leading the pack. It was descriptive and seemed to be accurate but it didn't have much of a ring to it. One egghead proposed the moniker Dr. Frankenstein, but nobody else understood what he was going for with it. Monster-faker was another option with little support.

Nicknames were not the Tromaville P.D.'s forte.

Clancy sat at a detective's desk he'd never earn, pressing ice to his broken face, and telling his story for the seventh time. His audience was officially the staff psychologist and an Internal Affairs detective. Unofficially, the entire force was gathered around. As were a few drunks and hookers waiting to be processed. As were a few solid citizens who had come by to bail out a few drunks and hookers.

Clancy told it again.

The run-in with Cigarface, Knuckles, and Knipples.

The beating from same.

The monster who appeared out of nowhere, killed Knuckles and Knipples, ran off Cigarface, and given him back his hat and gun.

The psychologist was ready to sign off on a case of post-traumatic stress disorder. The psychologist chalked up pretty much everything to post-traumatic stress disorder, whether it was a mild tension headache or an elaborate hallucination of a monster on a rampage.

Internal Affairs was ready to go back to sleep. He didn't know what really happened in Shinbone Alley. He didn't care. He just knew that Clancy had been offered a bribe and didn't take it. Good cop. Case closed. Whatever violence took place afterward had been in the line of duty.

Neither one wanted to be the first to call it a day. Standard operating procedure dictated that a story had to be told at least twelve times, so that any holes in the story could be probed.

Internal Affairs said, "Tell it again."

The shrink said, "Tell it again."

Clancy told it again. For the eighth time.

The door swung open and slammed shut. The murmured arguments in the back of the room over Clancy's new nickname sucked silent, like there was now less oxygen in the room. Indeed there was. The crowd parted and there stood the Honorable Mayor Peter Belgoody. All 350 pounds of him.

The mayor:

Five feet, ten inches of solid lard.

Black hair permanently slicked back, stuck to his scalp by self-produced grease.

Mustache lying limply on his upper lip. Possibly a caterpillar accidentally ingested at a picnic, attempted to escape, and died there.

The latest in a long, crooked line of heads of state.

The file on Peter Belgoody that no one in Tromaville could be bothered to start:

4/15/55: Born a bouncing baby boy to Bob and Betty Belgoody. Tips the scales at 17 pounds. Mother survives the delivery. Wishes she hadn't.

11/2/65: Bob Belgoody soundly defeated in first and last run at the mayor's office. Platform based on controversial proposal to ship entire graduating class of Tromaville High to Vietnam immediately. Belgoody's plan is surprisingly popular. His opponent, Frank Stimpson, leaks photos of Bob pouring the pork to a prepubescent Peter. Bob's response: "So? The boy's softer and more girlish than his mother."

11/3/65: Bob Belgoody banks a bullet in his brains.

11/4/65: Peter writes a heartfelt thank-you card to Mayor-elect Stimpson.

11/5/65: Stimpson replies by going public with long-term affair with Betty Belgoody. A June wedding is planned, following Stimpson's November divorce.

9/13/66: *Tromaville Times* banner headline: "Mayor's Stepson Wins Fattest-Boy Contest." Photo splash of Peter in a pig suit. The rigged event at the county fair allows 213-pound Peter to get a taste of winning. He likes it. No surprise. Peter likes the taste of most everything.

12/23/66: Peter asks Santa for a set of Sea Monkeys.

12/25/66: Santa gives Peter a set of Sea Monkeys.

7/8/68: The Summer of Love in San Fran. The Summer of Lunch in Tro Vil. Peter is shocked to discover drug use running rampant through Tromaville High. Peter is more shocked to discover that neither he nor his stepfather are making any money off it. Peter threatens to turn narc unless he's cut in on the wacky tobacco concession. The dealers don't like it but can't see they have any choice. Thirteen-year-old Peter becomes a drug lord.

9/26/69: Mayor Stimpson gives Peter a tour of city hall. Peter is impressed that stepdad can breeze through the cafeteria and take whatever he wants without paying for it. Swears that one day he, too, will be mayor.

2/29/72: Crippled 'Nam vets give Peter's drug trade a big boost. Inspires Peter to expand his franchise into other drugs.

6/4/73: Peter graduates from high school. Stimpson informs him that he'll be going to college in the fall. Peter isn't concerned. Professors from the college are among his best customers. Complimentary weed ensures that Peter graduates from Tromaville City College just three years later with straight As and a perfect zero-attendance record.

1/12/75: Peter loses his virginity. Sort of. An emaciated, broke heroin junkie offers Peter a blow job for a fix. Peter doesn't exactly know what a blow job is but agrees. The junkie makes a noble attempt, forcing her face between layer upon layer of sweaty, hairy flab. She finally finds a stub that may or may not be Peter's peter. She valiantly bobs her mouth up and down on the stub for several minutes before coming up for air and proclaiming the job well done. Peter doesn't know the difference and lives up to his end of the bargain. The encounter makes Peter realize that he can make even more money in the prostitution racket. Drug Lord Peter expands again. Now it's Peter the Pimp.

12/1/77: Inspired by a recent movie, Peter the Pusher-Pimp squeezes his 290-pound frame into a tight white suit and takes his crew into the city to check out the disco scene. Peter hates the music and thinks the dancing is retarded but does like one aspect of the culture: cocaine. Returning home, Peter decides to open a disco as a base of operations for the other aspects of his burgeoning empire. He cleverly decides to name it Snow Mountain. The police fail to notice.

3/17/85: Twenty years after his election, Mayor Stimpson begins to consider retirement. Term limits were never a popular concept among the lazy, apathetic residents of Tromaville. They'd do just about anything to cut down on the number of elections they had to endure. Stimpson endorses Peter as his successor. Peter begins to bone up on local issues.

3/17/88: An election year. Mayor Stimpson still just considering retirement but showing no signs of stepping down despite the fact that he has been officially diagnosed with Alzheimer's.

4/30/88: Tromaville begins to worry when the demented Mayor Stimpson signs a law requiring that all cats be shaved bald. When the law is enforced, Stimpson insists that all the cats in Tromaville be rounded up and arrested on charges of indecent exposure. More than two hundred cats are gassed before Stimpson does another 180, saying Tromaville has become worse than Auschwitz. He's disgusted and appalled at the way Tromavillians have behaved. Cats are not Jews, according to Stimpson, and he pardons every remaining feline. Henceforth, only Jews should be gassed.

5/7/88: Peter still enjoys the endorsement of his stepfather but is now concerned that an endorsement from a cat-killing, pants-soiling neo-Nazi won't mean much. Before things get out of hand, Peter decides to take Stimpson out of the picture. That night, Peter smothers his stepfather with a pillow. To get rid of the evidence, Peter eats the pillow.

11/7/88: *Tromaville Times* banner headline: "Local Club Owner Elected Mayor in Landslide." Subheadline: "Fattest-Boy Record Still Unchallenged."

Since 1988, Peter Belgoody had ruled Tromaville as a semi-benevolent dictator. Peter enjoyed his official mayoral duties, especially cutting the ribbons at supermarket openings. On 9/11, Tromaville watched as their familiar skyline changed forever. Peter calmed the public, vowing that no terrorists would attack Tromaville while he was in charge. No airplanes could knock over any buildings as long as he was in them and, weighing in at 350 now, that was probably true.

Peter the Pusher-Pimp delegated most of his extracurricular activities to an array of trusted captains. Snow Mountain closed down, to be transformed into a crack house. His right-hand man was Chuck Plotnick, the feared chief of police. On the streets, he kept an army of foot soldiers. Legions of lowlifes and losers loyal only to him. While not every single soul in Tromaville was under his direct control, Peter believed it was only a matter of time before they were.

Thanks to his close personal relationship with Plotnick, no one was surprised when the mayor arrived at the cop shop. It wasn't unusual for Mayor Belgoody to take an interest in police activity. And Clancy's story certainly qualified as one of the strangest to come out of Tromaville police lore since the Great UFO Scare of '78.

There weren't any chairs on the main floor of HQ that would support someone of Peter's carriage, so he placed himself heavily atop the desk and stared down at Clancy.

Peter said, "I hear you had a run-in with some bad guys, Clancy."

Clancy said, "Yes, sir."

Peter looked closely at Clancy's shattered nose. "I'd hate to see the other guys." He paused and looked around the room, waiting for the inevitable sycophantic laughter. It shook the room, right on cue.

"You taking any painkillers for that?"

Clancy shook his head. "No, sir. I wanted to be straight in my head when filing my report."

Peter frowned. "Then what's this I hear about a monster saving your life?"

Clancy looked at the floor. "I know how it sounds, sir. But I swear on my life. This thing was seven feet tall. Bald. Skin looked like it had been melted down with acid or something. All bubbly and loose."

The psychologist leaned in close to the mayor's ear, was surprised to find a patch of mustard behind it, and whispered, "Obvious post-traumatic stress, sir. I don't think we're going to find out what really happened out there tonight."

The mayor pushed the shrink away as if his words transmitted leprosy into his ear. "Fuck off, Freud. I believe you, son."

Internal Affairs snapped his pen in surprise, spattering ink over his desk. "You do? Sir?"

"Think about it, people. Do you really think Clancy here could shove a pipe through a guy's chest, bend it, and drown the guy in his own blood? No offense, Clancy."

"None taken, sir."

"Now I'm not saying that Frankenstein's running around Tromaville and we should all go grab pitchforks and torches. But obviously we've got some psycho vigilante type who thinks he's real bad-ass on the loose. Probably hopped up on speed or junk or one of those goddamn things. Haven't I always said that goddamn DARE program is a waste of taxpayers' money?"

Internal Affairs nodded. "Yes, sir. You have."

"Well, here's your proof. This kid probably went through that whole thing, got hooked on dope when some ex-junkie blew pot smoke in his face in the classroom, and look where we're at now. Find this psycho, boys. Priority number one."

The entire squad room snapped to attention. "YES, SIR!"

The mayor nodded. "All right, then." He rested a beefy hand on Clancy's shoulder. "Good work, son. Take care of that sniffer. We want you back on the street ASAP."

Clancy said, "I will, sir. Thank you."

"And have the doc fix you up with some pills. I'll bet that hurts like a son of a bitch."

Cigarface lay on the leather couch, looking warily at the hand that held the ice pack over his throbbing balls. "I could do that myself, y'know," he piped, his voice still unnaturally high.

Chief Plotnick shook his head. "You just take it easy."

The door swung open and slammed shut. Peter Belgoody stepped into his office, puffing a turd-shaped and scented cigar.

"All right, fuckers. I want answers and I want them now."

Peter stormed behind his desk, settled his bulk into his specially made chair. Despite its lifetime guarantee, the chair still creaked ominously whenever its owner lowered his colossal ass into it.

Peter said, "You had a simple job. Offer Clancy the money. If he didn't take it, which he almost certainly wouldn't, get rid of his useless ass. What went wrong?"

Cigarface said, "It wasn't our fault! It was the monster!"

Peter slammed his fist onto the desk, making everything and everyone jump. "Don't start with this monster bullshit!"

Cigarface said, "But boss, I swear—"

Plotnick said, "His story's been pretty consistent, Your Honor."

Peter said, "Clancy said the same thing."

Plotnick said, "What?"

Peter said, "I said Clancy said the same thing."

Plotnick said, "You said I said Clancy said the same thing?"

Peter said, "No, I said I said Clancy said the same thing."

Cigarface said, "You said Clancy said the same thing I said?"

Peter slammed his fist down again. "Stop that shit! Yeah, Clancy's singing the same monster tune as you are. So fucking what? You both got your asses handed to you and now you're trying to cover it with some bullshit story. I don't know who this guy is, but he's no monster.

It's just some fucking asshole trying to muscle in on our territory. Find him and stop him."

Plotnick stood, leaning his weight on the ice pack for support and making Cigarface squeak in pain. "Yes, sir. Of course. But . . . how?"

Peter grabbed the heavy ashtray off his desk and threw it at Plotnick's head. "You're the fucking chief of fucking police, dipshit! You tell me! How hard is it gonna be to track down a seven-foot-tall bald burn victim strung out on pep pills?"

Plotnick wiped the blood out of his eye. "Shouldn't be a problem, sir."

Peter exhaled a plume of smoke. "That's right, it shouldn't be a fucking problem. Now give me back my goddamn ashtray."

Cigarface said, "Hey. The monst . . . uh . . . guy used mops on Knuckles and Knipples. Think that means anything?"

Peter took the ashtray from Plotnick's hand and threw it across the room at Cigarface. "It means there were mops lying around the alley for some fucking reason! Now both of you, get the fuck out of my office!"

Cigarface and Plotnick tucked their tails between their legs and vanished from the mayor's sight.

Peter regretted not making Cigarface put the ashtray back on his desk before he left. He sighed and flicked ashes onto the floor, looking forward to watching the Mexican clean-up lady's ass jiggle as she bent over to sweep them up. He pulled the blinds and looked out at his city. Days like this made running a corrupt administration almost seem like a full-time job. There were only two things that would calm him down now: a sandwich and a massage.

11.

Melvin Takes a Dump[1]

Melvin wandered the streets of Tromaville, staring at the blood on his hands and wondering what the hell had happened back there. Not only had he never done anything even remotely like that before, he wasn't entirely convinced he had done it at all. Whose voice was that when he was talking to the cop? Not his, that's for sure. He remembered putting the words together and sending the "speak" command to his voice box, but the sound that came out was nothing like his voice. He felt like he was a character in a martial arts movie. His lips moved, but the voice that came out belonged to some carmel-tongued DJ in a studio three thousand miles away.

As the sun rose, he found himself walking along the riverbank on the outskirts of town. He stepped into the water and waded out to wash the blood and other bodily goo off. Melvin stood in the icy water, not feeling its chill and not realizing that what was now waist-deep used to be almost over his head.

1. Sorry, that should be "the" dump.

After a few minutes, steam began to rise off the polluted river water. He looked around in momentary panic as the water in his immediate vicinity rapidly began to churn and boil. When fish rose to the surface belly-up, Melvin headed back to shore. The water calmed immediately.

Melvin sat on the shore and looked back out at the horizon, sadly studying the trail of dead fish he'd left behind him. He hadn't meant to do that, and though he had no real proof, he knew deep down that he had killed those fish. He'd have to be more careful from now on.

Melvin lay down, watched the sun come up, and tried to take stock of his situation. He was bone tired but knew he couldn't allow himself to pass out here. As peaceful as it was, if anybody discovered him while he was asleep it would all be over. His mom had made it perfectly clear that he couldn't go home again. For the first time in his life, Melvin would have to fend for himself.

So let's see. He could try to break into the health club. He knew the place like the back of his hand . . . or like how the back of his hand used to be, anyway. There were places in the basement where he could hide out for a while. At least, he thought there were. Jerry's office was in the basement, and he was always bringing strange people down there for some reason. Why was that? The more he thought about it, the angrier he got. In fact, it felt just like it had last night in Shinbone Alley.

All right, forget that. The last thing he needed right now was to go off on another psycho trip. He had more pressing matters to deal with, such as sleep. Tromaville had more than its fair share of abandoned buildings, some of them pretty big, like that old disco. But he had heard rumors that those places weren't quite as abandoned as they looked. So why did the mayor keep them around? Shouldn't they all be demolished and Tromaville given a fresh start? That pissed him off, too. Maybe he should just go down to that old disco, clean it out, and shove a mop up the ass of whoever sold those poor bastards all those drugs. Yeah, that's what he'd do. Shove it so far up their ass that the handle came out their throat. Then he'd grab both ends and pull and rip the guy in half.

Where did that come from? Melvin stood up and started walking, hoping the activity would get rid of some of these weird thoughts that were popping up out of nowhere. He had to focus.

He found an old, worn dirt road leading out of town. That was the way to go. Obviously anytime he started dwelling on what was going on back at home, his blood started boiling. It wasn't safe for people to be around him right now.

As he walked, he forced himself to think of a pleasant memory, something that would distract him from the violence that kept creeping into his mind. He remembered an old Chad Everett record he used to listen to over and over when he was a kid. One song in particular was a favorite, and as he walked, he began to sing. "If you'll be my Dixie Chicken . . . I'll be your Tennessee lamb . . . and we can walk together down in Dixieland."

The song put a spring in his step and he sang louder and louder, twirling his mop around. Before long, the road led to a gate marked by a weather-beaten, bullet-ridden sign. "Tromaville City Dump . . . No Industrial Waste of Any Kind . . . Have a Nice Day."

He looked around. This was the dump? He'd never been here before. Maybe it was his situation, maybe it was the early morning light, but right now it looked like paradise. The dump overlooked the river and provided a magnificent view of Tromaville below and New York City across the water. The sun reflected off of discarded beer bottles and license plates. It probably helped that the toxic muck that had deformed his body also seemed to have destroyed his sense of smell.

Melvin walked through the dump, marveling at what people had discarded. He picked through piles of broken appliances, old magazines and clothes, and empty boxes. As he wandered through the maze of garbage, he stepped on a book. Melvin, like most friendless nerds, had always loved to read and was amazed that anyone would throw away a book. He leaned over to see what it was.

Dianetics by L. Ron Hubbard.

Okay, maybe some of this stuff really was garbage, but a lot of it was still perfectly useful. People gave up on things much too quickly, he thought. All it would take was a little work to get some of these broken-down machines back in working order.

Melvin planted his mop in the soft ground and looked around, a crooked smile forming on his crooked face. This could be it. Everything he needed to make a home for himself was right here. Okay, maybe not food. Or fresh water. But he felt reasonably certain he could somehow live off the land. Even if the land was filthy, polluted, and covered in garbage.

But all that would have to come later. Right now, Melvin was so tired he could barely stand up. He was deep in the heart of the dump, so it was unlikely that anyone would find him today. All he needed to do right now was find a place to collapse.

He found one behind a fly-covered mountain of medical waste, their biohazard stickers peeling away in the sun. Hidden away behind the hill was an intact, rust-covered Pinto. Melvin tried the door and was mildly surprised to discover that the car was locked. Who was going to steal this thing? He shrugged and tore the door off, tossing it over his shoulder without so much as a thought to the impossibility of what he'd just done.

The Adventures of Knipples' Left Eyeball: Episode II

The eye watched with interest as the police swarmed over the body of its previous owner. Knipples had forced the eye to look upon a lot of things it probably would have rather avoided, from diarrhetic bowel movements to Knipples' frequent moments of self-pleasure (sometimes simultaneously). But that didn't mean that the eye wanted Knipples dead. Knipples' skull was the only home the eye had ever had. They'd been through a lot together. And now the eye had to watch as its home was covered in a sheet, roughly tossed onto a gurney, and rolled off to the morgue.

Now, the eye was left alone in Shinbone Alley. Alone with its memories of last night. Alone with the image of the creature's fingers prying it out of its comfortable socket and tossing it aside. Alone with the memory of the creature stepping on its twin, the right eyeball, liquefying his brother, his partner, the only friend he'd ever really known. Alone with thoughts of revenge.

The eye was not stupid. The eye knew that without any means of transportation, the odds of it actually getting vengeance were heavily stacked against it. It had to find a way out of Shinbone Alley. Impossible? Not for the eye. For the eye had tricks up its nonexistent sleeve. The eye possessed a power of which even Knipples was unaware. How different would Knipples' fate have been had he known he was host to . . . The Hypnotic Eye?

When Knipples was a confused young lad of eleven, he studied the ancient art of hypnosis. He read countless[2] books on the subject, but the lessons never took hold. But the eye also read. And the eye learned. And now the hour was nigh. The Hypnotic Eye would emerge in full!

The only trouble was, in order to hypnotize someone, you have to be on eye level with the subject. And at the moment, The Hypnotic Eye was on eye level with no one. So it waited. It bided its time, waiting for an unsuspecting eye to roam its way.

Fifteen minutes after the law had removed the corpses and abandoned Shinbone Alley, The Hypnotic Eye felt its target. The Hypnotic Eye turned in the direction of the gaze. There. At last. Two beady blood-red eyes studied The Hypnotic Eye.

The red eyes emerged into sunlight, revealing themselves to be in the skull of a plump, ten-inch rat with greasy, matted gray fur. The

2. Well, two . . . which was certainly higher than Knipples could count.

Hypnotic Eye went to work. It narrowed its pupil and shot powerful hypnotic rays at the rat.

Within seconds, the rat fell under The Hypnotic Eye's spell. It shot forward and sank its forepaws into the eye's soft tissue. The Hypnotic Eye rejoiced. Calloo-callay! It worked!

The rat's sharp teeth bit into the eye, shooting sweet humors into its throat. Yes, thought The Hypnotic Eye. Eat, my pretty. Allow me to become one with you, body and soul. Together we shall track down the creature that did this to us. And then . . . we shall rule this entire town. Nay, the world! From this moment forward, we shall be The Hypnotic Rat-Eye!!!

Vengeance is ours!

In the infamous lost "lonely boy" scene, loosely based on Lloyd Kaufman's pathetic high school years, Melvin pitches his tent, warms up his weeny, and shoots out his soda.

In the infamous (and unfortunately, not lost) bathtub scene, we learn the repercussions of being a lonely boy who pitches his tent, warms up his weeny, and shoots out his soda. (HELL-O! We're making fun of masturbation, people!)

Before being cast in *The Toxic Avenger*, the struggling actor Shlomo Toxvengerberg stars as Stanley Kowalski in the Scranton Community Dinner Theater production of *A Streetcar Named Desire*.

Like Vin Diesel, one of Toxie's early jobs was as a bodyguard. Here he is blocking the paparazzi from taking pre-makeup shots of Julia Roberts *(left)*. Luckily, our photographer was able to take this snapshot, and little did Julia know that Toxie gave it to Sgt. Kabukiman, NYPD, who sold it to the publishers of this book to help finance his addiction to uncut wasabi.

After the cancellation of the *Toxic Crusaders* cartoon show, Toxie was down on his luck and forced to work at a local gas station. Unfortunately for Toxie, the gas station was located in Tromaville's Lavender District and was run by a man named Sodomy Stu, so the only thing not getting pumped was gas. (On the plus side, it did prepare Toxie for his numerous backdoor-entry scenes in *Citizen Toxie: The Toxic Avenger Part IV*.)

Lloyd "Deep Throat" Kaufman shows Toxie how his missing gag reflex helped him get ahead in Hollywood.

This photo holds the distinction of featuring more nudity from Andree Maranda *(seated)* than all 83 minutes of *The Toxic Avenger.*

Like James L. Brooks's 1994 blockbuster *I'll Do Anything, The Toxic Avenger* was originally going to be a musical before test screenings showed that people hated all the singing and dancing. The only remaining evidence of its musical origins are the tutu, the taco chips, and the retarded boy with his mouth *(pictured on left)*.

A scene from *Tox Capades: Toxie on Ice*, the only ice show besides *Muppets on Ice* to feature people actually getting decapitated by ice skates. The show closed after two weeks, once the last cast member had finally been killed.

The infamous "Father Toxie and the Catholic School Boy" scene, which was altered because pedophilia was not as accepted in 1984 as it is now. Using the magic of CGI (which had actually not yet been invented, and which Troma still cannot afford), the eight-year-old school boy was turned into a middle-aged female dwarf who gets killed. The slaughter of middle-aged female dwarfs has always been accepted.

On the night of *The Toxic Avenger* premiere, Toxie visits the Bijou All-Male Revue to see *The Man Who Blew Too Much*. Unfortunately, it was sold out. So he went to see his own movie instead.

12.

Hot Cross Buns and Dripping Wet Pussies[1]

While Melvin painted Shinbone Alley with a pallette of blood and puke, Bozo and his crew tried to forget the events of the day as only they could: by stealing a car and playing hit-and-run. It had not been a satisfying installment of the game. It was Slug's turn at the wheel, and even though they drove around Tromaville for hours, the streets were strangely deserted.

The best they could come up with had been a stray dog. The dog was so small that its body became hopelessly entangled in the wheel well of the car. It made for some terrific footage, especially since the dog hadn't died right away. There were several surreal seconds of half of

---

1. Greetings, fellow onanists! Remember back in junior high, all those long hours you spent trying to find the good parts in books such as *Tropic of Cancer*, *Wifey*, and *The Lustful Turk?* Boy, we sure do. That's why, as a public service, we've crammed a whole bunch of high-quality wanking material in a single chapter for your convenience! And to make it really easy for you, all the hottest stuff in this chapter will be printed in bold italics *(like so)* so you can flip right to it. Because every second you waste reading boring shit like this gives your mom more time to burst in on you in midstroke. So have a good time, kids, and shoot one out for your Uncle Lloyd!

the dog's head sticking out from beneath the car, whining and whimpering as its hind legs twitched uncontrollably directly above it. But after that, the wheels refused to turn, and they were forced to abandon the car and walk home. Julie and Wanda were understandably pissed and refused to even provide *hand jobs*. Slug was none too pleased himself. He had been awarded twenty points for the dog, but everyone agreed that he had to forfeit them for *fucking* up the car. All things considered, the evening had been a complete waste.

Wanda woke up alone the next day in a foul mood and a fouler smell. *She felt something* cold, clammy, and *moist* on her hair and neck. She grabbed a handful of wet hair, sniffed it, and promptly choked back a gag reflex. Her hair and pillow reeked of cat piss. *She jumped out of bed, her melon-heavy breasts almost throwing her off balance and knocking her back onto the mattress.*

Lying there on her pillow was her aged calico cat, Butters, fast asleep. Butters was almost fifteen years old and had suffered from incontinence for the past two. Last night had apparently seen Butters break his own personal best, unconsciously seeping urine for several hours. And now he lay there in a pool of pee, perfectly content.

Wanda was less than content with this scene and grabbed Butters off the pillow, provoking a halfhearted mewl from the arthritic cat. She marched into the bathroom and turned on the tap in the bathtub. She doused Butters in floral shampoo, scrubbed, and rinsed. The water brought the cat back to a semblance of his younger self and he writhed and hissed, trying to get away. *Furiously, she scrubbed her pussy, water soaking through her loose white T-shirt.*

Once Wanda was satisfied with the cat, she let him go and turned on the shower, *stripping off the clinging shirt and soaping up her own naked body.* Butters staggered off to a corner of the apartment, fur clinging to his body and spastically shaking water off his paws. He found a corner of the living room and sprayed urine all over the wall, piss spattering back onto his fur.

Wanda wrapped a towel around herself and headed into the kitchen. She fixed herself a huge breakfast. Waffles, cereal, cookies, and half a rasher of bacon. She wolfed it down, marched back into the bathroom, and plunged her favorite gagging stick down her throat. The semimasticated food returned, splattering into the toilet with a sickening plop. Satisfied, she brushed her teeth, gargled, brushed her teeth again, and tossed the towel aside. *Nude,* she stepped onto her bathroom scale. *She peered over her jutting udders* and nearly broke down sobbing when she read the numbers. No!!! She'd gained a pound!

Wanda kneeled down by the toilet and stuck her forearm halfway down her esophagus. She retched, but nothing came up. Exhausted, she leaned against the throne. This was shaping up to be one of the worst days of her life. At this rate she might actually have to exercise once she got to the gym.

Slug and Bozo probably wouldn't say this was shaping up to be one of the worst days of their lives. Neither of them was introspective enough to come up with such a judgment. But Bozo was surprised that a world without a mop boy could stress him as much as this.

They'd arrived at the health club at about four in the afternoon, eager to *feel the tight, binding spandex cupping their packages as they pumped.* But they didn't even have a chance to change clothes before the stress level began to rise. Standing outside the locker room were Plotnick and Jerry. Plotnick was counting a wad of cash, while Jerry sadly watched the money disappear into Plotnick's pocket, as if he'd just given Plotnick a gift certificate good for *one free blow job from his mother.*

Plotnick saw Bozo and Slug first and frowned as they approached. "Just the guys I was looking for. About time you showed up."

Bozo's brow furrowed. He didn't enjoy being surprised, especially not by cops. "What's up?"

Plotnick rolled his eyes at Jerry. "What's up? Give us a minute here, wouldja, Jerry, while I bring Dumb and Dumber here up to speed."

Jerry nodded, his eyes still on the money sticking out of Plotnick's pocket. "Sure. I've got some work to do upstairs anyway."

Plotnick waited until Jerry had disappeared before continuing. "So you guys haven't heard anything about what went down in Shinbone Alley last night?"

Bozo and Slug looked at each other vacantly, the only way they knew how to look at each other, really. "We weren't anywhere near that part of town last night," Slug told Bozo.

"That's right," Bozo translated for Plotnick. "What happened?"

"Oh, not much," Plotnick replied. "Knuckles and Knipples got themselves killed, and Cigarface was turned into a falsetto, but that's about it."

"Killed?" Bozo wasn't a part of their crew but knew they were high enough on the food chain not to be messed with. "Who'd have *the balls to fuck* with them?"

"We don't know. Whoever it is seems to have a fondness for mops. You know anybody like that?"

Slug scratched his head while he tried to puzzle this one out, but Bozo put two and two together almost immediately. "Mop Boy? Gimme a *fuckin'* break, Plotnick. He's a puddle of *goo* by now."

"I know that. But the mops are all we have to go on right now. Maybe the janitor had a friend who didn't like the fact that his little buddy turned into a crispy critter in front of half the town. And maybe this friend's looking for revenge. You guys know if this kid had any friends?"

To their credit, Bozo and Slug waited all of a second and a half before bursting into spontaneous, hysterical laughter. Plotnick stared granite-faced as the two muscle-bound morons draped arms over each other and doubled over in fits of uncontrollable giggles. But as the laughter continued unabated, it proved contagious, and even Plotnick joined in. Soon all three were holding their sides, slapping their knees, and cackling like dental patients hopped up on happy gas.

"Mercy," Plotnick sighed, wiping streaming tears away from his eyes. "Okay, okay. Seriously, though, I want you **two assholes** to keep your eyes and your ears open. We don't know who this guy is, but he's strong as a motherfuck and looks to have a bit of a hero complex. We don't know what the fuck the mops are all about. Maybe nothing. But it could be that there was somebody in on your little joke yesterday who didn't think it was quite as ha-ha-hilarious as you dipshits."

Slug pshawed, accidentally spattering Plotnick with spit. "Unlikely. Funniest fuckin' prank this town's ever seen. Back me up, Bozo."

"I gotta side with Slug on this one. Besides, there was something like fifty people in on it. Doesn't exactly narrow it down for you."

"No, it doesn't. Hey, you know what would narrow it down? If I focused my investigation on a couple of scumbag pudknockers who've always wanted to be part of The Big Man's crew and decided to knock off a couple of his chief lieutenants and make it look like the work of the wronged punk they supposedly killed but whose body mysteriously hasn't been found yet. Jeez, that'd narrow it right the fuck down now, wouldn't it?"

Bozo's forehead vein began to throb. "You can't pin this on us. We already told you we weren't anywhere near Shinbone Alley last night."

"Yeah, you did. But you haven't said where you were. Maybe I should have a team dust this abandoned stolen car we found this morning over on the East Side. Fuckin' mess. Had a dog all tangled up in its front tires. Maybe we find your prints on it, your alibi checks out. Of course, then you've got some other problems to deal with."

Bozo and Slug held their breath. As far as they knew, their game was a huge local mystery. Never mind the fact that they had pictures posted all over www.tromavillehitandrun.com.

Plotnick stabbed both of them in their beefy chests with a fore-finger. "Just be my eyes and ears. You find out anything about this guy, you call me. You help me, I might be able to help you."

Plotnick shouldered his way between them and disappeared down the hall. Bozo took three quick deep breaths. "That guy stresses me, Slug. He really stresses me."

Wanda's day had not noticeably improved. She arrived at the gym with one goal in mind: shed this pound that had leeched onto *her otherwise perfect body*. This goal was proving to be more elusive than she'd anticipated. She was well into her thirty-fourth spinning cycle when Slug, Bozo, and Julie turned up. They made a beeline for her, distracting her from her workout with their yammering about some mop-carrying psycho they were supposed to be looking for. Wanda tried to make it as clear as possible. She didn't care. She wasn't going to go out and help them search the streets for this guy or anybody else. Until she was back down to 112 pounds, she wasn't doing jack and/or shit.

Bozo wasn't listening. He was mentally dividing the town into sections and assigning each of them an area to canvass. It was moments like this that made Wanda regret ever joining up with this bunch. If it weren't for the fact that *both Slug and Julie had ways of making rivers of pleasure cascade between her legs,* she'd cut them off right now. As for Bozo, she'd never had much use for him. She and Julie had tried to entice the guys into *swapping partners* once, and Bozo hadn't done a thing. He seemed to take more pleasure out of watching Slug and Julie go at it than from anything Wanda did *beneath his waist*. And that would have been okay if she thought Bozo was simply *gay* or *bi* or *a voyeur* or *a foot fetishist* or something she was familiar with. But she honestly couldn't figure out what *stiffened* Bozo's *wick*. It was obvious to just about everybody except Slug that Bozo had some closeted *homosexual* issues to work out. But they seemed to be all mixed up with Bozo's inherent narcissism, sadism, and masochism. He was the only person Wanda had ever met who genuinely seemed to want to go fuck himself as hard and as painfully as he could.

Bozo had spent the better part of fifteen minutes talking about his master plan to find the crazy guy and the importance of following the plan to the letter, and Wanda had had more than enough. She climbed off the Exercycle, grabbed the towel off the handlebars, and draped the towel around her shoulders. "***Fuck*** off, Bozo," she told him.

An awkward silence draped itself around the workout room. Very few people had ever told Bozo to fuck off and walked away with a mouthful of unbroken teeth. Everyone waited to see if Bozo was enough of a freak to actually punch *a good-looking woman in the mouth.*

In point of fact, he was. But so thrown off was he by Wanda's remark that he didn't. Instead, he countered with the most intelligent question he could muster. "Huh?"

"You heard me. If you want to go out and look for this guy, help yourself. But count me out. I've got bigger problems."

"Like what?!"

"Just look at me, Bozo!" Wanda screamed. ***"Look at my ass!"*** Bozo glanced at it while Slug stared outright, breaking into a wolfish grin as his eyes focused on *the leotard riding into the crack of her ass.* "I'm a *fucking heifer!* I am one step away from another round of lyposuction here."

Bozo opened his mouth to protest but was silenced by Julie, who sympathized with Wanda. "Wanda's right, Bozo," she counseled.

"I am? I knew it!! I'm huge!!!" Wanda burst into tears and ran off.

"She has to take care of herself first. Let her go."

Bozo flexed his neck and gritted his teeth. "You girls are stressing me, Julie! I'm warning you—"

"Uh, you guys had better go on without me," Slug said, still day-dreaming about *Wanda's ass-crack.* "I oughtta check on Wanda. Make sure she's all right. She seems really upset."

"The fuck?!" Bozo watched in impotent fury as Slug chased after his girlfriend. He'd noticed *the stiff rod that had appeared in the front of Slug's shorts after Wanda offered up her ass for examination,* and while he certainly appreciated seeing *the outline of his hard-on,* he suspected that very little comforting was going to go on. "Does nobody give shit one that we all might go to jail if we don't track down this asshole?"

"Nobody's going to jail," Julie smoothed the thumping vein back down into Bozo's temple. "Plotnick just has *his panties in a bunch* because he actually has to do some police work for a change. He's covering *his ass*. He *doesn't have anything on* us."

"Yeah, but—"

"Shhhh. Let's you and me go see what we can dig up on this guy. We don't need those two."

Bozo allowed Julie to take him by the hand and lead him out of the health club. How had he lost control of everyone so quickly? He'd have to dream up a suitable reminder of who was in charge for the next time he ran into Slug and Wanda. Perhaps *he'd drip hot wax on Slug's schlong while Wanda ass-raped him with a strap-on.* But should Wanda be forced to ass-rape Slug, or Bozo himself? Decisions, decisions.

Wanda stepped into the sauna, her naked body wrapped in a soft towel, clutching a manila folder to her chest. She poured water on the hot coals, filling the chamber with hot steam. *The towel fell to the ground and she reclined on the wooden bench, allowing the hot, moist air to caress her smooth skin.* It had been a bitch of a day. All of the exercising, all of the bingeing and purging, none of that could take the place of a good steam and a big O.

She opened the folder and examined the pictures inside. Printouts of the digital pictures she and Julie had been taking of the hit-and-run game. There was little Skippy, his brains spread out over the asphalt like so much jelly. There was *Grandma* Pisspants, as they'd dubbed her, death pee shooting out of *her twat* at the moment of expiration. There was the college student with the antenna impaled through his eye, broken shards of glass embedded in his cheek like little diamonds. As she flipped through her precious memories, *her fingers absently tweaked her nipples, gently rubbing her breasts and belly.* The game was hot. The pictures were hotter.

She spread the pictures in front of her, freeing both hands. *As one hand continued to rub her tits, the other slid down through her carefully trimmed pubic hair into her slick, wet slit. A low moan of pleasure rumbled out of her throat as her fingers did their work.* Wanda's eyelids fluttered shut as images of violent vehicular homicide danced through her head.

It wasn't long before Wanda was completely lost in her masturbatory reverie. So it was no surprise that she didn't notice as the door to the sauna slowly creaked open. Nor did she notice the figure that lurched toward her, draped in an unclean bath towel until he was right on top of her. Literally. *With a gutteral roar, the cloaked figure dove for Wanda's open, pulsing vagina.*

Wanda screamed, partly from surprise, partly from pleasure. She grabbed the figure by the shoulders and pulled him up, hauling the towel off him to reveal a sex-crazed Slug.

"You *asshole!*" Wanda smacked him lightly on the head.

Slug distorted his face and spoke out of the side of his mouth. "I am not an *asshole!* I am a human being! I am . . . Mop Boy!"

"That isn't funny, Slug. When are you going to quit with that elephant-man shit?"

"When you stop liking it, *sweet tits.*"

And loath as she was to admit it, Slug had a point. She did like it. When she was a girl, the only things that turned her on more than that elephant-man movie were her repeated attempts to break her hymen on the pommel horse in gym class. She'd always wondered if John Merrick's deformities extended south of the equator, and if they did, what kind of *monstrous one-eyed wonder weasel* was he packing down there? It was one of her oldest fantasies. So when *Slug attempted to slide back down her body and replace her fingers with his tongue,* she covered him back up with the towel.

Slug was pretty useless at most everything, but to give him his due, he was a *master of the fine art of eating pussy.* Twice a day he gave himself a clean, close shave just in case he was called upon to perform emergency *cunnilingus. He gave the act everything he had, using his tongue, his fingers, his lips, his teeth (a little or a lot, depending on the woman), his nose, spit, and breath, and just to give her a little thrill she wouldn't get anywhere else, he liked to rub his cleft chin in there.* So among Slug's natural skill as a *beaver-eater,* Wanda's fantasy disguise, and the fact that her pictures had sent her halfway to Shuddertown already, it wasn't long before *Wanda was gasping for air and squealing in a sing-song way, "Oh . . . oh . . . ohgod . . . ohmigod . . . I'm cumming . . . I'm gonna cum, Slug!"*

Now, when most women shout this during a sexual act, it's either because they're in love with the sound of their own voice or because they're totally bored with what their partner's up to down there and want to get the whole tedious thing over with immediately. In Wanda's case, it was a warning. But this time it was a warning that came too late. *Wanda squeezed Slug between her thighs and held his face down between her legs and began to quiver. Slug knew what was coming, but Wanda held him fast. All he could do was close his eyes as a geyser of clear female ejaculate shot out of Wanda's fun hole. It was a heavy load, drenching Slug's face and hair as Wanda shouted out in ecstasy.*

When she finally released him, Slug collapsed onto the floor and pulled the towel off his head. She-cum dripped from his face. Dating a squirter had its risks, no doubt about it.

Wanda hauled him off the floor and gave him a deep, soulful kiss, lapping her juices off his face like an eager kitten at a saucer of milk. Wanda's hand shot down the front of Slug's shorts, finding his rod standing at full attention. Slug helped things along by sliding his shorts off, giving his mammoth love muscle some much-needed room to breathe. Then Slug had a momentary panic attack as he realized that Wanda's she-cum was rapidly drying and his eyelids were temporarily glued open. He allowed his concentration to shift from his dick to his eyes and forced himself to blink. His hard-on went down a bit as he winced at the sensation of his eyelids ripping away from themselves.

Luckily for him, Wanda wasn't about to let this one get away, as so many of Slug's stiffies had slipped from her grasp in the past. She knew if she wanted to keep Slug's undivided attention, she'd have to resort to desperate actions. While Slug exercised the muscles in his face, trying to prevent Wanda's cum from cementing it into one expression, Wanda's mouth plunged down onto his prick. A deep moan of excitement erupted from Slug's throat, his eyes rolling back in his head and his fingers weaving into Wanda's thick hair. Slug believed that if he held a woman's head down on his crotch while she was giving head, it could stay there for the rest of his life.

Wanda was almost as good at performing fellatio as Slug was at cunnilingus.[2] Maybe a little too good, because within a couple of minutes, Wanda realized that if she didn't stop soon, Slug was going to erupt and then he wouldn't be any good for anybody. But Slug held her head fast, swooning and moaning with every lick of his balls.

Realizing that she could only count on herself for a second orgasm, Wanda's fingers slithered back inside, doing the work of half a dozen penises. Nevertheless, Slug announced his intention to cum long before Wanda was ready. Indeed, even as the words were leaving Slug's mouth, semen was shooting from his schlong.

Wanda wrestled her head free from Slug's grasp as she tasted the first milky drops of sperm on her tongue. She leaned back and

---

2. Although if both Wanda and Slug had entered a poonani-eating contest, Wanda would probably take the prize. Sadly, the state fair had banned the poonani-eating contest shortly after the end of World War II when the men started coming home from overseas. It was one of those things that could only truly thrive in a primarily female society. Like girls' baseball or one-titted archery.

concentrated on her own masturbation, wrapping her feet around Slug's cock and stroking it with her toes. That was enough for Slug. He came with a vengeance, thick, white clumps shooting out and hitting him in the face and chest and, of course, all over Wanda's perfectly pedicured toes. The sight of Slug's penis erupting like Vesuvius sent Wanda over the edge as well. With a moan bordering on a scream, she succumbed to her second climax. Once again, streams of clear ejaculate squirted out of her vagina, aimed straight at Slug.

Overcome,[3] Slug fell off the bench, drenched head to toe in both his and Wanda's waters of love. He lay on the floor of the sauna, trying to catch his breath. Wanda, naturally, took it all in stride. She took one last deep breath before retrieving her towel from the floor. She wiped the sticky mess from her feet before stepping over Slug and out of the sauna.

"You should probably take a shower," she counseled Slug as she left. "You smell like overtime at the protein factory."

Slug nodded at Wanda's ass as it disappeared out the door. He was exhausted but satisfied. After all, this wasn't the first time he'd been left lying naked, semiconscious, and soaked in ejaculate. And this time, his rectum wasn't even bleeding. It had been a good day.

---

3. Or would that be overcum?

13.

Sarah, Hot and Blind

The blond girl sat alone on the park bench, a camera in her lap, her devoted German shepherd lying alert at her feet. She sat perfectly still, a smile never far from her lips. She smelled the clean park air. She felt the touch of a warm summer breeze against her cheek. Others enjoying the park that June day admired her from afar. She had a simple, homespun beauty that couldn't be faked with makeup, plastic surgery, or expensive outfits. She wore a plain floral summer dress and looked perfectly at peace with the world. She was the girl everyone wished lived next door. The others tried not to stare at her but a few couldn't help it, especially as it seemed the girl didn't seem to mind their gaze. In truth, she wasn't even aware of it. The girl was blind.

As she sat on the bench, she listened to everything that was going on in the park. She heard children playing on the swing sets. She heard some half-drunk college kids tossing a Frisbee around. She heard the rapid patter of joggers' feet as they ran past. Periodically she'd focus on one particular soundscape. Slowly she would raise her camera to her eye, more out of habit than necessity, and snap away at the sounds that entranced her.

Sarah Claire Parkinson[1] took up photography in her senior year at
Tromaville High. She could still see back then and had joined the staff
of the school paper, the *Tromaville Reactor,* and the yearbook committee. Class photographer was the job everybody wanted. It seemed
glamorous and cool, unlike all the boring writing jobs.[2] Sarah got the
job because she was the only one whom Mr. Goddard, the faculty
adviser, trusted with the school's camera.

As it turned out, Sarah had a natural eye for photography. At first Mr.
Goddard was simply impressed that all of Sarah's pictures were properly
exposed and in focus, something that couldn't be said for previous vol-
umes of the *Reactor.* But soon it became obvious to everyone that Sarah
had a gift. Her pictures won awards and comparisons to the works of
Dorothea Lange and Margaret Bourke-White. After graduation, Sarah
was the only student who had options beyond either going to college or
getting a job at the power plant. She could either accept a full-ride schol-
arship to NYU's School of Journalism, a low-paying but respectable job
at the *Tromaville Times,* or a high-paying but thoroughly reprehensible
job as a paparazzo.

At one of the many award ceremonies she attended that year, she
met Stan "Slam" Collins, one of the sleaziest and most notorious shutterbugs to ever strap on a telephoto lens. Sarah was easy pickings for
Slam. She was a small-town girl at heart, and Slam seduced her with
stories of high society and easy money. Oh, and also a liberal amount
of rohypnol in her diet soda.

Slam told Sarah she could be one of the greatest paparazzi in history.

---

1. There had been some confusion when Sarah was growing up as to whether her
first name was Sarah or Claire. Her mom had preferred the name Sarah, while Dad
was a Claire fan, and each parent confusingly referred to their daughter by the
name they liked best. But Dad had a stroke when Claire was only ten years old, so
Sarah eventually won out. Now the only people who called her Claire were her
father's old friends, and they were few and far between.
2. And you can take it from us, writing is neither glamorous nor cool.

Her innocent good looks would provide her with access to places scumbuckets such as Slam could only dream about getting into. The rich and famous wouldn't know what hit them until it was too late. So with her high school diploma in hand, Sarah decided to turn her back on Tromaville and enter the high-risk world of stalking celebrities.

Her first year as a paparazzo went extremely well. As Slam had predicted, no one expected this sweet-looking blond girl to be hiding in bushes with a camera, looking out for candid topless pictures of TV stars, or film directors cheating on their wives with their adopted underage Asian stepsons. Veteran shutterbugs would cheerfully inject their grandmothers with ovarian cancer cells in exchange for some of the pictures Sarah got. She made a small fortune in a short time, but the job weighed heavily on her conscience. She completely destroyed at least two careers that first year. First came the high-octane action star whom she outed after publishing some candid snaps of him in a passionate liplock with the equally macho producer of his latest multimillion-dollar crashapalooza. Sarah didn't really understand why anybody was surprised over that one. After all, in the love scenes in his previous movie, the guy looked like he was trying to suck his costar's face off with his lips. It should have been obvious to anybody who'd ever been in a heterosexual relationship that this guy had no idea how to kiss a woman.

The second one was more of a personal blow to Sarah. She'd been following around a pop star, one of her favorites, not so much to get anything to publish but just because she was a fan. One night after a sold-out concert in Chicago, she'd followed the young star to a run-down part of the city. The girl had been acting peculiar all night, and Sarah was horrified to watch as she lay down naked on a rust-colored mattress in an abandoned tenement and became the focal point of an all-night gang bang in exchange for vials of crack. But old habits die hard, and Sarah's disgust didn't prevent her from taking pictures of the whole sordid scene. Two weeks after the shots were splattered all over

the front pages of every tabloid in supermarkets coast to coast, the pop
star was found dead of an overdose. Sarah wanted to quit. Slam
wouldn't let her.

Slam kept pushing Sarah farther and farther. He told Sarah that she
was doing the Lord's work. She'd rid the world of two shallow, talent-
less morons in just over a year. Slam told her that the paparazzo's real
job was to keep the gene pool clean and bring down the undeservedly
famous. Sarah didn't quite believe that but knew she couldn't stop now.
The money and the lifestyle she'd earned were too much temptation for
anyone.

It all came crashing down one cold January night. She and Slam
had staked out the beach house of Tom Hues, one of the world's
biggest movie stars. Rumor had it that Tom was leaving his wife, Rita
Roberts, and had taken up with a much younger foreign starlet,
Emmanuelle Sopapilla. Pictures of Hues and Sopapilla together
would be worth more money than either Slam or Sarah had seen in
their lifetimes. The problem was that Hues fancied himself a crusader
for celebrity rights. He'd been outspoken in his campaign against the
paparazzi for years. Assault charges had been filed against him on
more than one occasion by photographers who'd had their cameras
smashed and lives threatened. The charges were always dropped
when Hues filed countercharges of trespassing and stalking. After
each vindication, Hues would tell interviewers that the law had basically given him a blank check to break as many photographers' arms
as he could.

Sarah knew that she and Slam were treading a fine line with this
assignment. Technically, they weren't trespassing. They were sitting in
their car on a public road. But Hues' popularity made it very unlikely
that any judge would allow technicalities to sway in Sarah and Slam's
favor.

By the time the gate to the compound opened, Sarah had dozed off.
A red convertible emerged and drove off down the hill. Slam woke

Sarah up as he gave chase. Sarah opened her eyes to see the landscape whizzing by at a dizzying speed. Slam ordered her to get her camera ready. Hues and Sopapilla were in the car just ahead of them.

Sarah buckled her seat belt as Slam drove faster and faster down the winding Pacific Coast Highway. They quickly caught up to the convertible, but their approach had forfeited their anonymity. Hues caught a glimpse of them in his rearview mirror and stepped on the gas. Slam grinned. "Let's get it on," he growled.

In his defense, Slam was usually an excellent driver and an ideal wheelman for a job like this one. But Slam was from the East Coast, whereas Hues had the home-court advantage. Slam pulled alongside of the car, giving Sarah the opportunity to take the pictures. Before she had the chance, Hues hit the brakes. The convertible disappeared in Slam's rearview.

"Fuck!" Slam shouted as he braked and cranked the wheel into a U-turn. But the twisting road proved too much for him. The car careened through the guardrail and over the side. Hues watched triumphantly as the car sailed through the air, Sarah's camera flashing all the way down.

Slam was killed instantly,[3] while Sarah's seat belt saved her life. She spent the next several weeks in the hospital, recovering from broken ribs, a shattered leg, and assorted other cuts and scrapes. Her wounds mended perfectly, all except one. The flash from her camera had reflected repeatedly off the mirror in the car and gone straight into her clear blue eyes. Her sight was gone forever.

---

3. Well, he was pronounced dead at the scene, anyway. Actually, the steering wheel had broken his ribs, piercing a lung from which he bled internally for a good half hour. He'd then been thrown from the car completely, glass slicing its way into every bit of exposed flesh. Landing on the jagged rocks below, he broke his back. He lay there for forty-five minutes, suffering horribly as crabs sucked the sweet jelly from his eyes. By the time the paramedics found his body, he was quite dead but had gone through hell on his way there. Which is just as well, because he really was a piece of shit, and Sarah was better off without him.

Most people[4] would fall into the depths of self-pity after an accident like that. Sarah's gifts were her eyes. Now they were gone. But Sarah believed it was the best thing that had ever happened to her. As far as she was concerned, she had seen enough. For most of her life, she'd seen triumph, beauty, and the best of the human condition. But for the past year, she'd seen nothing but people who had everything they could ever ask for but still weren't happy, including herself. If that was the American Dream, she just didn't want to see it anymore.

So Sarah returned home to Tromaville. She'd made enough money to buy herself a little house where she lived with her Seeing Eye dog, Charly. She'd always been a quick study and picked up braille without much trouble. Unfortunately, the accident had also thrown off her center of balance, so she was a bit clumsier than she used to be. But all things considered, she was content.

She'd even rededicated herself to photography as an art form instead of a trap. Most of her pictures were blurry, poorly developed, over- or underexposed, and occasionally just studies of the ass end of her lens cap. Even so, they were still good enough to get her a well-received gallery showing in SoHo called "Sarah Claire Parkinson—Leading the Blind." She'd attended out of politeness but didn't enjoy being back in New York and was glad when she got back to Tromaville.

So today, Sarah led a quiet, normal life on a quiet, normal street in Tromaville. She had no real friends except for Charly, her constant longtime companion.[5] And that was pretty much the way she wanted it. Most of the time, anyway. Sarah was an observer, and even without eyesight, she was a more astute observer than most. And Sarah believed that the best view came from without. She'd already been too close to

---

4. Including the authors of this book, you can bet your sweet ass on that. Hell, I feel sorry for myself after a bad haircut.

5. We should note that we do not mean "longtime companion" in the sense you're thinking, gutterbrains. Sarah was one of the few friendless blind people in Tromaville who did not fuck their dog.

the thick of things, and look at what it had cost her. No; from now on, she'd be perfectly content to keep herself to herself and chronicle the world as it went by.

Still, even the most detached and unaffected observer had to set foot in the circle of life from time to time. Sarah put her camera away, reached down, and gave Charly an affectionate scratch behind his ear. "I'm hungry, Charly," Sarah told him. "Let's get some tacos."

Santos pulled the flask out of the waistband of his brown polyester pants and helped himself to a long, deep drink of whiskey. His unfocused eyes swam down into the fryer full of bubbling oil. The fries looked tasty, but somewhere in his subconscious he remembered what happened the last time he reached in for a hot, fresh fried potato. If he'd get workmen's comp for the injury, it would be worth it. But that program had been cut about a year ago. Why was that? Oh, yeah. He'd cut it himself.

John Santos had not had an easy life. And the fact that everything he'd been through had led him to the height of his unchosen profession, manager of Tromaville's Taco Shack, struck him as a grave injustice. He'd started working at the Taco Shack part-time back in high school. No big deal. Lots of kids did that. But unlike the rest of the pimple-faced geeks who passed through the employee entrance, Santos was actually responsible, hardworking, and dependable. If he had a fault, it was that he couldn't say no. So if someone had to work overtime or pull a double or a split shift, it was always Santos. That didn't leave him with much time to pursue his real dream of becoming a heavy-metal übergod.

The pages fell off the calendar, and Santos climbed the corporate ladder at Taco Shack. He started to lose his long, curly, heavy-metal überhair. In return, he gained a round, firm, fast-food übergut. And now here he was, forty fucking years old, earning $9.35 an hour and reporting to some faceless corporate drone who wouldn't eat at the Taco

Shack on a thousand-dollar dare. Christ, if you worked hard and played by the rules, you were supposed to get a shot at the brass ring and the American Dream, right? Well, Santos had done all that, and all he got in return was a brown, grease-spattered uniform, a paper hat, and a peptic ulcer. So a few years back, Santos had decided to give himself something he really wanted: a drinking problem.

Unlike everything else he'd ever tried to get, the drinking problem came easily. He welcomed the smooth (and some not-so-smooth) whiskey into his system like an old friend. But if getting the old heave-ho from the Taco Shack had been his unconscious intention, that had proved difficult. As it turned out, sobriety was not a requirement for fulfilling his duties as manager. Indeed, corporate had applauded many of his drunkest, most half-assed decisions. Cutting workmen's compensation had been one of those decisions, one he had occasion to regret on more than one self-destructive night.

Santos sucked out another mouthful of booze before replacing the flask in his pants. He absentmindedly wiped at some grease on his nametag. "*¡Buenos días!* My name is John." Nice to meet you, John. You dick. Would you like fries with the shambles of your life?

About ten feet away from Santos (but, thanks to the liquor, completely out of his line of vision), the newest member of the Taco Shack team was cutting the cheese . . . literally, not figuratively. Bobby Mackleberry struggled with an enormous, fluorescent orange block of processed cheese, guiding it through the industrial slicer with an eye toward protecting his fingers. At sixteen, Bobby was the poster boy for Pimple-Faced Teens of America. His part-time job at the Taco Shack didn't help his complexion any. Everything he worked with oozed grease, from the overcooked shells to the hunk of cheese in his hand. That grease came off on his hands, and his hands inevitably ran over his face in exhaustion. As a result, his face was a bas-relief map of zits, blackheads, and ingrown facial hair.

This wasn't a huge issue for Bobby. He'd taken the job with one goal in mind: to save enough money to buy himself a car. Until he had the car, he wasn't going to be impressing anyone, anyway. Most girls at school were none too pleased if you picked them up for a date on a ten-speed. Once he got himself some wheels with a motor attached, he'd start to worry about his appearance, hygiene, and social skills. But until that day came to pass, those were luxuries he could not afford to concern himself with.

From where Bobby stood, he could see the kitchen and the counter area but could neither see nor be seen from the dining room. Best of all, he had a spectacular view of Diana's ass stuffed into her brown polyester slacks. Diana was the counter girl. She wasn't gorgeous by anyone's definition, but she easily trumped everyone else at the Taco Shack in the looks department, so she got the relatively easy job of cashier. She'd been working there about six months, and Santos, drunk as he was, was still clearheaded enough to give her a uniform a size or two too small. Customers were happy to order more just for another opportunity to stare down her cleavage. And Bobby was happy to slice everything in the goddamn restaurant as long as he could watch her ass bobble back and forth.

As for Diana, she didn't give a shit if every nerd, reject, booze hound, and deadbeat dad in Tromaville ogled her tits as long as it meant she didn't have to touch the food in this place. You couldn't pay her enough to eat this crap. The tacos were soggy. The burgers were worse, made as they were from wadded-up, unused taco meat. And the fries were so greasy they'd been known to eat through the plastic trays. But if everyone else in town wanted to poison themselves, she was happy to take their money and shake her maracas. Cashier was an easy, undemanding gig. At least it was until 3:15 P.M., when the calm of the Taco Shack was disrupted by the arrival of three grease-painted, gun-toting weirdos who announced their arrival with a simple command:

"OKAY, YOU FUCKING RETARDS! DROP YOUR TACOS OR I'LL BLOW YOUR BRAINS OUT!"

As we've seen, Tromaville is not exactly a town that thrives on law and order. Even so, it was highly unusual for three psychos with automatic weapons to hold up a fast-food joint in broad daylight. Most of the corruption and lawlessness in town were overseen and sanctioned by those who were ostensibly charged with keeping the peace, and even they were smart enough to realize their thin cover would be blown right off if Tromaville appeared to be the Wild West. So it might be worth taking a minute to see who these nut jobs are and why they've suddenly decided to interrupt our story.[6]

It's true that most everyone in Tromaville with an interest in criminality gravitated toward a career in law enforcement. The power elite had virtually all of the gangs and low-level scumbags sewn up tight and tucked away in their pocket. But there were a handful of crooks that even the mayor couldn't control. First there was the Mafia, which, needless to say, doesn't exist. But for the sake of argument, the nonexistent Mafia had nonexistent roots in New York and New Jersey that reached back generations. The mayor took some nonexistent kickbacks to keep him turning a blind eye toward their nonexistent affairs. But even he was unable to take the reins of their nonexistent organization. They operated (or didn't operate, since they weren't there) on a separate but equal playing field from the rest of the mayor's shady dealings.

More troubling was the new specter of terrorism. Ever since Osama Bin Laden decided to rearrange the view across the river, the country had been on edge, worrying about where they might strike next. Tromaville was certainly no exception. Indeed, unlike the paranoid

---

6. Or it might not, I don't know. If you don't give a shit, feel free to skip ahead. It's not like there's gonna be a quiz on this later. Unless, of course, this book has been assigned in one of those easy-A liberal arts "literature" classes in college where they make you read comic books and watch movies all day. If that's the case, here's the Cliff's Notes version. The answers are "three," "necrophilia," "hot sauce," and "The Warriors." As for the essay question, just toss the words "New Humanism" and "Zeitgeist" around a lot and you'll be fine.

residents of Rabbit's Ass, Colorado, Tromavillians actually had some reason to be concerned. Not that they dreamed they were a big enough target to become some future Ground Zero. But their proximity to the city made them likely recipients of fallout from a dirty bomb, anthrax attack, or poisoned water supply. And that could throw a damper on anybody's Ramadan.

Of course, while everyone was busy protecting themselves from people with complicated last names and towels wrapped around their heads, they'd completely forgotten about the possibility of homegrown terrorists. A decade ago, they'd been all the rage. They were blowing up federal buildings and barricading themselves inside compounds with miniarsenals and larders full of canned hash. Back then, we didn't need foreign-born terrorists. We had plenty of people more than capable of fucking things up right here in the good old U. S. of A.

In the months following 9/11, these homegrown anarchists became a wee bit envious of their more successful cousins from the Middle East. They'd ruined things for everyone. It was one thing to lock yourself inside your house and kill yourself and all your friends. It was quite another to hijack a plane, ram it into some great public building, and slaughter yourself, everybody on board the plane, and hundreds of innocent people. What was that supposed to prove? Where was the personal touch? Where was the love?

One person who longed for the good old days of in-your-face anarchy was LeRoy Tyche, resident of Tromaville. LeRoy worked for the IRS as a tax auditor, so he had plenty of reasons to hate the government. Like a lot of people, LeRoy hated his boring, tedious job. But unlike a lot of people, LeRoy was self-aware enough to realize that he was a genuinely boring, tedious person and therefore uniquely qualified for nothing except the job he already had. So instead of hating himself for taking the job, he hated the government for making it necessary. If he wanted to change his life, he'd have to overthrow the government.

So LeRoy formed a terrorist cell. In four years of active recruitment, he'd managed to attract two members to his cause. The first was Frank Bosch, who worked in the cubicle next to LeRoy. Frank didn't have any particular ax to grind with the system. He'd just always wanted a black friend to prove how open-minded he was, and LeRoy fit the bill. If his cool black friend also happened to be organizing a coup d'état, then that must be cool, too.

The third and most valuable member of the group went by the name of Rico. Just Rico. He'd never offered LeRoy and Frank any other name, and neither of them had the balls to ask. Rico appeared to be truly psychotic and interested less in changing the status quo than in just spreading violence for the sake of spreading violence. But he'd make a key addition to any start-up terrorist organization thanks to his ample collection of guns, knives, and explosives. Rico had it all. Assault rifles, sawed-off M1 carbines, M52 automatics, even some 9mm Lugers for the ladies. He had grenades, Bowie knives, crossbows, and a kitchen full of enough ingredients to stock a catering truck with pipe bombs, car bombs, and Molotov cocktails. Where he got this stuff didn't matter to LeRoy or Frank. Not as long as Rico taught them both how to use it all.

He did, too. Rico proved to be an excellent teacher, and both LeRoy and Frank were eager students. Before long, they were ready to do . . . something. They just didn't know what.

It was Frank who came up with the idea of robbing the Taco Shack. He'd been a regular customer for years and knew exactly when they'd have the most cash. He'd also been watching Santos carefully and knew that it was physically impossible for him to try to be a hero. LeRoy and Rico liked the idea. Their group could certainly use the money, as well as some publicity if they wanted to expand beyond three members. The Taco Shack was a soft, easy target. It would be the perfect place to practice their skills in the real world. Assuming everything went well, and there was no reason it shouldn't, next time they'd hit a bigger Taco Shack. Maybe the one in Queens. Before you knew it, their numbers would be legion and they'd be hitting the big score: the Taco Shack across the street from the White House.

Everything was planned to the last detail. They applied colorful makeup to their faces, partly to disguise their identities and partly because Rico enjoyed wearing colorful makeup. They were armed, they were dangerous, and they were ready to roll.

Meanwhile, this chapter has gone on a lot fucking longer than it was supposed to. If you've been reading this book on the toilet, there's probably been someone pounding on the door for a while now. If you're reading it in an airport, I hope they haven't announced the last call for boarding your flight. If you're reading it while drunk, you probably need another drink.[7] So wipe your ass, board your plane, freshen your drink, and we'll see you in the next chapter.

---

7. For the record, I've been writing the book while drunk on a toilet in the airport.

14.

Bloodbath at the International House of Paincakes

KAY, YOU FUCKING RETARDS! DROP YOUR TACOS OR I'LL BLOW YOUR BRAINS OUT!"

As an exclamation point to his command, LeRoy fired a single shot into the ceiling of the Taco Shack. Anyone whose attention hadn't been raised by being called a retard now turned their focus to the three gun-wielding maniacs spreading out through the restaurant. Rico stood guard by the door while Frank, who was most familiar with the Taco Shack's daily operation, headed to the counter. He stuck the barrel of his gun in Diana's face and shouted, "Everybody in the back get out front, now!"

Bobby turned to Santos just in time to see his ass heroically disappear into the walk-in freezer. He toyed with the idea of shouting at him just to see the crooks trot his boss out and shoot him in the neck but decided against it and instead joined the three other members of the staff with Diana behind the counter.

"How many we got back there, Frank?" LeRoy shouted, never taking his eyes off the paralyzed diners.

"Five!"

Rico risked a worried glance into the restaurant. "I thought you said there'd be six!"

"We're missing the drunk. Probably passed out in the produce. I wouldn't worry about him."

"Yeah, well that's why you're not in charge and I am," LeRoy commanded. "Go find him."

Frank scowled at the employees. "All right, fucks. Get out there with the rest of the cannon fodder while I go find your boss."

The Taco Shack team, none of them willing to risk their lives for $5.15 an hour, did as they were told and grumpily sat in an open booth.

In any large holdup or hostage situation, there will always be one person who tries to be a hero. Usually these are the first to die. Sure enough, the second Frank disappeared into the kitchen, a cell-phone-sporting, power-tie-wearing, self-important corporate drone stood up. Priority one was ending this immediately so he wouldn't be missed back at the office and have his choice corner cubicle given to the new up-and-comer in Market Research. Priority two was appearing to be a hero in front of that cashier with the big hooters, and the hot blond chick with the dog, eating alone in the corner. Priority three was not getting killed, although he didn't mind if he was hurt if it would make him more sympathetic to hooter girl and dog chick. Waaaaaaay down on the list of priorities was saving everyone's lives.

So the hero put down his beef, bean, and cheese burrito, wiped some guacamole off his cheek, and made his stand. He knew kick-boxing—well, he knew kickboxing movies, anyway—so he felt sure that he could take these two. Never mind the fact that they were both packing guns and the most lethal thing he had on him was the key to his SUV.

"Hey," the hero shouted to everyone's surprise, "leave these people alone. Take what you came for and get out."

"Who the fuck are you?" LeRoy asked, not really caring about the answer.

"Your worst nightmare, bee-yotch. An ordinary man who's had enough."

The hero may have been about to adopt a kickboxing stance half-remembered from a late-night Van Damme-a-thon. Or he may have been about to come to his senses and sit back down with a giggled, "Sorry. Lost my mind for a second." No one will ever know because before he could make a move, LeRoy tattooed his chest with a line of bullets. Blood burst from the hero's chest, raining down and mixing together with the hot and mild sauce. The hero fell backward, collapsing onto a cheap aluminum frame holding an ad for Taco Shack's limited-time Apple Pie Shake promotion.

Half the customers screamed. The rest trembled quietly and prayed their sphincters would hold.

LeRoy waved his gun over the crowd, allowing the smoke to waft aromatically out of the barrel. "Now," he said calmly, "anybody else want to be a hero? Rico, you got any heroes back there?"

Rico aimed his gun at the family sitting closest to the exit, a single mother, her six-year-old daughter, and a baby. He jammed the barrel of the gun into Mom's face. "I don't know, LeRoy. You gonna be a hero, lady?"

The mother fought back tears and shook her head no.

Rico moved on to the little girl, sticking the gun in her face. "How about you, kid?"

The mother screamed, "NO!" Her daughter burst out sobbing. Oddly, the baby remained perfectly calm. Rico found this highly suspicious and pointed the gun at the baby's soft head.

"It's always the quiet ones you gotta worry about."

The baby found the barrel of the gun extremely interesting and probed at it with his chubby fingers. Rico's eyes widened. "I knew it!"

With a single squeeze of the trigger, Rico vaporized the baby. Not a lot of people have seen the effect of a .357 Magnum on a six-month-old infant at close range, which is probably a good thing. Certainly the people in the Taco Shack won't ever forget the image. Even LeRoy thought the action was a little extreme, but at least the survivors knew they weren't fucking around now.

Frank came back from the kitchen with Santos in tow. "What's all the shooting?"

"Had to make a couple of examples of these assholes. I wasted the dickhead in the tie there and Rico blew that baby's head off."

Frank nodded. "Good thinking. Let's get the money."

LeRoy casually paced through the restaurant. "Yeah, take the boss man there and collect the cash. Rico and I should watch these fucks. Looks like we've got us some real cowboys here."

Rico was looking for another baby to shoot. "No shit, man! You see the look in that kid's eyes? He was tryin' to take my gun from me!"

"It was self-defense, man."

The mother and daughter were hysterical, screaming in grief and terror. Rico sneered at them. "Pull yourself together, lady. I did you a favor. You've obviously got more kids than you can handle anyway."

LeRoy wandered around and heard a low, threatening growl coming from beneath a corner table. He glanced down and there was Charly, teeth bared, chomping at the bit to tear out this asshole's throat but too loyal to his mistress to move. LeRoy looked Charly in the eye for a second, then moved on to the shapely legs next to him. He followed the legs up to Sarah's face. She trembled, visibly frightened, but wasn't willing to give these pricks the satisfaction of her tears.

LeRoy stood back and admired her. "Better get your dog under control, lady."

Sarah reached down and stroked Charly's head. "Take it easy, Charly."

Rico heard the conversation and glanced over. "There's a dog in here? Who brings a dog into a restaurant?"

"I dunno, Rico, but this chick's got one."

"That's fucked up, man. That ain't hygienic."

Sarah's eyes danced aimlessly around the room. "Leave my dog alone! He's clean!"

LeRoy reached down and waved his hand in front of Sarah's eyes to no effect. "Well, I'll be dipped in shit." He grabbed Sarah by the shoulder and hauled her to her feet. "Hey, Rico! This chick's blind, man!"

"So fuckin' what? Still shouldn't let some filthy dog into a place with food."

"Yeah, whatever," said LeRoy, leaning in close to Sarah and smelling her perfume. "This is turning into a great day, man. I always wanted to cornhole a blind bitch!"

LeRoy grinned and bent Sarah over the table, knocking her taco salad all over the floor. He lifted her dress up and reached for her panties. This was enough for Charly, who finally had the excuse he needed. The dog leaped out from his spot beneath the table and sank his teeth into LeRoy's foot.

"Fuck!" LeRoy howled. In one swift, smooth motion, he brought his gun down, aimed it at the dog, and squeezed off a round. The impact of the bullet sent Charly skidding across the room with a final, pathetic whimper of pain.

Sarah screamed as she heard Charly shot. "Charly!! No!!!"

LeRoy and Rico both laughed. Rico rubbed the front of his pants and said, "Hurry up, man. I'll take sloppy seconds but I can't last forever here."

LeRoy nodded and pulled Sarah's panties down. He licked his lips in anticipation as he undid his belt. Rico stared hard, eager for his shot at the blind girl.

With both of them fixated on Sarah's heart-shaped ass, they were taken completely by surprise when the seven-foot tall, mop-carrying monster leaped through the large picture window.

"What the holy fuck?" Rico yelled, too shocked to even point his gun. Melvin had landed nearest to Rico and grabbed him the second his feet hit the ground. Melvin lifted Rico over his head and threw him across the dining room. Rico hit the condiment area hard and lay stunned among the straws, napkins, and ketchups.

This all happened so quickly that LeRoy's hands hadn't moved from his belt. As Melvin moved inexorably toward him, LeRoy realized that he'd have a better chance against this thing if his hands were doing something else. He unshouldered his rifle and aimed it at Melvin's chest. Melvin reached out, took the gun from him, and wrapped the barrel into a curlicue.

LeRoy was now pretty sure that he was going to get his ass kicked but, not one to back down without a fight, threw a punch anyway. It was a good punch, and thrown at a normal person, it would have connected with their jaw and laid them flat. But it hit Melvin square in his barrel chest, instantly shattering the bones in LeRoy's hand. LeRoy yelled in pain. He yelled louder as Melvin grabbed his broken hand and squeezed it, grinding the bones into dust. And LeRoy set a new record for yelling volume when Melvin placed a hand on his chest for leverage and tore his arm clean off. LeRoy whirled around in blind panic, dousing tables in a warm arterial spray.

At this point, most of the customers and employees of the Taco Shack simultaneously decided to fuck this shit and get the hell out of Dodge. Most but not all. Sarah was obviously at a serious disadvantage without Charly. She had no idea what the fuck was going on. All she knew for sure was that she wasn't getting cornholed. She pulled up her panties and took refuge beneath her table, hoping for it all to be over soon.

Bobby also stayed behind, diving beneath his own table. Not that he thought he could help or do much of anything. It was just that shit like this didn't happen every day. Assuming he wasn't hallucinating the whole thing, he wanted to see what went down. Hell, even if he was hallucinating, it was pretty damn cool.

In the back office, Santos was still trying to focus his eyes long enough to master the combination lock on the safe. Frank heard the commotion in the dining room and didn't know what to do. It sounded like things were going to hell out there. Should he go out and lend a hand? Or should he keep his eyes on the prize back here? Goddammit, why couldn't anything be easy?

"Keep working on that thing," he told Santos. "I'll be right back."

Frank walked back through the kitchen and arrived at the counter just in time to see Rico come flying at him. Rico had recovered sufficiently to attempt an assault on Melvin and for his troubles had received another one-way flight through the restaurant. This time he hit the overhead menu and came crashing down on top of Frank.

Frank shook his head, pushed Rico and the broken menu pieces off him, and stood up behind the counter. He found himself eye-to-chest with Melvin. Frank's eyes traveled up, and he looked Melvin in the droopy eye. A low roar came from Melvin's throat as he took Frank's face in the palm of his huge hand and shoved. Frank fell back, crashing into the soda dispensers.

"Motherfucker!!" Melvin felt a chair break against his back. He turned around to see LeRoy, still gushing blood from his right armhole, hurling whatever he could grab at him. Melvin shook his head, somewhat impressed by LeRoy's tenacity. He was less impressed when LeRoy finally realized that his broken gun hadn't been his only weapon. LeRoy pulled a knife from his belt and rushed at Melvin with a fair approximation of a samurai yell.

Melvin didn't know how much punishment this new body of his could withstand and was certain that he didn't want to find out now. LeRoy thrust the knife at Melvin's stomach. Melvin barely deflected the knife with his mop in time.

For a one-armed guy who had to be bleeding to death, LeRoy proved to be surprisingly skilled with the knife. LeRoy hacked away, taking little slivers of wood out of the mop handle. Unfortunately, a mop is not the best defensive weapon against a hunting knife, as Melvin found out the hard way. LeRoy faked a jab at Melvin's face, then swept the knife toward his leg, slicing deep into Melvin's thigh.

Melvin growled in anger and pain. The injury forced him down, and as he went down, he swept the mop at LeRoy's feet. The mop cracked into his ankles, sending LeRoy to the floor. Melvin pinned LeRoy's remaining hand with the mop and kicked the knife away before kicking LeRoy's head into unconsciousness.

Melvin grabbed LeRoy by the shirt and tossed him over his shoulder like a sack of laundry. Better dispose of all three of these scumdogs at the same time, he thought. He hauled LeRoy back and leaped over the counter. Rico and Frank were gone. Melvin looked around, concerned. This can't be good.

He made his way back into the kitchen. Still no sign of the other two. Melvin set LeRoy out on the long counter atop the taco shells and mystery meats. Now, where could they have gone to? And more importantly, had he completely disarmed them?

As it happened, the answer to that was no. Once Melvin was in the center of the kitchen, Rico and Frank launched their ambush, emerging from their hiding places in opposite corners with guns blazing.

Melvin ducked down, taking refuge beneath the countertop. Bullets whizzed past, hitting pots, tubs of sauce, and walls. Melvin looked around and found a metal wheeled cart within reach. He grabbed the cart and sent it flying toward Rico, whom he correctly sized up as the better shot. The cart's corner hit Rico square in the crotch. He fell over the cart in pain, dropping his gun.

Melvin crawled along beneath the counter toward Frank, who had squeezed himself into the corner by the deep-fat fryers and was still shooting wildly. As he made his way through the kitchen supplies, Melvin found a large round baking sheet. He peered up over the counter and sailed the disc through the air. It hit Frank in the forehead. Not hard, but it stunned him just long enough for Melvin to pop up in front of him and yank the gun out of his hands.

Once Frank was disarmed, Melvin took a fry basket out of the hot grease. He grabbed Frank's wrists and forced his hands into the basket.

Melvin squeezed the sides of the basket together, trapping Frank's hands in a wire cage.

"No, man, what are you doin'?!" Frank whined as Melvin hooked the basket above Fryer A. Frank could feel the grease bubble up and spatter against his interlocked fingers, while his face was staring into the abyss of Fryer B. Melvin reached over and broke a pipe off the wall, bending it over Frank's body. Once it was secure, Melvin grabbed another pipe, repeating the procedure until Frank was securely locked in above the two fryers.

After Frank was stuck, Melvin unhooked the basket and lowered it down into the boiling hot grease. Frank's scream came from deep inside his stomach. His body spasmed as he instinctively tried to pull his hands out of the grease, but to no avail. To make matters worse, Frank hadn't eaten yet and he had to admit that the smell of his cooking fingers made his stomach grumble.

Melvin removed the basket from the fryer, hooking it up to allow the excess grease to drip back into the tub. "Order up!" he yelled before sprinkling seasoned salt onto Frank's red and black hands. The salt on the burns made Frank howl louder than before. But this time, the screams were cut off as Melvin forced Frank's head into Fryer B with his mop.

As Frank drowned in the hot grease, Melvin turned his attention over to Rico, who was still cradling his injured jewels. Melvin grabbed Rico by the throat and slammed him onto the counter next to LeRoy. Rico struggled as Melvin grabbed the first weapon within reach: a gallon of milk. Melvin poured half the jug down Rico's throat. As the milk bubbled out of his mouth, Melvin scooped ice cream in after it, giving Rico the worst ice cream brainfreeze of his life. Melvin followed it up with a healthy squeeze of chocolate syrup and a liberal spraying of whipped cream. Rico's face was covered with the sticky crap, chocolate and melting ice cream dribbling back into his nose. Melvin topped it off with a maraschino cherry before hauling Rico's head up to the shake mixer. He positioned the corkscrew where he guessed Rico's mouth might be and hit the switch.

The mixing blades came down, swirling into Rico's treat-filled maw and slicing into his tongue and upper palate. Rico's screams were muffled by the ice cream, but his suffering was plain enough. His legs kicked futilely while shards of broken teeth ricocheted up out of his mouth. It wasn't long before Rico stopped struggling altogether.

Two down, one to go. LeRoy was just starting to come to, and most people thought that even if he lived, the fight would have gone out of him by now. Most people would have been dead wrong on that score. The second LeRoy saw Melvin switching off the mixer, he reached into his pocket and pulled out a grenade. He brought the tiny explosive up to his mouth and put the pin between his teeth.

Melvin saw what he was doing and shoved the grenade into his mouth completely before he had a chance to yank the pin out. LeRoy gagged and spit the pineapple out. It landed harmlessly in his lap and rolled onto the counter. Melvin roared and grabbed LeRoy by the throat, hauling him over to the industrial slicer. The shiny metal still reeked of cheese as Melvin pressed LeRoy's face against the cold steel.

LeRoy's screams went on longer than most. Melvin guided his face back and forth over the blade, slicing off thin strips of flesh. LeRoy did not stop screaming until the metal scraped against bone.

Melvin let LeRoy go limp against the slicer and stood back to survey his work. Only one thing missing, he thought. He crossed through the kitchen to the utility closet and found a couple of unused mops. Santos had crawled out to the doorway by now and was certain that the monster was going to kill him next. In fact, Melvin didn't even notice him as he pulled the mops out of the closet and brought them back to the counter. He mashed the mopheads into what remained of Rico and LeRoy, then went back out into the dining room.

Sarah had left the safety of her table and was crawling around the dining room, looking for her dog. "Charly!" she called. "Charly, where are you?"

Melvin walked over to her and laid a comforting hand on her shoulder. "Are you all right, miss?"

"Don't hurt me!"

"I won't. You're okay. It's all over."

"But my dog . . . where's my dog?"

Melvin looked over at where Charly had fallen. The dog was completely still, lying in a large pool of blood. "I'm sorry, miss. Your dog didn't make it."

"What? No! Those bastards!" Sarah broke down in tears, hitting Melvin in the chest in her anger.

"I know," he said, paying her fists no attention. "I'm sorry. Those guys won't hurt anyone else, though. I promise. They're taken care of. Here, let me help you get home."

Ordinarily, Sarah wouldn't have accepted help from a stranger. But the excitement had her so turned around, she honestly wasn't sure she could even find her way out of the restaurant on her own, much less get home. And something about this man did make her feel better. His voice, maybe, or his strong but gentle hands. She allowed Melvin to lift her to her feet and guide her slowly but safely out of the restaurant.

Bobby watched them go, unsure if he should do something. After all, he'd just seen this creature tear apart three heavily armed psychos. Was it really the best thing to let this deformed, blood-stained giant walk off arm in arm with a blind girl? Possibly not, but he didn't think he could do much to stop him even if he wanted to. And besides, he didn't think the monster was going to hurt that girl. When he spoke, he sounded like an okay dude. And there was something about the way the monster had approached the blind girl. He'd seemed tentative, almost shy, when he rested his hand on her shoulder. Maybe he just didn't want to scare her, but Bobby thought there was more to it than that. He'd recognized the way the monster had acted around the blind woman. He'd acted that way himself whenever he'd attempted to talk to a pretty girl. Uncertain, waiting for the inevitable rejection. If he didn't know any better, he'd say that thing was as big a nerd as he was.

With sirens finally beginning to sound off in the distance, Bobby sat down to wait for the police. He couldn't wait to tell everybody that they'd been rescued by a monster.

15.

Thirty-two Short Films[1] about Tromaville

As Plotnick and his men tramped through the crime scene, helping themselves to tacos and fries, the police chief had to admit that the investigation was not going the way he'd hoped. When they'd first arrived, he was overjoyed. It appeared that the monster had struck again and this time had killed four men, a dog, and a baby. A fucking baby! Now they had a legitimate threat to public safety on their hands.

Only problem with this plan was all these fucking eyewitnesses. Even the mother of the slaughtered kid swore that it was one of the stiffs in the kitchen who had offed the baby. And the goon in the bad

---

1. Whoops. Sorry, force of habit. That should be . . . I don't know . . . scenes? Chaptettes? Whatever. Oh, and there're a lot less than thirty-two, too. Most of them had nothing to do with anything, so we cut 'em in editing. But you can access all of them in the "Deleted Scenes" section of this book, along with the authors' commentary, a making-of featurette, and a music video! What's that? What do you mean, books don't have bonus features? Goddammit, you mean people actually have to rely on the book itself for all their entertainment value? Fuck, being a novelist is hard!

necktie. They couldn't even pin the dog on the monster. The citizens were sticking to their story. The monster had broken in and saved their lives. The scumbags in the kitchen were the real bad guys. If the cops find the monster, they should pin a medal on him.

Matter of fact, Plotnick only had two eyewitnesses to the monster's actual rampage. One of them was Santos, who smelled like he'd spent the past two years in a distillery. He was no trouble. Nobody was going to believe that rummy's story.

This kid Bobby, on the other hand, was a real pain in the ass. Usually cops will go over a witness's story over and over again, making sure there are no holes in it. But Bobby was so eager to tell everybody what had happened, the cops got sick of hearing it before Bobby got sick of telling it. So after he'd been dismissed, Bobby went off to find people who weren't sick of hearing his story. And he found them. The press was swarming outside like maggots on a week-old steak. This disturbed Plotnick. He'd been able to keep the Shinbone Alley story out of the papers easily enough. But with something like this, he'd have to make a statement.

And then there was that fuckhead Clancy. He was supposed to be taking two weeks medical leave. Wouldn't you know it, the first direct order he'd decided to disobey had been that one. The second he saw those mops sticking out of the fried, shaken, and sliced heads in the kitchen, he knew exactly who had been responsible. And now he was out front, shooting his mouth off to the same reporters as that Bobby kid.

Plotnick dreaded hearing what Belgoody was going to say about all this. Fortunately, he had a couple of news friends himself who would report exactly what he told them to report. And Plotnick's friends did TV news. So let Bobby and Clancy spill their guts to that bleeding-heart shit-for-brains from the *Tromaville Times*. What was his name? Jackoff or Jerkwad or something like that. Plotnick would prefer that their side of the story remained under wraps completely, but if it just came out in the morning papers, the damage would be minimal.

Nobody bothered to read anymore. Besides, his side of the story would be broadcast at four, six, and eleven. God bless the media.

Ian Jakov was scribbling notes as fast as Bobby and Clancy could speak. He had his mini-tape recorder taking everything down, of course, but Ian didn't quite trust these things. A tape could tell you exactly what was said but it couldn't tell you how it had been said. It couldn't tell you the way Bobby and Clancy looked at each other, the look of recognition in their eyes when they realized they were describing the same creature. A good reporter never relied on just one source. And Ian Jakov was a good reporter. He'd just never had the chance to prove it until now.

The *Tromaville Times* had a reputation as a paper that toed the party line. This reputation was somewhat unfair. No, they hadn't run any major exposés on corruption in City Hall, or birth defects as a result of the power plant, or anything like that. But it hadn't been for lack of trying. Ian's editor, Paula Greyson, encouraged her writers to dig deep and get to the real stories behind Tromaville's shady history. But she wouldn't run a story unless it was airtight. And sooner or later, every major story began to have major holes. Sources were revealed to be drunks, drug addicts, or pedophiles. Reporters would be promised concrete evidence that somehow never materialized. So a six-part story about Mayor Belgoody's efforts to keep the nuclear plant running despite the fact that it was dangerously below code standards became a one-part story followed the next day by a retraction and an apology.

But this time would be different. This time Ian had plenty of eyewitnesses, including a cop who was willing to go on the record. And this time the story appeared to be so outlandish, it would probably fly under the radar for a while. This wouldn't be the first time a story about mutant creatures appeared in the *Tromaville Times*. The power plant had allegedly spawned freaks at the high school, weird amphibious things, and at least one giant radioactive squirrel. But this was the first time one of these things had appeared more than once. In front of reliable witnesses. As some kind of vigilante.

Ian thanked Bobby and Clancy for their candor and asked them if he could contact them for a follow-up. Ian handed them each a card and headed back for the office. He knew this story was a big one. He'd have to do it justice when he wrote it. And that would mean coming up with a good name for the creature. Something catchy . . . like The Monster-Hero.

By the time Melvin and Sarah reached her house, Melvin had learned just about everything there was to know about Sarah. Maybe it was the shock of losing Charly. Maybe it was the fact that she hadn't had an extended conversation with another human for about a year. Whatever it was, she just wouldn't shut up. And Melvin hoped she never would. He liked to listen to her talk. She was smart, funny, beautiful. Exactly the sort of girl he could have never talked to before his . . . whatever it was.

Sarah invited Melvin in. She didn't usually invite guys in on the first date, not that she had many first dates anymore. But Melvin seemed different. Besides, did this even qualify as a first date? If it did, then she could have sex with him next time and not worry about him thinking she was a slut. That cinched it. This was a date.

The first thing Melvin noticed about Sarah's house was the long row of white canes. Not because it was obvious, but because Sarah immediately selected one from the rack to replace the one she lost at the restaurant and knocked the whole thing over. Melvin tried to grab them but they clattered through his fingers and onto the floor.

"Whoops! Don't worry about those. That happens all the time," Sarah tossed over her shoulder as she tap-tap-tapped her way through the living room.

"You sure have a lot of canes."

"Yeah, they break really easily."

"They do?"

"Yeah, can you believe it? Just a couple of knocks on a guy's head and a jab to his crotch and it falls apart."

Melvin half-laughed, then looked around for a place to sit. The only thing that looked capable of supporting his weight was the sofa, so he decided to risk it. Four loud cracks later, the sofa was several inches shorter. Melvin winced at the broken couch and hoped Sarah wouldn't notice.

"So, Melvin," Sarah smiled, "I've been going on nonstop since we left the Taco Shack and you've barely said a word. I don't know the first thing about you other than your name."

"Oh." Melvin was not used to conversation and didn't pick up on Sarah's hint. The silence stretched out between them for what seemed like an eternity but really was probably only about fifteen to twenty minutes.

"What do you do, Melvin?" Sarah asked, more to make sure that Melvin was still in the room rather than out of genuine interest.

"Oh, well . . . I'm sort of . . . between jobs at the moment."

"Oh." Sarah wondered if blind people were forced to show the sighted the door.

"I mean I used to work down at the health club."

"Oh, really? I thought you probably worked out."

"You did?" Melvin couldn't fathom that one until he glanced over at his new biceps. "Oh, yeah. Yeah, I guess I do. Anyhoo, there was an . . . an incident there the other day. I haven't been back since."

Sarah nodded, not wanting to press Melvin for details he clearly didn't want to get into. "So what are you going to do now?"

"I'm still trying to figure that one out. I've been through a lot of changes recently. Big, big changes."

"Uh-huh. Well, whatever happened to you recently, I'm glad you were at the restaurant today. You saved a lot of people."

"Yeah, I seem to be doing that a lot lately."

"That's wonderful. It sounds like you have a gift."

Melvin wasn't too sure about that. If this was a gift, it was one of those crappy, useful gifts that your least favorite grandmother always stuck you with at Christmas.

"Melvin?" He had fallen into another silent reverie, and Sarah wasn't sure if he was still there.

"Yes?"

Sarah stood in front of him, gently taking his hand in hers. "I was wondering . . . would you mind if I touched your face? I'd like to get an idea of what you look like."

Her hand was inches from his warped cheek. Melvin stood up abruptly, knocking Sarah backward.

"Whoa, sorry about that. But hey, is that the time? I just remembered . . . I think I left the oven on at my place. Or . . . anyway, I've gotta go. It was really great meeting you, Sarah. I'll call you. If that's okay. Is it okay?"

Sarah tried her best to follow Melvin's voice as it rapidly headed for the front door. "Sure, but—"

"Great! You take care of yourself and I'll call you soon, okay? 'Bye!"

Sarah heard the door slam and Melvin's heavy footsteps running down the sidewalk. Well, that was weird, she thought. Maybe he's got acne. Or a really bad cold sore. Or a wicked cleft palate. Then again, from what she heard at the restaurant, he was a fighter. That opened up a whole new Pandora's crisper of potential disfigurements. Cauliflower ear. Rutabaga nose. Zucchini lips.

Sarah sighed and went to lay down on the sofa Melvin vacated so quickly. Her stomach gave a little flip as she went down, discovering the couch was several inches shorter than it used to be. Melvin was a strange one, all right. But for all his quirks, including the not insignificant fact that it seemed he had literally torn apart those three shitbirds at the Taco Shack, there was something about him she found irresistible. After all she'd been through, it was so nice to finally meet a normal, regular guy.

The past couple of days had been rough on poor Cigarface. The doctor told him that his genitals had been completely crushed in the Shinbone Alley fight and there was virtually no chance that they would grow back. The doctor gave him a choice. Either live the rest of your life in agonizing pain or have your deflated balls snipped off. To Cigarface, that was no choice at all. He'd take the agonizing pain, thank you very much.

On the street, Cigarface was not commanding the respect he once did. It was no easy thing to order the troops when your voice sounded like you were permanently hooked up to a helium tank. Once he'd been one of the most feared thugs in The Big Man's rogues' gallery. Now he sounded like he should be helping sew Cinderella's dress for the big ball.

He had one chance to get back on top. Find the monster before anyone else did. Find it and rip it to shreds. He hadn't had much luck with that, either. Not that he had much idea where to look. But still, how hard could it be to find a seven-foot-tall, bald, greenish-brown, deformed dude carrying a mop?

Pretty goddamn hard, as it turned out. So now, Cigarface sat alone at Murphy's Bar, sucking back shot after shot and focusing all his anger on the throbbing, insistent pain deep within his plaster underpants. Every so often, somebody at the end of the bar would yell out, "Hey, Cigarface! Find your monster yet?"

"Shut the fuck up!" Cigarface would chirp back and the bar would erupt into laughter. It was getting real old, real fast.

The final insult came late in the evening. Cigarface pulled his Zippo out of his shirt pocket and flipped it open. The flame danced in front of his eyes as he lit the stogie he'd been gnawing on all night. The smoke attracted the attention of Murphy himself.

"Hey! You can't smoke that in here."

"Since when?"

"It's the law now, Cigarface, you know that. No smoking in restaurants and bars."

"Yeah, but since when have you given a shit about it?"

"Since now, Chipmunk Boy. Take it outside."

Cigarface limped out the door and fumed, exhaling blue smoke into the night air and hating everyone and everything. Fuck The Big Man. Fuck Plotnick. Fuck Murphy and fuck the fucking voters of the great state of New Fucking Jersey. And most of all, fuck that fucking monster over there.

Over there?!

Cigarface nearly swallowed his lit cigar. Sure enough, there was the monster, big as life and twice as ugly, heading down a back alley. And it looked like he was carrying . . . flowers?

Whatever. Cigarface ran back into the bar.

"HEY! COME ON!"

The laughter crested and broke over Cigarface in a mighty wave. Goddamn voice was going to fuck him every time, wasn't it? Cigarface pulled a gun out of his waistband and fired a single shot into the ceiling. That shut 'em up.

"Listen up, fuckers! I found the monster!"

The crowd murmured at this news. "Murmur, murmur, murmur, murmur."

"He's right across the street. Now, do you wanna sit here and murmur all night, or do you wanna help me kick his ass??"

About half the bar giggled over Cigarface's high-pitched voice, working them up to go kick some ass, but eventually everyone agreed that they did want to go kick some ass after all. If it really was the monster, terrific. If not, they'd just kick Cigarface's ass. Either way, it was something to do.

Melvin had never put much stock in flowers' ability to predict whether one was loved or not loved before. But until now, he'd never had much reason to. So far it was a draw. Three flowers said she loved him. Three others said she loved him not. It all came down to this one.

Before the flower could be allowed to reach its decision, Melvin's path was blocked by a wall of gun-toting barflies. Melvin wasn't looking for trouble, so he stopped and slowly turned around. Guns were appearing all around him, carried by some of the most dangerous-looking drunks he'd ever seen.

Melvin was surrounded. And somehow he guessed that as tough as his new body was, it probably wasn't bulletproof. He tucked the flower into his tutu for safekeeping. This could really suck.

An unnaturally high voice echoed through the alley. "Hey, freak! Remember me?"

A few members of the gun line still tittered at the sound of the voice. An annoyed Cigarface stepped into the light and turned his attention to the gigglers. "Grow the fuck up, cocksucker. This is serious!"

Melvin stared intently at Cigarface. "Who are you calling a freak?"

Cigarface aimed his gun up at Melvin's head. "I'm calling you out, Mop Boy. Goddamn but you're one ugly son of a bitch."

Melvin squinted through his good eye, which made his droopy eye widen. "Don't call me Mop Boy. It makes me angry. And you wouldn't like me when I'm angry."

"I already hate your fuckin' guts, Mop Boy! And now I'm gonna spill 'em all over this alley. So long, freak-o."

Melvin had less than a second to make his move. And the only place he had to move to was up. As fingers squeezed down on the triggers and bullets exploded into the dank night air, Melvin leaped. He shot fifteen feet straight up, grabbed onto a fire escape, and hauled himself to safety.

His would-be assassins were not so lucky. The bullets needed homes, and they found them in the meat, brains, bone, and tissue of the shooters themselves. If they hadn't formed such a perfect circle around Melvin, maybe a few of them would have survived.[2]

2. There's a lesson here for you, kids. If you're thinking of pursuing a career in wet work, skip geometry class. It'll only hurt you in the future.

The only one not to be killed instantly was Cigarface himself, who had been standing just outside the circle of death. Bullets tore through his stomach, thigh, and crotch. Mostly his crotch. Suddenly he had another reason to be glad he hadn't wasted a lot of money on having his damaged nutsack surgically removed. In an instant, he had the exact same procedure performed free of charge.

Melvin watched all this from his perch, then leaped back down to confront Cigarface. He was getting awfully tired of people trying to kill him. Melvin planted a foot on Cigarface's bleeding torso and pressed down hard, squeezing a helpless squeak out of Cigarface's throat.

"So this was your idea?" Melvin asked.

Cigarface nodded, glanced down at Melvin's foot. It appeared that the pressure was forcing his intestines out through one of the bullet holes. That was a hell of a thing.

"And it was probably your idea to beat up that poor cop, wasn't it?"

Cigarface nodded again. Now that he looked closer, he could see that the intestines were actually snagged on Melvin's shoe. If Melvin stepped away, Cigarface would be disemboweled. He hoped he passed out before that happened.

He didn't. Melvin stepped off and stood in the center of the circle of corpses, Cigarface's intestines trailing off his shoe like a stray bit of toilet paper. Cigarface watched them go, rolled his eyes back in his head, and died.

"All right, then." Melvin was getting used to his new voice. He liked it a lot. "Listen up. Things are going to change in this town. Scum like you have been running things for too long, making life miserable for decent, honest, hardworking people. Those days are over. Tell your bosses. Tell everyone. We've had enough, and their days are numbered! The tide is turning in Tromaville, and I'm turning it. I'm not just a pretty face!"

Damn, Melvin thought, that was a good line! Probably should have made sure there was somebody left to hear it, though.

Melvin looked down and pulled the flower from his tutu. In all the excitement, he'd lost track of where he was. Better start over. . . .

She loves me.

She loves me not.

She loves me.

She loves me not.

She loves me.

She loves me not.

One petal left . . . so that means . . .

She loves me!

A crooked smile broke across Melvin's face. He dropped the stem in a pool of blood, then ran to a pay phone on the sidewalk. He dropped in some coins and mashed the numbers with his massive fingers.

He listened to the phone ring once . . . twice . . .

"Hello?"

"Sarah? This is Melvin. Melvin Ferd? We met this afternoon?"

"Yeah, I remember. You're kind of hard to forget, Melvin. I'm glad you called."

"I said I would, didn't I? So I was wondering . . . if maybe you wouldn't want to maybe go out with me? If you don't want to—"

"I'd love to, Melvin."

"It's okay, I understand. It was really nice meeting you and—"

"I said yes, Melvin. Is tomorrow night okay?"

Melvin's head was swimming with excitement. He had a date! With a girl! An attractive girl!

He looked at his feet and saw that Cigarface's intestines were still caught on his shoe, trailing back into the alley. He reached down and brushed them off with an embarassed glance around.

"Yeah, Sarah. Tomorrow night is perfect."

The Adventures of The Hypnotic Rat-Eye (Formerly Known as Knipples' Left Eyeball): Episode III

It had been no trouble for Knipples' eye to seize control of the rat's consciousness. And now that the eye had legs, finding the creature and wreaking its horrible vengeance should have been a simple matter. But in practice, The Hypnotic Rat-Eye was finding things much more difficult than that. The Hypnotic Rat-Eye had lived its entire life in Shinbone Alley. It did not know the ins and outs of greater Tromaville. The Great and Terrible Hypnotic Rat-Eye was forced to admit, it was lost.

If The Hypnotic Rat-Eye was to find the creature, it would have to find another host. One with greater mobility and powers of deductive reasoning. But where would it find such a being?

The Hypnotic Rat-Eye perched atop a garbage can and looked around, scanning the horizon for a new host. There. Off in the distance. A mangy, lost, starving dog sniffed through a Dumpster in search of scraps. The Hypnotic Rat-Eye smiled. Perfect.

The rodent leaped from the can and skittered down the street toward the dog. It stopped directly in front of it, fixing the canine with its irresistible gaze. The dog looked down and bared its teeth at the juicy rat. Yes, The Hypnotic Rat-Eye thought, that's right, my pretty. Feast. Feast on my sweet innards.

The Hypnotic Rat-Eye made no effort to escape when the dog raised its hackles and barked angrily at it. The dog sniffed the rat. The rat remained stock still, mesmerizing the dog with its stare. Come on, Fido. Eat the rat.

Unexpectedly, the dog turned away and moved on to another Dumpster in search of greener pastures. What the . . . ? The Hypnotic Rat-Eye was perturbed. This dog must have a stronger will than I expected. No matter. None can resist The Hypnotic Rat-Eye.

The rat chased after the dog and bit it lightly on the paw to draw its attention. The dog whirled around, barking furiously. This was the opportunity The Hypnotic Rat-Eye had been waiting for. It leaped directly into the dog's mouth. The canine's jaws snapped shut, fangs sinking into the rat's flesh.

The Hypnotic Rat-Eye relaxed and welcomed the sweet release. Yesssss . . . grow fat, grow strong. You will be my vessel, and I, your captain. We will find and destroy the creature. And then, the world! None will escape the fury of The Hypnotic Dog-Rat-Eye!! None!! NONE!!!!!

16.

Health Club Horror

"**M**ONSTER-HERO SAVES MOST IN MEXICAN RESTAURANT STANDOFF"

Jerry studied the *Tromaville Times*'s banner headline for more than a minute. He didn't bother venturing into the article it accompanied, but the headline captivated him. So this monster bullshit was true after all, huh? Plotnick had told him to cool it with the on-site pharmacy at the health club for a while. "Until this whole monster thing blows over, anyway," Plotnick had said.

Plotnick had laid some lame-ass excuses on him in the past. Everything from "I need a bigger cut this week because the policemen's ball is coming up" to "Sorry I couldn't make it to your party but my dog wrecked my transmission." Now it appeared that the "whole monster thing" might have a little ring of truth to it after all. Hell, they couldn't write a whole headline about it if it weren't true, could they?

Either way, Jerry didn't know what the monster had to do with him. Plotnick was worried that the thing was some sort of superhuman vigilante, running around town and wiping out lawbreakers. But Jerry was a legitimate businessman. Dealing drugs out of the gym may not be strictly legal per se, but Jerry felt sure it all depended on your interpretation of the law. As far as he was concerned, it was all part of the service.

A timid knock interrupted his study of the newspaper. "Yeah," he shouted, "come on in!"

A pretty young brunette entered his office, closing the door behind her. Jerry recognized her as one of his regular customers but couldn't place the name. One of those stupid names like Amber or Heather or Ashlee or something.

"Hey . . . honey. What can I do you for?"

Amber or Heather or Ashlee stepped up to his desk, her sixteen-year-old body pressing insistently against the confines of her magenta leotard. "Hi, Jerry. I've got a teensy problem."

"I'm a problem-solver, babe. What's up?"

"Well, there's this party tonight?" She was the type of teenage girl who made every statement sound like a question. "Like a rave? And I'm like totally out of everything."

"Everything, huh? What are you after? X? Coke? Crack? Feel the need for speed?"

"Yeah, all that. But the problem is . . . I can't really pay you? Money?"

"That is a problem, sweetheart."

"Yeah. So I was thinking maybe I could pay you something else?"

Jerry sighed and touched his index fingers to his chin in a pantomime of deep thought. "Hmm. I'd like to help you out, doll, I really would. But I can't pay my suppliers with what you want to pay me with. Know what I'm saying?"

Amber or Heather or Ashlee's face fell. She did know what he was saying, which wasn't often the case.

"Tell you what, though," Jerry continued. "You're a good customer. I know you're good for the money. So we can consider this a down payment. I give you the goods. You give me the cash in a week or so. That work for you?"

The girl hesitated for a second. This wasn't exactly what she had in mind. But given the circumstances, she didn't see that she had any other choice. She smiled, nodded, and slipped the straps of her leotard off her shoulders. Her not yet surgically plumped breasts tumbled free.

Jerry smiled and opened a desk drawer, inviting the girl to look inside. There was her pot of gold, a cornucopia of pills, vials, and powders. Her smile widened as she squeezed behind the desk, grinding onto Jerry's lap and thrusting her rosebud nipples into his face.

The girl slithered down beneath the desk, freeing Jerry's growing schlong from his sweatpants. Jerry leaned back in his desk and smiled. Yes indeed, it was very, very good to be a legitimate businessman. So many perks.

Melvin was very pleased with how well the shack he'd constructed had turned out. He'd been able to salvage a small refrigerator and a hot plate from the dump and put them in working order. There had been no shortage of chairs and tables. He'd been less enthusiastic about flopping on one of the many old, creatively stained mattresses lying around, but eventually he found one that was reasonably clean. Certainly clean enough for a mutated, radioactive creature such as him.

Now that he'd decided to pursue a career as a superhuman hero,[1] he had some things to figure out. He sat at his makeshift dining table, working on a to-do list. Somehow he seemed to be able to sense evil and corruption. That was helpful, but Tromaville had a lot of problems. He couldn't just wander around aimlessly and wait for trouble to find him. If he was going to make a difference, he would have to go on the offensive. And the more he thought about it, the more he

---

1. Legal restrictions prevented him from becoming a superhero, as Marvel and DC had a joint copyright on that term.

realized that Tromaville had plenty of places where he could go and be offensive. The schools were in real trouble. Kids were being sold drugs and bringing guns to class. There were entire parts of town honest people never set foot in. And then there was the movie theater. Maybe the crap they showed there wasn't a crime technically, but it sure seemed like one.

But at the top of the list was his old workplace, the Tromaville Health Club. Melvin knew all about Jerry's side business. And then there was Bozo and his gang. Melvin could sense that they had been up to something other than just picking on him. He wasn't sure what that was yet, but he could feel deep down that it had to be stopped. People were getting hurt.

Melvin stood up, straightened his tutu, and grabbed his mop. Time to go to work. As he started the long walk back to town, he realized this job would be a lot easier if he had some kind of souped-up supercar. Too bad the toxic waste hadn't given him flying powers, too.

Bozo was pissed. His usual demeanor was a simmering rage topped off with an unfocused sexual frustration, so casual observers could be excused if they didn't see much difference between pissed Bozo and normal Bozo. But Bozo felt the difference in his tensed shoulders and the throbbing veins in his forehead and neck. He didn't like it much.

His search for the mop killer had predictably turned up nothing. Not only did he not know where to look, he also didn't really know what he was looking for. He would have given up on it completely if it weren't for one thing. He was certain that Plotnick would send him up the river for the mop boy prank, the hit-and-run game, and probably frame him for the monster-hero shit, too, if he didn't find the real guy.

Bozo had a difficult time making the others understand this. Julie helped for a while but got bored sooner rather than later. Naturally, she'd assumed that Bozo would, too. So when Bozo's search stretched into a second day, she suggested that he shove the search up his ass. Bozo wouldn't have minded shoving most anything up his ass, but as he was fairly certain that his ass was the one place the monster-hero/mop killer/whatever you wanted to call him was not, he told Julie she was an unhelpful bitch.

Julie replied by informing Bozo that she would rather be an unhelpful bitch than Plotnick's bitch, which was exactly what Bozo was becoming by continuing to look for the alleged monster.

Bozo then asked if Julie would prefer it if Bozo became somebody's prison bitch instead.

Julie told him yes, she would. She would love to see Bozo get gang-banged in a prison shower by half a dozen foot-long cocks.

Bozo proposed that if that happened, she would end up lapping beaver in the women's prison at the same time.

Needless to say, all this talk of beaver-lapping and foot-long cock dogs erected hot spots on both of them. And ten minutes later, after a furious fight-fuck, Bozo was back out on the streets looking for the creature. Without Julie. But if he was gonna do this, he'd be good and goddamned if he did it alone. Bozo went straight over to Slug's place, and this time he didn't take no for an answer. Slug didn't want to help, but Bozo made it clear. He didn't care if Wanda had six vibrating cunts that played "Hava Nagila" when they came. Slug was going to hit the streets with Bozo. And they were going to track down this mop-monster-hero thing.

"And what do we do when we find it?" Slug asked.

Bozo shrugged. "I dunno. Run it over, I guess."

By the time Melvin made it to the health club, he was exhausted. He'd taken a long, circuitous route in an effort to get to his destination unseen. And he would have made it if circumstances hadn't forced him to come out of the shadows. Every few minutes he sensed . . . something that made his blood and bubbly skin start to tingle like it had in

Shinbone Alley and at the Taco Shack. Not quite as intensely, but he found he was unable to ignore it.

It first happened as he was making his way through a residential neighborhood. He followed the tingling sensation and found a little girl, about seven or eight, standing at the base of a tree calling up to her cat. Melvin worried that if he walked up to the girl, she'd scream bloody murder. He tried to walk away but couldn't. Especially after the girl began to cry.

Melvin walked over and looked up at the tree. "Is your kitty stuck up there?" he asked the girl.

The girl dried her eyes and looked at Melvin. She was a little afraid, there was no doubt about that. But her concern over her cat seemed to outweigh the fact that she was standing there talking to a tall, discolored, walking meltdown with a mop.

"Uh-huh."

"What's her name?"

"Dirty Sanchez."

"Okay." Melvin gripped the tree tightly in one hand. "Take it easy. I'll get your Dirty Sanchez for you, little girl."

Melvin shook the tree, bringing down leaves, a squirrel, two Frisbees, and Dirty Sanchez, who landed safely in his outstretched palm. Melvin handed over the cat to the little girl. She thanked him and ran off, holding her pussy tight and stroking its soft fur.

Melvin smiled as he continued on his way. "Now, there's a girl who loves a Dirty Sanchez," he thought, happy that he was able to help.

A few minutes later, Melvin sneaked past a grocery store. A man struggled with his car in the parking lot, jamming a straightened-out wire hanger into the keyhole in the trunk. "Of all the stupid fuckin' goddamn things to do," he muttered to himself.

Melvin wandered over and stood behind the man, leaning casually on his mop. "Lose your keys?"

The man sighed and kept working without turning around. "I locked 'em in the trunk after I put the groceries in there. Stupid."

"You'll scratch your car up doing it that way."

"Yeah, thanks, pal. Got any better ideas?"

"Maybe. Stand back a sec."

The man turned around and found himself face to face with Melvin's chest. He stood back, eyes widening. "Sweet-lovin' Jesus."

"It's okay," Melvin tried to reassure him. "I won't hurt you. Or your car, if I can help it."

Melvin sized up the car and squatted down, grabbing the rear bumper. Gently, he began to lift the rear end of the car. "You didn't buy any eggs, did you?" Melvin asked.

The man backed up some more, shaking his head and not believing what he was seeing. Melvin lifted the car three feet off the ground before letting it go. The tires hit the ground hard, and the trunk popped right open. Melvin reached inside for the keys and handed them over to the man.

"Uh, thanks," the man said, bending down to make sure his car was all right.

"No problem. Take care."

And so it went. Melvin would make a little bit of progress before that tingle came back. By the time he made it to the Tromaville Health Club, he'd helped a group of little old ladies across a busy street, frightened away two rapists and half a dozen muggers, given directions to a busload of lost Japanese tourists, and called a cab for a drunk businessman who was about to drive home. Melvin was surprised how much trouble people got into around Tromaville on a regular basis.

Most of the elderly ladies were too blind or senile to take much notice of Melvin's appearance. For their part, the Japanese tourists, used to their cities and villages being decimated by humongous radioactive thunder lizards, found nothing even remotely unusual about Melvin's new body. Each and every rapist and/or mugger Melvin encountered filled their drawers with steaming piles of fear-shit, as was the plan. Unfortunately, so did most of their would-be victims once they caught sight of the hideously deformed creature of superhuman size and strength stepping out of the darkness in front of them. Melvin felt bad that he'd inadvertently freaked out the very people he was saving but was sure that the greater good outweighed their momentary discomfort.[2]

Melvin entered the health club through the back door at the same moment someone else was exiting. She was young, nervous, dressed in a magenta leotard, and zipping up a black gym bag. She was pretty. Looked like her name was Amber or Heather or Ashlee or something like that.

The girl ran smack into Melvin and dropped the bag, spilling its contents everywhere. Vials of crack and multicolored pills tumbled onto Melvin's feet. He knelt down and picked one up.

The girl's eyes engulfed her face, and for once, Melvin couldn't tell if she was scared of him or of the fact that she'd been busted. "Oh, shit!" she cried, then repeated, "Shit, shit, shit!"

"Take it easy," Melvin said. "What's your name?"

"Brandi."

Melvin nodded. He'd been close. "Where'd you get all this?"

"Are you a cop?"

"Do I look like a cop?"

"I guess not."

---

2. As for the drunk businessman, he swore off the sauce after Melvin's impromptu intervention. After he sobered up, he attended his first AA meeting. Unfortunately, none of the judgmental pricks in the group believed that Burt F. had his life turned around by an eight-and-a-half-foot-tall monster with glowing red eyes who called a taxi for him. Like a lot of recovering drunks, Burt F. wouldn't keep his mouth shut about his last day as a drinker, and eventually the story cost him his wife, his job, and his house. Now, if this were a comic book series, we'd bring Burt F. back when we started to run out of ideas (probably right around issue 66 or so) and start to raid this story for minor characters we could transform into supervillains. But since this is a novel, you'll just have to take our word for it. Burt's story becomes really fucking stupid and convoluted, involving radioactive booze and clones. If it's ever told, you'll be horribly disappointed. We swear.

"So where'd you get it?"

Brandi chewed her lip and weighed her options. Melvin didn't feel like waiting and prodded her out of her reverie.

"Was his name Jerry?"

"Yes." She looked a little sick at the mention of his name.

"Thought so. Listen, Brandi. You don't need this stuff. Now, I want you to get out of here and never come back. If you want to exercise, use the gym at your school. Okay?"

"But I still owe Jerry! If I don't pay—"

"You don't owe him anything. Leave this stuff here. Never use it again, okay? And you might want to get some mouthwash. Your breath smells a little funky."

Brandi snapped her palm over her mouth and nodded. She looked like she could either kiss Melvin or kill him. But since she couldn't kill him and really didn't want to kiss him, she simply released her grip on the gym bag and ran off.

Melvin took the bag inside and made his way to his old utility closet. He dumped the drugs down the drain of the big industrial sink, allowing the tingle to wash over him. He let himself go, getting angrier and angrier by the second. As the last of the cocaine swirled down the drain, he grabbed a pair of mops and set out. Time to do some good.

Julie and Wanda loitered by the treadmills, admiring hit-and-run photos and complaining about Bozo and Slug. It had been almost a week since the last hit and run, and they were jonesing for another go. They were nearly at the point where they'd consider getting behind the wheel themselves. But that would truly be a last resort. Neither of them was overjoyed about going out without the guys. As long as one of those two idiots was driving, Julie and Wanda had plausible deniability. Not that they would have called it plausible deniability. They just thought it was common sense not to get your hands dirty if you could help it.

Jerry strutted into the workout room, oblivious to the shiny patch of dried semen on his sweatpants. "Hey," he called over to Julie and Wanda, "if you aren't gonna use those things, stop hangin' all over 'em."

The girls glanced at each other, then stepped off their treadmills. "Jesus, Jerry," Wanda sneered. "Had that stick up your ass long?"

"Nah. It's new. Like your tits."

The girls brushed past him. Julie glanced down and said, "I'd tell you to go fuck yourself, Jerry, but it looks like you already did."

Jerry looked at the front of his pants and saw the cum stain. He rubbed some spit on it, to no avail. He spun around and attempted to yell a witty retort at Julie, but it was too late. They'd already disappeared.

"Fuckin' cunts," he muttered and lay down on the bench press. One good thing about running this place was that he knew how all the machines really worked. So he could adjust the bench press to make it look as if he were pumping two hundred pounds, when in reality he wasn't even doing twenty. If he had his way, he'd never touch any of these useless, backbreaking torture devices. But appearances were everything. Hell, he was selling that philosophy at seventy-five dollars a month (base membership). Jerry strapped on a pair of headphones, cranked up some music (anything was better than the canned New Age crap he pumped into the gym), and began his "workout."

Perhaps if Jerry played better music over the PA system in the first place, he would have lived. But because he couldn't hear anything, he didn't notice any of the panicked screams that ricocheted through the workout room when Melvin walked through the door.

Melvin barely noticed the screams himself. He was fixated on the plump pusher pretending to exercise. The man who had helped to make his life a living hell for the past several years. The man who had done his best to hook everyone who came his way on one drug or another, whether it was steroids or heroin. The man who was about to find out what pressing two hundred pounds was really like. Because although nobody would have believed it, Melvin had been paying attention all those years working at the health club. And he knew how the machines really worked, too.

Jerry lifted the weight easily, over and over. Up and down. Back and forth. How long should he keep doing this today? He should at least break a sweat, he supposed. So not too much longer. Probably just until this song was over. He kept going. Up. Down. Up. Down. Up . . .

"Jesus' balls!" he shouted. All of a sudden, this thing weighed a ton. His arms felt like cold, wet spaghetti. He couldn't hold it. The weight came crashing down, pulling every muscle in his arms.

Jerry sat upright, yanking the headphones off. "All right, who's the—"

His question remained unasked as a pair of strong, massive hands pushed him back down and yanked him backward. Jerry looked up and found himself staring at Melvin's twisted face, albeit upside down.

Melvin lifted the weight easily with one hand, keeping Jerry pinned to the bench with the other. Jerry stared straight up and saw himself reflected in the metal spike that held the weights. His eyes flicked from the spike back to Melvin's crooked eyes.

"You're through," Melvin said and let go of the weight.

The spike shot down, straight through Jerry's nose. His head was split clean in half. Well, not so clean, maybe. Blood and snot burst onto the black weights. Jerry's body spasmed uncontrollably. Suddenly the cum stain was the least of his laundry problems. His sweatpants filled with piss and shit.

Melvin ground a mop into the lower half of Jerry's skull, pinning his flopping tongue like a fish on the deck of a boat. Those few people who hadn't fled the scene immediately upon Melvin's arrival now filled the room with fresh screams before joining their friends in getting the hell out of there.

Melvin took a step back and surveyed the familiar, now empty room. Well, he thought, that was satisfying. But he wasn't done yet.

The tingle hadn't gone away. He still had business at the gym. Melvin rolled his shoulders and allowed himself to follow his instincts. Wherever they might take him.

Steam billowed around the sauna, almost obscuring Wanda's view of her treasured photos. She wiped the condensation away, admiring the vivid reds, the deep blacks, and the putrid yellows of her death shots. After a hard day, there was nothing better than a long, slow finger fuck accompanied by images of blacktop brutality. Hell, even after an easy day it was pretty damn good.

Wanda massaged her erect nipples, floating mere centimeters atop the silicone Dr. McKinlay had inserted. Had her boobs been this sensitive back when she was just a B cup? She didn't think so. Thanks to the good doctor, she'd blossomed into the full flower of her sexual renaissance. And while her real passion was laid out in front of her in stark images of red asphalt and tires jammed with digestive systems, she also took great pleasure in imagining herself under Dr. McKinlay's knives and lasers. Her chest sliced open, waiting to receive their cargo. Her legs splayed wide, hungry for the sharp, hot touch of vaginal rejuvenation. She had recurring fantasies of being fucked by Dr. McKinlay on the operating table in midprocedure, her body being penetrated everywhere at once. At times she wasn't sure if these really were fantasies and not actual memories.

The steam and Wanda's masturbatory reveries were so thick, she scarcely noticed the door creak open. A massive male figure stood silhouetted in the fog.

"Slug?" Wanda asked, squinting through the steam and working her fingers deeper inside her.

The stranger took a silent step forward. Though he was still obscured by the clouds of hot steam, Wanda could see the figure was draped in a giant towel.

"Slug, if you're wearing that fucking elephant man getup again, you can forget it. I want you now."

In fact, Wanda was fairly certain that whoever this guy was, it wasn't Slug. For one thing, he was about a foot and a half taller. And broader. And presumably bigger all the way around. Which was fine by her. She was jonesing for a guy whose dick didn't need help from her fingers to fill her up. What Slug didn't know wouldn't hurt him. Good thing, too; otherwise he'd be dead from all the shit he didn't know.

Wanda reached up, grabbed the shrouded figure's hand, and pulled him down to her. The towel brushed against her face. She placed her hands squarely on the stranger's shoulders and pressed him south, hoping this guy wouldn't need a road map to figure out what he was supposed to do down there.

The figure crouched between her legs and remained still. Wanda felt his shoulders trembling a bit. Great, she thought. All the guys in the world and I get stuck with the world's only seven-foot-tall virgin.

"Come on, baby," she purred. "Let's get this horse blanket off you and put that tongue of yours to work."

She pulled the towel off the figure. As she did so, the stranger rose. Wanda found herself face to misshapen face with the elephant man of her younger dreams. Melvin's droopy eye seemed to wink at her as his mouth wrinkled into a grin.

"Hi there," Melvin said.

EDITOR'S NOTE: Okay, Kaufman. Hold it right there. Maybe in your little two-bit movies you can get away with illogical shit such as this. But this is a novel! Unlike you, we have certain standards. You're going to be sharing shelf space with the likes of John Updike and Ethan Hawke. Now, we've cut you a lot of slack so far because this is your first novel and you're clearly developmentally disabled somehow, but enough is enough. What possible reason could there be for Melvin to be wearing the same stupid towel Slug was wearing before? I won't even get into the fact that it didn't really make sense for Slug to be wearing the towel in the first place. But you either go back and explain why Melvin's wearing it, or the book is canceled.

KAUFMAN: All right, all right, fine. No reason to get excited here. This is why I've got my trusted coauthor, Adam Jahnke, here. Adam, tell her why Melvin's wearing the towel.

JAHNKE: Uh . . . because he was wearing it in the movie. I don't know why the hell you did that.

KAUFMAN: Oh, yeah. Well, it was the go-go eighties. Lots of people were wearing towels back then to hide their massive cocaine use.

EDITOR: So Melvin was doing blow at some point in the past few pages?

KAUFMAN: No, no, no! Melvin's a good guy, he wouldn't do that. He was . . . uh . . . hang on. Come on, Jahnke, help me out here or I swear to fucking Christ I'll give your cheese sandwich to some homeless fuck.

JAHNKE: No, Lloyd, please!

KAUFMAN: Well, then—

JAHNKE: All right, fine. So let's go back a couple of pages. Melvin's just finished killing Jerry in the workout room. . . .

Melvin left the workout room, following the now familiar sensations that filled his mind and chest. There was a tingle that played around his mind that carried him to people in trouble. But more troubling was what he felt in his gut. It was a weight crushing his heart, and it inevitably led him to the face of evil. And once he saw it, he simply lost control.

The weight led him downstairs, past the swimming pool. Where it all began for him in some respects. He could still see the goat, the crowd. Could still feel the lice jumping from the goat's wool into his hair. Was that what he was feeling now? Maybe this was a false alarm. Maybe the gym was deserted and all he was experiencing now was the memory of his past humiliation. Maybe not. The weight wasn't getting any lighter. He couldn't leave without checking it out.

He followed his heavy heart to the saunas. All were empty except one. This was it. But the steam was so thick, he couldn't see through the tiny window on the door. He paused with his hand on the latch. This was still pretty new to him. He could be wrong. There might not be anyone in there except for some totally innocent man or woman enjoying a steam. He didn't want to scare anyone unnecessarily.

Melvin went to the adjacent sauna and found a discarded towel hanging on a hook. He draped it over himself as best he could. It didn't cover him completely, but at least it covered his face. If it turned out this was nothing, he'd apologize and say he didn't realize there was anyone in here.

Suitably disguised, Melvin returned to the closed door. As he eased it open, pillows of steam billowed out. He heard a low moaning inside. A girl's voice. "Fuck me with your scalpel, Doctor," she murmured.

No doubt about it, Melvin thought. This must be the place. He stepped inside.

JAHNKE: How's that?

   KAUFMAN: Brilliant! Madam Editrix? What say you?

   EDITOR: Pretty fucking convoluted and lame, but I guess it'll have to do.

   JAHNKE: Woo-hoo! Now, where's my cheese sandwich?

   KAUFMAN (wiping crumbs off his chin): Uh . . . it's coming! Soon! Here, have some goldfish crackers in the meantime.

   JAHNKE: Wow, thanks, Lloyd!

   EDITOR: Guys, literary circles also frown upon interrupting the narrative for pointless asides that break the continuity of the story.

   KAUFMAN: Really? Jesus, literary circles have a pretty fucking big stick up their collective ass, don't they?

"Hi there," Melvin said.

Wanda screamed, a natural enough reaction, and squirted, an unavoidable reaction considering how worked up she'd been. She-cum splattered on Melvin's chest.

Melvin roared and lifted Wanda off the bench, depositing her ass-first on the bed of hot coals. Her screams went up an octave as she squirmed. Melvin took no pleasure from his revenge. In fact, his attention was diverted by the folder that had scattered its contents on the floor as he lifted Wanda up.

He released Wanda, who tumbled off the coalbed and lay whimpering on the floor, and knelt to examine the photos. It was a phantasmagoria of grisly mutilations. Elderly people, kids, animals, pregnant women, people from every walk of life splayed out beneath the wheels of a variety of cars. And in a few of them, posing next to the pools of blood and crippled limbs, were a few other faces Melvin recognized. Slug. Bozo. And Julie.

Melvin focused on the picture of Julie, pointing at the outline of a hard-on in the slacks of an overweight businessman whose legs were pinned beneath an SUV. The weight in his chest was doubled. She was here. Somewhere in the building.

Melvin stood and tossed a towel to Wanda, still cowering nude in the corner of the sauna. "Put something on," he advised, "and hang tight. I'll be right back."

He stepped out of the sauna, slammed the door, and wedged his mop in the latch, locking Wanda in. Melvin headed off in search of Julie as Wanda hammered her fists futilely against the door.

Julie stood in front of her locker, methodically applying a combination of creams, powders, antiperspirants, and perfumes chosen for their ability to make the maximum olfactory impact upon entering a room. It had been said that Julie smelled like a French whorehouse. Not to her face, of course, but even if it had, she undoubtedly would have taken it as a compliment. At least she didn't smell like an East Jersey whorehouse.

She wasn't sure what she was going to do after she left the health club. Bozo was almost certainly still out there trying to find that whatever-it-was. Stupid asshole. So the chief of police made a couple of wild threats. So fucking what? Obviously Plotnick was the one in trouble here. If he didn't find this so-called monster, he'd probably be out of a job. And if he was out of a job, how was he going to follow through on those threats? Bozo just didn't think these things out. But he was good behind the wheel. And a good lay. Well . . . he was an okay lay. All right, he was a pretty shit-poor lay unless he had a stick of butter and a flagpole stuck up his bung. But he was good behind the wheel, and that was really all Julie cared about.

Maybe she should try to track Bozo down and explain how things were to him. Somebody had to. Otherwise he'd spend the rest of his life trying to track down Sasquatch or whatever this monster thing was. Poor idiot bastard. He wasn't going to find any monster. The thing didn't even exist. She was sure of that.

Julie closed her locker, revealing Melvin, who was leaning against the wall, watching her. Melvin waved his fingers at her.

"Hello, Julie."

Amazingly enough, Julie did not scream. She didn't have a chance. Even as she was trying to figure out an appropriate response, an attractive brunette walked in, fresh from the showers, wrapping herself in a towel. She saw Melvin and froze in her tracks.

Melvin noticed her standing there. "Hey! You're Marisa Tomei!"

Marisa was used to being recognized in unusual places but not by unusual creatures. She shrieked, turned on her heels, and ran as fast as she could.[3]

This was all the opportunity Julie needed. She followed Marisa Tomei's lead and started running. Melvin realized he'd made an error in judgment. Until now, everyone he had revealed himself to had stood their ground and wanted to fight. It hadn't occurred to him that

---

3. Marisa Tomei ran straight out of Tromaville, in fact, and back to a very nice career collecting Academy Awards from drunk cowboys.

someone might just choose to run away. That certainly wasn't how it worked in any of the comics he'd read. It was a good thing he knew the health club so well. She could run, but there was no place she could hide. Particularly with all that stinkum she wore.

Hiding, however, was not what Julie had in mind. Julie had never run and hid from anything in her life, and she wasn't about to start now. But she was smart enough to realize that in a fair fight, she'd never lay a hand on that thing. Fortunately, she'd never participated in a fair fight before.

Julie ran out of the locker room and found her way to the free weight room. She grabbed a ten-pounder and crouched down out of sight. She did not have long to wait. Melvin burst through the door moments later. He paused and looked around, sniffing the air.

Julie stood and threw the weight. It flew clumsily through the air and hit Melvin in the groin with enough force to drive him to his knees. Julie grabbed another weight. This one was heavier, and she knew she'd have to get closer to do any damage. She stepped forward, preparing to bring the weight down on the creature's bulbous head. It was a good target, almost as good as that ridiculous tutu. . . .

A bolt of recognition hit Julie, making her hesitate just long enough for Melvin to reach out and grab her ankle. He yanked and Julie fell, smacking her head on the weight intended for Melvin. She fell into darkness . . .

. . . coming out moments later, feeling herself being carried, slung across the monster's shoulder. Her eyes opened, focused on the floor going past. Melvin and Julie arrived at their destination quickly. The creature stopped at a door, pulled a mop out of its latch, and stepped inside.

Melvin deposited Julie on an empty bench. Wanda stood nearby, unable to sit, sweating profusely, and looking decidedly less glamorous than she had before. Melvin stood back, folded his arms, and pointed at the pictures still spread out in front of them.

"Care to explain those?"

Wanda glanced nervously at her friend. Julie simply sat still, unfazed, rubbing her sore head.

"Nothing to explain," Julie said calmly. "At least not to you, Mop Boy."

Both Melvin and Wanda were taken aback. "Mop Boy?" Wanda looked carefully at Melvin. "You think that's the janitor?"

"I know it is. I recognize the outfit."

Wanda looked him up and down, then barked out a dismissive laugh. "Jesus fucking Christ! It is, isn't it. And I was almost going to let you eat my pussy."

Melvin squirmed under their laughter. "Him?" Julie chuckled. "He couldn't give good head with a feather tied to his tongue."

Julie stood and draped an arm around Wanda's shoulders. "I think we're through here. Step aside, Frankenstein."

A low rumble began in Melvin's throat as he put a hand on each of them and shoved them back down onto the bench, making Wanda squeal in pain. "Not quite. You might have noticed, I've been through some changes."

Some of the girls' cockiness began to evaporate as they stared up at Melvin's angry face. Melvin continued, "I wasn't too happy at first. But I've come to realize how important it is to let nature run its course. Not that you two would know anything about that. But I can help you get rid of all those unnatural things you've put in your bodies."

Julie and Wanda's eyes widened in fear. "You. Wouldn't. Dare." Julie looked him right in the upper eye, sure that she'd intimidate the old Melvin with her glacial stare.

Melvin stared her back, gathering her hair into his massive fingers. "Julie," he rumbled, "this isn't your natural hair color. Is it?"

With a single pull, Melvin ripped Julie's hair out by the roots. Julie's scream was ear-piercing and made all the worse by Wanda's sympathy shriek. Julie's hands shot up to her scalp and came away bloody.

"Fuck you, you fucking freak!" Julie yelled, tears streaming down her face.

"And Wanda," Melvin said, keeping both girls trapped on the bench, "those breasts of yours. You know, if they burst, they can pose a serious health risk. See, watch."

Melvin latched on to Wanda's right teat and squeezed until everyone heard a muffled pop. Screams reverberated through the sauna. Melvin took his hand away, leaving Wanda's chest looking purplish and deflated on one side.

"You gonna tell me what I want to know, Julie?" Melvin inquired.

Julie took her hands away from her bloodied scalp and covered her chest. "I'm all natural, I swear!"

"Yeah, right," Melvin sneered. "How long has this hit-and-run thing been going on?"

"Almost a year!" Julie whined. "But it wasn't our idea! It was Slug and Bozo! They came up with the game!"

"And all you two did was ride along, take pictures, and get off on it?"

Julie pointed at Wanda. "She took most of the pictures! And she totally got off on it! Sick bitch!"

"You lying cunt!"

Wanda lashed out at Julie, shattering her nose with a lucky punch. Melvin stepped back as Julie leaped for Wanda's throat. They tumbled off the bench, Julie landing on top of Wanda, choking the life out of her. Wanda's knee shot up directly into Julie's crotch. Blinded by pain, Julie fell aside. Wanda paused just a second to catch her breath, then rolled over and began a new assault.

Melvin stood by the door, shaking his head at the catfight. If everybody did this, his job would certainly be much easier. He retrieved the folder full of pictures, then poured some more water on the coals, refilling the sauna with steam before stepping back out into the hall.

He could still hear the two girls going at it as he shut the door. Melvin shoved the mop back into the latch just as Wanda's head slammed against the window. The head disappeared for a second, then was slammed against it again and again, Julie's fingers visible in her rat's nest of hair. Somehow Wanda broke free, leaving the cracked window empty save for the billowing steam and some traces of blood.

Melvin tucked the folder under his arm and walked away, leaving the health club empty and silent except for the muffled sounds of the fight behind the locked sauna door. He couldn't believe he'd ever been attracted to either of those shrieking harpies.

17.

Love Means Never Having to Say You're Surly

Ian Jakov, ace reporter, had no time to reflect in the glory of having his story printed on the front page of the *Tromaville Times*. He'd spent most of the day on the phone with scientists from various universities, attempting to formulate a theory about the monster. Who was he? What was he? Where, when, why, and how?

This was no easy task. Most of the eggheads he contacted laughed and hung up. Others didn't even laugh. The few who had been willing to discuss the possibility of a monsterfied hero in Tromaville had been . . . how to put it delicately? Crazy. Rambling on about chaos theory, butterflies, and cosmic rays.

Only one had made any sense. Dr. Flem Hocking, the wheelchair-bound genius from T.I.T. (the Tromaville Institute of Technology), was familiar with the town and the story from the paper. He theorized that the monster was a by-product of all the toxic waste in town. Not much of a stretch there. Lots of things in Tromaville were by-products of the toxic waste. But Dr. Hocking suggested that the Monster-Hero was once just a regular, good-hearted person and that exposure to the waste had mutated him into what he was today. If the subject had not been an inherently decent person, they'd have ended up with a Monster-Villain instead.

Dr. Hocking further suggested that the toxic waste most likely mutated the subject's sense of right and wrong as well. So his sense of morals and ethics, previously a purely abstract concept, had been mutated into a physical one. Dr. Hocking called these new electro-chemical morals Tromatons, because if he was wrong, he didn't want them named Hockatons. The Monster-Hero's Tromatons steered him toward finding and eradicating evil.

Yep, that was the best theory Ian could come up with. It wasn't much, and it had no real scientific basis since Dr. Hocking had never even seen the Monster-Hero. But it kind of made sense, and as long as Ian established that Dr. Hocking's field was theoretical science, he wouldn't need to clutter the follow-up piece with details such as proof and data.

Ian's editor, Paula, marched up to his desk, trailing cigarette smoke behind her. "Jakov!" she yelled. She often yelled. "How's that follow-up coming?"

"Almost there. Just putting the finishing touches on it."

"Well, make it shine. We actually sold papers today with this story. The TV stations are spinning the Taco Shack massacre so that your monster looks like the real menace."

"What? That's the exact opposite of what every witness there told me."

"So you might have a real story on your hands. Bully for you. Just make it snappy. Oh, and that whole 'Monster-Hero' name? Sucks shit. Change it."

"To what?"

"I don't care! You want him to be a hero? Name him something heroic! Like 'Mop Man' or 'the Meltdown' or 'Supermuck.' "

Ian flipped through his notes from the Hocking interview. "How about the 'Toxic Avenger'?"

Paula thought it over, rolling it around on her tongue. "Pretty bad, but it's slightly better than the 'Monster-Hero.' Keep working on it."

Ian turned back to his computer and set to work deleting every instance of the phrase "Monster-Hero." Too bad. He'd kind of liked that one.

Ian wasn't the only person in Tromaville with theories about the artist formerly known as the Monster-Hero. Plotnick had his own ideas, and they were somewhat more down to earth. He couldn't shake the notion that the thing with the mops was somehow connected to that dorky janitor who'd been dipped in shit. Unfortunately, he had just one lead on the nerd. And while he didn't want to play that card, he was afraid his options were running out.

Plotnick stepped up to the front door in his finest dress uniform. He gave himself a breath test in his cupped palm, shined his shoes on the back of his pants, steeled his nerves, and rang the bell.

A solid minute went by, giving Plotnick ample opportunity to turn tail and run. Maybe she wasn't home. Maybe she wasn't accepting visitors. Maybe . . .

The door swung open. Mrs. Ferd stood behind the screen door, giving Plotnick her most suspicious fish-eye.

"You again?"

Plotnick smiled and revealed his secret weapon, a bouquet of roses that cost the Tromaville P.D. $4.99 at the Piggly Wiggly. "Mrs. Ferd!" he beamed. "Good evening."

"Yeah, save the sales pitch. What are you after?"

"Nothing! I just felt someone should check in on you. With your son missing, no one to look after you . . . I was concerned."

Mrs. Ferd squinted at the flowers. "What are you doing with those?"

"They're for you."

"Don't you bring those in this house. I'm allergic."

"Oh," Plotnick said, tossing the roses to the ground and brushing his hands on his jacket. "I apologize. I had no idea."

"Uh-huh. Well, you may as well come in as not."

Mrs. Ferd disappeared back into the house, leaving the door open. Plotnick wagered this was as close to an invitation as he was going to get and followed her in.

"So," he ventured as he stepped into the living room. "Have you heard from little Melvin since I saw you last?"

Mrs. Ferd refilled her tumbler with apple Schnapps and gazed at a picture of her son. "No. He's probably scared to come home."

"Why do you say that?"

"He should be! After the mess he left that bathroom in? And don't think I won't remember to paddle him for it the next time I see him."

"Right. Of course."

"Children need to be raised with a firm hand, no matter how big they get."

"I completely agree. So nothing? No phone calls or letters?"

"Well"—Mrs. Ferd sipped her drink—"there was one caller. Left a message on the machine. He said it was Melvin but it wasn't. Didn't sound anything like him. Probably some brat kid who found out Melvin was missing and was trying to play a prank on a poor old lady."

"Probably. If you still had the message, I could try to identify the culprit. If you want to press charges, that is."

Mrs. Ferd looked warily at Plotnick. "As a matter of fact, I did save it. Don't know why. I guess . . . well, it was a nice message, even if it wasn't Melvin."

Plotnick tried to contain his excitement. "May I hear it?"

Mrs. Ferd sized him up, then nodded. "The answer phone is in the bedroom. This way."

Plotnick followed her into her dimly lit, perfectly kept room. He leaned against the dresser as she sat down on the bed and pressed "Play" on the twenty-year-old machine resting on her bedside table.

The tape rewound and hissed to life. "Mom," a deep, authoritative voice came from the tinny speaker, "it's Melvin. I'm fine. Everything's okay. I . . . I met a girl. Her name's Sarah. You'd like her. Oh, and I've got a new job. I guess you're not home. I'll explain everything later. I know this doesn't sound like me but it is. I'm sorry about the mess in the bathroom. I . . . uh-oh. Gotta go. 'Bye."

BEEP!

Plotnick chewed his lip in thought. "And that wasn't Melvin's voice?"

"Ha! Are you kidding? My Melvin's voice is this high, mewling thing. That man sounds like that cable news guy."

"How do you figure he knew about the bathroom?"

"I don't know. That's why I kept it, I suppose. Even though it's probably all bullshit. I can tell you right now my Melvin has not met a girl. And even if he did, he knows I probably wouldn't like her."

"Mmm. Well, thank you for playing the message for me, Mrs. Ferd."

Plotnick began to go back out into the living room, but before he took two steps, Mrs. Ferd said, "Where do you think you're going?"

"I . . . well, I thought—"

"Chief Plotnick, I wasn't born yesterday, you know."

"Yes, I'm well aware of that."

"You come by with roses, pretend to be interested in the message on my answer phone? Which just happens to be in my bedroom? I know how the game is played."

Mrs. Ferd grinned and with frighteningly practiced hands, dropped her housedress to the ground. Plotnick repressed a shudder as he studied her naked body, ninety-two pounds of wrinkled flesh and bone.

"Well? Aren't you going to arrest me, Officer?"

"Mrs. Ferd, you're trying to seduce me, aren't you?"

Mrs. Ferd lay spread-eagled on the bed and pointed to her withered clam. "Bring it on over, Chiefy."

Plotnick marched forward without enthusiasm, hoping he wouldn't find dust and cobwebs down there. Well, he thought as he unbuttoned his pants, in for a penny, in for a pound.

Melvin knew what it was like to be nervous. Most of his preaccident life had been spent in a state of perpetual anxiety. But as he stood staring at Sarah's back door,[1] fidgeting with the daisies he'd picked for her, he entered a new realm of jangled nerves. His heart raced. His palms were slick with sweat. He was fairly certain that if he attempted to speak, his tongue would leap backward down his throat in panic.

Melvin took a deep breath. Come on, he thought. You saved this woman from a trio of gun-toting lunatics without breaking a sweat. You can knock on her door and enjoy dinner with her. Can't you?

Probably not. She's probably forgotten all about their date anyway. She's probably not even home. Girl like this probably has all sorts of guys chasing after her all the time, guys with hair and smooth skin and two equidistant eyes. So that's that. I'll knock, she won't answer, I'll go back to the dump, polish my big, hairy mop, and go to sleep. End of story.

Melvin stepped up, rapped lightly on the door, and started to back away. Seconds after his barely audible knock, the door opened. Sarah stood framed in the doorway, backlit by the glow from the kitchen, wearing a simple but beautiful floral dress.

"Melvin? Is that you?"

Just as he'd feared, he couldn't make his voice work for a moment. He could only stare, wondering if he hadn't died in the accident and this was his form of heaven. Melvin cleared his throat and forced out a yes.

"Well, come in. Dinner's almost already."

---

1. That would be the back door to her house, of course. Melvin won't feel comfortable enough to stare at her actual rear entry for another couple of chapters.

Melvin ducked his head and squeezed his shoulders through the too-small door into the kitchen. The table had been set for two. Everything was perfect, except that Sarah had put two breadsticks in the candleholders on the table. Their blackened tips suggested that she'd also tried to light them. Melvin looked around for the bread basket that undoubtedly held the candles and hoped he could make the switch before dinner.

"I brought you some flowers," Melvin said, offering the daisies to Sarah.

"That's so sweet. Thank you." She reached out for them and, after a couple of exploratory grabs, found them. "They smell beautiful."

"Would you like me to put them in some water for you?"

"No, I can manage."

Manage she did. She reached into the cupboard for a vase, found something that was its approximate size and shape (not a vase, however, but a tube of Pringles), filled it with water (dousing the remaining BBQ crisps), and gently placed the flowers in their new home.

"There," she said, placing the soggy chip-vase on the table. "I hope you like steak. As big as you are, I just assumed you weren't a vegetarian."

"No. I mean, yes. I do like steak. No, I'm not a vegetarian."

The microwave dinged. "That'll be the bread," Sarah informed him, reaching into the oven and removing a straw basket covered with a towel. "Careful. It's hot."

Melvin peered inside and saw a puddle of melted red wax. He folded the towel over it and plucked the bread out of the candlesticks, plopping them into the basket.

Sarah took Melvin's plate over to the stove and loaded it up with food, furrowing her brow at the smell. "Well," she said, bringing Melvin his plate, "this should be steak and twice-baked potatoes. But it smells a little . . . off."

Melvin looked down at the offered plate. There was a steak, all right, but it appeared to have been seasoned with drain cleaner. And instead of twice-baked potatoes, Sarah had whipped up some twice-baked apples. Which might have made a nice dessert if it hadn't been for the copious amounts of bacon, cheese, and sour cream Sarah had slathered atop them.

"I'm sorry," she said, wiping her hands on the tablecloth. "I don't cook much. I usually eat out since . . . well, since the—"

"Sure, I understand. It's okay. I'm not really hungry anyway," he lied, eyeing the steak and wondering how much drain cleaner his mutated digestive system could handle.

"To tell you the truth, I'm a little nervous," Sarah smiled shyly. "Okay, a lot nervous. I haven't seen anybody since the accident. I mean, obviously I haven't seen anybody. I mean—"

"You mean you haven't dated anyone?"

"Right. And you seem really nice and . . . well, you saved my life. But still, I don't even know you. And after what you did to those guys at the restaurant . . . not that they didn't deserve it . . . whatever you did do to them. You see? I don't even know exactly what you did to those guys! I feel like I ought to be scared to death of you."

Melvin nodded and absent-mindedly took a bite of twice-baked apple. Not bad, actually. "But you're not. Are you?"

Sarah hesitated just a moment before she smiled. "No. I'm not."

Melvin walked up to her and gently took her hands in his. He knelt down, then slowly, nervously, brought her hands to his face.

Sarah explored the contours of Melvin's lumpy face with her fingers. He winced as she accidentally poked his melted eye. "I'm sorry!" she exclaimed, but kept her hands on him.

"Not your fault," Melvin said, blinking his eye. "I should have warned you about that. So . . . not exactly the man of your dreams, am I?"

"Does it hurt?"

"Not anymore."

"Good. It feels like you've been hurt enough in your life."

Sarah leaned forward and gently kissed Melvin's misshapen lips. Melvin, needless to say, felt bursts of excitement coursing through his every fiber at his first real kiss. As for Sarah, it was a kiss like none other. Her heart soared and her stomach leaped as she threw her arms around Melvin's muscular torso and kissed him deeply, passionately. Maybe it was love. Maybe it was just the trace amounts of radiation she was absorbing.

That night, Melvin told Sarah everything. He told her about his thankless job at the health club, his life with his mother, the prank that had been played on him and its aftereffects. He told her how he now seemed able to sense trouble and felt compelled to help. He explained his plan to clean up Tromaville. Sarah took it all in without interruption or judgment.

Melvin also broke three chairs that night, since Sarah's furniture hadn't been constructed with a seven-foot-tall mutation in mind. So the next day, Melvin offered to bring Sarah to his place.

Melvin swung open the door to the shack and led Sarah inside. Sarah stood for a moment and declared, "Needs a woman's touch."

Melvin was a little stung that the shack he'd worked so hard on didn't even pass muster with a blind person but knew better than to argue. So as she set to work, Melvin traipsed into town for some food and other supplies.

He returned a little over an hour later and was surprised and a bit annoyed to discover that Sarah had actually made the place look better. She'd moved the furniture around. The layout of the shack now made more sense instead of just looking like a bunch of discarded crap that had been dragged inside (which, of course, it was). She'd even brought in some wildflowers, although Melvin didn't even want to think about where she'd found them. The shack had more light, it was airier, and it smelled better.

Sarah looked up from the window treatment she was working on. "What do you think?"

"I'm impressed," Melvin said honestly. "This place looks great. How'd you manage to do all this yourself?"

Sarah just smiled. "I have my ways. Did you bring food? I'm starving."

Melvin handed her a sandwich. The kid Bobby from the Taco Shack had seen Melvin in town and provided him with plenty of food as thanks for saving his life. As Sarah dug in, Melvin unfolded the newspaper he'd dug out of the trash on the way back.

"Sarah," he said, examining the front page, "listen to this. It's a story on the front page of the *Tromaville Times*. I think it's about me."

" 'Who is the Toxic Avenger?' " he read.

" 'Tromaville Police remain baffled as to the identity of the mysterious monster-hero who ended a dramatic hostage situation at the Taco Shack on Wednesday. But local scientist Dr. Flem Hocking has watched the developments unfold with keen interest. In an exclusive interview, Dr. Hocking shared his insights with this reporter.' "

Melvin read the entire article aloud to Sarah (skipping over the bit about the two bodies found locked in a sauna at the Tromaville Health Club, their fingers entangled around each other's throat). When he finished, he folded the paper and smiled at his new girlfriend.

"Sounds like I've got a name now."

"The Toxic Avenger," Sarah repeated. "I like it. I guess you're a real hero now, Toxie."

18.

Bring on the Bad Guys

June sucked.

This thought was foremost in Mayor Belgoody's mind. And not June Sakamoto, the comely masseuse who was hard at work on Peter's oil-slicked, lard-protected shoulders at the moment. Unfortunately, June wouldn't even finish him off by hand, much less suck. No, it was the month of June that plagued Belgoody. That June sucked thirty-one flavors of hot 'n' spicy shit. Thank fucking Buddha it was over.

Peter reached over and helped himself to another section of six-foot party sandwich. Yes, sir, there was nothing like a grinder and a massage to help ease your troubles. He took a deep drag off his cigar, exhaling a noxious cloud of tobacco, pickles, and mustard.

June, long practiced in the art of massaging Belgoody's problems away, saw the smoke rising and held her breath for ninety seconds. She'd learned the trick the hard way. The first time she'd worked for Belgoody, she hadn't been prepared for the variety of odors his body excreted and almost ended up choking to death on her own vomit. She wouldn't even have come back if she had any other choice. But the money was very, very good. And after just a few weeks of deep-sea diving training, she was ready to assume her duties as Belgoody's regular masseuse.

The intercom on Peter's desk buzzed to life. "Mayor Belgoody, Chief Plotnick is here to see you."

An annoyed sigh pooted out between Peter's pursed lips. He found his reaching stick on the ground beneath him, thrust it in the general direction of his desk (June narrowly avoided having one of her lovely brown eyes gouged out with it), and jabbed it at the talk button on the intercom. "Send him in!"

Plotnick strode into the office, saw the beached sea creature lying spread out and greased up on the table in front of him, and failed to suppress a shudder. Plotnick despised Belgoody's massage meetings. Recovering from his initial revulsion, Plotnick put on his game face and beamed out a hearty greeting.

"Mr. Mayor. Happy Fourth of July."

"Fuck you and fuck your happy fucking Fourth. What in the name of Mary's drippy cunt is going on out there?"

"Sir?"

"Shut up! Have you seen today's paper?"

Belgoody smacked his reaching stick down on a newspaper sitting atop his desk.

Plotnick glanced over at it, taking care to stay just out of jabbing range of the stick.

The banner headline read simply, "Happy Independence Day." The front page was covered with innocuous puff pieces about picnic areas, ambrosia salad recipes, and fireworks displays.

"You see that?" Belgoody demanded.

Plotnick knew that if he said no, Belgoody might get so pissed off that he actually stood up. Plotnick didn't want to see that, so he simply made a noncommittal grunt.

Belgoody didn't know how to interpret that. He simply went on as if Plotnick had agreed with him. "That, asshole, is the newspaper of a happy, normal little town. No stories about crime or corruption or pollution or any of that shit. Just happy, normal people living their lives and celebrating the fact that they were lucky enough to be born in a country where they don't have to pick flies off their babies' eyeballs."

Plotnick nodded, not entirely sure where this was headed but fairly certain it was not a destination he wanted to visit.

Belgoody pressed on. "The problem with that, major asshole, is that Tromaville is not a happy, normal little town. Or at least, it's not supposed to be. It's supposed to be a place where the wants of the few . . . or the one"—he pointed at himself to make sure that the point got delivered—"outweigh the needs of the many. It's supposed to be a place where nothing happens unless it's controlled by the handful of people in positions of power. It is not supposed to be a place with a loose-cannon superfreak running around. It is not supposed to be a place where the chief of fucking police can't track down, capture, and/or kill one lousy fucking monster. It is NOT, you major bloody pus-dripping asshole, supposed to be a place where the people feel safe enough at night to leave their homes and go out for a FUCKING FIREWORKS DISPLAY!"

With that, Plotnick's worst fears came to life. Belgoody had worked himself up into such a frenzy that he managed to get off the massage table and stood there, naked, wet, and greasy, jabbing his reaching stick into Plotnick's chest.

"Do you have any idea how much a fucking fireworks display is going to cost?" Belgoody covered his shame with a massive sheet.

Plotnick did not know exactly how much it would cost but had to agree that Belgoody had a point. The Tromaville Chamber of Commerce advertised a Fourth of July fireworks show every year, but until now it had been an empty promise. The best view of the show would have been from a city park overrun with junkies, hookers, trannies, and

rats the size of pintos (the horse, not the car). Everyone knew that
nobody would show up for such a display. So every year, the cops just
gathered down in the general vicinity of where the fireworks were supposed to happen and fired their guns into the air for fifteen minutes or
so. Tromavillians pretended they were listening to fireworks, and everybody was happy. But this year, thanks to this so-called Toxic Avenger
thing, people might actually come out.

"Just look at this bullshit, Plotnick." Belgoody settled his lard into
his desk chair and pulled a manila folder full of reports out of a drawer.[1]
Plotnick recognized them at once. He'd sent the reports over himself.
They were crime figures for the month of June. If you were a law-
abiding citizen, the picture they painted was one of sunshine and rain-
bows. There was a noticeable and severe drop-off in criminal activities
right around midmonth.

"I mean for fuck's sake, man"—Belgoody shook his head sadly, as if
he were speaking to a mentally challenged intern—"with stats like this,
I almost feel safer out there myself. You wanna clue me in as to what
exactly you're doing to track down this monster-hero?"

"Actually, sir, it's the Toxic Avenger now. Nobody calls him the monster-hero anymore."

Belgoody smacked Plotnick's ear with his reaching stick. "I don't
give fuck one if he's called the Amazing Cum-Guzzler. What are you
doing to find him?"

Plotnick laid out everything he'd done so far. After Cigarface had
been so messily killed, Plotnick had had a great deal of difficulty convincing other foot soldiers to go after the creature. In fact, a lot of

---

1. As usual, Belgoody had completely forgotten about June Sakamoto the second
he stopped feeling her hands on his flesh. And so, as usual, June quietly sat down
in a chair in the corner, lit a cigarette, and listened to everything that was said.
Unbeknownst to anyone, June Sakamoto was the most powerful person in Tromaville. She was privy to all of Belgoody's secrets and was smart enough to understand
all of them, even the ones Belgoody didn't understand himself.

former Tromaville criminals had decided to relocate to safer pastures, such as New York and Iraq. His carnal knowledge of Mrs. Ferd hadn't exactly borne fruit either. Melvin hadn't come anywhere near his old house. He had managed to convince Mrs. Ferd that the Toxic Avenger was a menace to society and that she should call Plotnick immediately if she should ever run across it. But it was beginning to look like Plotnick would actually have to marry the old crone to get her son to come out of the woodwork. And he wasn't quite ready to leap into that abyss. The one between her legs was dank and bottomless enough, thank you very much.

Then there were Bozo and Slug. That plan had backfired almost as badly as the car they were now living in. After Julie and Wanda had been found dead in the sauna, Bozo went off the deep end. He no longer gave a shit about the fact that Plotnick knew they were behind the hit-and-run game. It was an open secret at this point. As a matter of fact, hit-and-run "accidents" were the only part of the June crime report that had not been affected by the appearance of the Toxic Avenger. They'd actually gone through the roof. And there wasn't much the cops were willing to do about that, either. Since Bozo and Slug never left their car anymore, the cops couldn't get to them without running the risk of getting hit themselves.

Belgoody took all this in, chewing on his cigar and frowning until the talk turned to Bozo and Slug. Finally, a smile crawled onto Belgoody's face. "Okay, now we're getting someplace. These ass-pirates in the car . . . you know where to find them?"

"Not exactly, but they're not hard to track down."

"Find 'em. Tell 'em about the fireworks show tonight. Tell 'em that pretty much every Joe and Susie Q. Public and all their screaming brats are gonna be at the park tonight. I want those dipshits to plow right into the middle of that crowd."

"Wouldn't it be easier to just cancel the fireworks if you don't want to spend the money?"

"Fuck the fucking fireworks! The Toxic Boy Scout isn't gonna let everybody in town get smooshed by a couple of assholes in an old car. If the hit-and-run boys are there, then he'll be there. And you and every cop in town will be there waiting for him. Get it?"

"Got it."

"Good. Make it happen."

Plotnick left the office, leaving Belgoody stroking his greasy mustache. Moments like this, Peter thought about growing his facial hair out into a handlebar 'stache. Then he could really go to town, twirling it and filling his office with an evil "Mwoo-hoo-hah!"

The Adventures of The Hypnotic Dog-Rat Eye (Formerly Known as Knipples' Left Eyeball): Episode IV

Grudges aren't easy to hold on to. Now, the object of a grudge, that's another story. You can remember who it is you hate until both of you are in the ground with maggots crawling around your brains. But the grudge itself, the why part of the equation, that's a lot more elusive. In the fullness of time, most people are fucked up the ass so often and so hard that it becomes difficult to tell one ass rape from the other. And if that's how it is for people, imagine how difficult it is if you're the vengeful spirit of a disembodied eyeball that's been digested by a sewer rat that's been digested by a stray dog.

The Hypnotic Dog-Rat-Eye (or D.R.E., as it had decided to call itself) had not had an easy time of it over the past ten days or so. Dogs were not so easy to hypnotize, it turned out. D.R.E. had investigated every trash can and Dumpster in Tromaville, humped a few dozen dogs and at least one surprised cat, and licked its balls until they glistened with saliva, but none of these activities, pleasant though they had been, had brought D.R.E. any closer to his dream of revenge.

Only once had D.R.E. caught sight of the creature that had started him down this path. D.R.E. was asleep in an alley (he found he needed a lot more sleep now that he was a dog) and woke up to see the creature itself, towering overhead, stuffing a would-be rapist's head up his own ass. The vision awakened the spirit of vengeance lying dormant within The Hypnotic D.R.E.

The dog snarled and came racing up to the creature, barking loudly. The monster stopped what it was doing, glanced down, and scratched D.R.E. behind the ear. The indignity! D.R.E. barked louder and sank his jaws into the creature's ankle.

The monster looked down, startled. It rapped D.R.E. gently on the snout and shook its deformed head. "Bad dog," it rumbled. "Stop that. Go on home now."

The creature had finished its work and stomped off down the street. D.R.E. chased after for a few blocks, barking loudly, but it had no effect on the creature. Finally, The Hypnotic D.R.E. was unable to keep its host focused on the target. The dog part of D.R.E.'s brain caught the scent of a pizzeria. The Hypnotic D.R.E. put up a mighty struggle, but to no avail. The dog regained control of its will and took D.R.E. away from the creature, heading toward the intoxicating aroma of sauce and cheese.

Since it had lost that battle, D.R.E. had fallen into a deep depression. It was too small in this form to pose any threat to the creature. And the dog didn't have enough reasoning power to help D.R.E. stay on the monster's trail. As long as it was in this host, D.R.E. was doomed to be forever one step behind the creature. He could only hope to stumble across the thing and, if he did, hope that he could keep the dog focused long enough to leap at the monster's throat.

As D.R.E. was adding up the sorry register of his life and trying to figure out how to get a new host, the problem was suddenly taken out of his paws. It was late at night, and as D.R.E. crossed the street, a mint green sedan emerged out of nowhere and crushed D.R.E. beneath its speeding tires. The car didn't even slow down, and as it sped off into the night, D.R.E. could have sworn he heard a voice say, "Dogs are fifteen points, dude. Mark it!"

D.R.E.'s twisted canine host lay dying in the gutter. As the dog's life ebbed out, the power of The Hypnotic Dog-Rat-Eye returned. Now it has the strength to control the host! Unfortunately, the host was about two minutes away from finding out if all dogs really did go to heaven. D.R.E. needed a new host. But how?

Truly, Dame Fortuna smiled upon The Hypnotic Dog-Rat-Eye, for out of a nearby alley stumbled the drunkest and filthiest of all of Tromaville's drunk and filthy homeless. D.R.E. felt the man's presence and smiled inwardly (which was, let's face it, the only way he could smile). This was the host he needed. It had everything. Size, mobility, opposable thumbs, reasoning, and almost no free will.

The drunk kneeled in the gutter next to D.R.E. and stroked its fur. "Poor little fella," he slurred. "Kinda bastard'd fuckin' run over a li'l doggy, anyway?"

Indeed, my inebriated friend, D.R.E. thought as it concentrated all its hypnotic ability on the drunk, *wouldn't you like to help this poor little doggy in this, his ultimate hour of need? That's it, good sir. Help the doggy.*

The drunk cradled D.R.E.'s head in his lap and gently but forcefully snapped his neck. "There ya go, buddy," he said. "No more sufferin' for you."

The drunk hefted the dog over his shoulder and carted it back to his campsite down by the abandoned railroad tracks. With a grim determination, he started a fire and set to work cleaning the dog's body. "Waste not, want not," he muttered.

Later, as the drunk feasted on greasy hunks of dog flesh, The Hypnotic Dog-Rat-Eye rejoiced. It had been ridiculously simple to bend this man to his will. Surely this time, vengeance would belong to . . . The Hypnotic Bum-Dog-Rat-Eye!!!

19.

Gore on the Fourth of July

Plotnick stood on the edge of the park, watching the waves of people arriving. Families, friends, happy smiling fuckers toting picnic baskets, blankets, and lawn chairs. Where the fuck where these assholes coming from, anyway? Plotnick had lived in Tromaville his entire life and had never seen most of these shitheads before. He was finally beginning to appreciate what a good job they'd done keeping people scared all these years.

As he'd suspected, Bozo and Slug had been stupid easy to track down. They were living in that crappy green Pontiac all the time now, and as much as they might have wished it could be otherwise, it was physically impossible to keep the car moving twenty-four hours a day. Both the car and the guys themselves ran out of gas sooner or later. He'd found them in the first place he looked. Just above the nuclear plant, it was a scenic overlook that had been used as a make-out spot by teenagers for generations. Plotnick wisely decided not to point out the homoerotic implications of their chosen hideout.

The boys were fast asleep when Plotnick rapped on the rolled-up

window. Bozo, who was passed out in the front seat, tried to start the
car immediately, but once he saw that Plotnick had his gun aimed right
between his eyes, he thought better of it. "I just wanna talk," Plotnick
assured him.

Bozo rolled the window down, and that was almost enough to over-
power the cop right there. These guys really had been living out of their
car. The funk that wafted out of that window was worse than anything
Plotnick had whiffed in Belgoody's office. Plotnick staggered back a
step but, to his credit, kept the gun pointed at Bozo.

"The fuck do you want, pig?" Bozo demanded, making no move to
get out of the car. The shock of fresh air coming into the backseat reviv-
ified Slug as well, and he was now wiping the cobwebs (literally) away
from his eyes and trying to figure out what the hell was going on.

"You kinda fucked me on our deal, Bozo," Plotnick said.

"Yeah, well," Bozo shrugged. "Once your whole life goes to shit, it's
kinda hard to give a fuck about shit like that, know whut I'm sayin'?"

"News flash for you. Your whole life was shit way before your
slutbag girlfriends tore each other apart."

Slug looked like he wanted to say something, but the click of the
hammer of Plotnick's gun being eased back shut him up.

"Anyway, I've got a new deal for you shitheels. And all you have to
do is exactly what you've been doing."

Bozo's eyes narrowed at him. "And if we don't? What are you gonna
do, toss us in jail?"

"No, I'll just shoot both your sorry asses right here and now."

Slug leaned forward to confer with Bozo. "Shit, Bozo, that don't
sound too bad. Nobody dies from getting shot in the ass."

"Shut the fuck up, Slug." Bozo pressed his palm against Slug's face
and shoved him back in his seat. He studied Plotnick carefully before
saying, "So what exactly did you have in mind?"

And that was that, really. Once the plan was explained to them . . .
several times . . . both Bozo and Slug seemed genuinely eager to

participate. Plotnick told them they didn't even have to stop the car. Just start mowing citizens down, and once the Toxic Avenger showed up, Plotnick and the boys would move in on him. After that, Bozo and Slug could drive off and nobody was going to pursue them.

But for now, all Plotnick could do was wait and watch the future subjects of tomorrow's memorial service arrive. It was a good plan, Plotnick thought. He was so happy with it, he'd almost entirely convinced himself it had been his idea in the first place.

Bozo and Slug parked their car about a mile away from the park. They ate cheeseburgers and washed them down with warm beer and cheap whiskey mixed with watery cola. Thanks to Tromaville's lax attitude toward liquor laws, the town was still home to one of the few remaining drive-thru liquor stores in the country.

Since they'd been living out of their car, things had gone from bad to worse. Slug would still get out once in a while to stretch his legs and take a shit, but Bozo hadn't left the front seat for days. His legs were beginning to atrophy in strange and fantastic ways, since the only muscles he used down there were in his feet.

Slug didn't have enough imagination to know what would happen after tonight's adventure, but Bozo knew the score. No matter how things went, this was their final hurrah in Tromaville. If everything went down according to Plotnick's plan, they'd hit the road and never come back. If Slug had a problem with that, he was more than welcome to get out of the car. Especially if they happened to be tooling down the interstate at ninety miles per hour at the time.

But Bozo didn't really think Plotnick's plan could be followed to the letter. Moreover, he wasn't sure he wanted it to be. Assuming the mop boy came out to put the brakes on their slaughter, Bozo didn't think it was going to be all that easy for the cops to grab him. And that was fine by him. Bozo had scores to settle with this walking sludge pile.

Yes, sir, no matter how things played out, this was shaping up to be one memorable evening. Not only were they going to get a bead on the freak that killed Wanda and Julie, they also had carte blanche to smack down as many lame-os as they could squish beneath their chassis. The whole thing made Bozo feel stiff and powerful. As he sipped his beer, he furiously rubbed at his erection through his jeans.

Slug noticed this, shrugged, and kept on eating his fries. As far as he was concerned, as long as Bozo was taking care of himself, he wouldn't have to worry about waking up to the now-familiar sight of Bozo fucking a hole in the upholstery tonight.

Plotnick glanced at his watch: 7:30 P.M. So far everything was looking good. They had a huge crowd milling about aimlessly, buying cotton candy and Sno-Kones, and clustering together in a huge, empty field. If worse came to worst and Bozo decided that this whole setup was a trap for him instead of the Toxic Whatsit, Plotnick figured he could go get his own car and take out a few of these sorry fuckers his own self.

Part of him assumed he'd have to do just that. At first glance it was a fine plan. But the very second you began to examine the details, it started to fall apart. First off, he was depending on two psychotic drunks who'd already burned him once. Then he was assuming that their reign of terror would be stopped by a superhuman creature he'd never actually seen for himself. And nobody knew how to find the creature and tell him he might want to drop by the park around dusk to do some crime-fighting. It was just taken as a given that he'd be there. These superfreaks always seemed to show up on cue in the funny papers. Maybe he should have put together some sort of tox signal to shine on the clouds and summon him.

Well, it was too late to worry about the little picayune details of the plan. The crowd had gathered. The sun was setting. The cops were carefully stationed around the park to swarm on top of Toxic Man the second he showed up. And unless Plotnick missed his guess, he thought he could hear a loud, angry motor getting closer.

Melvin had been hoping for a quiet evening at home with Sarah. He'd been awfully busy recently, cleaning up Tromaville and keeping the streets safe and all. He was pleased that he really seemed to be making a difference. Thugs were leaving town right and left, while the people he was trying to help no longer freaked out at the mere sight of him. He had that reporter fellow to thank for that, he suspected. The stories in the *Tromaville Times* were overwhelmingly pro-Toxie. As soon as he had a moment, he might have to send the guy a muffin basket.

Anyway, now that things were finally beginning to quiet down for him, Melvin thought he might put his feet up and relax. Unfortunately, Sarah had other ideas. She wanted to go down to the park to see the fireworks. Well, hear the fireworks, anyway. Melvin tried to convince her that this wasn't such a great idea. The Toxic Avenger was still something of a man of mystery in Tromaville, and Melvin didn't think he wanted to go public quite yet. It's one thing for a civilian to be grateful to see a huge mutant when it's saving their ass. It's another to share a corndog with it and see it making out with its blind girlfriend.

But Sarah had a way of helping Melvin overcome his inhibitions. She pointed out all the great press he'd been getting and was sure that everyone in town would be thrilled that the creature walked among them. It would give them a chance to thank him personally. If it weren't for Melvin's efforts, they wouldn't even be having this celebration.

This was all certainly true, but Melvin still wasn't convinced. Sarah, however, had saved her trump card for just such an occasion. She promised Melvin that once they got back, they'd make some fireworks of their own, if he knew what she was saying.

Melvin did not know what she was saying and expressed reservations about Sarah's ability to handle gunpowder.

Sarah sighed. She loved Melvin, but his naïveté could be more than a little tiresome. Spelling it out for him, she lifted her top and gave Melvin an eyeful of her creamy white breasts. "I want you to fuck me tonight, Melvin," she said, stroking his mop handle for emphasis.

Now, you might think that Melvin wouldn't need any more convincing after that. After all, we're talking about a guy who was the world's most frustrated virgin even before he had his raging libido mutated into a hard-on of superhuman size and strength. But Melvin had been burned before. Literally, the last time someone had told him they wanted to be fucked by him, he'd ended up a bigger blaze than a protesting Buddhist monk. So Melvin still had some reservations.

Toxie Needs Your Help!

If you think Melvin should respect the sanctity of sexual intercourse and wait before going to bed with Sarah, turn the book on its side!

If you think Melvin should get bizay with this beauty-full buxom blind bimbo and go to the fireworks display, continue with the book as written!

WHAT ARE YOU, GAY?! THIS ISN'T A DEMOCRACY, FUCKFACE. BESIDES WHICH, IF WE DID THINGS YOUR WAY, THEY WOULDN'T GO TO THE PARK AND THE WHOLE FUCKING STORY WOULD COME TO A SCREECHING HALT. TOXIE'S GETTING LAID TONIGHT WHETHER YOU WANT HIM TO OR NOT. ANYWAY, NOW EVERYBODY KNOWS WHAT A FUCKING PRUDE YOU ARE BECAUSE YOU'RE READING THE BOOK ALL BASS-ACKWARD.

Bozo stepped on the gas and felt the purr of the engine all the way up through his nuts. Slug rode shotgun, giggling maniacally. He didn't know much about art (or science or politics or even personal hygiene), but he knew what he liked. And this here, Slug liked. He liked it a lot.

Bozo aimed the car at the biggest target he could see, a vendor selling those shiny Mylar balloons. The vendor pissed him off for a lot of reasons. First off, those balloons were a fucking overpriced rip-off. Plus, the vendor had the misfortune of dressing in bright red pants, rainbow suspenders, and a funny hat. He was the closest thing to a clown in sight. It might not have been written up in the official rules, but as far as Bozo was concerned, hitting a clown was worth the maximum amount of points possible. Especially clowns surrounded by a bunch of kids.

Unfortunately for Bozo, he wasn't exactly sneaking up on anybody. At least three people noticed him barreling down on the poor balloon vendor. One was Plotnick, who was happy that at least one part of the plan was coming together.

Another was the balloon man himself. He had just finished apologizing to another disgruntled parent for his lack of change when he heard the car. A lot of parents were momentarily upset with the balloon man when he yelled, "HOLY FUCKING SHIT!!" Days later, as they replayed the incident in their mind's eye, they forgave his outburst. It may have been obscene, but it probably saved at least a few lives.

The third pair of eyes that saw Bozo's car belonged to Melvin Ferd. It took them longer than expected to make the trek from the dump to the park, mainly because Melvin had to stop every few minutes and adjust his tutu to accommodate his toxic hard-on. These fireworks couldn't end soon enough for his taste.

They were about a block away from the park when the car raced past them. Melvin didn't like how fast they were going and liked it even less when he recognized Slug leaning out the passenger side window.

"What was that?" Sarah asked, immediately sensing the change in Melvin's mood.

"Trouble," Melvin said. "Will you be okay here for a few minutes?"

He didn't wait for an answer. Melvin took off running after the speeding car. He was fast . . . but not fast enough. He knew he'd never make it in time to save everybody. His legs pumped harder than ever, but his mismatched eyes could only widen in horror as he saw the car leap the curb.

Families scattered every which way. Bozo gripped the steering wheel tight and wondered if he could have cum if he hadn't already spilled his seed inside his jeans. Tires rolled over tiny limbs not fast enough to clear the area.

The worst of it was bought by the balloon vendor. The car's grille shattered his knees, and a split second later, his grease-painted face splintered the glass of the windshield. The air filled with screams and shiny helium-filled balloons.

Plotnick wasn't much of an actor, so it was his good fortune that nobody was really paying attention to his attempt to act shocked at this turn of events. Everyone was far too busy screaming, crying, and howling in pain to take any notice of the cop standing on the periphery of the action, palms slapped against his cheeks and his mouth a huge "O" of feigned surprise. But before he had a chance to follow up his pose with a practiced "oh, the humanity," he noticed the huge green creature with the mop running onto the scene. And the creature's expression of fury and horror seemed all too genuine.

Plotnick hesitated for only a second before fumbling for his radio. "All units," he barked, "target is in sight! Swarm! Swarm!"

From out of nowhere, police units converged on the chaotic scene. Melvin barely noticed, so focused was he on the car now doing dough-nuts in the blood-stained grass. But before he knew what was happening, the cops had him surrounded, separating him from the target.

Inside the car, Slug looked out the back window and saw the cops surround the mop thing. "Bozo, they've got him!" he yelled, poking the back of Bozo's head. "We've gotta go!"

Things were happening fast. Too fast for the Tromaville P.D., which was used to things happening very, very slowly. They hadn't even had a chance to draw a bead on Melvin before he planted his mop in the ground and easily vaulted over the top of the police cruisers. Plotnick saw Toxie sail through the air and knew deep down that things were not going to go as planned.

Toxie landed with a tremendous slam atop Bozo's car. Slug

squeaked like a lab rat upon impact, while Bozo reacted somewhat more forcefully. He cranked the wheel hard to the left, spinning around in the emptying field. Toxie dug his fingers into the car top and hung tight.

The cops sat impotently inside their cruisers, watching the spectacle and glancing over at Plotnick for direction. They'd been told explicitly not to engage the hit-and-run driver. Their target was the monster. Now that the monster was on top of the vehicle, they didn't know what part of the order to listen to. Plotnick wasn't sure either but knew that if the creature stopped the car, he'd be an even bigger hero than he was already. Suddenly this plan didn't seem all that carefully thought out at all.

Bozo hit the gas and went bouncing up and over the sidewalk and back out onto the street. Once his tires hit asphalt, he punched it, exploding down the street and out of sight, like a Formula One racer. The cops shrugged and looked at their chief.

Plotnick's shoulders slumped as he spoke into his radio. "Help the injured," he commanded. This new jumping trick of the monster's had made things a whole lot more difficult. Who'd have thought capturing a seven-foot-tall radioactive superbeing would be so hard?

Bozo, on the other hand, was finding it equally hard to get rid of the seven-foot-tall radioactive superbeing. He was swerving all over the road at speeds approaching eighty, but still he clung to the roof. And Slug wasn't being particularly useful. He cowered in the middle of the car, narrating the action with a high-pitched "He's still there, man! He's still there! Jesus fuckin' Christ, he's still up there, Bozo!"

"SHUT! UP!" Bozo hollered. "I know he's fuckin' up there! Help me try and get him off!"

"How?!"

"I dunno, but do somethin'!"

Slug looked around frantically for something resembling a weapon. And while their time spent in the car had provided them with a huge collection of burger wrappers, drink cups full of piss, and porn newspapers smeared with shit, it hadn't done much for their arsenal.

A muscular green arm smashed through the window. Broken glass flew everywhere while the arm's fingers groped wildly for something to grab ahold of. They found Slug. Slug sissy-slapped Toxie's arm. Unsurprisingly, it had no effect. Toxie grabbed Slug tight and yanked him out through the window.

For a moment, Slug believed a man could fly. He saw the road streaking by beneath him while Toxie held him aloft. Slug craned his neck and saw Toxie lying face down on top of the car, holding him with one hand. Toxie smiled and with a nod of his head, indicated that Slug should check out something in front of them.

Slug forced his eyes forward and saw a bumper sticker on a parked SUV that read "My Child Has Perfect Attendance at Tromaville Elementary." He wondered fleetingly if things might have been different for him if only his parents had put a bumper sticker like that on their car when he was growing up. But then his head smashed into the SUV's taillight and his spine was shooting through his brain and Slug didn't wonder anything after that.

Once Slug was dead, it was as if a cloud was lifted from Bozo's mind. Bozo immediately had a new perspective on the situation. This thing on his roof wasn't going anywhere as long as Bozo kept driving. But if he stopped . . .

Bozo strapped his seat belt around him and braced himself as best he could before he slammed on the brakes with both feet. Sure enough, Toxie went flying off the roof, landing painfully on the street about thirty feet in front of the car. The stop was so sudden that Bozo hit his own head against the steering wheel, and for a moment they both sat where they were, dazed.

It was a moment too long for Bozo. He shook his head and wiped the blood from his eyes, then looked out the window to see Toxie up and marching straight toward him. Toxie did not look happy.

Bozo scrambled to shift the car into reverse. He found the gear and punched the gas. Toxie, however, had seen what he was trying to do and closed the gap between himself and the car in a heartbeat. He grabbed onto the front bumper and held tight.

The tires spun and made a horrible screeching noise on the asphalt. Foul, acrid smoke rose into the air, but the car didn't move. Bozo looked back through the windshield at Toxie. The eye that was still in its proper place was a narrow slit of determination, while the other eye was wide open.

As Bozo stared at Toxie, the supermutant released the car. It took off like a shot, careening wildly out of control. Bozo fumbled for the wheel, the brakes, anything that would help. The car smashed into a bus shelter, shattering glass and whipping Bozo around the interior of the car like a BB in an aerosol can.

Bozo coughed and peered up over the dash through the shattered windshield. Toxie dusted his hands off on his tutu, retrieved his mop from the street, and calmly walked toward the car.

Bozo shook his head in disbelief. No fucking way was that goddamn mop boy going to take him out. He'd rather be ass-raped by seventy disease-ridden spider monkeys than let that fuckin' mop boy have that satisfaction. He spat blood onto the floor, revved the engine, and drove straight at Toxie.

Toxie couldn't believe it. What kinda batteries was this guy running on, anyway? He took a deep breath and easily jumped out of the way of the oncoming car.

Bozo braked, spun around, and came back for another shot. This time Toxie was ready for him. He stepped aside and grabbed ahold of the passenger door, yanking it off as if it were held together with chewing gum and paper clips.

Bozo braked again, spun around again, and waited. He revved the engine menacingly. Toxie held his mop out like a sword and wielded the car door as a shield. *All right*, he thought. *Time to put a stop to this. For starters, this might look cool, but the door shield is totally useless.* He tossed the door aside and gritted his teeth, an ominous but excited growl escaping from his throat.

As if responding to some signal heard only by the two of them, Bozo and Toxie charged at each other.

Toxie ran straight at the speeding car. At the last moment he stuck his mop into the grille and vaulted over the hood, through the windshield, and into the car.

"GAAAAAHHH!!" Bozo cleverly screamed. "How the fuck did you do that?"

"How are you keeping this car going after all I've done to it?"

"It's a good car! Made in America, motherfucker!"

"Yeah, well, so am I. You ready to pull over and surrender?"

"I'm never giving up to you, Mop Boy!"

Toxie shook his head sadly. "Well then, I guess I'll just have to pull you over."

He reached over and ripped the steering wheel out of Bozo's hands, not to mention out of the dashboard completely.

"What the fuck?!"

"Take it easy. I'm just looking for . . . ah, there it is."

Toxie pointed out the window at a ramp curiously set up all by itself in the middle of the street.

"I knew that was around here somewhere," Toxie smiled.

Bozo watched helplessly as Toxie jammed the steering wheel back into place and pointed the car at the ramp.

"Hold on!"

Bozo and Toxie grabbed ahold of their seats as the green sedan went straight up the ramp, flipped over twice in midair, and landed with a final crash in the street.

Bozo, literally scared shitless, looked over at Toxie. Toxie was counting on his fingers.

"Get ready: one-one-thousand, two-one-thousand, three-one-thousand . . ."

BOOM!!!!!!!!

Tromaville might not get the fireworks display they expected that Fourth of July, but the fireball that went up on that deserted street was a thing of beauty. Fire and smoke billowed into the twilight. It was exactly the kind of incredible, once-in-a-lifetime explosion that you want to see over and over again in all sorts of different contexts.

Toxie sat in the heart of the fireball and looked over at Bozo. He burned well, skin flaking off in dark, pork-scented hunks. And while he felt he could sit there and watch his nemesis burn all night long (literally, since the heat and the fumes weren't bothering him at all), he had a more important engagement.

He emerged from the burning car, shaking the burning fuel off his limbs. Phew. His tutu reeked of gasoline. Looked like a shower was in order before he kept his date with Sarah. Didn't blind people have an acute sense of smell? Or was that just hearing?

20.

Everything You Always Wanted to Know about Sex with a Hideously Deformed Creature of Superhuman Size and Strength* (*but Were Afraid We'd Tell You)

A t this point in the book, one of two things would usually happen. The previous chapter concluded with Toxie going off to meet up with his lady fair to engage in some much-needed rutting. Ordinarily we would either discreetly jump ahead in the story and allow you to fill in the details with your lurid imagination. The other option would be to fill in the details for you in prose worthy of *Penthouse* Forum.

However, the Troma Team is nothing if not single-minded in our pursuit of academic excellence. Toxic sex scenes have been a staple of the Toxic Avenger series ever since we first drunkenly decided we wanted to see a monster fuck a blind girl back in the eighties. But certain questions have always nagged at us, questions we would be unable to answer within the context of a motion picture.[1]

So in the interest of putting minds to rest, we've put together a list of frequently asked questions regarding Toxie's ability to make the beast

---

1. Well, at least not a motion picture that doesn't have multiple Xs all over the poster and a crew of fluffers.

with two backs with Sarah. We trust this will be of interest to those of you who draw pornographic cartoons involving popular animated characters and superheroes.

Q: If the toxic waste deformed Melvin everywhere else, what did it do to his manhood?

A: Rest assured that the accident that caused an enormous growth spurt everywhere else did not leave his genitals untouched. When fully erect, Toxie's big, hairy mop is bigger than any you've ever seen. Even larger than the authors of this book, making it well over four inches long.

Q: Yeah, but is it all gross and pus-filled and oozing toxic goo like the rest of him?

A: No, indeed. Apart from the same slight discoloration that affects the rest of Toxie's skin, his love rocket is an ideal specimen. And the only time it oozes toxic goo is at the same moment of release that anyone's prick oozes toxic goo.

Q: What about foreplay?

A: What, you mean the excellent movie *Fore Play* directed by John G. Avildsen and starring Zero Mostel, available now on Troma DVD wherever movies are sold and at www.troma.com?

Q: No, I mean between Melvin and Sarah. Getting each other in the mood.

A: Aha. Well, this first time, it was kind of a moot point. Melvin was a virgin, and Sarah had been celibate for so long, a stiff wind could have brought her to climax. But subsequently, Toxie is a gentle and understanding lover. Those powerful hands that are capable of such violence are also capable of great tenderness.

Q: How about oral sex?

A: Yes, please!

Q: Between Melvin and Sarah, asshole.

A: Oh. Yeah, they're all over each other. Sarah's a master of the French arts. She could deep-throat a kielbasa. And little Melvin surprised himself at his instant familiarity with Sarah's velvety cooch. In that case, his mismatched eyes helped him out. One eye could see exactly what was going on down there while the other one could see how Sarah was reacting to it.

Q: What about anal?

A: Well, it would be my first time, so if you're gentle . . .

Q: Not you! Them. And I don't believe it would be your first time.

A: No, at this point, Melvin's just happy to be fucking the old-fashioned way. Maybe someday their relationship will need a little extra zing to it, but not yet.

Q: Isn't Toxie radioactive, though? Shouldn't Sarah get cancer or something after having sex with him?

A: Actually, fucking Toxie is like the greatest chemotherapy in the world. You get to have an orgasm and your hair stays in. If anything, Sarah would now be immune from all cancers.

Q: How long can Toxie last?

A: The toxic waste gave Melvin superhuman stamina as well as size and strength. So his staying power in the sack is much, much greater than that of the average man. However, this still doesn't make it any greater than that of the average woman. Sarah can easily wear him out.

Q: What happens when Toxie cums? In the movies, you show all kinds of weird shit going on.

A: Ah, yes, the toxic orgasm. What you're referring to is what we call the meltdown. Toxie shudders and green foam cascades out of his mouth. What you do is get some Bromo-Seltzer . . .

Q: I know how you do it, dickhead, I've read your first two books! What's it supposed to be?

A: Oh, uh . . . green . . . love foam . . . of some sort or another. You know. It's green 'cause it's Toxie and he's radioactive. Regular love foam, of course, is white.

Q: The fuck are you talking about? Love foam? What kind of freak are you?

A: Hey now, let's not make this about me. This is about Toxie and Sarah.

Q: How do Toxie and Sarah prevent unwanted pregnancies?

A: With tremendous difficulty. Toxie's spunk is extremely powerful and just shoots through most over-the-counter condoms. If he pulls out, he has to be extremely careful to aim it away from the face; otherwise it could cause some serious damage. Birth control pills are effective, but Sarah has to take double the usual amount.

Q: Have you been touching yourself through this whole chapter?

A: Absolutely not! I've been touching myself through this entire book.

21.

The Little Old Lady from Passett Cleaners

Frank Passett had been Tromaville's premier dry cleaner for more than twenty years. His convenient location, reasonable prices, and outstanding service made him the cleaner of choice for both the rich and powerful and the poor and lowly. Frank considered himself to be something of a father confessor. It was his job to absolve Tromaville of their filthy stains. Frank had seen it all. Blood, cum, grass, puke, wine, you name it. If it stained fabric, Frank could wash it away. After twenty years, Frank could tell you some stories.

None of them, however, were stories that would be of any interest to anybody except another dry cleaner. Still, Frank was a nice enough guy and didn't deserve to have his shop turned into a crime scene. Yet that's exactly what happened on the fifth of July.

Louise Carmichael stepped up to the counter with a bag of laundry as big as she was. This was not as impressive as it sounds. Most things were as big as or bigger than Louise. Topping out at three feet, Louise appeared to be either six or sixty-six, depending on how far away she was when you first saw her. She'd been Frank's customer for as long as he'd been in business, so he knew that she was closer to sixty-six and possibly much older than that.

Frank saw the laundry bag below him, reached over the counter, and relieved Louise of her burden. "Morning, Mrs. Carmichael."

"Good morning, Frank."

"Have a good Fourth?"

"Oh, fine, fine. Shame about what happened down at the park, though."

"Yeah, that was a real tragedy, all right."

"I don't know that I'd go quite that far."

"No?"

"As far as I know, there were a lot of young people hurt, but the only one to die was that awful balloon clown."

"No, it just came over the radio. A couple of kids who were in critical condition just died this morning."

Louise Carmichael tsk-tsked the news. "Oh, that is too bad. But I did hate that balloon clown."

"We all did, Mrs. C. We all did. How're the girls?"

Louise rolled her eyes. "A handful and a half! You know that age."

"Teenagers," Frank chuckled pointlessly, having almost completely exhausted his repertoire of small talk. "Just dropping off today or picking up?"

"Do I have something to pick up?"

"I think so."

"Oh, fiddle-faddle. I'm afraid I don't have the ticket. I swear I'd forget my head sometimes . . ."

"Not a problem. Let me just have a little look-see around back."

"Frank Passett, you're a dear."

Frank smiled, hefted the laundry bag over his shoulder, and disappeared into the back. Louise sat in the little waiting area, found a new issue of *Plumpers* she hadn't seen before, and began to leaf through the pages.

She'd barely had a chance to see if she recognized this month's Big Butt Mama when a metal trash can came hurtling through the picture window.

Louise screamed and looked up to see the infamous Toxic Avenger she'd read so much about stepping through the shattered windowpane. The creature looked around and shouted, "How come you got no pictures of bruthas on the wall?"

Louise made herself even smaller than she was, hoping the monster wouldn't notice her there. But the thing looked directly at her, pointed its mop at her face, and growled, "You."

Louise Carmichael wasn't a spry woman by any stretch of the imagination, but it's amazing what a threatening mutant in your face can do for your physical abilities. She disappeared beneath the coffee table and skittered back behind the counter, out of the creature's grasp.

She buried herself among some low-hanging clothes, pulling the plastic around her and praying that the thing couldn't see her. She could see his huge feet tramping past, pulling clothes off the rack. The creature jabbed its mop into the lower spaces, narrowly missing Louise at one point. She held her breath and waited for the thing to go by.

Then the rack began to move. Louise felt hooks dig into her shoulders as she was lifted up and away, off the floor, and on a circuitous route through the shop. A squeal of surprise escaped her lips. From her new vantage point, she could see the Avenger, standing by the controls of the movable rack and looking directly at her.

Louise cruised the shop, struggling to free herself at first but then realizing she'd suffer a painful fall if she got loose at this point. She looked around and called out for that useless Frank Passett, but he was nowhere to be found. The back door stood wide open. She assumed that Passett must have bolted the second he heard the window break. What a hero. She could only hope he'd run for help and not just home to Mommy.

Now the conveyor belt was carrying her back toward the front of the shop. She tried wiggling free of the hooks, but she was held fast. And there was the creature, waiting for her. Louise twisted and turned, but it was too late. The monster had her around the waist, lifting her off the rack.

Louise kicked and screamed and hit, but these annoyances were less than nothing to the beast. It carried her over to one of the industrial washing machines. The creature tossed the thrashing woman into the machine and slammed the door shut.

Louise scrambled around, looking for some way out. Through the glass door, she saw the creature fiddling with the controls. Within seconds, scalding hot water began to fill the chamber. Her screams reverberated through the metal tomb, piercing her own ears as her lungs filled with hot steam.

The last thing Louise Carmichael saw before she drowned was the hideous face of the monster, grinning at her through the glass door. She was glad she'd be dead before the spin cycle kicked in.

Sarah sat alone in the shack, reading her braille *Kama Sutra*. She had not officially moved in with Melvin. She still had the house in town, and a lot of her stuff was still there. But she certainly spent most of her time in the shack these days. Of course, that was kind of unavoidable. She'd spend the night and then Melvin would go off to work, leaving her there by herself. She had no idea how to get back to town on her own.

Melvin walked in and immediately Sarah knew something was wrong. She could hear his feet dragging as he walked (although she was pleased to note that whatever was wrong, he wasn't so far gone that he forgot to put his mop back in the umbrella stand she'd found for them). Without saying a word, Melvin sat down heavily upon a stack of tires. Sarah stood up and moved toward him.

"Melvin? What's wrong?"

"Don't come any closer," Melvin warned.

"What? Why not? What's happened?"

"I'm afraid, Sarah," Melvin said. "I don't know what's happening to me. I'm afraid I might be losing control of myself."

"That's ridiculous," Sarah said, although she took Melvin's advice and stayed at the table. "Why do you think that?"

"I just killed someone, Sarah."

"You've killed a bunch of people, sweetie. That's your job."

"Yeah, but this was just some little old lady. She wasn't doing anything. But I couldn't help myself. I . . . I don't know . . . I sensed her and I had to kill her. And I don't know why."

Sarah finally came over and sat on Melvin's lap, running her hands over his face. "Well, there must have been a reason."

"What if there wasn't? What if I really am turning into some kind of monster? You could be in danger just being out here with me."

"I know you could never hurt me," Sarah assured him, kissing him gently on top of the head.

"I hope you're right. But when they find that old lady . . . they'll come after me, Sarah. The people in town were just starting to get used to me, but when they find her . . . they're gonna chase me with pitchforks and torches. And they'll come after you, too."

"I think you've been working too hard lately. We should go away for a little while. Get you away from all the evil and corruption in Tromaville and let your system recharge itself. Then, when everything's back to normal around here, we'll come home. How's that sound?"

"Great, but where would we go?"

"I know the perfect place just a few miles outside of town. My dad used to take us camping there all the time. I remember it had this weird name because a lot of writers would go out there to concentrate on their work and get away from it all."

"What's it called?"

"It's called the End of the Book."

22.

Angels, Demons, and Other Assholes

Plotnick was sick and tired of seeing Peter Belgoody naked.

He'd been spending a lot of time in Belgoody's office lately, the two of them trying to figure out what to do about the Toxic Monster Mop Hero thing. And because Belgoody was under so much stress, every time Plotnick came to see him, June Sakamoto was there working on his flab. That girl deserved some kinda medal for going above and beyond, Plotnick thought. Maybe before she took this job, she worked with diarrheic babies or vomiting monkeys or something. She had a gut of steel, that one.

At any rate, things were going from bad to worse as far as Plotnick was concerned. The whole hit-and-run thing had been a total fiasco. The Toxic Avenger was an even bigger hero now for putting an end to the hit-and-run game. The only thing that kept the cops looking like total assholes was Bozo's piss-poor aim. If he'd been a better driver, he might have killed more people at the park. And with Bozo and Slug gone, Plotnick was almost out of foot soldiers.

And now they'd discovered the purple, bloated body of Louise

Carmichael in the industrial washer at Passett Cleaners. That boring cocksucker Frank Passett had run all the way to the police station babbling about the monster tearing up his shop, and won't somebody help that poor old woman? *Poor old woman, my dimpled ass,* thought Plotnick. Louise Carmichael was the biggest scumbag in Tromaville. Had been for going on three decades now. The least of her offenses was that she ran a sex tourism agency out of her basement, arranging visits to places such as Thailand for horny businessmen to go fuck underage girls (or boys, if that's what yanked their crank). At least that shit didn't affect Plotnick's job. As long as the pedophiles were spilling their seed in Third World countries and not in town, he could turn a blind eye to that.

Of course, there were plenty of other strikes against Louise Carmichael that took place right here in Tromaville. She was also a drug smuggler, a white slaver, a bookie, a counterfeiter, arranged murders for hire, and had a huge collection of pirated DVDs. If she hadn't lined Plotnick's pockets with so many kickbacks over the years, he might have had to do something about some of that. Aw, who was he kidding? He could have never brought himself to bust Mrs. Carmichael. She was just so nice!

Much to Plotnick's surprise, Mayor Belgoody was taking the news of Mrs. Carmichael's death quite well. In fact, the more grisly details Plotnick provided, the wider Belgoody's grin became until finally (godfucking-dammit, Plotnick thought, I knew this was gonna happen) he leaped off the massage table in happiness, spilling the sheet and June Sakamoto to the floor.

"Yes! Plotnick, this is it. This is the fucking break we've been waiting for!"

"It is?"

"You're goddamn skippy. He fucked up this time."

"I don't see how."

"What was the old bat doing when the Toxic Fuckface showed up?"

"Waiting for her dry cleaning."

"Exactly. This is an unprovoked attack, pure and simple. The monster's gone crazy. We have to put a stop to it."

"I don't know, Mayor. I mean, this woman was about as close as you can get to pure evil. She set kittens on fire that wandered into her yard."

"That was never proven. Besides, the law-abiding dipshits of Tromaville don't know jack about her history. They just know that she was a tiny, harmless old lady sitting in a dry cleaners, minding her own business, who got horribly slaughtered by a horrible monster."

Plotnick thought it over. "You think people will fall for that? They love this thing."

"It just takes one misstep to make people forget all about their heroes. Clinton gets a blow job from an intern, his approval ratings sink like the fucking *Titanic*. O. J. Simpson is acquitted, mind you, of killing his wife, and people shun him like yesterday's garbage. Neil Armstrong eats human flesh just once, just ONE TIME! You'd think the man never walked on the moon."

"Maybe you're right," Plotnick rubbed his chin. "What the hell. Nothing else has worked."

"I want a press conference, and I want the fucking army on the line. We've got an international supermenace in our backyard, and I want it eliminated."

"Yes, sir. Might I also recommend a pair of pants before the press arrives?"

Ian Jakov sat at his desk at the *Tromaville Times,* drinking cold coffee and playing with his lighter. Now that he was the go-to guy for Toxic Avenger stories, his stock around the office was through the roof. Unfortunately, all the Toxic Avenger stories tended to be kind of the same. Hero saves innocents from evildoers, usually hero ends up killing said evildoers, hero vanishes.

What Ian really wanted was a sit-down interview with the hero himself. Hell, he'd given the thing its name. It owed him that much. Well, he'd tried to give the thing a name, anyway. Thanks to repetition in the paper, the Toxic Avenger was fast becoming the most common name, but there were still a few holdouts for Monster-Hero. Odds were good that bootleg T-shirt sales would end up deciding the issue. "I Heart Toxie" was outselling "I Heart the Monster-Hero" by at least three to one.

Ian's phone rang. He couldn't decide whether to be annoyed and ignore it, or happy for the break in the monotony of the day. He picked up the receiver.

"Ian Jakov."

"Mr. Jakov," a smoky, feminine voice replied. "Please listen. I don't have much time."

"They're your minutes."

"Very soon, you'll be sent to a press conference at city hall this afternoon. I want you to go to that press conference, then meet me in the parking garage afterward."

"Who is this?"

"No names. I have important information about the Toxic Avenger."

"Hey, you're using my name!"

"Will you meet me?"

"Sure, sure, I'll be there. But how—"

The line went dead. Ian sat there, staring at the receiver. Cloak-and-dagger stuff, eh? Cool. And she sounded hot, too. Of course, that could be deceiving. Remember that time the phone sex chick turned out to be a dude?

"Jakov!"

"I didn't!"

Ian's editor, Paula, glared at him. "Pull your head out, Jakov. I just got off the phone with the mayor's office. Big press conference down at city hall in one hour. Something to do with your Toxic Avenger. Let's go! Chop-chop!"

Ian nodded and finally put the receiver back in its cradle. Well, the mystery caller had been right so far. Let's see what else she has to say.

Mayor Belgoody stood in a cramped office, peering out a slightly open door at the distinguished members of the press setting up their cameras and lights. It wasn't quite the media circus he'd hoped for, but considering it was short notice, he couldn't complain too much. The usual local muckrakers were there, of course. But there were also a couple of satellite trucks parked outside. Even if he hadn't seen the trucks, it was pretty easy to tell which ones were from the big cable networks. They had bigger lights, fancier cameras, nicer suits, and had no qualms about shoving the local guys (who'd been set up and ready for twenty minutes) out of their way and back to lesser positions.

Hovering near the back of the room, trying to stay out of the way of the TV crews, stood Ian Jakov. Belgoody was worried about that one. Jakov had been responsible for shaping public opinion in favor of the monster, and it would probably take more than one hurriedly assembled press conference to get him to change his tune. Belgoody thought he might have to go over Jakov's dandruff-flaked head before the day was through.

"Mr. Mayor!"

Belgoody turned away from the door to see Chief Plotnick and a starched, ramrod-straight military official marching toward him. Plotnick saluted nobody in particular, then said, "Mayor Peter Belgoody, this is General Colin Oskippie."

The mayor put on his most official look of greeting, shook the general's hand, and immediately regretted it. General Oskippie looked like he was about a day away from retirement and two days away from burial, but his grip was bone-shattering. The general had learned from experience that an amazingly painful handshake helps dispel the immediate impression most people had that they were dealing with a feeb.

"Your man's filled me in on the situation, Mayor," the general spat through clenched teeth. "Sounds like you've got a real creature feature on your hands out here."

"Yes, sir." Belgoody nursed his wounded paw and nodded.

"Well, you've called in the right platoon. I've led monster-hunts from Normandy to 'Nam. We'll get your boogeyman, Mayor. Rest easy on that score."

Belgoody glanced nervously at Plotnick, who could only grin and nod for reassurance. Turning back to Oskippie, Belgoody replied, "Not a doubt in my mind. So. Are we ready to meet the press?"

Ian was hard at work chewing on a pen when the door finally opened and the men of the hour strode out to the podium. It was difficult to see anyone behind Belgoody's mass, but Ian recognized Plotnick and saw someone else in uniform he couldn't place. This already didn't bode well. The last time Jakov attended a press conference with this many stars and bars, he ended up spending six weeks in Afghanistan.

An ear-splitting whine of feedback exploded out of the speakers as Belgoody smacked each microphone with the palm of his beefy hand. "Is this thing on?" he asked. "How about this one? This one? How about now?"

Once he was satisfied that each and every microphone was in good working order, Belgoody cleared his throat and squared his shoulders. "Thank you all for coming on such short notice. For those of you who don't know me, my name is Peter Belgoody, and I'm the mayor of Tromaville. For several weeks now, our fair town has been plagued by a creature erroneously dubbed the Monster-Hero by the press."

Ian squirmed uncomfortably. Apparently his name hadn't been embraced by the powers-that-be.

Belgoody continued. "We now have irrefutable evidence that this creature is no hero. May I have the first slide, please?"

Behind him, a large image of a pleasant-looking older lady appeared.

"This is Mrs. Louise Carmichael, longtime Tromaville resident and pillar of society. Yesterday, Mrs. Carmichael stopped by Passett Cleaners on Eighth and Collins. According to Frank Passett, the owner, Mrs. Carmichael was a regular customer, coming in once a week without fail, often bringing in homemade cookies. As it turned out, this would be Mrs. Carmichael's last visit to Passett Cleaners. Next slide."

The next image was still Mrs. Carmichael, but she didn't look quite so pleasant anymore. Her purple face was smashed against the glass door of a washing machine. Her tongue protruded. Her limbs stuck out at odd angles. Most disturbingly, a mop was wedged into the handle of the machine, locking her in.

"Mrs. Louise Carmichael was murdered at approximately 3:00 P.M. yesterday afternoon. The evidence is consistent with that found at other crime scenes known to have been perpetrated by the so-called Monster-Hero. This clearly refutes the ignorant claims of certain sensationalist reporters that the alleged 'Toxic Avenger' is a force for good in Tromaville. This creature is a menace running amok in our little town. The best efforts of our local law enforcement have proved to be no match for this superhuman threat. Therefore, Chief Plotnick and I have agreed to call in outside assistance. General?"

The four-star general stepped up to the podium. "Thank you, Mr. Mayor. Ladies and gentlemen of the press, I am General Colin Oskippie, U.S. Army. While I'm pleased to be of help in this town's time of need, I only wish we'd been called in earlier. Radioactive monsters are no laughing matter, people. I can't tell you how many times I've seen this same scenario play out in towns just like this one. At first, everyone's pleased as party punch to have their own radioactive monster. Of course, the first to die are always bad guys. They're the only ones ignorant enough to try to pick a fight with a thing like this. But that doesn't make the thing a hero. The bloodlust rises, and the next thing you know, you've got little children floating face down in ponds and old ladies trapped inside washing machines."

"Amen to that, General," Belgoody nodded sagely. "Rest assured that the military will have the full cooperation of Tromaville. All our resources are at your disposal."

Ian couldn't take much more of this. He stood and waved his pen to indicate a question. "Excuse me, General. Mayor. Ian Jakov, *Tromaville Times.*"

Belgoody sighed heavily. "I don't believe we've opened the floor to questions yet, Jakov."

"I'm sorry, I just have one question for all of you. Is this a joke?"

The general put on his sad dad face and replied, "I wish it were, son. I wish it were."

Ian felt himself shoved aside by an impossibly tan woman with blond highlights in a tight business skirt. "General! Rachel Cicatrix, World News Network."

"Rachel, good to see you again."

"General, will martial law have to be imposed in Tromaville?"

"Why, that's a fine idea. Mayor?"

"You have my full support, General. I think we could use some martial law around here, sure."

"Follow-up question, General?"

"Sure thing, darling."

"Are those new boots?"

"No, no, I've had these for quite some time. Just shined 'em up, though. Thank you. Any other questions?"

Ian stood up again. "Just one more, please. Correct me if I'm wrong, but so far, nobody in Tromaville has been able to find the Toxic Avenger unless he comes out himself. How are you going to track him down?"

"I'll field that one!"

All eyes turned to the new voice. Its owner was a ruggedly handsome man in a safari jacket with overflowing folders full of documents tucked beneath his arm. Every woman and not a few men swooned when they saw his crystal blue eyes and disarming smile. He'd suddenly emerged from the same cramped office where Belgoody and the rest had been hiding before the conference, although his entrance was stylishly backlit and, unless it was Ian's imagination, accompanied by a fog machine and a subtle musical theme.

"Who the fuck are you?" Ian asked the question on everyone's lips.

"You think you're the only one who consults experts," Belgoody sneered. "Everyone, meet Professor Hank Stone."

"Hank Stone," Rachel purred to Ian's left, barely concealing the orgasm she was having. "Adventurer. Explorer. Symbologist."

Ian's eyes rolled. "Symbologist?!"

Stone planted his strong hands on the podium and leaned into the microphones. "That's right. I search art and artificats for hidden clues that broaden our understanding of the world around us. Mayor Belgoody has brought me in to consult on the Toxic Avenger problem. And what I've learned will amaze and astound you."

Thus began a seventy-eight-minute lecture with slides, graphs, and statistics that mesmerized everyone except Ian. Stone showed details of paintings and sculptures by Da Vinci, Rembrandt, Michelangelo, Dali, Toulouse-Lautrec, and Jack "King" Kirby. Stone displayed religious icons dating back to the fourteenth century. He translated Babylonian texts and dazzled the crowd with stories of his narrow escape from a pirate ship buried beneath the sands of the Sahara. He tore open his shirt and displayed scars from innumerable sword fights. By the time he was through, there wasn't a pair of unstiffened nipples in the house.

The upshot of all this was, according to Stone, that the Toxic Avenger was a creature of pure evil, that he had seduced and kidnapped an innocent blind girl named Sarah, and that the military would find these two at the End of the Book. "Oh and also," Stone concluded, "Jesus Christ was gay."

Once the thunderous ovation died down, Belgoody stepped back up to the podium. "So there, Mr. Ian Doubting Thomas Jakov. Satisfied?"

Ian looked back over the pages and pages of rambling notes he'd made. "Not really, no. How exactly is Professor Stone qualified to have an opinion on the Toxic Avenger? His conclusions completely contradict those made by Dr. Flem Hocking. Dr. Hocking is an actual scientist, not just a glorified art history major."

"Flem Hocking?" Belgoody was incredulous. "Fuck you! Your guy can't even talk properly! Were you listening to any of that lecture? This guy ate broken glass to earn the trust of a tribe of Pygmies in Africa. How fucking cool is that? Hocking can't even wipe his own ass!"

Stone cleared his throat and nodded. "I have nothing but respect for Dr. Hocking, but it is true that he is incapable of wiping his own ass."

"And that's good enough for me!" General Oskippie enthused. "Ladies and gentlemen, thank you all for coming out today. We're scheduled to begin Operation Kill Mutie at oh seven hundred tomorrow. Hope to see you there!"

The general, the mayor, Hank Stone, and Chief Plotnick made no move to leave the podium at the conclusion of the press conference. They stood and posed while a barrage of flashbulbs exploded in their faces.

Amid all the confusion, Ian Jakov stood up, tossed his useless notes into the trash, and went off in search of the parking garage.

CLICK CLICK CLICK CLICK.

Ian's footsteps echoed like gunshots through the darkened parking garage, which was odd, since he was wearing sneakers. What was it about garages, Ian wondered, that made everybody sound like they were wearing high heels?

"Mr. Jakov," a familiar voice whispered.

Ian looked around and saw the red glow of a cigarette emerge from behind a puff of bluish smoke. Ian walked over to the woman, a beautiful Asian with a portable massage table leaning against the wall behind her.

"Are you the one who called me?" Ian asked.

"Were you followed?"

"No; everybody's too busy posing for photo ops. Who are you?"

"My name isn't important. Call me Deep Tissue."

"Aren't you June Sakamoto?"

"What?!" June nearly choked on her smoke. "How did you—"

"It's written on your massage table along with your address, phone number, and Web site."

"GodDAMMIT!" June kicked the table over. "Never mind that. The Toxic Avenger is in great danger."

"Yeah, I know," Ian nodded. "The press conference—"

"Lies. All lies. Louise Carmichael is no harmless old lady. She was a ruthless criminal mastermind responsible for untold death and suffering both here and abroad. The mayor and the police know this."

"I'm not surprised," Ian said, "but I can't prove anything."

"Yes, you can." June handed over a computer disk. "Everything you need is right here. Names, dates, addresses. The entire history of Tromaville's corrupt government is on this disk. It's up to you to bring it down and save the Toxic Avenger."

Ian took the disk and quickly stuffed it in his pocket. "How'd you get all this?"

"I've been working for the mayor for some time now. I listen. I take notes. And he's computer-illiterate. Has no idea how to work the damn thing, so he asks me to help."

"This is unbelievable. I don't know what to say."

"Say you'll run the story."

"Of course I will. But what's in this for you?"

"I don't want anything," June said, lighting up another smoke, "except your paper's endorsement when I run for mayor this fall."

"You want to be mayor?"

"Actually, I'd rather be prime minister of Canada, but since I can't do that, I figured I'd start here. Do we have a deal?"

"Absolutely," Ian said and shook hands on it.

"But remember," June cautioned, "no one can know I'm Deep Tissue. At least, not until I'm ready to sell the movie rights."

"What movie rights? You met me one time in a garage. How is that a movie?"

"I've seen movies about less."

"Yeah, me too, I guess. Thank you. Will we meet again?"

June smiled. "Not like this. Go. And don't forget to tip your valet. He's my cousin. He'd like to be comptroller."

23.

You Say You Want a ~~Resolution~~ ~~Execution~~ ~~Prostitution~~ ~~Lilliputian~~ Revolution

Ian sat at his desk at the *Tromaville Times,* chewing a pencil eraser like it was gum, his mind a frenzy of conspiracy theories, cover-ups, and dark deals. He'd spent hours poring over the documents on the disk Deep Tissue had given him. He couldn't say any of it had been news, exactly. Tromaville's movers and shakers weren't subtle when they moved or shook. But it was the hard, concrete evidence he'd dreamed about for so long.

There had been a lot to go over, but first and foremost was the Louise Carmichael story. Once he had a grasp on her criminal empire, Ian began to write. It was the easiest article he'd ever written. It was as though his brain had sensed the urgency of the situation and moved down south to take up residence in his hands. His fingers flew across the keyboard, spelling out the truth behind harmless Mrs. Carmichael and why the Toxic Avenger's actions had probably been the best thing he'd ever done for this town.

Ian had turned the article in and sat back to digest the rest of the information. He had material here to do follow-up articles for months.

Since the police department was equally corrupt, he couldn't expect anyone there or the mayor to be brought up on criminal charges. All he could do was expose the truth, and once the people found their voice, the protests would kick Plotnick, Belgoody, and the rest of the crew to the curb faster than Ian had ejected his college roommate after the deadbeat smoked the last of his weed during their junior year.

Ian was so lost in thought that when his editor called his name from across the office, he was so startled that he swallowed a good-sized hunk of eraser. He looked up and saw Paula standing in her office doorway, holding a mock-up of tomorrow's paper in one hand and waving him over with the other.

Ian stepped into the office, and at Paula's command closed the door behind him. "Sit," she barked, not meeting his eyes.

Ian took the chair across from her desk and saw the pages of his article spread out in front of her. Paula spread out the mock-up next to it. The banner headline read, "MARTIAL LAW."

"What's going on?" Ian said, giving the paper a cursory glance.

"I should be asking you that question," Paula said, pouring herself a glassful of bourbon and pointedly not offering one to Ian. "What the fuck do you think you're doing with that article you turned in?"

"What do you mean? I mean, I know it isn't the most well-written thing I've ever turned in, but the deadline was pretty tight."

"Who gives a sloppy fuck how well written it was? We can't run that even if it's got fuckin' Shakespeare's byline on the copy."

"Why not? It's all true."

Paula waved away the word like a tsetse fly. "That's not what they said at the press conference, and your job was to report on what they said at the press conference."

"I thought my job was to report the news, and if they spoon-feed us bullshit at a press conference, to dig deeper until I find the news."

"Well, aren't you the intrepid young go-getter? What are you, stupid? You think it's 1971 or something? Your job and my job is to tell stories that people want to read. Not to tell them that for the past couple of decades they've been stupid enough to elect and reelect a corpulent leech to the office of mayor over and over again. If the mayor says the Toxic Avenger is a threat killing innocent old ladies, then guess what, Lois Lane? Your little pet is a fucking threat killing innocent old ladies! End of story!"

"But you know that isn't true."

"I know what I'm told."

"But this is exactly the opposite of everything we've been saying in this paper about how Toxie's a hero!"

"It's 'Toxie' now? Look, we let you run with the 'Toxie' story as long as we did because nobody gave a shit, really. The mayor's office didn't have a position on it, so neither did we. Now he does. Besides"—Paula helped herself to another glass—"nobody reads this thing beyond maybe the first couple of paragraphs of a few main stories and the TV listings. Our parent company was taking your stories and repurposing them for use on the television branch. That's where everybody gets their news from these days."

"What parent company? What television branch?"

"Jesus wept, he is stupid. The *Tromaville Times* is owned by News Services International. They own tons of papers and TV and radio stations. The main TV branch that's been getting your stories is—"

"World News Network."

"There you go! And if you'd played your cards right, News Services International probably would have made a movie through their Hollywood branch. Not that you'd have gotten any money, of course, but I bet you'd have made a helluva talking head for the talk show circuit."

Ian eyed the bourbon hungrily. "So now what? I can't rewrite the article. It's past deadline."

"Yeah, don't worry about it. The mayor's office had some concerns, so they sent over an article earlier today. It's all taken care of."

"You're just gonna publish a press release as a news story?"

"Don't look so shocked; it happens all the time. You honestly think we have a Washington Bureau chief? There's like three guys that cover the White House. Everybody just changes the bylines and some of the adjectives."

"I think I'm going to be sick."

"Oh, please, you are not. Anyhoo, you're off the Toxic Avenger beat, needless to say."

"I thought you were firing me."

"Oh, hell, no. You're under contract, sweetie. You're not going anywhere."

"I don't understand."

Paula sighed, as she often did at home when scolding her illegal-immigrant housekeeper. "You'll continue to draw a paycheck until your contract runs out, and you'll keep writing for the *Times*. Whenever you turn in some inflammatory rhetoric like this here, it just goes in the old flaming circular file. Sooner or later, your writer's ego will kick back in and you'll miss seeing your name in print and you'll start turning out stories about pandas mating or anorexic pop stars or something like that."

"It's just that easy, huh?"

"Well, it could have been easier. I could have not told you anything and let you just get more and more frustrated as story after story got killed."

"Well, you're a peach," Ian sighed. "Can I at least have a drink?"

"I don't think so." Paula shook her head as she polished off the bottle. "I think we're through here."

Ian dragged his sorry ass back to his desk, wondering how he could have been so stupid. He plopped down in his chair, rummaged through a drawer, and found an old pay stub. The checks were from the *Tromaville Times*. No indication of any corporate lineage there. He grabbed the morning's paper and found the masthead. Yep. There it was in black and white, albeit in microscopically tiny print. "A Division of News Services International."

Fuck. For the first time in his life, Ian actually had something to say but didn't have a voice. He had a disk full of incriminating evidence but nowhere he could bring it. The *Times* was useless. All the TV stations were owned by one corporation or another. Same with the publishing houses, although by the time he got a book together, this whole thing would be a moot point anyway. He had to get word out to the people now. Tonight. But how?

Ian smiled. They thought they'd won, but he wasn't licked yet. There was still one bastion of free speech left. One place where he could speak his mind and let the people decide. The Internet. He would harness the power of the blog.

Ian turned to his computer and uploaded his article and other supporting documents from the disk to his personal Web site. For kicks, he also added a few dancing bananas and some music. To finish it off, he added the following:

PEOPLE OF TROMAVILLE. Mayor Peter Belgoody, Chief Chuck Plotnick, and the *Tromaville Times* are launching a campaign to destroy the Toxic Avenger. The army will either capture or kill him tomorrow morning at 7:00 A.M. WE CANNOT LET THIS HAPPEN! If you want to help, please meet me at my apartment at 1:00 A.M. to formulate a plan of attack. LET'S TAKE BACK OUR TOWN!

Ian finished his posting and logged off. One way or another, he'd let the truth be known. The mayor and their powerful friends might have control of virtually every mass medium there was, but there was one thing they hadn't counted on. Mayor Belgoody, prepare to tremble before the awesome power of the blogosphere!

The blogosphere was a piece of shit.

It was a quarter to two, and a bleary-eyed Ian sat on his couch, nursing a glass of Wild Turkey and watching the counter on his Web site not move. Nobody had come to his apartment at 1:00 A.M., and the only comment anyone had left on his blog was some pervert asking for nude pics of Deep Tissue.

It had been a long, discouraging day. Ian was finally beginning to drift off to sleep when he heard a soft, tentative knock on his door. Ian sat on the couch, not moving. The knock came again.

Ian sighed. Why bother? At the rate things were going, it was probably the cops, there to arrest him for inciting a riot or something. Still, there weren't many alternatives left. He got up, opened the door, and found a police officer standing in the hall.

The cop looked him up and down. "Ian Jakov?"

"I knew it," Ian muttered. "Yeah, that's right." He held out his wrists, waiting to be cuffed.

"I saw your Web site. Am I too late? My name's Jake Clancy."

"Clancy? You're the cop that the Toxic Avenger rescued in Shinbone Alley. Jesus, I didn't recognize you. Last time I saw you, you were pretty badly beaten up."

"Yeah, well, I, y'know, healed. Can I come in?"

"No! I mean yes! Come in. No, you're not too late. How'd you find my site?"

"I was just doing a Google search for my name and your blog came up."

"Well, I'm sure glad to see you. Unfortunately, you and I are about it."

"Nobody else came?"

"Afraid not. So I'm not sure what just two of us can do."

Clancy nodded. "They'll come."

Ian laughed bitterly and tossed back some more booze. "How? I was stupid to think anybody would find my Web site. The only way I could have reached fewer people would be if I called into a liberal radio station."

"Well, you found me," Clancy said, taking a seat. "And I believe in what you're doing. The Toxic Avenger's a hero. If it weren't for him, I'd be dead. And there're a lot of people just like me around town. We owe him our lives."

"Sure, but how do we reach them?"

"That's why I was late. I had a few stops to make."

Another knock came on Ian's door. Ian glanced from the door to Clancy.

"Better get that," Clancy said. "That'll be some of them now."

Ian went to the door and was greeted by Bobby, Santos, and the rest of the crew of the Taco Shack, each of them weighted down with greasy bags of tacos.

"Sorry we're late," Bobby said. "We figured people would want food."

And so it began. Over the next hour, people swarmed over to Ian's apartment. Men, women, and entire families who had been helped by the Toxic Avenger. They all had stories to tell. How the Toxic Avenger had saved them from a fire, had freed them from a kidnapper, had opened a stubborn jar of pickles for them. Some stories were big, some small, but they were all important to the people who lived them.

As the night wore on, the meeting moved outside as the apartment could no longer hold the crowd. Ian was just drunk enough to wipe away a tear of gratitude and give Clancy a hug before they left the apartment.

Before long, the group was ready for action. And as night gave way to dawn, Ian looked once again in awe at the number of supporters who had responded to his (or at least Clancy's) call to arms. One guy in particular caught his attention—a wild-eyed, shabby-looking homeless person whom Ian half-suspected had been eating dog recently. The bum saw Ian staring at him, grinned, and walked over.

"We're goin' to get the monster soon?" the bum mumbled.

"To help him," Ian corrected.

"Yeah," the bum giggled. "Lots of help. I got somethin' for him."

"That's super," Ian said, and quickly found someone else to talk to.

The bum stood alone, giggling. At long last, he thought, I shall come face to face with the creature I do not know and whose death I seek for reasons I no longer remember! Truly, it is a glorious day to be The Hypnotic Bum . . . Rat . . . Eye . . . something or other. Whatever . . . vengeance is mine!

24.

Showdown at the End of the Book

A nd then Toxie killed all of the bad guys. He and Sarah lived happily ever after.

The End

EDITOR: Um, hello? Lloyd?

LLOYD: Hello! What did you think?

EDITOR: That's it?

LLOYD: That's it! Less is more, right?

EDITOR: No, I think actually you might want to flesh this chapter out a little bit.

LLOYD: What? Why? We're letting the readers use the power of their own imagination! It's much more powerful than anything we could ever come up with.

EDITOR: That may be true, but after slogging through this whole book, that might come across as a little anticlimactic. Why don't you and Jahnke put your heads together and come up with a real final chapter?

LLOYD: All right, fine, but I told him you wouldn't go for it! Goddammit, this is really asshole time! Adam! Adam Junkie! We've got to fix the last chapter of the book!

ADAM: What book? Make Your Own Damn Movie?

LLOYD: No. The Toxic Avenger, goddammit! Fix this fucker or I'll show you what the "ghost" in ghostwriter is all about!

ADAM: Okay, fine. What is it, like the last two minutes of the movie? Great. That should be another fifty pages or so. . . .

The Real Chapter 24

Showdown at the End of the Book

M elvin woke up holding Sarah's nude body in his green tree-trunk arms, her hair flowing over his face, into his mouth, and down his throat.

He rolled her over gently and quietly hacked up a hair ball. There were definite pros and cons to this whole girlfriend situation. But most of the cons so far revolved around getting hair from various parts of her anatomy in the mouth and between the teeth, so those tended to be far outweighed by the tremendous pro of getting laid on a regular basis.

And since coming out to Sarah's idyllic campsite, that had been a very regular basis indeed. You could set your watch by it. They'd been going at it like captive monkeys in heat. Like drunk teenagers whose parents left town for a holiday weekend. Like drunk parents in Atlantic City, leaving behind their ungrateful brats for a holiday weekend. Like a computer nerd with a high-speed connection and a lifetime supply of lotion and Kleenex. Whatever metaphor you could come up with, they were fucking like it.

Melvin rolled out of the sleeping bag, taking care not to wake Sarah. He stood, forced to hunch over in the cramped confines of the tent, stretched as best he could, and yawned. Sarah had been so right. This was a brilliant idea. He felt so much better since getting out of town, he could barely describe it. Maybe the entire town of Tromaville was so corrupt, he couldn't tell where one evil stopped and another began. He'd been constantly on edge for weeks now, and that had taken its toll. But out here in the country, there was just him, his girlfriend, and unspoiled nature. Speaking of which, unspoiled nature was calling Melvin's name at that moment.

He quietly unzipped the back of the tent and stepped outside. He cast his eyes over the countryside as he whipped out his one-eyed tutu-snake and got rid of some toxic waste. It really was a beautiful country, he thought, and worth protecting.

Just then, his morning constitutional was interrupted by the hiss of static and a booming, tinny voice: "KEEP YOUR HANDS WHERE WE CAN SEE THEM."

Jeez, he hadn't heard that while he was taking a whiz since he'd moved out of his mom's house. He slowly raised his hands and tilted his head slightly to look behind him. There were about two hundred cops and soldiers stationed around the front of the tent, with a dizzying array of pistols, rifles, machine guns, and antitank weapons pointed right at him. It had simply been dumb luck that they'd chosen a campsite against a cliff face, making it impossible for them to be completely surrounded.

Melvin sighed and turned back to his business. He was pretty sure they wouldn't shoot him in the back, and they must know Sarah was with him, otherwise they would have taken him down already. All things being equal, Melvin figured, he'd might just as well finish his piss.

After a solid minute, the voice came back over the megaphone: "AREN'T YOU FINISHED YET?"

Melvin waved back to the men. "Just one more second!" It was actually more like thirty seconds before he was through. He turned back and yelled, "Mind if I zip up?"

There was silence while the men consulted with each other; then, "GO AHEAD."

Melvin tucked himself back in, straightened his tutu, and turned to face the opposition. It was worse than he'd thought. Everyone was armed to the teeth, and a tank was parked in the center of the action, its colossal gun aimed straight at the tent.

Melvin stepped forward, putting himself between the tank and the tent. "Let's take it easy here, fellas," he called. "There's an innocent girl in there, y'know."

General Oskippie sat in a jeep parked next to the tank and addressed Melvin again through the megaphone. "ARE YOU THREATENING HER?"

"No, no! I'm just saying let's not lose our heads here."

The flap to the tent opened, and Sarah emerged, barely dressed in a diaphanous babydoll. "Melvin, what's going on? Who's out there?"

The second Melvin heard that flap unzip, he'd started to warn Sarah to stay inside, but once he got an eyeful of her taut body in that see-through negligee, the words caught in his throat. It did not, on the other hand, render the cops or the soldiers speechless, although it did have an effect on their aim. Sarah's appearance was greeted with cat-calls, wolf whistles, and more than a few "I love my job"s. Melvin was going to have a talk with Sarah when this was all over about what was appropriate to wear when company was over.

General Oskippie got back on the megaphone and addressed the whistling troops. "OKAY, ENOUGH OF THAT SHIT." A little bit of that kind of behavior was fine. Hell, it was mandatory in the don't-ask-don't-tell military. But by God, they had a job to do, and no trim in a peekaboo nightie was going to keep them from it.

Sarah found her way over to Melvin, who wrapped his arms tightly around her. "It's gonna be okay," Melvin assured her despite every appearance to the contrary. "Nobody's going to get hurt."

"What do they want, Melvin?" Sarah asked nervously and a bit too loudly. One of the nearby soldiers overheard and began to giggle.

"Melvin?! Your name's Melvin?" Before long, the entire company was doubled over with laughter, leaning on their rifles for support. Even General Oskippie had to admit it was pretty funny and barked a dry laugh into the megaphone.

Melvin was used to being laughed at, but this was the first time he realized the absurdity of matching his old name with his new body. He chuckled along with the troops. "I guess it is pretty funny, isn't it?"

About a hundred yards away from the outer perimeter of the soldiers, Pete Belgoody was holding court in a makeshift media tent. Naturally, he'd turned the craft services table into his desk. He sat behind the smorgasbord, answering questions for the cameras (he'd decided not to take any chances and didn't invite any print journalists) and punctuating important points with a bite of doughnut.

So far things seemed to be running smoothly. They had all the men and hardware they needed. They'd made it to the End of the Book in record time.[1] The caterers were available at short notice and were now hard at work on those delicious French toast dippin' sticks that Pete loved so much. The only thing that worried Pete even slightly was the minor point that he hadn't heard any loud ker-pows, rat-a-tat-tats, or long, low whistles followed by deep, rumbling ka-booms come from the target area yet. But the morning was still young after all.

But then Belgoody heard something far more disturbing than all the gunshots and mortar fires in the world put together. He unwedged

---

1. Although there were those who would dispute that. Many critics would later suggest that it took them much, much longer to get there than was necessary.

himself from his deck chair, stood at the edge of the tent, and cupped a hand around his ear. Why, they were . . . laughing.

Belgoody shook his head and listened again. They laugh without gunshots! They laugh without knives! They laugh without tasers, bazookas, and mines!

The mayor hurriedly turned back to the media and apologized. "I'll be back soon. I just . . . something's come up." He waddled off, leaving everyone to assume he'd developed a case of the squirts.

As Pete huffed and puffed his way up to the campsite, he punched a number into his cell phone. "Plotnick," he gasped, "the general's about half an ass cheek away from screwing the pooch on this one. Time to bring Plan B up the hill."

Belgoody barged through the line of armed men and found his way over to the command jeep. The general wasn't there. Instead, he was sitting at a nearby picnic table with the monster and the blind chick!

"EXCUSE ME, GENERAL," Belgoody spoke into the microphone, "BUT WHAT THE FUCK?"

"Mayor!" the general greeted him. "Come on over. This guy here, he's all right! You didn't tell me about his sense of humor. He's got some funny stories."

The Toxic Avenger grinned and shrugged his shoulders at Belgoody, then waved. Belgoody shook his head. "I'M SORRY, GENERAL, I MUST HAVE FORGOTTEN TO TELL YOU ABOUT HIS JOKES WHILE I WAS DEBRIEFING YOU ON ALL THE PEOPLE HE'S SLAUGHTERED."

"Oh, yeah." General Oskippie snapped his fingers, suddenly all business again. "That's true. What about that, Melvin?"

"Well, sir," Melvin nodded, "I won't deny that I can be a little aggressive. But I think you'll find that anyone who met their end at my hands deserved what they got. My methods are sometimes . . . extreme.

But that's why Sarah and I came out here. So I could try to get my instincts under control."

"TELL THAT TO LOUISE CARMICHAEL," Belgoody barked in to the megaphone.

"Who?" Melvin asked the general.

"The midget lady in the washing machine."

"Actually, General," Sarah pointed out, "I think they prefer to be called little people."

Melvin nodded. "That's right. And I honestly can't explain that. All I can say is that I was sure that what I was doing was right at the time. If that's not true, if she was an innocent victim, you should arrest me right now."

The general frowned. He'd been hoping for a more straightforward answer so he could call this whole thing off and go back to the base. "I think you know we can't just arrest you, son. What prison would hold you?"

Melvin shook his head. "I don't know. But if I deserve to go to jail, you have my word I would not try to escape. Or don't you have some kind of government facility where you could study me?"

The general cleared his throat. "Well . . . yes and no. All our facilities are set up for postmortem studies. Autopsies, brain probes, that type of thing. Our scientists have become really quite skilled at cutting open aliens over the past fifty years."

"Wouldn't you learn more from them if they were alive?" Sarah asked.

"Funnily enough, no," the general answered jovially. "This one time we shot down a UFO over Seattle and one of the aliens lived. Tried to study him alive and after about six weeks everybody was bored shitless. Even the alien was begging to be dissected."

"GENERAL," Belgoody shouted, "COULD I HAVE A MOMENT, PLEASE?"

The general stood up and slapped the table with his palm. "You two sit tight. We'll figure this thing out."

He walked over to the jeep, signaling to his men to maintain their positions. Belgoody frowned. "So?"

"I don't know. He thinks there must have been some reason he killed that woman."

"No!" Belgoody whined. "No reason! It's a monster! Kill it!"

"What about the girl?"

"She seems very nice, but if she didn't want to get ripped apart by a zillion bullets, she shouldn't have gone camping with a monster!"

The general jabbed his forefinger into Belgoody's chest, where it promptly sank in about three-quarters of an inch. "Look here. I'm not going to have my men murder an innocent girl and a potentially not-as-guilty-as-you-say-he-is . . . thing just on your say-so. I want to know more about this woman. Or at least proof that he's responsible for the deaths of other clearly innocent people and not just drug dealers, pedophiles, and serial killers. Get me?"

Belgoody deflated a bit and waved his arms at Melvin and Sarah. "But what about them? You've got them right in your sights!"

"They're not going anywhere and neither are my men until I get some answers."

At that moment, Belgoody's cell phone began to chirp the theme to *Cabaret*. Pete smiled and said to the general, "You may be getting them sooner than we thought." He answered the phone. "Yes? Outstanding. Bring her right up front, Chief Plotnick."

Moments later, the men parted and Plotnick appeared at the jeep with Mrs. Ferd. She was dressed in her usual uniform of housedress, curlers, and lipstick-stained cigarette dangling from her lips. General Oskippie took a step back at her approach. "Who's this?"

Plotnick ignored him and squeezed Mrs. Ferd's shoulders. "Eunice, do you see the creature that killed your boy?"

Mrs. Ferd looked over at the picnic table. She and Toxie saw each other simultaneously. Her eyes widened and sobered. "That's it. That's the thing that killed my Melvin!"

"Melvin?" the general turned on his heel and looked back at Toxie.

"Mom?" Toxie asked, standing next to his girl.

Mrs. Ferd went into hysterics, babbling about how the creature broke into her home, smashed all the fine things in her bathroom, and kidnapped, killed, and probably raped and ate her son. Toxie listened to all this with alarm. "No, Mom, listen! I am your son! It's me! Melvin!"

This just made Mrs. Ferd even more hysterical with grief and terror. Belgoody patted her on the back with compassion, then looked at the general with contempt. "That enough proof for you, or do you want to wait until more grieving mothers show up?"

The general shook his head. "But he says he is Melvin."

Belgoody threw up his hands in exasperation. "Christ on a cracklin' nut bran, Oskippie, he's a psychotic monster! The thing's crazy! Now, are you gonna do the right thing or do I have to do it myself?"

The general gritted his teeth and gave the order to his men. Weapons went to shoulders, aimed at Melvin's bald, bulbous head.

But no sooner had the rifles been made ready than the scene was invaded yet again. The soldiers were jostled every which way by an arriving horde of civilians, led by Ian Jakov. "STOP!" Ian shouted.

Toxie couldn't believe what he was seeing. Virtually the entire population of Tromaville had come out and was making their way through the phalanx of armed soldiers, placing themselves between him and harm's way. Toxie recognized them all. Once they had been victims, but thanks to his efforts, that was no longer the case. Now they were fighting back. They were fighting for him.

Soon the soldiers found themselves aiming their weapons at a wall of civilians. Average men, women, and children locked arms and formed a barrier between Toxie and the guns. Santos, the drunk manager of the Taco Shack, had the misfortune to be in the middle of this human wall and was face to face with the gun barrel of the tank. He tried to move left and right, but there was nowhere to go. Santos craned his neck and shouted, "Anybody want to trade places?"

Ian walked over to the general and Belgoody. "You're through, Mayor. The people of Tromaville know all about your campaign of lies and corruption, and they know what you're trying to do to Toxie."

The general interjected, "Wait now. Who's Toxie?"

Melvin raised his hand, just visible behind the wall. "That'd be me, General!"

"Oh, I see. Carry on, son."

"General, Louise Carmichael was no innocent old lady, and I can prove it. I can also prove that Mayor Belgoody has defrauded the city of Tromaville out of millions of taxpayer dollars, is responsible for the crime that has plagued our city for so many years in association with Chief Plotnick here, and is in cahoots with organized crime across the country keeping our town full of toxic waste and an unsafe nuclear power plant."

"Okay, for starters," the general said, "when you're pissed off, you should try not to use words like 'cahoots.' It just sounds silly. For seconds, I don't know what the fuck is going on in this town. I think you're all nuts. But I have no trouble believing that this slimy bag of sweat and lard is as corrupt as a . . . uh . . . help me out here, son, you're the writer."

"As an oil baron on an environmental advisory board?"

"That'll do, I guess. But what about this lady's claim that Toxie here killed her boy?"

"I can answer that, General," Toxie said as he made his way through the crowd. He stepped forward and told the whole story of his origin, even the humiliating bits, which certainly lent him credence. After all, who'd fess up to almost fucking a goat if they didn't have to?

Once the story was told, Mrs. Ferd looked shaken. "I . . . I just don't know."

"Mom," Toxie said, "look into my eye. The good one. You'll see I'm still Melvin."

Toxie crouched down and looked his mother in the eye. She focused on it, doing her best to block out all the bubbly green flesh and veiny muscles that surrounded it. Finally, she gently touched Melvin's cheek and wiped away a tear. "Melvin!" she cried. "It *is* you!"

The crowd erupted in a heartfelt "AWWWWW" that would not have been out of place on the most syrupy very special episode of *Full House* as Melvin and his mother embraced. Melvin lifted her off the ground in happiness. Even the cantankerous old general brushed away a sentimental tear.

Belgoody, on the other hand, was fit to vomit with rage. This was not the way this was supposed to go. He whirled as best he could and grabbed Plotnick's gun away from him. Blindly, he turned and pulled the trigger.

BLAM! The bullet went wild into the crowd and sank between the eyes of The Hypnotic Bum-Dog-Rat-Eye, who was moments away from sinking a knife between Toxie's shoulder blades. The bum sank to the ground, dead.

The mob screamed in panic. The general shouted, "Stand down!" But the gunshot triggered a Pavlovian response in the soldiers on the front line. Within seconds, triggers were being squeezed, and bullets filled the air.

Toxie wasted no time. He dropped his mother and leaped into the air. He spun his mop feverishly, deflecting bullets away from the crowd. For thirty seconds he was a whirling dervish of fury, batting away bullets like flies and knocking rifles out of the soldiers' hands. Finally the general's orders sank in and soldiers holstered their guns.

Toxie stopped and looked around. "Is anyone hurt?" he called out.

Ian crouched down by the bum. "Just this guy!"

The crowd of townspeople cheered! But Toxie still felt his anger coursing through his veins. He stormed over and confronted Belgoody, pressing his flabby body against the jeep.

"It takes a lot of guts to fire into a crowd of unarmed people, Belgoody," Toxie sneered. "Let's see exactly how much."

Toxie plunged both his hands deep into Belgoody's vast stomach and probed around with his massive fingers. The mayor's body twitched as Toxie yanked out yard after yard of intestine. Blood sprayed out in force, hosing down those who were closest to the carnage. Belgoody stared in panic as his vital organs were exposed and scrambled to grab them back from Toxie and stuff them back inside. But it was no use. Within moments the mayor sank to the ground, face first in a puddle of his own blood.

Toxie wiped his hands on his tutu and turned to the general. "You see what I was saying about impulse control? Sorry about that."

Ian shook his head. "Don't be. You just saved the taxpayers of Tromaville the time and expense of a tedious recall election."

The crowd cheered again!

General Oskippie hooked a thumb over his shoulder at Plotnick. "What about this douche bag? What do you want us to do with him?"

Melvin's eye narrowed in anger at the man who'd tried to turn his own mother against him. He advanced on him but was stopped by Mrs. Ferd herself, who threw herself on Plotnick and kissed his cheek.

"Please, Melvin, don't hurt him. I think this could be your new daddy!"

Plotnick tried to pry Mrs. Ferd off him, but she held tight. He stared at Toxie and mouthed the words, "Please kill me now."

Toxie just smiled and shook his head. "I hope you'll be very happy together. That reminds me, there's someone I want you to meet! Sarah!"

"Melvin!"

The crowd parted again and guided Sarah through. Toxie ran over to her and they embraced, smothering each other in passionate kisses. The crowd cheered yet again, although by now they were getting a bit tired of cheering every time something like this happened.

"Mom, this is Sarah. Sarah, this is my mother."

"I'm very happy to meet you, Sarah," Mrs. Ferd said, staring disapprovingly at her outfit.

Ian grinned and clapped the general on the shoulder. "Well, General, all's well that ends well, eh?"

"Yes, I suppose our work here is done. I'll leave it to you folks to wrap up the loose ends. Little things like rebuilding your city government from scratch, figuring out a way to live in peace and harmony with a radioactive man, and patching up the massive code violations in your nuclear plant. Stuff like that."

And that's just what he did. Sure, the media were still controlled by corporate giants who never allowed any real news to leak out. Yes, there was still crime and poverty and misery both in Tromaville and around the world. And okay, maybe the shine started to go off of Toxie and Sarah's relationship and they actually had to work at being a couple, just like everyone else. But for now, for that one moment on that July morning at the End of the Book near Tromaville, there was a happy ending. And nobody had had to tip their masseuse to get it.